Try Me
Tempt Me
Take Me

One Night with Sole Regret Anthology
Volume 1

Olivia Cunning

CONTENTS

Other books by Olivia Cunning

Sinners on Tour Series
Backstage Pass
Rock Hard
Hot Ticket
Wicked Beat
Double Time

One Night with Sole Regret Series
Try Me
Tempt Me
Take Me
Coming Soon:
Touch Me
Tie Me
Tell Me

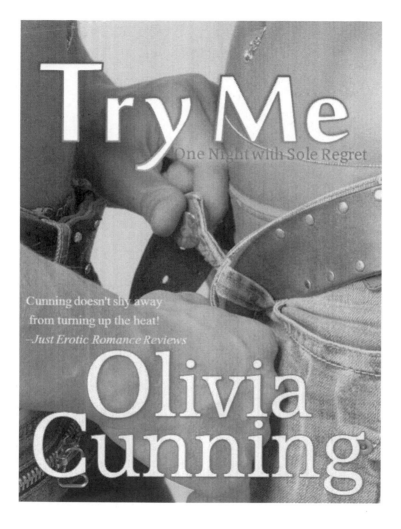

Try Me

One Night with Sole Regret

Cunning doesn't shy away
from turning up the heat!
–*Just Erotic Romance Reviews*

Olivia Cunning

Try Me
One Night with Sole Regret #1

CHAPTER ONE

Melanie caught the gleam in Nikki's eyes in the public restroom mirror they shared. Oh crap. She knew that look. What was the woman scheming now? Melanie was not in the mood to deal with her drama tonight.

The long drive to Tulsa, followed by a parking nightmare, overpaying a scalper for tickets, and standing in line through high winds for two hours had Melanie out of sorts. Okay, she admitted it; she was downright bitchy. Her hair looked like it had lost a fight with a raccoon—a rabid raccoon with a powerful nesting instinct, and her toes, crammed into highly insensible high-heeled, strappy sandals, felt like they'd were being whacked with tiny pickaxes wielded by miniature coalminers.

Nikki, on the other hand, looked her typical polished self, except for the unsettling extra dose of deviousness in her big blue eyes. Melanie paused with her tube of pink lipstick halfway to her lips, her Nikki-is-about-to-get-us-into-trouble alarm sounding in her head.

"What's that look for?" Melanie asked.

"Tonight's the night," Nikki said. She tucked a strand of silky chestnut-brown hair behind one ear and turned to catch her good side in the mirror. Both sides were gorgeous, but Melanie had never convinced Nikki of that or that she was worth more than a string of one-night stands with losers.

"That's what you said last night," Melanie said and focused her attention back on her lipstick application.

Nikki wrinkled her nose at Melanie's hair and yanked a brush from her purse to try to free the nest of raccoons from the tangled mass.

Good luck with that.

There was a reason Melanie wore her hair up most of the time. Only the sturdiest of hair clips kept the thick and wavy waist-length tresses under control. Nikki had talked her into keeping it down tonight, saying that it made her look gorgeous. Melanie never looked gorgeous when standing next to Nikki— a simple fact that she'd learn to live with when they'd attended college together. Men flocked to Nikki. Melanie faded into the background. She was used to it.

Nikki went at Melanie's hair with determination and immediately caught the brush on a tangle of snags. With a sigh of defeat, she handed her brush to Melanie. Melanie supposed she should try to calm the mess into something less offensive. She didn't want to frighten the band.

"I mean it this time." Nikki rearranged her boobs in her push-up bra, unfastened another button on her skintight white blouse to show off more cleavage, and checked out her bad side. "I almost got back stage last night. If I'm lucky, that cute roadie I talked to in Wichita will remember me. The band had to leave right after the show, or I'm sure Jack would've introduced us to the guys last night."

And now they were in Tulsa, trailing after a band like a pair of desperate Sole Regret groupies. Melanie wasn't a serious fan, but she was positive the cute roadie would remember Nikki. Nikki was the kind of woman men drooled over. Wanted. Dumped.

Melanie guessed the roadie would ask Nikki for a sexual favor in exchange for introducing her to the members of her latest band obsession and Nikki would use sex to get what she wanted. It saddened Melanie. None of the men who used and discarded her friend knew how much they hurt her. Melanie already dreaded having to lift Nikki out of her cloud of self-doubt and despair in the morning. She didn't understand why

Nikki continued to put herself in these situations. She was a sweet girl. A pretty girl. A smart girl. Until she found herself in the company of any asshole in the music business, then she acted as if she'd been lobotomized. With only ten lobes to draw upon, Nikki had to be running low on brain parts by now.

"You are not bailing on me again," Melanie said, still trying to tame her hair. She was looking less like a lightning-strike victim already, though her scalp protested each tug. *Gorgeous, my ass.* More like ridiculous. "I'm not going to wait for you out in the car while you get laid by some guy who won't remember your name by the time he blows his load."

"Of course you're not going to wait out in the car."

Well, at least they agreed on something.

Nikki ran her tongue over her teeth and caught Melanie's gaze in the mirror. "You're coming with me."

"Oh no, I'm not. I don't even like musicians." Especially not the tattooed metal-head freaks Nikki lusted after. Nikki had a serious bad-boy complex. Maybe her father should have paid more attention to her as a child.

"Please." Nikki clasped her hands together in front of her chest and managed to make her already wide blue eyes appear even larger than usual.

"Why would you even ask? You know tattooed guys give me the creeps."

Nikki shook her head at her. "If you'd take the time to get to know them, you'd recognize how hot they are."

Doubtful. Just seeing men with tattoos made Melanie's heart race with fear. Her reaction wasn't intentional. She'd been scared by a group of bikers when she was a teen. Had she been older, she probably would've recognized they were only teasing and meant her no harm. But they'd terrified her. Her parents had intensified her fear by saying she could've been kidnapped, raped, murdered, or worse. She hadn't even wanted to know what was worse than being raped and murdered. Her thirteen-year-old mind had associated her parents' warnings with men who looked a certain way. Men like those bikers who'd cornered her in the entryway of an abandoned storefront.

As she'd been too afraid to actually look at their faces, all she remembered was their body art and their words. The one with a skull tattoo had and told her all the lewd things he wanted to do to her pretty mouth. She hadn't understood what he'd meant at the time, but now that she was older, she knew she'd had a reason to be uneasy and disgusted.

One with a barbed-wire tattoo around his arm had touched her hair. She'd screamed, and they'd laughed at her, but ultimately had left her alone. She knew that tattoos didn't make a person bad, but that incident had left a lasting impression. Attending rock concerts was an exercise in keeping her fear at bay. Unfortunately, going to concerts was Nikki's favorite thing to do, so Melanie's fears got a fairly regular workout.

"I don't want to get to know them; I just want to stay away from them."

Nikki wrapped an arm around Melanie's shoulders and assessed them in the mirror. "You'll be fine, Mel. I promise. Besides, I need you to help me pull off my ruse."

Melanie's inner alarm clanged even louder. "What ruse?"

The crowd in the stadium roared with enthusiasm.

"Sole Regret's set is starting!" Nikki scooped her cosmetics and hairbrush into her purse, grabbed Melanie by the wrist, and rushed from the bathroom, nearly knocking a tough-looking biker woman to the floor in her haste.

"Watch it, bitch."

"Sorry," Melanie said as she was yanked into the stadium's causeway, her heels clicking rapidly on the cement.

There were many benefits of being friends with Nikki. She was fun. Afraid of nothing. Men liked her. So while they started out at the back of general admission, with several dozen coy looks, a bit of exposed cleavage, and some well-placed hands on the male metal-heads in the crowd, Nikki miraculously managed to work her way to the area just in front of the stage without being punched in the face. Melanie was allowed to join her only because Nikki refused to release her wrist. Along the barrier fence in front of the stage, Melanie purposely positioned herself between two women and turned away from the man hanging over the railing. The thrusting of his fist in the air drew attention to the skull tattoo on his forearm. One glimpse of that bit of body art had the hair on the back of her neck standing on end. Melanie forced her attention to the stage to keep her gaze from straying to the man's arm.

She supposed she should be excited to be so close to the stage, but Melanie much preferred stadium seats to the pit. She liked to listen to the music, not defend herself from injury. The pit was hot and sweaty: crowded, loud, lewd, and dangerous. Nikki called it exciting. Melanie called it painful. Nikki spent the next forty-five minutes trying to get the attention of the band's lead singer; Melanie spent her time avoiding elbows in the face by two enthusiastic fangirls and keeping the guy behind her from squishing her against the metal bars of the barrier fence and prodding her in the ass with his junk. How could Nikki *enjoy* this?

Melanie watched the lead singer—the current object of Nikki's obsession–prowl the front of the stage. He could've been a gorgeous man. Tattoos ruined his otherwise good looks. Had he been dressed in a nice suit and discussing philosophy instead of wearing ripped denim and screaming something about descending into Hell, Melanie might have admired the wide cut of his shoulders and his strong, handsome profile. But, yeah, the ink completely turned her off. She wondered what color his eyes were. He had yet to take off his sunglasses. The stage lights were blinding, but she figured the shades were part of his image. He'd worn them onstage the night before, too, and by the way the two fangirls were screeching Shaaaaade every time he stalked in their direction, she assumed he'd been named after his fondness for eyewear. Melanie had a heck of a time keeping the names of the band members straight even though Nikki had gone on and on and *on* about them on the drive down from Wichita.

Melanie did enjoy watching Shade and the other band members interact with the crowd and each other. The bassist was surprisingly popular with the audience; Melanie found most bass players to be obscure by default. This one had a softer look than the two guitarists— handsome, even features, a normal haircut sans black dye, a perpetual smile, and gentle eyes. Had he not decorated his every inch of his hard-muscled arms with tattoos and bore piercings in his eyebrow and lip, Melanie might not have crossed the street if he'd approached her in public. Why did these men insist on destroying their looks with permanent accessories? It was a damn shame.

The lead guitarist, who had an inordinate fondness for black, was big on chains and trying to upstage the vocalist. They competed for the crowd's affection with an active rivalry. The rhythm guitarist, who had a gorgeous mane of long, straight hair and no shirt—much to the delight of any female who didn't mind a fully inked torso—mocked the competing stage hogs behind their backs. The bassist found his antics so hilarious that he had to pause a few times to catch his breath from laughing so hard. Melanie doubted she would've noticed the nuances of their dynamic from stadium seats, so at least she had something interesting to watch as she tried to convince the guy behind her that her ass was off limits and not designed as a pincushion for his boner.

Near the end of the final song of their set list—the same set list they'd played the night before—the lead singer hopped off the stage and walked the narrow path on the other side of the barrier fence, slapping hands with fans in the front row as he passed them. Nikki used Melanie for leverage so she could stretch her body into Shade's path. She got a hand on his skintight T-shirt, but was unable to keep her hold as he blazed past. He returned to the stage just as the song ended on a long, wailing guitar note.

"I touched him," Nikki squealed excitedly and covered her mouth with her rock-god-blessed hand.

"Congratulations," Melanie said.

"God, I want him."

"What about the rest of the band? They're all totally your type."

"They're my backup plan, but Shade is the one I really want." Nikki's eyes rolled upward, and Melanie suspected she was in the throes of an orgasm. Melanie took a deep breath and shook her head at her friend. What was the appeal?

When the band pretended their set was over and the crowd began to chant for an encore, Nikki started tugging Melanie toward the side of the stage. Melanie accidentally stomped more than one toe in the darkness. She spouted a litany of sorries as she was given no choice but to follow her determined friend, who had an iron grip on her wrist. The crowd was bathed in darkness to excite them for the final song as well as let them know the show wasn't actually over: Sole Regret's biggest hit was yet to come. Even Melanie had noticed they hadn't played "Instigator" and they'd blown the roof off the stadium with their high-energy rock anthem the night before.

Melanie had no idea how Nikki managed to see well enough to slip past security, but they were suddenly free from the crowd and standing next to the stage. They were so going to get caught. Melanie clung to Nikki's hand, hoping they didn't get chewed out too severely when one of the distracted security guards noticed them. In the darkness, Nikki managed to find the cute roadie she'd been talking to the night before. Melanie wondered if Nikki was wearing night vision goggles. Her own eyes were still trying to adjust to the lack of illumination after she'd stared up at bright stage lights for almost an hour.

"This is her," Nikki said. She tugged Melanie against her and kissed her on the mouth with heated, seeking lips. It wasn't one of those *you're my bestie and I've had a too much to drink, so I'm feeling affectionate* kisses. It was more a *we go down on each other, wanna watch* kind of kiss. Melanie was too shocked to do anything but breathe. And even that was a struggle.

What the fuck? Was this the ruse Nikki had mentioned?

"Oh yeah," the cute roadie said when Nikki ended her plundering assault on Melanie's lips. "That's totally hot, tater tot." He reached into the front pocket of his mega-baggie jeans and pulled out a backstage pass on a lanyard. He draped it around Nikki's neck. "I only have one left."

"But what about my friend?" Nikki directed her morose-puppy look in his direction. The guy didn't stand a chance.

"Show Tony what you just showed me, and he'll let you both backstage. Trust me."

The stage lights flashed on and the band started their encore with a hard and heavy drum progression. Melanie covered her ears with both hands.

"It's loud," she yelled.

Nikki grabbed Melanie's wrist again and led her behind the stage to where a man stood guarding a door. Nikki flashed her pass at him and he opened the door, but stuck out his arm to bar Melanie's entry.

"Jack said you'd let us both in," Nikki said. "He only had one pass for us to share."

"Why should I believe you?"

Melanie was secretly hoping he refused to let either of them in. What in the world was Nikki thinking? Kissing her on the mouth. Letting that guy think it was natural for them to make out. Just so she could meet some weird lead singer who called himself *Shade*, of all things.

"Because we want to see Shade," Nikki said. "Both of us."

And the next thing Melanie knew, her best friend had her tongue in her mouth and her hand on her ass. Melanie jerked away. She'd been shocked the first time. Now she was just pissed.

"What the *fuck*, Nikki?"

"She doesn't like to do it in public," Nikki explained to the security guard. She cupped Melanie's breast and gave it a squeeze. The guy groaned and shoved them both into the backstage area and shut the door behind them.

"What is *wrong* with you?" Melanie slapped Nikki's hand away from her breast.

"I knew you wouldn't agree with my plan if I asked." She shrugged. "Last night, I sorta told that roadie guy that I was into threesomes and I had this hot girlfriend I wanted to share with Shade."

"You sorta told him that?"

"Yeah, he thought it was sexy and knew Shade would be interested."

"But *I'm* not interested, Nikki."

"Duh. I know that. That's why it's a ruse. I didn't think you'd actually want to sleep with him. Or me."

Nikki's bottom lip jutted forward, and she gave Melanie her please forgive me, bestest best bestie look, her I can't help but be impulsive look, followed by her you know you love me look. The bitch. She knew Melanie would forgive her because

Melanie did love her and worried about her impulsiveness getting her into big trouble someday. "I can't believe you'd use me just to meet some rock star, Nikki. I'm not sure why I'm friends with you. All you do is cause me grief."

"But I'm a good kisser, right?" Nikki winked at her and laughed. "I never realized what great tits you have, Mel." Nikki lifted both perfectly manicured hands and made squeezing motions in front of Melanie's boobs. "Can I suck on them?"

Melanie crossed her arms over her chest. Nikki was always making stupid remarks like that. Good thing Melanie didn't take her seriously.

"Don't be mad." Nikki dropped her hands and released a heavy sigh. "I got us backstage didn't I?"

"I didn't even want to come backstage."

"Sure you did. Let's go find some alcohol. I'm going to need a little liquid courage to approach Shade."

"Go by yourself. I'm going to go wait in the car." Melanie turned to find the nearest exit.

"No, you're not." Nikki wrapped an arm around her shoulders. "You'll just end up worried about me in here with a bunch of—what do you call them again?"

"Freakish assholes?"

Nikki laughed. "Among other things. Just do this one thing for me, Mel, and I'll never ask you for anything ever again."

Melanie snorted. "Uh huh. Yeah. Sure."

"I won't." Nikki hooked Melanie's pinky finger with her own. "Pinky swear."

Melanie released a frustrated sigh. "Where's the booze?"

CHAPTER TWO

Gabe climbed out from behind his drum kit, both thighs weary with fatigue. He stretched his aching back, wincing as he twisted to one side. Thirty years young and he could safely say he was getting too old for this shit. Jack tossed him a hand towel, and Gabe wiped the sweat off his face.

"Great show, man," Jack said. He took the towel and offered Gabe a handful of used drumsticks to throw into the audience.

"Thanks."

Gabe joined his band mates at the front of the stage. He flung a dozen sticks into the crowd, took a bow to the screaming fans, and made a beeline for the dressing room. He needed a beer, a nap, and a shower, not necessarily in that order.

"Don't forget we have an after-party tonight," Owen said as he handed off his bass guitar to one roadie while another disconnected his wireless transmitter.

Gabe had forgotten about the after-party. That meant the first thing on his agenda had to be a shower. No one wanted to smell him after he'd been swimming in his own sweat for an hour. And maybe if a hot piece of ass caught his attention at the party, he'd add *get laid* to his list of priorities.

"See you there," Gabe said and headed for the dressing room to shower.

The steamy water felt like heaven against his weary flesh. He considered blowing the party and just hanging out in the shower by himself for the entire night. His bunk on the tour bus sang a siren's song to his exhausted body. Gabe was proud to be known as one of rock's fastest drummers, but his signature aggressive style wore his ass out at every live performance. Still, he knew the guys would give him hell if he didn't make an appearance at the party, so he'd show his face for five minutes, have a beer, and then catch that nap. Alone. He was much too exhausted to chase pussy tonight.

He found his bag among the pile of the band's overnight luggage and tossed on a pair of well-worn jeans, a T-shirt, and his favorite boots. He didn't bother spiking his still wet hair as he planned to go to bed soon, so he tugged on a baseball cap and headed to the conference room at the end of the hall. The room was packed wall-to-wall with guests.

Gabe headed for the bar. One beer. That was all he needed to unwind, and then he could disappear. He made a concerted effort to greet everyone who recognized him. Shake hands. Pause for a photo. Smile and bullshit. Sign an autograph. Laugh at a joke. Accept praise. Enjoy the excitement. Seek out the familiar faces of his band mates in a sea of strangers and exchange a nod of recognition. Finally, he reached the bar.

"Corona?" Jordan asked.

He knew damned well that's what Gabe wanted. He'd been with the crew all summer.

"Yeah."

Jordan disappeared beneath the bar and emerged with a bottle. He popped the cap and handed it to Gabe, who took a long swallow. It went down smooth. Good stuff.

He caught movement out of the corner of his eye, and he turned his gaze on the sweet piece of ass beside him at the bar. Long, brown curls fell to the middle of her back, and her jeans clung to her curvy backside in a most distracting fashion. High-heeled sandals accentuated her long legs, which would look perfect wrapped around his hips. If the front of her looked half as spectacular as the back, he was definitely interested in hanging around a while longer. He wasn't *that* exhausted.

CHAPTER THREE

Melanie took the glass of whiskey out of Nikki's hand. "You've had enough." Even though they'd arrived in Nikki's car, Melanie realized she'd be the designated the driver tonight, so she'd stopped drinking after one apple martini. They had a three-hour drive just to get home. But while Melanie showed restraint, Nikki used the open bar to its full potential. She had yet to request one of everything, but each time Shade laughed or said something loud enough for her to hear, Nikki ordered another drink.

Nikki stole a glance over Melanie's shoulder at her current obsession, who had yet to notice her. Probably because she was standing out of his line of sight. His inattention had Nikki reliving her college party days—get drunk, sleep with some jerk, wake up not knowing where she was, call Melanie to come get her, cry on Melanie's shoulder, eat chocolate ice cream, rinse and repeat. Melanie had thought Nikki had finally outgrown the pattern. Apparently not.

Melanie's patience was at its limit. Nikki had behaved like a lunatic to get backstage and now she was too chicken to even approach the guy. Maybe if Melanie introduced her to Shade before she was completely wasted, she wouldn't start throwing herself at the nearest dick, which happened to be attached to the greasy bartender. Determined that her friend would set her sights on more attractive man-meat, Melanie took her by the arm. She knew Nikki would lament for the next thirty years about how she'd missed her chance if she didn't at least talk to Shade.

"Wait, wait," Nikki pleaded as Melanie dragged her away from the bar. "I need to check my make-up first."

When Melanie stopped in front of the lead singer of Sole Regret, Nikki's elbow began to tremble uncontrollably in her hand. Shade paused in midsentence, his handsome face turned in their direction, and then he took a nonchalant swig of his beer. Melanie watched his Adam's apple move as he swallowed. She couldn't tell for sure if she had his full attention because he was still wearing sunglasses. Indoors. At night. He was taller than she'd imagined—over six feet—and built. Between all the booze and women, Melanie wondered how he found the time to work out. But he had to. Black leather pants clung to muscular thighs, and his white T-shirt strained to contain his well-defined chest as he moved his beer bottle away from his sensual mouth.

"Hi," Melanie gushed before she lost her nerve. She now understood why Nikki had needed copious liquid courage. *Intimidating?* That was an understatement. "I'm Melanie and this is my best friend, Nikki." Melanie tugged Nikki forward. Nikki tripped over her own feet, and Shade took her by one shoulder to steady her.

Nikki swayed toward him and pressed the back of her hand to her mouth. "I don't feel so good."

The only thing worse than having Nikki miss her chance at talking to Shade would be Nikki throwing up all over him.

"Are you gonna be sick?" Shade asked, setting his beer down on the table he was leaning against and taking her by both shoulders.

"I think . . . " Nikki swallowed queasily. "I think I need to lie down for a bit."

"I'll take her home," Melanie said. She should have cut her off from the alcohol earlier.

"No," Nikki said and stomped on Melanie's foot. "I'll be okay. It's just a little loud in here." She glanced up at Shade, her long lashes obscuring her eyes, her body in a completely submissive stance. "Is there a place where I can lie down for a bit?" she asked. "With you on top of me?"

Melanie blinked and turned her head to mouth, *Wow.*

"If you bring your friend with you," Shade said.

Melanie's head snapped up. Was he serious? "Having kinky sex with my best friend and some *freak* I don't even know is

14

not my idea of a good time," she blurted.

A guy behind her burst out laughing.

Nikki elbowed her in the ribs.

Shade just smirked. One eyebrow appeared above the rim of his dark sunglasses. "Then what *is* your idea of a good time?"

She didn't think watching tear-jerkers in her jammies would convince him of her fun-loving nature, so she settled for making a sound of incredulous frustration, turned in the opposite direction, and stalked off. Or tried to. She took precisely one angry step before crashing head-on into a hard body.

The man steadied her with both hands on her upper arms, his cold beer bottle pressing into the flesh of her biceps. She didn't lift her gaze to look at him, but stared at his green T-shirt, feeling like a complete tool.

"Where's the fire, baby?" he asked.

"In my pants," Shade said and laughed.

Melanie shoved away from the man and headed for a nice safe corner to collect her thoughts. She half-expected Nikki to come after her—to either berate her for calling Shade a freak to his face or because she'd ruined Nikki's chances with the egomaniac—but several minutes of staring at the wall convinced her that Nikki had deserted her for a guy she didn't even know. *Again.* A quick glance over her shoulder confirmed her suspicions. Nikki was laughing and hanging all over Mr. Rock Star Jerk, who seemed to have his gaze trained on Melanie as he suckled a spot right behind Nikki's ear. When Melanie narrowed her eyes at him, he took Nikki's hand and led her out a back door.

Melanie scrubbed her forehead with two fingers and turned to stare at the wall again. She considered leaving, but she couldn't desert Nikki without backup. They'd arrived together, they'd leave together. Besides, the woman's love life was a disaster. What if she needed Melanie's help? Considering who she'd left with, the chances that she would need Melanie to bail her out of trouble were all but guaranteed. Melanie supposed attending an after-party alone with a crowd of tattooed metal-heads was better than waiting for Nikki in the car by herself, but not by much. Resigned to her fate, Melanie found the free end of a sofa and sat to wait, keeping her eyes diverted from the people milling about the room.

Her gaze trained on the door that Nikki had just exited, she didn't notice the man sitting next to her until he spoke. "I'm surprised you didn't go with them."

She tore her gaze from the door to look at him. His striking green eyes captured her attention from the shadow beneath the bill of his baseball cap. He was quite possibly the most attractive man who'd ever spoken to her without Nikki at her side. She recognized his T-shirt as the one belonging to the guy she'd careened into a few moments earlier. "Huh?"

"Jacob and your friend." He pointed the neck of his beer bottle toward the door that Melanie was so fixated on.

"Jacob?"

"More famously known as Shade."

"Oh." She settled her hands on her knees. "I didn't realize he had a normal name."

He laughed. "You didn't think his mother named him Shade, did you?"

She shrugged. "Never thought about it." Her attention moved to the door again. "What kind of a dork uses a lame stage name anyway? And why Shade? Because he wears sunglasses all the time?"

"Yeah, he has to wear them. He has vision problems."

Melanie's stomach dropped and she covered her big, blabbering mouth with one hand. "He does? Shit. Now I feel bad."

The guy chuckled. "I'm just fucking with you. He wears them because he enjoys looking like a douche twenty-four seven."

Melanie laughed. It felt good. Her severe case of anxiety decreased substantially, and her bitchiness finally took its leave. "I'm not usually this disagreeable. I just really would rather be anywhere else than waiting for Nikki to finish her fun. I honestly don't understand why she thinks he's so hot. He looks like a prison inmate."

When the guy didn't speak, she turned her head to look at him again.

He traced his bottom lip with his middle finger as he assessed her. "You don't seem too enamored with the band. What brings you backstage?"

"A friend I can't tell *no*." She sighed. "I'm such an enabler."

"Or maybe you're just a good friend."

"More like a *dumb* friend. If I'd quit sticking my neck out for her, maybe she'd learn some responsibility."

"But if something really bad happened to her, you'd feel responsible."

She gawked at him, surprised he understood the truth behind her actions so easily.

He smiled, revealing a set of perfect white teeth. That simple expression transformed him from gorgeous to dazzling.

Melanie's breath caught. Wow. Now this guy . . . She could understand wanting to jump in bed with him on short acquaintance. Please and thank you.

"Yeah, I totally get it. I'm one of those enabler types too," he said.

"So you admit you're as dumb as I am?"

He chuckled. "I guess so. Would you like a beer?"

She shook her head. "I have to drive and I'm already at my limit." She was pretty sure her sudden lightheadedness was caused by the company, not the alcohol.

"How about a Coke then?"

She smiled at his thoughtfulness. "Water?"

He nodded. "Jordan!" he yelled at the man at the bar. "Bring the lady a water."

"Got it!"

He turned his attention to her again. "So are you going to tell me your name?"

She relaxed into the sofa cushions, glad she'd found a normal person to talk to. She'd thought she'd have to spend the entire night pretending to be invisible. "Melanie Anderson. Yours?"

He laughed. "You really aren't enamored with the band, are you, Melanie?"

What did that have to do with telling her his name? "I like their music, but they're not my favorite band or anything. A bit too heavy for my tastes. Nikki is the one obsessed with them.

17

She dragged me here against my will."

A glass of water was pressed into her hand. "Thanks," she said to the bartender. She took a sip and waited for her gorgeous companion to speak again.

"I see. I'm Gabriel Banner." He grinned at her and suddenly overwarm, she wondered if someone had switched off the AC. "Call me Gabe."

A totally normal name for a totally normal guy. She would have felt uncomfortable talking to any of the other men in the room—tattooed, pierced, strange haircuts, chains and leather—but Gabe looked as normal as she did. His only notable flaw was the Texas Rangers ball cap he wore. The Angels' fan in her wanted to poke fun at his team loyalty, but she could forgive one little fault.

She smiled and offered her free hand in greeting. His hand slid into hers. Though he clasped her hand with a gentle grip, she could feel the strength in those long fingers. Her heart fluttered when his fingers brushed the back of her hand. "Nice to meet you, Gabe. How did a normal-looking guy like you end up backstage with all these, erm, *interesting* folks?"

He hesitated and then laughed as if he thought she was joking. "They're great, aren't they? Are you from Tulsa?"

She shook her head. "Kansas. Nikki wanted to meet Shade so badly that she made me drive here with her. She couldn't get backstage last night. I guess she got what she wanted tonight though. Where are you from?"

"Austin."

She did recognize a hint of a drawl in his speech, but she wouldn't have pegged him as a Texan—his jeans weren't tight enough to cut off the circulation to his balls. She supposed the Rangers ball cap should have given her a clue. "Did you drive all the way from Austin just to see Sole Regret?"

He laughed again and tugged on one earlobe. He was certainly easy to amuse. And the deep, rich sound of his amusement had her considering clown school to keep him laughing regularly.

"Yeah, I guess you could say that," he said.

Gabe took the final draw of his beer, extended the empty bottle, and gave it a little shake. Within twenty seconds it had been replaced with a fresh brew.

Sipping her water, she wondered why the bartender was so eager to do Gabe's bidding. "So, do you know the band?"

He smiled again and Melanie feared she'd melt. She was very interested in putting a permanent smile on his handsome face.

"We've met. What do you do with your time when you aren't enabling your friend?"

"I'm an accountant."

"That must be . . . " His eyebrows drew together. "Boring as shit."

She laughed. "It pays the bills. Besides, I like numbers. They're predictable."

"I suppose you don't have an unpredictable bone in your body."

She reached up and ran a finger down the side of his neck. His pulse leapt against her fingertip. "I wouldn't say that."

"Are you coming on to me, Melanie?"

Oh yes, yes, yes. "Maybe," she said. No sense in Nikki having all the fun tonight. Melanie was suddenly up for a little fun of her own.

"I hate to bother you," someone said from the other side of Gabe.

A stud piercing spanned the bridge of the guy's nose and a palm-sized black skull tattoo covered the side of his spindly neck. At the sight of the tattoo, Melanie's heart rate kicked up. Most tattoos made her feel uneasy, but skull and barbed-wire designs always freaked her out. Melanie took a huge gulp of water and returned her gaze to Gabe, wondering how he'd deal with a confrontation.

"I'm a huge fan of yours, Force," the fashion-nightmare gushed. "You're hands down the best drummer on the planet. Can I have your autograph?"

Perhaps Nikki hadn't thrown up all over Sole Regret's lead vocalist, but Melanie managed to spit water all over their drummer.

CHAPTER FOUR

Melanie jumped to her feet and searched for something to wipe the water from the side of Gabe's face. Chuckling, he lifted the hem of his T-shirt and rubbed the droplets from his skin. She couldn't help but gape at his washboard abs. It was bad enough that she'd spewed water all over a famous drummer; spitting all over a *hot* famous drummer with dreamy green eyes and a gorgeous smile was a tabloid-worthy disaster. Her gaze fixed on the hint of a tattoo peeking out above his wide, leather belt near one hipbone. She couldn't make out what it was before he dropped his shirt to cover his belly. She expected that feeling of unease to settle over her now that she knew he had a tattoo, but she only felt undeniable attraction when she looked at him.

Gabe took the CD from his excited fan and signed it before turning his attention back to Melanie.

"I am so sorry," she said. "I had no idea who you were. "And how much of an ass I was making of myself as I criticized your band.

His eyes flipped skyward. "Yeah, I kinda figured that much."

"I recognized the other guys in the band because I saw them on stage, but you . . . "

"Were the blur behind the huge drum kit."

"Yeah." And he looked like a regular gorgeous guy, not a rock star. She touched her cheeks with her fingertips and found them hot. "I really am sorry I spit water on you. You must think I'm a psycho."

"Actually, I think you're charming," he said. "I've never met a woman with the balls to turn down Shade and call him a freak in the same breath."

Melanie groaned. "I can't believe I did that." She plopped down on the sofa beside Gabe again and buried her head in her hands. "I don't really think he's a freak. He's just so . . . "

"Arrogant?"

"Yeah." She turned her head to look at him. "But you don't seem to be."

"I'm just the drummer." He touched the center of her back, engulfing her in his body heat and the clean fragrance of soap and hot-blooded male as he moved closer. "Do you have a boyfriend?" He stroked her left ring finger just above her first knuckle. "I know if you had a husband or a fiancé, he wouldn't let you out of his sight without a ring on your finger."

Her heart skipped a beat. Was he hitting on her? She was pretty sure he was. Did she mind? Hell no. Even though he was a musician and had a tattoo, she loved what she saw. And she wanted to do so much more than look.

"I'm currently single," she said. *Yay!* she added silently.

"I thought maybe that's why you rejected Shade, that you were madly in love with some lucky jackass. You honestly aren't attracted to him?"

She shook her head.

"Not even to his notoriety?"

"It doesn't make him any more special than any of us. So he's famous. Big whoop. It doesn't give him the right to behave like an ass. You're famous and you don't act like that."

"Are you sure about that?"

She nodded resolutely.

Gabe leaned closer still, his gaze so intense she felt frozen to the spot. He lifted a hand to brush his fingers across her cheek. Melanie's heart thundered in her chest.

"I'm going to kiss you," he said.

She couldn't drag her gaze from his. She'd never seen such green eyes. The contrast of those bright irises against his dark lashes was mesmerizing.

"You are?"

"Yes."

"But I'm not attracted to guys like you."

"Guys like me?"

"Guys with tattoos."

"Hmm," he murmured close to her ear.

Her eyelids drifted closed.

"What about guys with mohawks?"

She gasped and her eyes flew open. "Never."

Gabe pushed his ball cap off, revealing that the sides of his head were not only clean-shaven, but tattooed with black and red tribal patterns. The strip of hair down the center of his head was a couple inches long and jet black with crimson tips. So not her type. Then why was her belly tightening with need and why were her panties uncomfortably damp?

"And I suppose you'd never be attracted to a guy with a body piercing."

His warm breath caressed her ear. She stifled a groan. Why was everything about him turning her on? She really wasn't attracted to these bad-boy types. She was likely to cringe in fear when confronted by someone who looked like him. Now, even though Gabe had her cornered against the arm of the sofa, she felt no fear at all. She wanted to touch him. Stroke his mohawk, rub his scalp, caress his tattoos with her lips. How had those desires been spawned? She should be flinching away from him, not swaying toward him. He was exactly the type of guy she avoided as a rule. Yet she wasn't the least bit afraid of Gabe. She wanted him.

"My navel's pierced," she blurted. One moment of recklessness on her twenty-first birthday.

"I don't believe you."

She lifted the hem of her top to show him the jewelry dangling from her belly button. His breath caught, and his fingers traced the slender chain around her waist. A pulse of pleasure converged between her thighs, and she clenched her legs together to ease the building ache.

"God, that's sexy." His pinky dipped beneath the waistband of her jeans as he traced the gold chain again. "What other secrets are you hiding, sweet Melanie? I want to discover them all."

Melanie covered Gabe's hand before he delved any deeper into her pants. "You have piercings?" she asked, staring up into his eyes. She didn't see any in his ears or face. It was one of the reasons she hadn't recognized that he was one of them. His clothes covered his body tattoos. His ball cap hid his unconventional hairstyle and the ink on his scalp. She'd let her guard down with him before she'd realized he was frightening. That *had* to be the difference. She'd talked to him before she'd known she should be afraid. "Where? I don't see any."

"You'll have to feel it." Gabe took her hand and directed it to his chest. Her fingers brushed against a hard ridge within his nipple.

"Oh!" She rubbed her tongue against the edge of her teeth, wondering what that bit of metal would feel like if she flicked her tongue over the barbell she fingered under his T-shirt. His muscles tautened beneath her touch and she silently prayed that he was as attracted to her as she was to him. She wanted him to fist her hair in both hands, drag her beneath his long, hard body and press himself firmly against the throbbing ache between her thighs.

"Melanie." Her whispered name was like a silken caress. "You're gorgeous."

The corners of her mouth turned up. "So are you."

Their gazes locked and everything resembling rational thought vacated her skull. Gabe shifted forward and claimed her mouth in a plundering kiss. Dear God, he had strong, demanding lips. Her fingers curled into his chest, and her breath caught in her throat. When his tongue brushed her upper lip, her entire body ignited. The taste of beer. The scent of his body. The hard barbell of a nipple piercing against her fingertip. All so foreign. So dangerous. So fucking sexy. He tugged his mouth away and looked down at her. Her hand slid down his belly toward his hip.

"Show me your tattoo," she demanded breathlessly. Part of her wanted to prove to herself that she wasn't afraid. The other part just really wanted to get another eyeful of his great body.

"Which one?"

"The one on your hip. Are there more?"

He grinned. "I thought you didn't like tattoos."

She shook her head, her gaze moving to the design on the left side of Gabe's scalp. On closer inspection, the tribal pattern looked like a dragon. Not realistic. Artistic. The thick, black lines that made up its long, slender body arched along the edge of his hairline. Red fire spewed from the beast's terrible mouth inches from his temple. The dragon's claws seemed to be reaching for his ear. "I don't. I'm curious is all. It's not a skull design, is it?" She gulped. What would she do if it was?

"No. Not a skull."

She went limp with relief. "Then what?"

"I'd be happy to show them to you. All of them. But not here."

He turned his head to remind her that they were in a fairly secluded corner of a very crowded room. Melanie sat up abruptly and tugged her shirt down over her belly. Had anyone noticed what they were doing? She should be mortified by her reckless behavior, but it excited her instead.

"Force!" someone yelled from across the room and waved wildly at Gabe.

Gabe waved back.

"Why do they call you Force?" she asked.

"That's my lame stage name." He adopted a menacing expression—lip curled, brows drawn together—and cracked his knuckles. "I'm a force to be reckoned with." He grinned and lifted her hand so he could capture her fingertips in sucking kisses.

"Oh." An aching throb continued to build between her thighs, and she knew there was only one thing that was going to alleviate it. And only one man she wanted to drive it away. The excitement of being with Gabe, of overcoming her ridiculous fears, was far too seductive for her to deny. "I'm not normally attracted to guys like you."

"So you said."

Her heart thudded faster and faster as she gathered courage. She wished she could be more like Nikki and make it perfectly clear what she wanted. "If I tell you that I want you, would you believe me?"

"Try me."

"I want you."

He caught her gaze and held it for a long moment. "Do you want to get out of here?"

"Will you show me your tattoos?"

"That would require me to get naked."

She grinned at him. "I'm okay with that."

CHAPTER FIVE

Gabe wasn't sure what it was about this woman that had him so fired up. Yes, she was attractive, but that didn't explain it. He knew innumerable attractive women. Maybe it was because she liked him despite him being a rock star and not because of it. Or maybe it was because she'd turned down Jacob—no one ever turned down Jacob. Or maybe it was because there was something naughty and wild just beneath her conventional exterior, and he very much wanted to unleash her inner vixen. Whatever it was, he was hooked. He never questioned his little head's instincts. His dick had excellent taste.

He followed Melanie out of the stadium to a convertible, melon-orange Volkswagen Beetle wedged between two gargantuan SUVs in a parking garage.

"Cute," he said when the she pressed her key fob and the Bug's lights flashed. He'd hoped one of the gas guzzlers was hers. No such luck. Normally he wouldn't be caught dead in such a feminine car, but he wanted to show her more than his tattoos. He had the pressing need to be alone with her. To figure out what made her so appealing. Yeah, that belly chain and navel piercing of hers had turned his thoughts thick with lust, but it was more than that.

"It's Nikki's. I should probably text her and let her know I took off without her. Or maybe I should let her worry about *me* for a change." She paused to squint at him with assessing eyes. "Does she have a reason to be worried?"

"Only if she plans to see you before morning."

"Just how many tattoos do you have? It shouldn't take you all night to show me."

She offered him a challenging smirk. It made him want to kiss the sass out of her.

"But it will take me that long to work you out of my system."

Her breath caught. After a moment she closed her gaping mouth and squeezed her tight little body between the SUV and the Bug on the driver's side of the car. "Are you hungry?" she asked as she inched open the door and sidled into the car. "I'm starving. I missed dinner so we could stand in line for two hours. There has to be an open restaurant around here somewhere."

He took note of her rapid words. He hoped she didn't freak out and leave him hanging. Well, actually, he was more hard than hanging. Did she have any idea what he had in mind? It had been a while since he'd had to work at seducing a woman. They tended to fall out of their pants and into his. Maybe he was off his game. She wanted to have *dinner* first? For real? He was wondering how she was still clothed.

Gabe squeezed into the car with her and closed the door. Folded into the small space, he felt he was in danger of kneeing himself in the eyeballs. "Does the thought of being alone with me make you nervous?"

"No," she squeaked.

"Good. Then we'll order room service," he said, fiddling under the seat for a lever to give himself some room. He sighed in relief when the seat shifted and offered him a few extra inches for his legs.

"But—"

"You do realize I plan to fuck you, don't you?" No sense in pretending this was something it wasn't. "If you're playing games with me—"

"I'm not playing games, Gabe. I plan to fuck you until you can't move. I just thought we could get to know each other a little better first. I've never had a man seduce me this quickly. I feel kind of . . . um . . . *slutty*." She whispered that last word as if it had never applied to her before.

Heat flooded his groin. Fuck, yeah. She did want him after all. He was used to women coming on to him, making their intentions clear, and being blunt. He just wasn't used to women like Melanie doing so. Damn, his balls ached. There was no way in hell he'd make it through a polite dinner with her. He was perfectly fine with her feeling slutty. Especially because he didn't think she let herself feel that way often. Convincing her to do something she wouldn't normally do stroked his ego until an inferno of lust blazed inside him.

Melanie started the car while Gabe struggled to form coherent thoughts. They were pulling out of the parking garage before he managed to fire a rational synapse.

"Um, where to?" she asked.

He gave her the name of the hotel and she searched for it on the car's navigation system. It began to spout directions in a robotic voice.

"You have until we get to the hotel to get to know me," he said. "It isn't far. You'd better get started."

"How often do you do this kind of thing?"

"What kind of thing?"

"Have women you don't know drive you to your hotel room?"

"Less often than you think."

Her full lips pursed skeptically. She lifted an eyebrow at him, before returning her attention to the road. It was mostly deserted at this hour, which meant the short trip to the hotel would be especially quick. A good thing. If he caught the scent of her fruity shampoo one more time, he was going to unzip his pants and show her the effect she had on him; indecent exposure laws be damned.

"I usually take them to the tour bus," he said, forcing his mind to keep up with the thread of their conversation. "It's easier to get rid of them that way."

She laughed. "At least you're honest."

"How often do you do this kind of thing?" he countered.

"Before or after I graduated college?"

There was a distinction? "After?"

"Not often."

"Before?"

"Whenever I felt like it," she said. "Which wasn't often."

"So why are you doing this now?"

"I figure I'm entitled to a little slutty fun every now and

then."

She turned her head to smile at him. She had a great smile. It made his heart swell in his chest. And other things swell in his pants.

"And I really want to see that tattoo on your hip."

He didn't understand why a tattoo on his hip was such a big deal to her. It wasn't anything spectacular, just his astrological sign. "I think your *idea* of who I am and who I *really* am are entirely different things."

"Duh. That's why I wanted to get to know you first," she said.

Maybe he was the one who was nervous. He didn't know if she'd be impressed with the *real* him. Usually the rock star thing did all his work for him. Gabe ran his knuckles down her bare arm, and she shuddered. "And that's why I'm in such a hurry to occupy you with other things."

She glanced at him and asked, "So, do you have family?"

Well that topic definitely pulled the brakes on his libido. "Yeah. Doesn't everyone?"

"I suppose most do. Are they huge fans of your music?"

He laughed. "Not especially. Hate isn't a strong enough word to describe how they feel about my music. I had a strict, religious upbringing. My family is very conservative."

"You don't talk to your family then?"

"I didn't say that. They don't necessarily approve of how I live or the career I chose, but they love me. As long as I grow my hair out to cover the ink on my head before Thanksgiving, we get along just fine." And while he mostly did whatever he wanted to do, he respected his parents enough not to flaunt his liberal attitudes in their home. As far as he was concerned, it was a fair compromise. His family's comfort meant more to him than showing off his tattoos. He hadn't discovered his wild side until he'd gone off to college. He didn't have ink out of rebellion against his upbringing but because he'd legitimately liked all the designs enough to have them permanently etched on his skin. To him tattoos were art, not a statement.

Melanie pulled into the hotel drive and stopped the car near a waiting valet. Gabe tensed with anticipation.

"The ink looks good on you though," she said, her eyes

fixed on his scalp. "I'm not sure why."

He knew exactly why. "Forbidden fruit."

"So you think the reason I want you so bad is because my father would shoot you on sight?"

"That sounds about right," he said. And he had no issue with exploiting her daddy issues.

"Well, seeing as he'd shoot any man I hooked up with before a wedding band strangled my finger, don't think you're so special."

The door opened, and the valet offered Melanie a hand out of the car. She exchanged her keys for a valet ticket while Gabe mentally cursed himself for abandoning his manners and not being the one to open her door. When had he started sucking at impressing women? Around the time a sexy accountant had careened into his chest and didn't even have the decency to be hot and bothered the instant he'd touched her.

"Charge that to my room," Gabe said to the valet as he hurried around the car to claim Melanie's elbow.

"Yes, Mr. Banner."

Melanie managed to look impressed. "He knows you by name?"

"I'm a VIP," he said, "it's his job to kiss my ass."

Unable to keep his hands to himself for another minute, Gabe draped an arm across Melanie's lower back and drew her warmth against his side. She allowed him to lead her toward the grand entrance of the hotel, but apparently she was still in get-to-know-you mode.

"So if your parents were against you becoming a musician—"

"I didn't say that. They were never against me becoming a musician. It's the *type* of music I chose that they don't appreciate. They wouldn't have minded if I'd become a gospel singer." He winked at her.

"So how'd you become a drummer? It's not exactly a church choir instrument."

"I was the percussion geek in marching band. I'm not talented enough to play a *real* instrument."

"Are you making that up?" she asked as they entered the lobby through a revolving door. She didn't even gawk at the opulence. She was too busy sticking her cute nose into his business. And he was batting zero with dazzling her.

"Why would I make up embarrassing shit? If I was going to lie, I'd make myself out to be cool and irresistible, don't you think?"

She tilted her head, appraising him as if he were some column of numbers that didn't add up. He wondered if her limited view of the world served her well in Kansas. She seemed to like putting everything in a neat little box. And he was pretty sure she was still desperately searching for the right box to store him in.

As it was well after midnight, the lobby was empty except for the desk clerk smiling to himself indulgently as he pretended not to watch them. The elevator stood waiting.

"Tell me something else that makes you *less* cool," Melanie said.

"Gee, Mel, do you have all night? Don't you know that most rock stars began life as outcasts who didn't want to be weird but found a bunch of kindred outcasts to make music with? A few of us somehow manage to make a living off it. Most of us have to supplement our music habit by delivering pizzas."

"But being an outcast makes you normal."

He shook his head in confusion. "If you say so."

"What were you like in high school?"

He groaned inwardly and considered making shit up. He'd been a walking disaster. "Braces."

"That explains your perfect smile."

She thought his smile was perfect? Maybe all those painful visits to the orthodontist had been worth it.

"What else?" she pressed.

"Tall and skinny." Was she trying to talk herself out of sleeping with him or what?

She lifted the hem of his shirt to flash his belly. "Not an ounce of fat on those abs, but not skinny. Fit. And you are tall. I suppose that's a benefit for a drummer."

"I was so not attractive, Mel, I didn't touch my first boob until I was twenty."

"And how many boobs have you touched since?"

He grinned. "I don't grope and tell."

Inside the elevator, Gabe retrieved his room card from his wallet, glad that they'd checked in early and his belongings were already up in his room. He swiped the card over a panel to access the penthouse. The band had rented out the entire upper floor for the night. He had hoped something like that would turn Melanie's head, yet she insisted on asking him to share secrets about his less than head-turning past.

As soon as the elevator door slid shut, she turned to face him. She rested both palms on his chest and gazed up at him with sultry, hazel eyes. He hadn't noticed the blue and green flecks in them earlier. He opened his mouth to compliment her, and she interrupted him by saying, "Just tell me one more personal thing about yourself. I'm much more comfortable with Gabe than I am with Force."

"Force equals mass times acceleration," he said.

"Huh?"

"The reason they call me Force is not because I bang things hard—though I do. It's because I planned to major in physics before I dropped out of college my sophomore year. I was going to become an engineer and invent things." Actually, he invented things despite his lack of degree. That was something he was definitely keeping to himself, however. No one knew about his inventions. It was bad enough he'd shared the secret behind his nickname with her; only the band knew how he'd picked it up. So why was he telling Melanie? She had the strangest effect on him. He felt vulnerable. Exposed. She'd stripped away all of his cool. It wasn't a feeling he was accustomed to, and he wasn't sure he liked it.

She slapped him in the chest. "So *that's* why I'm so attracted to you," she said. "I knew it couldn't be the famous musician thing."

She raised up on tiptoe to kiss his neck. Every muscle in Gabe's body went taut.

"Melanie?" he whispered.

Her warm breath tickled his neck. "I do love a man with brains."

Brains that ceased to work when a certain sexy accountant suckled the pulse point in his throat. He didn't put the geek in "band geek" anymore. He'd hated being that awkward, meek guy. He no longer entertained dreams of building mechanical hearts and artificial limbs. He was a rock star. Success hadn't been handed to him on a bronze cymbal. He'd earned it. Melanie had better get used to the idea that the thing she was trying so hard to reject was a huge part of who he was.

Gabe reached over and pressed every button from the first to the tenth floor. The elevator jolted as it stopped on the next floor and then the door slid open.

Melanie jerked away, her gaze nervously darting to the empty corridor. No one was there. She stared up at him with wide eyes. "Do you think there's something wrong with the elevator?"

"I pressed all the buttons."

"Why?"

"Because I don't march anymore."

The elevator doors slid shut and they started upward again.

Her eyebrows drew together and nose crinkled in confusion. Gabe moved his hands to her shoulders and slipped the spaghetti straps of her tank and her bra straps down her slender arms. He used the lightest of touches on her silky skin, watching for her reaction.

"What do you like?" he asked.

"Huh?"

"Do you like a gentle, easy touch?" He stroked her skin with a feather-light caress and then curled his fingers to apply more pressure as he moved his hands along the back of her shoulders. "Or something rougher?"

Eyes wide, she shook her head. "I don't know."

The elevator stopped, and the doors slid open again.

He slid his hands to her breasts and freed them from her bra.

"Wait," she gasped. "Someone might . . . "

He cupped one perfect mound of flesh and gently stroked her hardened nipple with his thumb. "Gentle."

When no one joined them on the elevator, Melanie released a soft sigh, and her eyelids fluttered closed.

Gabe squeezed her other breast and pinched her nipple between his thumb and forefinger, rubbing the straining tip with an increasing pressure. "Rough."

"Oh!"

As soon as the elevator doors closed again, he leaned forward and drew his tongue over her pretty pink nipple. "Gentle," he said, blowing a slow breath over her puckered flesh before drawing it into his mouth and sucking with tender care.

Her fingers clung to his scalp. He still couldn't tell what she preferred; she seemed to enjoy both. He released her breast with a soft sucking sound and turned his attention to the other one. "Rough." He nipped her reddened nipple and then sucked it into his mouth, flicking his tongue over the hard tip. He scraped her flesh with the edge of his teeth.

"Gabe!"

The elevator doors opened again. This time she didn't notice. Gabe smiled to himself. *That's better.*

He drew away and waited for her to open her eyes before he cupped her pussy through her jeans. When the heat coming off it registered in his addled thoughts, his cock began to throb in anticipation. He stared into her beautiful eyes as he slid his fingers between her legs and pressed the heel of his hand against her mound. He rubbed his palm against her, stimulating her clit with just enough pressure to remind her that it was there.

"Gentle?"

The doors shut again, and the elevator carried them closer to their destination.

"Can I have both?" she asked breathlessly.

He grinned and backed her into the wall. He grabbed her ass and pressed his cock against her mound, grinding with hard, rigorous thrusts of his hips. "Or rough?"

She clung to him, rubbing her heat against his throbbing cock. If she'd been wearing a skirt, he would have surged into her body right then. He could almost feel her slick heat engulfing him, imagine her gripping him as she clenched with release. Almost.

"Oh God, Gabe, fuck me," she groaned.

His balls tightened with excitement. Drunk with desire, he rubbed his open mouth over her throat. "Did you decide what you want, Melanie?"

"Yes. *You.* I want *you.*"

He gave the black lens of the surveillance camera a long hard stare and then bit his lower lip considering what it would mean for her if he went with his instincts and gave her what she wanted right there. Tempting as she was, she deserved better. He could wait. A couple minutes. Max. His gaze shifted to her eyes. "I like a woman who knows what she wants."

He stepped away and noted they still had five floor stops before they reached the very top, which promised him heaven. Melanie gawked at him for a moment and then struggled to cover her exquisite breasts before the elevator doors opened again. He nonchalantly pressed the button labeled "close doors" trying to hide his eagerness, trying to pretend he was in control and had maintained his cool.

Yes, he liked a woman who knew what she wanted. He also liked to leave a woman flustered and disoriented, craving his body the way an addict craves her next hit. He stole a glance at Melanie noting she was flushed, disheveled, and glowing with a delicate sheen of perspiration. Gabe ducked his head to hide a self-satisfied grin and focused his attention on his fingernails to curtail his urge to gloat. Yeah, mission accomplished.

CHAPTER SIX

Melanie stole a glance at Gabe, who was leaning against the wall of the elevator car, inspecting his fingernails. She'd been ready to yank off her pants right there in the elevator so he could pound her with that big, hard cock he'd rubbed so vigorously against her mound. She hadn't even cared that the elevator doors kept opening. Thinking they might get caught had excited her even more. She'd known a few cock teases in her life, but she'd never met a pussy tease before. Maybe it was his way of teaching her a lesson for prying into his personal life. Why else would he suddenly start ignoring her? Had she been too needy? Too desperate? Had she done something to turn him off? *Shit!*

Melanie crossed her arms over her chest and turned her back to him to face the front of the elevator car. If he thought she was going to beg him to fuck her again, he would be sorely disappointed. She hoped he got a raging case of blue balls. She was going to take him up on that room service, take a look at his tattoos to prove to herself that she was brave, and then leave him with nothing but his hand for company. Maybe next time he'd think twice about getting a woman all hot and bothered and then pretending she didn't exist.

By the time the elevator doors slid open on the top floor, Melanie had almost convinced herself that she really was going leave. What was she thinking anyway? Yes, Gabe was the sexiest thing on three legs and yes, her entire body was still throbbing with lust after encountering leg number three, but dammit, she wasn't going to beg him to put her out of her misery no matter how attractive she found him. She took a step forward and then stopped, blinking repeatedly as she took in what was going on in the hallway next to one of the guest room doors. A couple was going at it right there in front of God and everyone. Well, she and Gabe were the only mortal witnesses, but really. . . And then it dawned on her that the bare ass with a pair of leather pants lowered just beneath the rhythmically clenching and relaxing flanks belonged to Shade and the shameless slut with her legs wrapped around his waist, her jeans dangling from one slender ankle and her back pressed against the wall, was none other than Nikki.

"Nikki," Melanie sputtered. "What the hell are you doing?"

Shade turned his head. He was still wearing his sunglasses, for fuck's sake. He didn't even pause his deep, rigorous thrusts as he grinned at her. "Decide to join us after all?"

"Screw you," she said. A hand settled against her lower back, and her nipples tightened as if her body couldn't help but respond to a certain drummer. Dammit, anyway. She couldn't deny that she wanted him, even though his inexplicable inattention in the elevator had pissed her off. She wasn't going to leave him alone with his hand, because she didn't want to be alone with hers.

"Don't you think you should take this elsewhere, dude?" Gabe said. "There are security cameras in the halls, you know. And those surveillance videos tend to end up on the Internet when they catch a celebrity fucking a hot, anonymous chick in public."

"I couldn't get my key to work," Shade said.

"We couldn't wait," Nikki added. "I needed his tasty cock inside me." She licked her lips and then trailed sucking kisses all along his jaw, as if it were completely natural to fuck a rock star in the hallway before a pair of witnesses. "He has the biggest, most beautiful cock I've ever sucked."

"That's not your room," Gabe said. He pointed across the hall. "That's your room."

Shade glanced from the door labeled 1012 to the one across the hall, 1021. He actually flushed. "Oh. My bad."

He grabbed Nikki's ass and held her impaled on his cock as he shuffled across the hallway. She banged against the wall but made no protest as he searched the pocket of his leather jacket and eventually produced a white plastic card. He managed to insert it into the slot upside down. When the little light on the door flashed red, he groaned in protest and, as if unable to resist, began to thrust deep and hard into Nikki's body. Gabe took pity on the pair of lust-crazed maniacs and opened the door for them.

"Thanks," Shade said breathlessly as he hoisted Nikki off the wall.

"See you tomorrow," Nikki said and waved at Melanie. "Force is gonna rock your world."

Melanie caught her wink just before Shade kicked the door shut. A loud thud pounded on the inside of the door.

Gabe turned to offer Melanie an apologetic grin. He rubbed a hand over the back of his head and stared at the carpet. "Sorry you had to see that. He's a horny bastard, but he has a good heart."

"Where's your room?" She would never admit it, but she was disappointed that Gabe wasn't so turned on by her that he needed to plow her in the hallway.

He diverted his gaze and tilted his chin, but she saw the smirk on his sensual lips. "In a hurry?"

Apparently he wasn't.

"You promised me room service." She wasn't cold, but she hugged herself and rubbed her hands up and down both arms. She still wasn't sure if he was even interested in continuing what they'd started. She'd never encountered a man who could go from full throttle to full stop in three seconds flat. He'd seemed to want her when they'd first entered the elevator. She'd felt his excitement pressed against her and still felt the uncomfortable wetness of her panties. When she'd admitted she wanted him, he'd pushed her away. What game was he playing anyway? She didn't have enough experience with worldly men to figure out how to proceed. Should she play hard to get, tear her clothes off, or jump him? Retreat? She glanced at the elevator, weighing her options. If she was the one to call this off, it wouldn't be quite so devastating to her already wounded ego.

Gabe wrapped an arm around her back and directed her across the hall. He slipped his keycard into a slot and a tiny light turned green. "I think I'm gonna have to go back on that promise, Melanie," he said and opened the door.

Was he really going to tell her to get lost? Why had he even brought her here? She glared up at him. "Why? Do you think it's funny to—"

He pushed her into the room and closed the door. Her heart rate kicked up as he gazed at her in the soft lamplight. There was no mistaking the heat in his appreciative stare. He was back to full throttle. *Oh, thank God.*

"I usually have better control." He reached for the hem of her top and pulled it over her head. "But I can't wait any longer. If it wasn't for the security camera in the elevator, I would have done you right there." He traced the lacy edge of the cup of her bra, his gaze riveted on her chest. "When you asked me to fuck you, I almost came down my leg, Mel. Fuck, I'm hard for you."

And she'd thought he was either playing hard to get or not attracted to her. Her confidence surged. "Take off your pants, Gabe." She flipped on an overhead light with the wall switch. "I want to get a good look at that tattoo."

He grinned and stripped off his shirt. She could stare at him shirtless for an eon and never tire of the sight of his toned body. He was beautiful.

Two tattoos decorated his chest. The one on the right was an amazingly realistic image of a gray wolf. The one on his left pec was an equally realistic image of a cougar. Melanie's gaze slowly made its way down firm pecs, over chiseled abs, to rest on one sexy ridge at his hip. Again the hint of his tattoo above the waistband of his low-slung jeans caught her attention. Again she couldn't fathom what it was. She reached for his belt. He caught her hand.

"Maybe you should familiarize yourself with the ink on my back first. The one on my hip might be too much for you to handle."

She chuckled. "Oh really?"

"There's no way to show it to you and keep my cock in my pants."

She snorted with amusement. "Oh no, I definitely wouldn't want that."

Gabe turned slowly and faced the wall. When the gorgeous

phoenix tattooed over the entire surface of his back came into view, Melanie's breath caught. Wow. The work was stunning. The skin it decorated, irresistible. Melanie approached him, splaying her hands over his enticing flesh. She didn't know what she expected tattooed skin to feel like. To find that it was as warm and smooth as regular skin surprised her. Gabe's muscles twitched beneath her palms; an excited rasp laced each rapid breath. The scent of his body beckoned her and she stepped close, inhaling deeply. Her tongue begged to sample his flesh, to determine if he tasted as good as he smelled.

"I love it," she said. "The details in the feathers are amazing." She took a closer look. "The eyes look so realistic. Why a phoenix?"

"It's a symbol of my rebirth," he told her. "From the man that everyone wanted me to be into the one I was meant to be."

She pressed her lips to a shoulder blade decorated by an extended wing inked in red, orange, yellow, and black. "Nice choice," she said. She drew her tongue over his skin.

"Thanks, I had it custom drawn."

"Not the tattoo," she said, "though it is beautiful. Nice choice on choosing the man you were meant to be."

Melanie slid both hands around his body to stroke his chest. She couldn't detect his ink by touch, but when her fingertip brushed the barbell piercing his nipple, a surge of liquid heat converged between her thighs. Engulfed by desire, Melanie pressed her lips to his spine and rubbed the bit of metal in a gentle circle with her thumb. She wondered what it would feel like to have her nipple pierced and Gabe's lips tugging at it. Would she be able to feel that pull inside and out? Her breasts suddenly heavy and aching, she crushed them into his back and ran her hands down his lean, hard stomach.

"So you're no longer lusting over the awkward band geek with braces?" he asked.

Unable to resist the temptation, she pushed her hand into his front pocket and shifted his cock in her palm. So long and hard and huge. Her pussy throbbed with longing. "I don't know. Was that guy as well hung as you are?"

His breath caught and his abs tightened beneath her other

exploring hand. She trailed kisses over his back while gently stroking his cock through the soft cotton of his pocket lining.

"Yeah, but he didn't know how to use it." He grabbed her wrist and pulled her hand out of his pocket before turning to face her. "Fortunately, I do."

As his heated gaze roamed her chest, her smart remark died on her tongue. His hand moved to her back to unfasten her bra with practiced ease. He removed the bit of pink lace and underwire and dropped it on the floor. "Beautiful," he murmured. His fingertips brushed over her taut nipples, and her back arched involuntarily. Gabe's hands slid down her belly and unfastened her belt. The button of her fly popped free. He tugged her zipper down, inch by inch.

Slowly.

Slowly.

Too fucking slowly.

She was on fire.

Melanie reached for his belt. She unfastened it and opened his fly. Before he could stop her, she jerked his pants down his thighs to reveal the tattoo on his hip. She squatted in front of him for a closer inspection—a lion?—but found the gorgeous hard cock in front of her far more interesting than any artistic design. Veins bulged beneath the darkened skin of his dick. The tip curved upward pleasingly. Its swollen head glistened with a hint of pre-cum. Melanie's tongue darted out to sample a taste of him and Gabe groaned in torment. Smiling at his response, Melanie pressed her palm against his hip and used her other hand to direct his cock into her mouth. She rubbed her tongue against the thick ridge on the underside. Sucking hard, she pulled back until her lips bumped over the crown of its head, before surging forward to take him deep within her mouth.

Gabe drew a sharp breath through his teeth. "Melanie . . . Wait."

She tilted her head back to look up at him. He stroked her hair from her face with one hand.

"Don't get me anymore worked up than I already am. I have surprises for you." He glanced over his shoulder into the suite. "In my luggage."

She tugged her head back, releasing him from the tight suction of her mouth. "What kind of surprises?"

"I'll show you. Just . . . if you keep doing that, I'm gonna come and then I'll probably fall asleep afterward."

She stared up at him in disbelief. "I've never known a guy to turn down oral sex before."

"At least let me reciprocate."

He wrapped both arms around her, pressing her bare breasts firmly into his chest. The piercing in his nipple rubbed against her areola, and she thought she'd explode with lust. That forbidden piece of jewelry made her feel so naughty. So reckless. He made her feel that way. She loved all the unconventional things about him. She was starting to see why Nikki was so attracted to bad boys.

Belly-to-belly, Gabe walked her backward into the large open living area of the suite. When she turned her head to take in the lushly decorated room, he paused. She looked up at him in question and he caught her mouth in a deep kiss. Melanie wrapped her arms around his neck and kissed him in return, making no protest when he pushed her jeans down over her hips. He grabbed her ass in both large hands and pressed her more securely against him, his thick cock prodding her in the belly.

He started moving her backward again. This time he didn't stop until her legs came in contact with the bed. He eased her down onto the mattress, still kissing her. When he had her where he wanted her, he lifted his weight onto his hands, tugged his mouth free of her eager lips, and stared down at her.

"Your pants are in my way," he murmured.

She tried to struggle out of them—they were in her way as well—but their bellies were plastered together and he had her jeans trapped against the edge of the bed with his lower body.

"Don't rush," he said. "I want to look at you first."

He shifted away and climbed to his feet, leaving her alone and disoriented with her legs dangling off the bed. He grabbed her jeans and pulled them off in one tug. He left her panties and her high-heeled sandals in place. She squirmed toward the middle of the bed, using her elbows and heels to propel herself across the mattress. He seized one ankle just above the strap of her shoe, and she stopped.

"Show me how you like it," he said.

"What?"

"I couldn't tell if you like it gentle or rough, so show me."

"How am I supposed to show you?"

"Touch your breasts."

"Gabe, I'd like anythi—"

The look he gave her threatened to melt her panties right off her body. "Show me, Mel."

She flopped onto her back and grabbed her breasts in both hands. Wasn't the entire purpose of having a partner to get her off so she didn't have to do it herself? She plucked at her nipples until they were sufficiently hard and then dropped her hands.

"Satisfied?"

He chuckled. "Not even. Take off your panties."

"Gabe . . . "

"Take them off."

She huffed and reached for her panties, jerking them off over her butt.

"Not like that." He leaned across the bed and covered her hands with his to slow her motions into a leisurely, deliberate tease. "Look at me while you slip them off," he said. "So I can't decide if I want to stare into your eyes or catch my first glimpse of your swollen pussy. Is it wet?"

"Dripping."

His gaze shifted down her body and he shuddered, his teeth worrying his bottom lip as if he was restraining it from seeking the heated flesh between her thighs.

How decidedly delicious that Gabe was telling her what he liked; telling her in the same way he'd asked her to tell him. She'd never been with a man who gave instructions, and she'd never bluntly told a lover exactly what she wanted from him in bed, but maybe with Gabe it wouldn't be awkward. Maybe for once she wouldn't have to fake her orgasm.

"I understand," she whispered. "I'll follow your instructions."

Their eyes met, and she tried to hold his gaze as she slowly worked her panties down her legs. He glanced down to check her progress and took a stuttering breath before returning his gaze to her eyes.

"That's sexy," he whispered. "I want to look at your body, but denying myself makes me want you more."

She tugged her panties past her knees and wriggled to open her thighs, to bathe her heated flesh in the cool room air.

He inhaled deeply and then grabbed his thick cock in one hand. "Fuck," he said breathlessly, "your scent is driving me insane." He stroked his length slowly from base to tip. "Tell me what you like, baby. I want to please you."

Melanie closed her eyes. It made it easier to talk to him. "I liked it when you were gentle with one breast and rough with the other. It made me hot. Can you do it both ways at the same time?"

She cracked an eyelid open to see if he'd been paying attention. His gorgeous smile made an appearance.

"What else makes you hot?"

You asking *what makes me hot makes me hot.*

She slowly slipped her panties off one foot and spread her legs wide. Trembling with a mixture of nervousness and excitement, she held herself open with one hand and traced the inner folds of her pussy with two fingers of her other hand. He watched her motion with his bottom lip trapped between his teeth, his breathing harsh and raged.

"I like a man to stroke my lips until I'm dripping wet and I feel I'm going to die if he doesn't fuck me soon. Even if I'm begging for him, he just keeps teasing and teasing until I don't think he'll ever give me what I want. Then he slips a finger inside me." She traced her opening with her fingertip. Dipped the tip of her finger inside. Her pussy clenched, trying to draw it deeper within. "He keeps it buried deep while he strokes my clit." She slowly drew her finger to her clit and then rubbed it in circles. Pulsations of pleasure radiated from her core, begging for a more rigorous touch. Faster strokes. She denied herself the relief of a quick orgasm, keeping her motions deliberately slow and gentle. The mesmerized way Gabe watched her motions, while matching her pace as he stroked his length, spiked her lust into the stratosphere. She'd never been more turned on in her life and he'd scarcely touched her.

She didn't know what excited her more: her fingers on herself or Gabe watching her as if hypnotized. But she was lying about what a man did to make her hot. That's how she got herself off; she'd never had a man figure it out. But telling him. Showing him. There was no way he could get it wrong.

"Then," she said, her voice low and husky, "when I start coming and my pussy is clenching, he pounds two fingers into me over and over again, as hard as he can. Driving me higher and higher."

"I can smell how turned on you are, baby," Gabe said. "I want to taste you. What do you want me to do with my tongue?"

She never expected to like this openness in the bedroom. She'd imagined it would be embarrassing. It wasn't as hard to tell him what she enjoyed as she'd thought it would be. And showing him? It just made her even hotter.

"I want your tongue firm and writhing against my clit until my juices are dripping down my ass, and then I want you to lap up the hot mess you created." She captured her juices on the tips of her fingers and brought them to her mouth. "I want to taste myself on your lips when you kiss me afterwards." She licked the cum off her fingers. "Mmm. Dirty."

He dove onto the bed with her, catching her thighs on his shoulders as he buried his face between her legs. His tongue brushed against her clit, and she cried out. Talking was sexy, but doing it was so much better. He rubbed his tongue against her clit and shifted so he could trace her inner folds with two fingers the way she'd showed him.

"Oh yes, Gabe." she gasped. He pleasured her so much better than she pleasured herself. His lips latched onto her clit and he sucked. "I love that," she said. "No one's ever done that . . . Oh God! Wait. I think . . . "

He released her clit, leaving her orgasm just out of reach. "Don't come yet," he said. "You just told me you like to be teased."

"Maybe I'm multi-orgasmic."

"Are you?" His tongue brushed her clit, and he continued to trace her aching opening with two fingers.

"I don't know. No guy has ever made me come before."

His eyes widened. "Never?"

"Not unless I help him out by touching myself."

"You're kidding."

She shook her head. "I wish I were. I usually just fake it." Why had she told him that? Her face heated with embarrassment.

"Don't fake it with me, Mel. If what I'm doing isn't working for you, tell me."

"It's working for me. That sucking thing *really* worked for me." She hoped he took her hint without making her beg him to suck her clit again.

"Do you like a finger in your ass when you come?" he asked before his tongue flicked her clit again. Her entire body jerked in response.

"I don't think so."

"Have you ever tried it?"

"Well, no, but . . . "

"I'll do it. You tell me if you like it or not."

Her already thundering heart raced out of control. What in the world was she agreeing to? "Okay."

He fell silent as he concentrated on pleasing the flesh between her legs with his lips. His tongue. His hands. The suckling sounds were almost as erotic as the feel of his mouth on her. He traced her slippery lips with his fingertips, teasing her until she bucked against his hand.

"Fuck me, Gabe. Please. Just . . . Just put it in and pound me. Pound me hard. I want you so bad."

His finger slid deep, and she took a strangled breath. She rocked against his hand, wanting him to thrust his fingers in and out of her though she knew damned well she'd just told him she'd like him to hold his hand still at this point. He sucked her clit into his mouth and rubbed it vigorously with the flat of his tongue. *Ah. Wow.*

Yes. Like that.

Oh. Fuck.

Gabe!

Her womb clenched. Spasms of release coursed through her pelvis and spread through her body. Mouth open in ecstasy, Melanie forgot how to breathe. Gabe slid a second finger into her clenching pussy and the tip of a third finger into her ass. He pressed all three digits deep and then pulled them free and pounded them into her again and again and again as she came. And came. She was still shuddering with aftershocks of pleasure when he pulled his hand free and used his tongue to clean the come from her quivering pussy. Cleaning up the hot mess he'd made. She sucked a deep breath into her lungs.

She was completely limp by the time he moved up the bed to lie beside her. He kissed her, giving her a taste of her own cum on his lips. She suckled his tongue until she could no longer taste herself, though she could still smell her sex on his skin. She wasn't sure why it turned her on. Why she'd never admitted that fact to anyone. Not even to herself.

"You didn't fake that did you?"

She chuckled weakly. "I wouldn't know how to fake that."

He smiled. "Well, now I know one thing you like."

"That only counted as one thing?" It had felt like ten blissful experiences in one.

"Mmm-hmm." He trailed gentle kisses along her jaw and throat. "Let's figure out what else you like."

"Let me catch my breath so I can figure out what *you* like."

"I'm not finished with you yet." He slid down her body and gently licked and suckled one nipple while he squeezed and tugged on the other. He continually stimulated her left breast with harsh, rough motions of his fingers and mouth until it was reddened, sore, and aroused, while her right breast was pampered with tender touches and kisses that left it yearning, achy, and excited. And her breasts weren't the only parts of her body that were throbbing with need. Her pussy was wet and swollen again already. She had no doubt that he could make her come a second time. This time she wanted him inside her when she came.

"Gabe," she pleaded, "I want you inside me. I want to wrap my arms and legs around you as you thrust deep and grind against me."

"We both want that, baby, but not yet. First, I want you to suck on my sac and tease my ass. Get me really worked up."

Suck on his *whozit* and tease his *what?* "I don't. . . know how."

"That's okay. I'll tell you how I like it."

Only fair, she supposed. He'd listened to how she liked it and hadn't hesitated in pleasing her. He rolled onto his back, and her pussy throbbed when she saw how hard and swollen his cock was. She needed to hurry up and get him worked up so he would fill her with that monster. She'd never seen a cock that big, much less had one inside her. Her vibrator would have felt inadequate in its presence.

Gabe propped a few pillows beneath his shoulders and head, lay back, and spread his legs. "Gentle," he said. "They're really sensitive."

She settled between his thighs and lowered her head to draw her tongue over the seam that ran between his nuts. His entire body jerked, and he clenched the covers beneath him in tight fists. She moved her head to suckle the skin over one ball and flick it with her tongue.

"Ah," he gasped. "I thought you said you didn't know how. That's perfect. I love it."

And she loved the way he was reacting to her unpracticed motions. She moved her mouth to the other side.

"Wet, um . . . wet your finger in your mouth and . . . "

When he didn't continue, she lifted her head and slipped her finger into her mouth. "Do what?"

"God, you're good," he whispered. "Don't stop. Wait. What was I . . . Um . . . " He pressed the heels of his hands against his eyes. "Not sure if I can take much more. Just rub your wet finger against my ass. Don't put it in. Just . . . rub."

His ass? Unsettled by his request, she tentatively stroked his sensitive hole with her fingertip. He sucked in a startled breath and nearly leaped off the bed.

"Did I do it wrong?" she asked.

"No, baby. You almost made me explode. I can't wait any longer." He rolled off the bed and landed on his knees. He unzipped a suitcase and began searching through its contents. Clothes and toiletries went flying in all directions. "Need a condom. Where the fuck *are* they?"

Within seconds he'd found one, opened it, and unrolled it over his massive cock. He rejoined Melanie on the bed.

"Are you ready?" he asked.

She was tired of talking. She grabbed him by the arm, tossed him onto his back, and straddled his hips.

He grinned up at her, looking all dangerous and irresistible. *Fuck*able. "I'll take that as a *yes*."

Gabe grabbed his cock in one hand and directed it into her opening. She sank down with a relieved sigh, rising and falling over him in a slow, deliberate motion. Growing accustomed to his girth. His length. Oh God, how he filled her. Again. And again. And again.

His back arched off the bed. "Faster, Mel. Faster and harder."

When she didn't pick up her pace, he sat up, wrapped both arms around her, and flipped her onto her back. Still buried inside her, he began to move. She got a new perspective on his stage name. There was a hell of a lot of *force* behind each rhythmic thrust, and that was exactly what she needed: a rigorous, hard *fuck*.

Melanie wrapped her arms and legs around him, mindful to not gouge his thighs with her shoes, and hung on for the ride. A pressure built inside her. Pleasure. Need. Connection. Gabe lifted his head to stare into her eyes. He slowed his strokes, grinding his hips each time he plunged deep. Stimulating her clit. Bumping against her cervix deep inside. Rubbing her front wall in just the right spot. Her pleasure became bliss. Her need, desperation.

Her mouth fell open in disbelief as bliss became euphoria. Desperation became release. She clung to Gabe, crying out in ecstasy as she came.

In the same instant, his body went taut. She watched as he let go. His breath caught in his throat. Eyes squeezed shut. Face contorted in bliss. He shuddered, pulled back one last time, and thrust deep, rocking against her as if he longed to be buried even deeper. He cried out between hard, shaky gasps before collapsing on top of her. She pulled him close, holding him securely to her chest as she kissed his temple. He murmured the sexiest little sounds of contentment as he regained his bearings.

Or maybe that was her making all those noises of delight.

"Did you fake it?" he asked.

She chuckled and gave him an affectionate squeeze. "I didn't have to. That was amazing."

"Are you kidding? I didn't even last very long. I told you that you had me too worked up."

She grinned as if getting him excited was some sort of accomplishment that deserved a trophy.

"I wish I wasn't so tired," he whispered. "I want to be with you longer, but I'm afraid I need some sleep. The shows wear me out."

"There's always tomorrow morning," she said, her heart thrumming. Maybe he was telling her to leave, to find her clothes and get lost.

He lifted his head and smiled down at her. "You wanna stay the night with me?"

She nodded and had to look away from his ear-to-ear smile. Why did her spending the night make him look so happy?

Gabe pulled out of her body and kissed the tip of her nose. "I'm glad. Don't go anywhere. I'll be right back."

Gabe disappeared into the bathroom, sliding the condom from his softening cock as he walked. Water rushed from a faucet.

Melanie struggled to find the strength to climb beneath the covers. She removed her shoes before she settled on the far side of the bed, leaving the sheets turned back on the other side of the expansive king-sized mattress. Gabe returned a moment later and smiled when he saw her waiting for him.

He joined her beneath the covers and despite the large area of empty bed, immediately spooned against her back and cocooned her in tranquil warmth. He kissed the edge of her ear. "I'm glad you decided to stay," he murmured. His deep voice sounded loud because he was so wonderfully close. "I hope you don't mind if I hold you all night."

Her heart warmed and felt as if it were enlarging in her chest. "I don't mind. I like it."

"If you get hungry, order room service," he said lethargically. "Just charge it to the room."

"What if I get horny?" she asked, threading her fingers through his and holding their combined hands against the center of her chest.

"Wake me up."

CHAPTER SEVEN

Gabe blinked and lifted his head from the pillow. Something had woken him. His first thought was that Melanie, who was still cuddled against his body, had decided she was horny. Now that he'd caught some sleep, he was pretty damned horny himself.

When he shifted, she started awake.

"What time is it?" she grumbled, stretching her lithe body and rubbing her delicious rump against his interested cock.

There was a knock at the door. "Gabe! You up? We have to be on the road in a couple hours. You want breakfast?"

It was Shade. And *no*, he didn't want breakfast. He wanted more of Melanie.

Her belly rumbled, and he covered it with one hand. "Yeah, we'll meet you in half an hour," he called to Shade. Melanie wriggled her ass against him and while he might not have been out of bed yet, he was definitely up. "Make that an hour," he yelled.

"I'm starving," Melanie complained.

"So am I." Hungry for her. And he was no longer tired. Not even a little.

He dove under the covers, delighting in the sound of her laugh as he cupped her breasts in both hands and kissed her flat belly. He caught her navel jewelry in his teeth and tugged gently. He wished they could spend all day in bed. Making love. Talking. Getting to know more about each other. Like a real couple. Always on the road, he never had time to get close to a woman. Different night. Different city. Different lover. Even if he found a woman he really liked—a woman like Melanie—he had to say goodbye to her before he could make a lasting connection. It had felt so good just to hold her through the night. He couldn't remember the last time a woman had stayed in his arms for more than a couple hours. Knowing that he'd have to let her go so soon left a raw achy feeling in his chest. Gabe wondered if she had any interest in trying something long distance. Unlike most of his one-night stands, Melanie was relationship material. And she didn't want him because he was a rock star; she wanted him for that closet geek he worked so hard to conceal. It would be nice to share that part of himself. To be accepted for it. Dare he think cherished for it? Even so, Gabe was afraid to ask her to commit. It wouldn't be fair of him to keep her hanging on when he knew he wouldn't be able to see her more than a couple times a month. And that was if they were lucky.

"Is something wrong?" she asked, pushing the covers down to look at him.

He glanced up at her sheepishly. He hadn't meant to stop pleasuring her. Sometimes he thought too much with his big head, when he'd be better off just going with the instincts of his little head. Maybe she'd be willing to try a relationship. He'd never know until he asked. Or maybe he should start with something a little less confining.

"I was just thinking."

"Ah," she said. "You were *so* turned on by my body that you started thinking."

Was she teasing? He couldn't tell. "I was thinking about us, actually."

"*Us?*"

"I like you, Mel. I thought maybe we could stay in contact. Keep seeing each other when we can. Maybe try to make a go of it."

"You mean, like a *relationship?*"

"If you don't want—"

She covered his lips with two fingers. "I like you too, Gabe. I just didn't think anything lasting would come from this. Continuing what we've started here is much more than I bargained for."

"Oh."

She smiled. "But I'm glad you're opening up that

possibility."

He couldn't help but smile in return. "You are?"

"Yeah. Sometimes you just know that you're compatible with someone."

"Would you have discovered that if you'd known who I was when you first started talking to me?"

"Probably not," she admitted. "And I would have missed out on getting to know a fascinating and complex man."

"Not to mention having two fantastic orgasms."

She laughed. "Well yeah, that too."

"Want to go for three this time?"

"I don't think—"

He moved his hand to cover her lips with two fingers. "I do."

He eyed his suitcase, wondering if he should treat her to one of the inventions he had stowed inside.

Her stomach rumbled again, and he paused. Maybe there were more important physical needs than sinking into her tight little body. He honestly couldn't think of any.

"Gabe, can we eat first? Also, I need to go to the bathroom and brush my teeth. I feel gross."

"There is nothing gross about you."

"I can't relax. At least let me pee."

He sighed. "Okay. I'll wait. I won't like it, but I'll wait. Might as well go get some breakfast. You're going to need your strength."

CHAPTER EIGHT

Melanie wasn't sure why meeting the band made her body quake with nerves. She'd spent the night with their drummer. She couldn't imagine the rest of the guys would be much more intimidating than a man with a black and red mohawk and tattoos on his scalp. Sure, Gabe and his comrades looked like a group of thugs, but thanks to Gabe, she'd let her guard down and discovered that he wasn't so different from the regular Joes she usually dated. Well, that wasn't exactly true. Gabe was far sexier. Far more interesting. Far more tender. Loving. Wonderful. And the man knew how to rock a mattress.

"We could have breakfast in bed," Gabe said near her ear. "There's still time to turn back."

"I'm cool," she lied.

As the hostess directed them into a private dining room, Melanie prayed Nikki was already at the table for backup. No such luck.

Three members of the band and two other guys were seated in one of four enormous booths in the room. There were dozens of additional square tables and chairs, each with neat white table cloths, forest green napkins, and silver-trimmed place settings. Even if the entire crew joined them, they wouldn't need this much space. A dance floor took up the far half of the room. She was pretty sure the place was used for wedding receptions. Melanie wondered if the hotel staff kept the rockers separate from the main dining room so people didn't trample them as they tried to get autographs or because said rockers were so noisy that they were sure to disturb the other, more conservative, hotel guests. Perhaps a little of both.

"Do you want to sit with them or on our own?" Gabe

asked, nodding toward the occupied booth.

"We can sit with them." She wanted to prove to herself that the rest of his band didn't make her a nervous wreck.

So far, not so good. Her stomach was working on a new gymnastics routine.

Gabe rested a hand against her lower back as they stopped next to the table. "Did you already order?" he asked the guys.

"Not for you," one member of Sole Regret said.

He had a shaggy, spiked arrangement of jet black hair that went quite well with his all-black attire. Melanie knew he was the lead guitarist, but could not for the life of her remember his name. His steel-gray eyes swept over Melanie's rumpled clothes and tangled hair before settling on her face. "Your sexy sweetheart can sit next to me." He scooted over in the booth and patted the seat beside him. Melanie hesitated before sliding in next to him.

Gabe sat on her opposite side, and she had to shift closer to the guitarist. He wore enough chains to tow a truck. His spicy aftershave had her wanting to bury her face against his neck and inhale repeatedly.

"Aren't you going to introduce her?" the guitarist asked.

"Melanie," Gabe said flatly.

She glanced at Gabe and found him examining a menu. He seemed to have lost all interest in her. Why? Was she not *cool* enough to hang out with his rock-star buddies?

She turned her attention to the guitarist. "Hi," she said, "you would be. . . "

He laughed and slid a hand over his face. "Where in the hell did you find this one, Force? I didn't think there was a woman under sixty who didn't know my name."

Another rock-star type reached across the table to shake her hand. "I'm Owen," he said. "Don't judge the rest of us by Adam's giant ego."

"You play bass," Melanie said, as if she were on a quiz show and was pretty sure she was going home empty-handed.

He nodded. "That's right."

He had the prettiest blue eyes she'd ever seen. And the bone structure of a movie star. And the tattoos and face piercings of a side-show act.

"Most people know him as Tags," the ego named Adam informed her.

She vaguely remembered Nikki telling her that the band's pretty boy went by the nickname Tags. Though in all honesty, it was hard for her to look past the tough-guy accessories to the gorgeous face beneath. She was working on it. Her heart rate had *almost* returned to normal. She had *almost* convinced herself that she had nothing to fear from these guys.

"Do you prefer to be called Tags or Owen?" she asked, noticing the beat-up set of military dog tags on a slender chain around his neck. Was that how he'd picked up the nickname? She was much too intimidated to ask.

"He'll answer to anything," the other guitarist in the group said. He grinned at Owen and then turned his attention to Melanie. "Cuff," he said, shaking her hand. He was wearing a thick cuff on one wrist that looked like something out of a bondage convention. "Or Kellen," he added.

"Kelly," Owen corrected. He grinned as if he was in possession of some guarded secret. Again, Melanie was much too intimidated to pry.

"Chicks don't like the name Kelly," Kelly said. "I told you to start calling me Kellen in front of the ladies or just stick with Cuff."

"But she's with Gabe," Owen reminded him. "You don't have to impress her."

Melanie wasn't sure how anyone could tell she was with Gabe. He'd started ignoring her the instant they'd sat down.

"I like the name Kelly for a guy," she said.

Kelly had long, black hair and a raw sensuality that seemed to reach across the table and grab her by the womb. She definitely remembered him playing on stage the night before. And poking fun at Adam and Shade. She wondered if his hair felt as silky as it looked. It was definitely better kept than her own unruly tangle of locks.

"See, I told you that chick was just a bitch," Owen said. "Not everyone thinks your name is a *girl* name."

"You're the only one who still insists on calling me Kelly," he said.

"You'll always be Kelly to me," Owen said with a sweet

smile.

"How did you end up with Gabe anyway?" one of the other guys interrupted.

Melanie recognized him as the cute roadie who'd given Nikki her backstage pass the night before. Jack.

"I thought you and that other hot chick were both supposed to hook up with Shade last night. She said you two were in love but still liked to double-team a guy because even a double dildo is never as good as sharing one *real* dick."

Melanie chuckled nervously. All the band members were gazing at her with interest now. Even Gabe had lowered his menu. "Nikki made that up. We're not lovers, just friends."

"You sure? The way she kissed you. . . "

"I'm sure. She completely caught me off guard or I never would have allowed it. We've never double-teamed a guy. Or a dildo."

The roadie frowned. "But you two were so hot together. I walked around with a boner half the night just thinking about it."

Kelly reached over and slapped him in the arm. "Don't talk like that in front of a lady."

Melanie assessed Kelly a little more closely. She wasn't really attracted to men with long hair—or mohawks, until recently—but he was gorgeous too. Strong features. Dark mysterious eyes. A woman could get lost in those eyes for hours.

"So what do you want to eat, Mel?" Gabe asked. "I thought you were starving."

She settled her hand on his thigh and leaned closer to share his menu. When he planted a gentle kiss on her hair, she looked up at him hesitantly. He smiled. There was a longing in his gaze she didn't understand. It differed from the look of sexual longing that made her crave his body. This one made her want more than a single night with him. But that was stupid. She knew a relationship with him would never work out. Why would he even suggest it when he could have as many hot-and-heavy, no-strings-attached affairs as he wanted?

"What are you having?" she asked.

"Steak and eggs."

"That sounds good. Will you order for me too?"

"Of course. How do you like your steak?"

"Medium-well."

"Eggs?"

"Over medium."

"What do you want to drink?"

Gabe was still staring at Melanie as if this totally normal conversation meant the world to him. She cupped his strong jaw in one hand, delighting in the roughness of his beard stubble against her fingertips, and lured him closer for a tender kiss. When she drew away, she stared up into his green eyes and released a dreamy sigh. It took her a moment to remember he'd asked her a question.

"Cranberry juice, if they have it," she said.

"If they don't, I'll make sure they get it."

He ran a hand over her hair and twined one curl around his index finger. The dead silence around the table became noticeably uncomfortable. Melanie's face warmed when she realized everyone was watching them. Gabe's brow furrowed as he turned his gaze to the other men in the group. They were staring at him as if he were a pod person.

"What are you all lookin' at?" Gabe grumbled.

In unison, five pairs of eyes turned upward to gaze at the ceiling.

A waitress approached and set plates of food in front of those who'd arrived before Melanie and Gabe.

"Force!" The waitress whipped a black Sole Regret T-shirt from her apron pocket and handed him a silver paint pen. "Will you please sign this for me? All I need is Shade and my collection of signatures will be complete."

"Sure," Gabe said.

"The concert last night was awesome! I was stoked when I found out you all were staying here."

"Glad you enjoyed the show." Gabe signed the T-shirt, and the waitress took his order while the ink of his autograph dried.

He ordered for Melanie first—which made her feel special, cherished even—and then for himself.

"And can I get some fresh fruit as well?" Melanie asked. She didn't usually eat such a heavy breakfast, but her stomach was up for it this morning.

"No problem," the waitress said. "What I wouldn't give to be in her shoes," she muttered under her breath as she walked away with her autographed Sole Regret T-shirt draped over one shoulder.

Melanie was suddenly delighted to be sandwiched between two sexy rock stars and having breakfast with most of the members of Sole Regret. Thanks to Nikki's impulsiveness, she had an *amazing* story to tell her grandchildren. She'd skip the sex parts, of course.

Apparently, Melanie wasn't the only one who was starving. Everyone with food fell silent as they devoured their meals. Gabe held her hand under the table, stroking the sensitive skin below her knuckles with his thumb.

"I wonder where Nikki and Shade are," she said.

"Screwing in the sauna," Adam said.

Melanie turned her head to look at him.

"He took two security guards with him to ensure their privacy."

"Sounds hot," Melanie said. "And I don't mean sexy hot. Hyperthermia hot."

"I'm sure it's hella sexy hot," Adam said. "And I'm sure Shade will tell us all about it later when we're bored on the tour bus."

"I'm sure Nikki would prefer he didn't," Melanie said, embarrassed for her friend. Yeah, Nikki could be slutty, but she made no excuses. If she wanted to fuck a guy in the sauna, she fucked him in the sauna. Melanie sometimes envied Nikki's lack of inhibition, but Melanie also pitied her, because she knew that what Nikki really wanted was for someone to love her. She was just going about it all wrong. Melanie recognized that she was going about it all wrong too, but then she'd never expected to feel anything for Gabe besides lust. She was feeling things for him that she had no business experiencing, much less expressing.

"I have some time after breakfast," Gabe whispered in her ear. "Are you planning on sticking around until the bus leaves?"

"Do you want me to?" she asked.

"That's a stupid question."

"You don't want to fuck in the sauna, do you?" She crinkled her nose.

Beside her, Adam inhaled sharply and then started choking. The guy who was sitting on his opposite side pounded him on the back. Adam's chains rattled in time with the pounding.

"Are you okay?" Melanie asked.

He nodded, still coughing, and reached for a glass of water. He knocked it over when his attention diverted to Nikki, who danced into the room, positively glowing with happiness. Or maybe her face was rosy from all the time spent in the sauna. Everyone at the table stood in unison, piling fancy cloth napkins on the puddle of water spreading across the table. Nikki trotted across the room and wrapped her arms around Gabe's neck.

"Did you have fun with Mel?" she asked, giving him an affectionate squeeze. She tilted her head to the side, grinned at Melanie, and offered her a little wink.

Shade stopped behind her and cleared his throat. Nikki untangled her arms from Gabe's neck and hugged Shade around the waist, resting her head against his broad chest like a docile kitten. He cupped the back of her head in one large hand.

"I suppose you thoughtless assholes didn't bother ordering for the rest of us," Shade said. Melanie couldn't tell who he was looking at, because he was wearing his damned sunglasses again. She wondered if he wore them to bed. And while fucking in the sauna.

"You're the only asshole I see here," Adam said and sat in the booth again. He tackled his omelet with vigor.

There was an uncomfortable moment where everyone stared at Shade, and then, when he didn't engage further with Adam, they all sat down again to continue their breakfast. Shade sat next to Owen, who shifted closer to Kelly to make room. Nikki perched herself on Shade's knee.

"Where are you heading next?" Nikki asked.

"Dallas," Shade answered.

"Can I come with?"

"Not this time, kitten."

Nikki's bottom lip jutted forward, but Shade squeezed her shoulder, and she smiled again. Though Melanie had told the guys that Nikki wouldn't want Shade to share all the dirty details of their night together, Melanie was sure she'd be getting an earful of naughtiness on their drive back to Wichita. The waitress delivered Melanie's cranberry juice and Gabe's cup of coffee before insisting on an autograph from Shade. He obliged her and then ordered for Nikki without asking her what she wanted. Melanie watched her friend for signs of distress, but she looked as pleased as an honor roll student receiving a shiny gold star.

Gabe squeezed Melanie's knee. "She's a big girl," he whispered into her ear. "She can take care of herself."

Was her concern for her friend that obvious? Rather than deny that she was obsessing over Nikki's personal life, Melanie took a sip of cranberry juice. Gabe slid his hand up the inside of her thigh. When he brushed her mound with the side of his hand, she sucked juice down her windpipe.

Her hacking resulted in vigorous whacks on the back until she finally stopped coughing and her rescuers—Gabe and Adam—were satisfied that she'd live.

"I'm fine," she assured them, fearing they'd fracture her ribs if they kept at it.

This time when Gabe's hand disappeared beneath the table she maintained her composure. At least outwardly.

Her breakfast arrived and though she was hungry enough to gnaw off her own arm, it meant that Gabe pulled his hand out from under the table to use his utensils. She instantly missed the feel of his fingers against her. Every touch delighted and unsettled her. She was going to have a difficult time saying goodbye to him.

Wanting to have him to herself for as long as possible, she made short work of her exquisite meal. The filet mignon practically melted on her tongue. Her eggs were covered with a hint of buttery sauce that delighted her taste buds with an explosion of flavor. Nikki stole her cup of fruit and began to eat it with her fingers. With rapt attention, the rest of the band watched Nikki suck and lick strawberry juice from her fingers. Shade cupped her breast and rubbed his thumb over the tip.

"You're getting me worked up again, kitten."

"Good," she said in a slow purr.

Melanie checked to make sure Gabe wasn't gawking at Nikki— he wasn't—and focused on her plate. Nikki had unintentionally gained the interest of Melanie's dates in the past. At least, Melanie was pretty sure it had been unintentional. She didn't want Gabe to be sucked in by Nikki's blatant sexuality as well.

"Is your kitten up for a gang bang?" Adam asked.

Before Melanie could punch him in the mouth, Nikki shifted forward, giving Gabe, Melanie, and Adam a straight-line view down her shirt. She'd lost her bra at some point since Jack had given them that backstage pass.

"I'm getting all the banging I can handle from Shade," she said. "Though I would be okay with Mel joining us. I'm craving taco."

Melanie's eyes widened, and she shook her head. "No thanks," she squeaked. Was Nikki really into girls or was she playing at it for the sake of these rock stars and their perpetual hard-ons?

Nikki laughed and sat up straight on Shade's lap. "I tried, baby," she said to him. "She's too much of a goody-goody."

"What about that waitress?" he asked.

Melanie expected Nikki to refuse, at the very least. And if not that, to tell Shade what he could *do* with his suggestion. She sure as hell didn't expect Nikki to climb off Shade's lap and whisper, "I'll go ask her."

He slapped her on the ass as she trotted off toward the kitchen.

"Don't use her like that," Melanie sputtered as soon as Nikki was out of earshot. "She's going to get hurt again."

"She just wants to have a good time," Shade said.

"She wants someone to love her. Desperately. And I know that someone isn't you."

"How do you know that?"

"You just want her to fulfill your twisted fantasies."

He smirked at her. "Sweetheart, all my twisted fantasies have already been fulfilled."

Sweetheart? "Don't patronize me," Melanie growled.

"He pisses me off too," Adam grumbled. "Thinks he's hot shit."

"Nikki knows we're just having a good time," Shade said. "You're the one who can't separate sex and love. Stop projecting that onto your friend." He turned his head toward Gabe. "Tough luck, dude. She's hot and all, but I'm glad she landed on your dick and not mine."

Melanie's jaw dropped. She didn't even know what to say to that. Gabe's body tensed. A muscle in jaw tightened as he clenched his teeth together. For a second Melanie thought he was going to punch Shade in his smug face.

"So am I," he said. He tossed his silverware onto his plate with a loud clatter, chugged his glass of water in three long gulps, and then stood. He extended a hand toward Melanie. "I need to be alone with you right now."

Stunned, she stared up at him. The intensity in his expression made her heart melt and her panties ignite. If she hadn't been confusing sex and love before, she sure as hell was now.

She placed her hand in his and rose to her feet, never taking her eyes off his.

He led her to the elevator and used his card to send them toward the top floor again.

"Something wrong?" she asked him.

"No. I just want to show you something."

"What kind of something?"

"The surprise I mentioned last night."

She racked her brain for memories of what he was talking about, but came up lacking. "I don't remember. What surprise?"

"I have a little hobby," he said. "It's sort of perverse."

Her muscles tensed. "*Good* perverse or *bad* perverse?"

"You'll have to tell me."

"Gabe. . . "

"Don't look so freaked out. If you like me enough to put up with my band mates' bullshit, this will be easy."

She wasn't so sure.

He took her hand and kissed her knuckles. "I think you're going to find this to be a treat. Of course, it's still a prototype."

Her thoughts swirled with confusion. "A prototype?"

He flushed, and she had to stifle the urge to kiss him. She loved to see him flustered.

"I have this hobby," he said quietly. "I build things."

"What kind of things?" She was picturing some lifelike android or a drumstick polisher.

"Things that make a woman feel real good."

She was already feeling real good, but had to wonder what he thought would intensify her experience. "What? Like sex toys?"

"I guess that's what you'd call them. Does it weird you out? I've used my creations in the past, but I've never told a woman I designed them. I thought maybe. . . since you know I'm sort of a geek in wolf's clothing. . . "

And that's what she liked best about him—the geek hiding just beneath the surface that only she seemed to appreciate. "Are you just going to show me or are we going to actually use them?"

"I have a couple new ones I haven't tried out yet. How do you feel about being a test subject?"

"Your test subject?" She already knew he could make her come like no one else.

"You can say no," he said.

As if the thought of refusing had even crossed her mind. Gabe Banner brought out her adventurous side and she couldn't wait to see what he showed her next. She wrapped her arms around his neck and rubbed the tips of her nipples against his chest.

"Let's see what you've got, Dr. Kink E. Inventor."

He laughed and nuzzled her neck, making her giggle with ticklish delight. "I'm glad you're up for some experimentation. I promise you won't regret it."

She slid a hand up the soft strip of hair at the center of his head and tugged him closer, her throat closing off with unexpected emotion. Her sole regret was that her time with him would have to end far before she was ready to let him go.

CHAPTER NINE

The elevator let them out on their floor. A mixture of anticipation and trepidation settled in Melanie's belly. She reminded herself that Gabe was a fantastic lover and that they didn't have much time left together. If these toys of his were important to him, she wanted to be open to them. Open to him.

Apparently her willingness to participate excited him. He had her shirt halfway off before they made it into the suite and all the way off by the time the door shut behind them. Her bra followed.

He cupped her breasts. "You have the perfect nipples for this," he said.

"For what?"

"I'll show you."

He shifted behind her and drew her back up against his belly, massaging her breasts and suckling the side of her neck as he slowly walked her toward the bed. His hands moved to her belt. He had her naked and sprawled across the mattress in less than a minute. He paused to stare down at her.

"You're beautiful," he said.

She smiled at him. "You make me feel beautiful."

Gabe watched her for a long moment. "I think we'll try two things at once. I want you screaming my name. You'll never have to fake an orgasm with me."

He was practically grunting like a cave man.

She grinned up at him. "Is that some sort of macho vendetta against my girlie bits?"

"Damn straight."

He opened his suitcase and rummaged around until he

found two packages securely wrapped in thick canvas. He laid them on the bed beside her and unwrapped the first. Three thin chains formed a Y-shape. Each end of the chain had strange-looking clips attached—one clip was larger than the other two and had some sort of suction cup affixed to it. Melanie lifted her head to get a better look, but couldn't even guess what the contraption was for.

"This is why you have perfect nipples," he said. "Exactly the nipples I had in mind when I dreamed this up."

"What is it?"

He didn't answer her. Still fully clothed, he climbed up onto the bed and straddled her thighs. He cupped her breasts in both hands, rubbing her nipples with his thumbs until they pebbled under his attention. He fastened one clip to her left nipple and the other to her right.

Her back arched off the bed. "Oh!"

"Are they tingling?" He tugged the chain.

"Aching."

"Must not have a good connection." He removed one of the clips and wet her swollen nipple with his tongue. She held the back of his head to keep him from moving away. While the clip on her nipple was stimulating, it in no way compared to the warm, wet pleasure his mouth gave her. He pulled back and returned the clip to her wet nipple. A delightful tingle swept through her flesh.

"Wow!"

"It's working?"

"It feels sort of like when you stick your tongue on a nine-volt battery."

"Do you like it?"

It felt different from anything she'd experienced. "I think so."

He went to work on wetting her other nipple, tilting his head so he could hold her gaze as his tongue flicked against her sensitive skin. When he had both clips in place, they released rhythmic pulses to both breasts. He tugged the chain between them, and Melanie's womb tightened.

"Gabe! I think I'm almost there."

"I don't even have it all the way on yet," he said. "Try to

hold back."

She'd never had a man tell her not to come. She tightened all the muscles between her legs, longing for something inside her to alleviate the throbbing ache, and clung to the covers in torment. She tried focusing on the top of Gabe head instead of the maddeningly pleasure flowing through her body, but it was no use. "Oh God," she cried.

He released the chain from his grip, allowing it to rest between her breasts. He stretched out the final chain, which was attached to the middle of the one connected to her nipples, so that it lay down the center of her belly.

"Hold really still, baby. I've got to get this just right."

His head disappeared between her thighs. His mouth found her clit and began to suck until there was no way even a tranquilizer would keep her still. Her hips bucked involuntarily against his face. He lifted his head and pressed something over her clit. It tightened, gripping her excited flesh. She squeezed her eyes shut, the erotic look of him working between her thighs more than she could endure. He adjusted his contraption until it was held in place. It pulled a bit, as if the only thing keeping it attached was suction. Gabe then used his finger to move it around. *Oh fuck*, what was he trying to do to her? Drive her insane? Melanie bit her lip to keep from screaming in blissful torment.

"Does it have a good seal?" he asked. "I don't want it to hurt you."

"It doesn't hurt," she assured him breathlessly.

He shifted over her to kiss her sweat-moistened belly worshipfully, tracing the chain resting against her stomach with his nose.

"When I first saw your belly chain, I immediately thought of how this invention would look against your skin. I knew you'd do it justice. I'll get the vibration going in a minute."

"Vibration?" Holy Hell, he *was* trying to drive her insane.

He grabbed the chain that was resting against her belly and gave it a firm tug. It pulled on both nipples and her clit simultaneously. Her breath caught as ripples of ecstasy radiated through her pussy in teasing spasms.

"I think it'll hold. Wait for me, baby. I have to get myself ready now."

Get *himself* ready? She had no idea what he meant. He reached for the second, smaller package but hid its contents from view. He offered her a crooked grin and her heart rate kicked up another notch, ready for whatever else he had in store for her. "Hurry, Gabe," she whispered. "Please."

He climbed from the bed and pulled his shirt off over his head. She drank in the sight of his well-formed muscles contracting beneath his skin as he unfastened his jeans and removed the rest of his clothes. Her hand trailed to her belly to toy with the chain. If she pulled it just a bit, the pleasure intensified, making her breasts ache and muscles deep inside twitch uncontrollably. She couldn't imagine how amazing Gabe's invention would feel if it actually vibrated.

Admiring the ink on Gabe's hip, which now aroused her instead of frightening her, she watched him wrap a thin leather cuff around the base of his cock and snap it in place. He stroked himself until his cock was thick and erect. She longed to trace the torturous veins beneath its smooth skin with her tongue. To feel the swollen head rubbing against her inner walls and his tight balls bumping against her twitching ass as he fucked her deep. Deep and hard. She wanted dig her nails into his back, her heels into his ass, and take it as good as he was willing to give it. She groaned at her own thoughts, praying he hurried. She couldn't wait much longer. She feared she'd implode if he didn't fill her soon.

The raspy hitch of his breathing as he stroked himself had her dripping wet in an instant. She rhythmically tugged the chain in time with his hand as he rubbed his length. God, watching him make himself hard for her was such a turn-on. Everything. Everything about him was a turn-on.

He applied a condom and then attached a slender rod to the top of his modified leather cock ring. The attachment was several inches long, had a small knob on the end, and ran parallel to and a few inches above his cock. The small attachment appeared to be made of highly polished wood. She couldn't begin to guess what the hell it was for. Did it interact with the contraption on her clit? While she let her imagination run wild, Gabe crawled up on the end of the bed with something hidden in his hand that he wouldn't let her see. His intense gaze sent a trickle of apprehension down her spine. She'd never seen him look so serious. So *determined*.

He rolled her onto her belly and then lifted her up onto her knees. Before she could let him know that doggy style was not her favorite position, he entered her several inches.

She whimpered.

"I just need to adjust this, baby. Hold still for me."

She felt the rod he'd attached to his cock ring press against her ass, and then something cold squirted against that bit of virginal territory. With the exception of his finger the night before, she'd never had anything in her back door. He rubbed the slippery substance over her tense opening, using his fingers to work it inside. Lube. If he rammed his enormous cock in her ass, it would probably kill her.

"Wait," she gasped.

He shifted forward, and the ball at the end of the slender rod popped into her ass while his cock pressed deeper into her pussy.

"Gabe, wait, I. . . "

"Does it hurt?"

No, actually it felt fucking amazing. But she didn't like things in her ass. At least that's what she'd anticipated. She wasn't exactly an expert at anal play.

"Melanie?"

"I'm not sure," she admitted, rubbing her hot face against the covers. She concentrated on what she was feeling back there. The rod was so slender and his cock was so thick, she couldn't feel much of anything inside her ass at all. It felt cool and wet, but she felt no pressure inside. "I can't really feel it much now."

He pulled back and the knob at the end of his attachment popped out of her ass. She cried out in bliss.

"Did you feel that?" She could hear the smile in his voice.

"Y-yes."

"And did it feel good or did it hurt?"

"Good." It was the longest sentence she could manage.

"Okay, I'm going to turn on the vibration now. Are you ready?"

"Good." She rocked backward, seeking double penetration again. "Feels good."

He reached around her body and pressed something between her legs. The device attached to her clit hummed to life. Her entire body went taut, and she moaned. "My goal is to make you scream my name. Give me what I want, but make me work for it."

He leaned against her back and reached under her, gathering the chain that was dangling from her belly into one fist. The pull tugged on her nipples and clit with just enough pressure to send jolts of pleasure through her breasts and womb, yet it put a stop to the vibration against her clit. Gabe then loosened his grip, which eased the pull on her sensitized flesh but buzzed her clit again. He alternated between pulling the chain and allowing it to loosen—between tug and vibration—over and over again. It brought her to orgasm in seconds. Before she recovered, he began to pump his hips, filling her clenching pussy with thick cock and popping that little knob in and out of her ass until tears were streaming from both eyes and she was begging for mercy. He tugged the chain with each thrust, pleasuring so many parts of her at the same time that her body was lost to sensation and ecstasy.

God, she was coming hard, so hard, and she couldn't stop. "Gabe," she cried. "Gabe! Gabe! Too much. Please." And then she really was screaming his name. Loud and repeatedly. The only other word she could manage to scream was "fuck".

When her voice grew hoarse and eventually failed her, she comprehended he was chuckling at her insanity. "You need to practice some orgasm delaying techniques, Mel," he said. At least that's what she thought he said. Her ears were still ringing with her own screams. She fought to catch her breath, whimpering now, still consumed with pleasure, but too drained to scream anymore.

He reached between her legs to shut off the vibrator and allowed the chain to sway beneath her with each of his powerful thrusts. He pounded against her cervix with each plunge inward and popped that maddening device out of her clenching ass with each outward stroke. She couldn't decide which motion gave her more pleasure.

She clung to the sheets beneath her face and closed her eyes, her entire body quivering. His concentration absolute, he didn't seem close to finding his own release at all. Apparently, that cock ring of his assisted him with orgasm delay. She moaned as her pleasure began to rebuild. It felt so good. He felt so good. Filling her. Pressing deep. She rocked against him, encouraging his steady strokes.

And as if his powerful thrusts weren't enough, that little knob popping in and out of her slickened ass was driving her insane. He rested one hand on her ass to make sure it plunged into her at just the right angle. It teased her. Made her crave something larger inside there. Something thicker. Deeper. Made her think maybe she'd like him to fuck her there, too. Ram his huge, thick cock in her ass. Would it hurt? Would she be able to take it? Just thinking about it made her pussy tighten and her ass strain for increased stimulation. Soon she was coming again and screaming his name even louder. When the quaking of her body began to subside and only the occasional aftershock of pleasure pulsed through it, she lifted her face from the covers.

"Please, Gabe. I can't take anymore."

"Shh, baby. Almost. I'll try to hurry for you."

His fingers dug into her hips, and he fucked her harder. Harder. She rocked back to meet his thrusts, because despite what she said, she wanted more. *More Gabe. More. More.*

"More," she sputtered, rubbing her sweaty face over the mattress. "Oh yes, please more."

"That's it. Take all the pleasure I give you, baby. Take it."

He fisted his hand around the chain, yanking hard on her nipples and clit. Fuck. It hurt so good after all the pleasure he'd given her.

"Spank me," she pleaded.

He landed one hard smack on the cheek of her ass and sent her flying over the edge again. She clung to the bedclothes and let the pleasure wash over her. She didn't know if his name was echoing in her mind or if she was still screaming it aloud. One thing was for sure, she was unequivocally lost in the man and never wanted to be found again.

CHAPTER TEN

Watching Melanie get off so hard excited Gabe almost as much as the feel of her pussy clenching around his plunging cock. He couldn't believe she was coming again. He'd heard of multi-orgasmic women—he'd even fucked a few—but this was ridiculous. Of course, it was his devices that had her so overwhelmed with pleasure that her body was drenched in sweat, her words had become incoherent, and she was drooling all over the bed.

He had honestly thought his perversion would turn her away. What kind of guy thought about how to make a woman come so much and so hard that he not only imagined devices to get the job done, but designed and made them? He'd expected her to head for the hills in terror when he'd told her about his unusual hobby. He was sure most women would have freaked the fuck out. It was probably why he'd told her in the first place. His way of driving her away. But Hell, if she was okay with it, he was more than eager to share it with her.

Seeing her mingling with the band had scared the ever-loving shit out of him. It had made her real. Not just some nice girl he could remember fondly while whiling away the long lonely hours on the tour bus. Not some girl he'd spent one night with, hoping for more. She wasn't some fantasy in his overactive imagination; she was real. And not just to him, but to everyone.

And not only had she not called him a *freak* for inventing sex toys, she seemed to be perfectly okay with his hobby. She'd not only screamed his name, she'd screamed in pure, bone-deep pleasure. And when the pleasure became too much, he'd showed her how a little pain made it even better and she'd fucking liked it so much she'd erupted with another orgasm. She was perfect. He wanted to use every prototype in his collection on her. Wanted her trembling with pleasure again and again and again. Wanted to fuck her every which way he'd ever imagined.

He had to get her to visit him in Austin.

Gabe cringed as he unsnapped the leather band at the base of his cock. It would take him an hour to come with that strap squeezing his dick closed at the base, and she really did seem to be at her limit. She shuddered as he tugged the knob free of her ass for the last time and set the gadget aside.

"Love that thing," she whispered, her voice raw.

"I'll use it again next time," he promised. "I have them in all different shapes and sizes. We'll figure out which one feels the best."

"Next time. . . I hope there are many, many next times."

He pulled out and encouraged her to roll onto her back. He wasn't sure why, but he wanted to look into her eyes as he came. And he didn't want any of his devices in the way. It had to be all him this time. He carefully removed the clips from each reddened nipple. Her body went limp beneath him.

"Are you finished?" she asked, her words slurred, as if she'd had too much to drink.

He shook his head. "I haven't come yet. I need to take the suction off your clit now. It will probably bruise."

"Worth it." Her eyelids fluttered. "Totally fucking worth it."

He grinned. "You liked it?"

She made a sound halfway between a laugh and a moan. "Where did you get it?"

"I told you. I made it."

"Fucking genius. You need to patent it. And that ass teaser too. Dear lord, it tugs just right. Makes me want you to fuck me in the ass."

He grinned. "And you were so hesitant at the beginning. I knew you'd like it."

"I'll never doubt your judgment again."

He moved down her sweat-slick body and released the suction on the cup attached to her clit. Her body jerked, and she sucked a breath through her teeth. He lowered his head and soothed the overstimulated flesh with soft caresses of his lips. "You're going to remember this for a few days," he said. He shouldn't have kept it attached for so long.

She laughed and covered her eyes with both hands, her elbows pointing toward the ceiling. "Gabe, I have no doubt that I'll remember this for the rest of my life. You've ruined me for all other men."

"Good. I don't want other men touching you." He shifted his arm so he could stroke her red and swollen lips with his fingertips. "Kissing you." His pressed his lips to her heated flesh. "Tonguing you." He plunged his tongue inside her opening.

"Ohhh . . . "

He crawled up her body and used his hand to guide his cock into her receptive pussy. He sank deep and his balls throbbed with their need for release. "Fucking you."

She wrapped her arms and legs around him. "What about holding me?"

He drew her closer. "No. No other man can hold you either. Just me."

"Just you," she whispered. Their eyes met. Locked. He began to thrust into her gently. It felt so good, but he knew it could feel even better.

"I want to fuck you raw, Mel."

She smiled and clasped the sides of his head between both hands. "I think I've already been fucked raw, Mr. Banner."

He grinned at her. "I mean without a condom. I'm clean. Are you?"

She nodded.

"Do you trust me to pull out in time?"

"You don't have to. I'm on the pill. Come inside me."

"Do you trust that I'm clean? I am, but if you're worried, I won't."

"I do trust you. You haven't lied to me yet. I want... to feel... *closer*."

He smiled and brushed the hair from her sweat-damp cheeks. Kissed her gently. "I'm crushing on you so hard, Melanie Anderson." In his adult life, he'd never asked a woman to have sex without a condom. Melanie was already special to him, but *this*, this trust, this flesh touching flesh, cemented their connection. He wanted nothing separating them.

He eased out of her body, removed the condom, and then slowly slipped inside again. He sucked a stuttering breath through his teeth. Her slick, tight heat was his own piece of heaven on earth.

He claimed her with slow, deep thrusts, delighting in each stroke. The skin along his spine began to tingle. The soles of his feet dampened. Every muscle in his body tightened. He never wanted it to end, this time with her. He never wanted it to fucking end.

There was a loud knock on the door.

"Force," Adam yelled from the hallway. "The bus is about to leave. Get your sorry ass downstairs!"

"Shit," Gabe muttered under his breath.

He lifted his head to look down at Melanie, stunned to see her lips trembling and her eyes watery. A lone tear slipped from the corner of her eye and glided down one smooth cheek. She hugged him and buried her face against his neck.

"Finish," she whispered.

"What's wrong?"

She shook her head. "I'm not ready to let you go. I'm sorry. I knew this was coming. I just didn't expect it to hurt."

He eased away so he could kiss her tears, kiss her lips, kiss her lovely face while he slowly thrust into her welcoming warmth. He wasn't fucking her anymore, he realized, he was making love to her. He not only felt the pleasure her body provided, but the comfort her soul offered his.

"We'll see each other again," he promised.

She clung to his shoulders and nodded. "I want that. You. I want you. Gabe."

A hard spasm gripped the base of his cock, and his mouth dropped open in wonder as he claimed his release inside her. She stroked the skin of his back as he shuddered. Her touch was so tender. So loving. Exactly what he needed. Even if the sweetness of it did rip his heart in two.

His body went limp, and she wrapped both arms around

him. He turned his face into her throat and inhaled deeply.

They lay like that for several moments, entwined in the aftermath of togetherness.

"Gabe?" she whispered.

"Hmm?"

"I think I want to get a tattoo. Will you go with me to get one?"

He lifted his head and looked down at her, framing her lovely face with hands tangled in her thick curls. "I thought you didn't like tattoos."

She swallowed and avoided his gaze. "Actually, I was sort of afraid of them. I... when I was thirteen, these four bikers cornered me and said all sorts of suggestive things. I used to have nightmares about their tattooed bodies and gruff voices surrounding me. Trapping me against the wall. I couldn't get away."

He kissed her cheek. "You should have told me sooner. I would have kept my shirt on."

Her eyes flashed. "Like *hell* you would. I love your body." She bent her head to kiss his collar bone. "Including your tattoos." Her small hands glided over his back and the tattoo of the phoenix which decorated the skin there. "Why are they all animals?"

He frowned, not sure how to answer. "I don't know. No one's ever asked me that before."

"Are you a nature geek too?" she asked with a grin.

He laughed. "Maybe. You'd better keep that just between you and me."

She smiled. "I like learning all your secrets. Tell me more."

He kissed her. "Next time," he promised. "I want to keep you coming back to me."

Her arms tightened around him. "As long as you're sure there will be a next time."

"I guarantee it."

CHAPTER ELEVEN

Gabe climbed the tour bus steps, walked down the aisle, and tossed his overnight bag into his bunk. Owen and Kelly were already sprawled on the semicircular caramel-colored sectional in the seating area near the front of the bus, but there was no sign of Shade or Adam. Gabe pulled his cellphone out of his pocket and checked his messages. He had a few texts from friends in Austin and a voicemail from his mother asking him when he'd be in town. She said she had a nice girl she wanted to introduce him to. Gabe was pretty sure his mom thought it was her duty to find him a woman or she would never be a grandmother. He wondered what she would think of Melanie. Would Melanie count as a *nice* girl even though she had a deliciously naughty side?

"Don't you dare call her yet, dude," Shade said as he dropped his bag on the floor next to his bunk. "She'll know your balls belong to her."

"I wasn't going to call her," Gabe insisted. At least not for thirty minutes or so. He'd secretly been hoping she'd called him by now. He missed her voice already. *Shit*, Shade was right. He *hated* when Shade was right.

Despite all of his talk about relationships, he hadn't really been sure if he'd ever call her. Hadn't been sure if the complications would be worth it for either of them, but especially for her. When he'd seen the tears in her eyes, he'd known he couldn't stay away. Until that moment, he hadn't been positive that she'd really want him to keep in touch. Now he was sure; she wanted him as much as he wanted her. He hoped she was strong enough to have him in her life. Few women had what it took to love a man who was married to the road and a music career.

"I don't believe you," Shade said as he snatched the phone out of Gabe's hand.

Gabe shrugged and sat next to Owen on the sofa. He knew how Shade ticked—you didn't spend ten years of your life living in close quarters with someone and not know how his mind worked. Well, Gabe understood Shade, but Adam was clueless and let Shade push all his buttons. Gabe knew Shade pretended to be cool so no one figured out how insecure he was about certain things. Not about women. Not about his singing. Shade had absolute confidence in those arenas. Shade had become a master of hiding secrets about himself that he was not open to sharing, but Gabe saw through his façade of cool. And he knew the best way to deal with Shade was to never rise to his bait.

"Are you going to call that little hottie you hooked up with, Shade?" Owen asked. "What was her name? Nikki?"

"Darling Nikki," Kellen said. He reached into the mini-fridge near his end of the sofa and hauled out two bottles of water. He handed one to Owen and kept one for himself.

"Maybe we should do a remake of that song," Owen said. "It could be metal."

"Been done," Shade said.

"You're not going to call her, are you?" Gabe asked. He didn't want his newfound relationship with Melanie sabotaged by Shade fucking things up with her best friend.

Shade shook his head. "She didn't want me to." He shrugged. "You know how it is."

Gabe took a deep breath and nodded. Owen and Kelly exchanged knowing glances.

"Whatever," Shade said. "She did say next time we come to Wichita she'd love to hook up again. Maybe she'll get her stick-in-the-mud friend to open herself up to a little fun next time."

"She's not a stick in the mud," Gabe said, a bit more perturbed by Shade's taunt than he should be. He didn't usually let Shade's bullshit bother him.

Shade chuckled. "As if you would know the difference. You're a dud in the bedroom yourself. Probably think doggie style is adventurous."

Gabe forced a puzzled look on his face. "What's doggie style?"

Owen laughed. Kellen just rolled his eyes. Adam came out of the bedroom at the back of the bus. "Are we going to hang around here all day? I need to get to Dallas. Like yesterday." "Just waiting for the driver," Owen said.

Adam sat in one of the captain's chairs across from the curved sofa.

"Can I have my phone back now?" Gabe asked.

"Are you going to call your mommy?" Shade asked. He tossed Gabe's phone in the air and Gabe caught it in one hand.

"Later," Gabe said. "I need to call Melanie first."

Owen leaned across Gabe's body and snatched the phone out of Gabe's hand before he could find Melanie's picture and name in his long list of contacts.

"Twenty-four hour rule," Owen said.

"Rock stars live too fast for the twenty-four hour rule," Adam said. "Our average life expectancy is equal to one-half normal divided by number of addictions minus the number of small craft flights per month, the number of fast cars owned, and the number of miles driven on a motorcycle without a helmet. I'd say the three-second rule better applies to Gabe here."

Gabe chuckled. "See? I'm already late calling her."

"Nah," Owen said, "you have fewer addictions than Adam and don't own a motorcycle. You have at least twenty more minutes."

The bus driver, Tex, climbed up the steps and did a head count. "Y'all ready t'go?"

Most of the band and crew had lost their Texas drawls after traveling around the country and the world for ten years, but not Tex. Gabe figured he took refresher lessons. And when Gabe hung around with him too much, he started talking just like him.

"We're ready," Adam said. "Let's go. I so need to get laid."

Adam had a regular hook-up in Dallas. Not a girlfriend, exactly. None of them had girlfriends, exactly. Kind of depressing.

Shade headed for his bunk. "I guess I'll get some sleep.

Sure didn't get any last night. Darling Nikki has some serious stamina." He took off his sunglasses, revealing weary ice blue eyes. He tucked his shades into the neckband of his T-shirt. "Don't let Force call that chick while I'm out."

"Why are you so worried about him calling her, Shade?" Kellen asked.

"He'll get all pussy-whipped on us if he lands himself a steady girlfriend." Shade climbed into his bunk. "Besides who would want to be stuck with the same chick all the time when there is so much delicious variety available?"

"Me," Kellen said.

"Yep. Me too," Owen agreed with a nod.

"Fuck that. For once, I agree with Shade," Adam said. "The more variety, the better."

"Man whores," Owen said and shook his head at them. "Both of you."

Shade grunted and slid his bunk's curtain closed. An instant later his boots dropped out of his bunk onto the floor.

"You don't have room to talk," Kellen teased and punched Owen in the shoulder.

"You either."

"At least we're ashamed of our whorish ways," Kellen said, leveling his most serious look at Owen.

Gabe snorted and burst out laughing. "Yep, you're a regular pair of cloistered nuns."

"Nuns?" Kellen said. "I think you mean cloistered monks."

"I wouldn't mind being cloistered with a bunch of horny nuns for a couple days," Owen said.

"As long as they were horny," Adam said with a thoughtful nod.

Kellen laughed. "They'd think you were possessed by demons and try to exorcise you."

"I'm more likely to exercise them." Adam slipped two fingers in and out of the loose fist in his opposite hand and smirked at Kellen.

Were they seriously discussing defiling nuns? Sometimes Gabe wondered why he hung around with these guys. Oh yeah, he had no choice.

"Owen might get some nun action," Kellen said. "He's the

one with the angel face." Kellen grabbed Owen's face in one hand and squeezed. "They'd think he was cute."

"Until they saw how he's mutilated his junk," Adam said.

"Not mutilated," Owen protested through his squished mouth. "The ladies like it."

Gabe didn't care how much the ladies liked it; he'd never get his cock pierced. He could invent less painful ways to keep his woman satisfied.

"The ones who aren't terrified of it," Kellen said and released Owen's face. He gave Owen a thunk on the side of the head as an afterthought.

Owen punched Kellen in the thigh and turned his attention to Gabe's cellphone.

"Owen?" Gabe said.

Owen's warm, blue eyes rose to meet Gabe's gaze. "Huh?"

"I think you should give my phone back now."

He looked down at the screen and started scrolling through Gabe's apps. "Why?"

"Because I have a lot of blackmail material on you and I'm not afraid to use it."

Owen found the game he wanted to play and started flinging birds at pigs. "Not half as much blackmail material as I have on you," he said calmly. "And you care what your mama thinks of you."

"You don't want me to call in a favor from Cuff, do you?" Gabe didn't have to explain what he meant. Owen knew if Gabe called Kellen "Cuff" in the privacy of the bus, it meant he wanted to use Kellen's *special* talents.

Kellen sat up straighter on the sofa, a devilish glint in his dark eyes. "Do you want me to tie him up or tie him down?"

Owen glanced at Kellen as if Gabe's threat was reward rather than punishment. While he was distracted, Gabe snatched his phone out of his hand.

"I think I'll take this to the bathroom so you guys don't bother me," Gabe said.

"What?" Adam called after him. "Are you going to jerk off for her with video rolling?"

Gabe sighed heavily and rather than correct Adam's lewdness, he said, "Yep. Twice. So do not disturb."

CHAPTER TWELVE

"Are you driving?" Nikki asked Melanie as they waited for the valet to retrieve Nikki's Bug.

"It's your car."

"I'm not sure if I can sit still for that long. I'm a bit tender down there." Nikki's eyes rolled southward. "Shade fucks like an animal."

"And you think Force doesn't? Why do you think they call him Force?" Melanie would never tell her the secret behind Gabe's nickname. She liked that there were things between them that were not widely known. She was sure half the planet knew more about his life than she did, so what she alone knew, she'd keep to herself. Something to treasure. She couldn't wait to get to know him better. To learn all the nuances of his personality and history that weren't part of the public record.

They'd exchanged numbers and said their goodbyes in the hotel suite, mostly because she didn't want to cry in front of his band mates. She'd felt stupid enough crying in front of him.

"I'll take the wheel at the halfway mark," Nikki promised.

"Fine."

Before they were even out of the hotel's drive, Nikki had her shoes off, her seat reclined, and her feet up on the dash.

"That was fun, but I don't think I could handle more than one night with that man. I'm exhausted," Nikki said.

"I figured you'd be sobbing by now," Melanie said. She almost laughed at the irony. She was the one who was almost in tears, not Nikki. And Nikki didn't even recognize that Melanie was upset.

Nikki rubbed her crotch through her jeans. "I'm tender, but I'm not *that* sore."

"I mean like you used to in college. You'd call me to come pick you up, cry on my shoulder, and then we'd eat ice cream. Remember that?"

"God, don't remind me. I was such an idiot, thinking the way to a guy's heart was through his dick." She rolled her eyes and shook her head. "I think I fell into that pattern just so we could do the ice cream thing together afterwards. You've always been so good to me, Mel. I'd start missing you while you were spending all your time studying, so I'd get drunk and sleep with some loser because I knew you'd come rescue me. Anytime I just called and asked if you wanted to hang out, you were always too busy, but if I was upset over a guy, you'd be there for me in an instant."

Melanie stopped at a red light and looked at Nikki. She had that needy puppy look on her face and yeah, Melanie, liked it. She wanted Nikki to need her. She had *never* wanted Nikki to sleep with jerks just to gain her attention though.

"I had no idea, Nikki. I'm sorry I didn't make more time for you when you weren't in crisis."

Nikki shrugged. "It wasn't all bad. I had some great sex in college. And a *lot* of mediocre sex. Still, nothing compares to last night. And this morning." She fanned herself. "That man knows his way around a vagina. And no wonder he likes threesomes—he's too much for one pussy to handle."

"Did you really ask that waitress to double-team him?"

Nikki grinned. "She was happy to join us. You missed out on some serious fun, Mel. Ever had a woman go down on you?"

Melanie flushed and her gaze automatically went to Nikki's lap. "Uh. No."

"You *don't* know what you're missing."

And Melanie was pretty sure she didn't *want* to know. She *did* want to change the subject. She'd known that Nikki was wild, but she'd had no idea she'd go to those kinds of extremes.

"So you don't want to be in a real relationship with Shade?" Melanie asked.

Nikki laughed. "Hell no. I just wanted to fuck him. Do you know how hard it is to maintain a relationship with a musician

TRY ME – One Night with Sole Regret #1

while he's on the road? With so many girls like *me* trying to get in his pants?"

Melanie turned her attention back to the road as she searched for a sign pointing the way to the interstate. "I guess I'm about to find out."

"What's that mean, Mel?"

Melanie shrugged. "Gabe wants to try a relationship."

Nikki slapped her on the thigh with the back of her hand. "Shut up. Are you serious?"

"Probably not. I doubt he'll even call me."

She couldn't believe she'd become such an annoying, needy pest that she'd actually shed tears at the thought of leaving. He was probably glad to be rid of her. Ten more minutes in his presence and she'd have attempted to have herself surgically attached to him.

"If he breaks your heart, you know who to call for ice cream."

Melanie smiled. "You know, even without the broken hearts, we can just hang out. Like this. Even have some ice cream."

"Yeah?"

Melanie nodded.

Nikki sat quietly for a long moment, as if she were trying to get her courage up. "Um, Mel?"

"What?"

"Do you need a roommate?"

Melanie stifled a wince. "Not really. Why?"

"I sorta spent my rent money on scalped concert tickets." She grinned sheepishly. "Again."

Melanie released a frustrated huff of air. "I suppose you don't have anywhere to go?"

Nikki shook her head. "I could try to find some guy with low self-esteem to take me in. They're easy enough to find and manipulate."

"You can stay with me." *I'll help you get your finances in order,* she added silently.

Nikki launched herself across the car and hugged Melanie. Melanie swerved halfway into the left lane, earning a well-deserved blare of a horn from the truck she'd almost hit. "Hug me later!"

Nikki kissed her cheek and then slid over to her side of the car. "I do love you, Mel."

Melanie smiled. "I know."

"If that rock star hurts your feelings, I'll hurt him."

"He's a good guy," Melanie assured her.

After they'd traveled about twenty miles and Nikki had told her several shocking stories about her night with Shade, Melanie's ringtone played from inside her purse. "Will you see who that is?" she asked Nikki. "I wasn't planning to be out of town all night. Someone might be worried about me."

Nikki fished the cellphone out of Melanie's purse and checked the screen. "Someone named Gabriel Banner."

Yes! Melanie almost cheered aloud.

Nikki chuckled and slapped Melanie's thigh. "Oh no, he's *never* going to call you. I can't believe he waited a *whole* half hour." She pushed a button. "Hi!" After a pause she said, "No, this is her friend, Nikki. She's driving. Do you want me to give her a message?" Nikki laughed. "You want to do *what* to her tits?"

Melanie snatched the phone out of her hand. "Hi. It's me. I'll call you when we get home, okay?"

"Okay," Gabe said. "And Mel?"

"Yeah?"

"Thanks for giving me your real number."

"Thanks for actually calling me."

"I missed your voice."

She smiled. Her heart fluttered and foolish tears prickled her eyes. He might not look like one on the outside, but on the inside, Gabe was a total sweetheart. "I wish I could talk right now, but I'm a road hazard when I use the phone and drive."

"Drive safe," he said, "but call as soon as you can."

"I will. I can't wait to see you again."

"Me too, baby. Me too."

She hung up and knew she was grinning all goofy, but she couldn't help it. After only one night, she found herself falling hopelessly for a rock star. She was so glad she'd given him a chance, that her fear and ignorance hadn't gotten in the way of getting to know a remarkable man. A remarkably intelligent, talented, gorgeous, and inventive geek of a man.

Gabriel Banner was perfect: tattoos, piercing, mohawk and all.

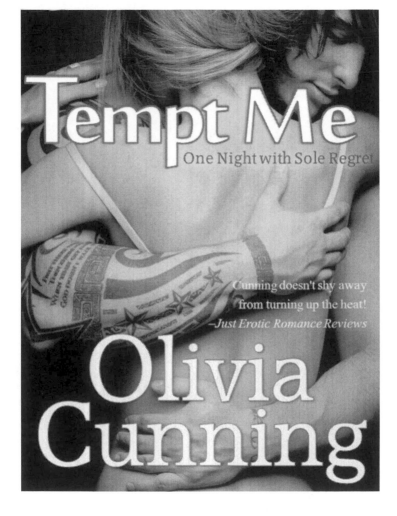

Tempt Me

One Night with Sole Regret

Cunning doesn't shy away
from turning up the heat!
—*Just Erotic Romance Reviews*

Olivia
Cunning

Tempt Me
One Night with Sole Regret #2

CHAPTER ONE

Adam's heart raced as he waited for Madison to answer her phone. Just the anticipation of hearing her voice thrilled him. He had no problem playing a guitar solo before fifteen thousand fans, but the prospect of speaking to one sweet woman made his palms sweat. Fucking pathetic. If his bandmates caught wind of his infatuation, they'd ridicule him nonstop. The entire group tended to gang up on whichever member happened to be jonesing over a woman, and Adam didn't want to be their current target. That was Gabe's role this week.

Standing near the back of the tour bus in the passageway between the bunks, Adam turned his back to the common area. Owen and Kellen had stolen Gabe's cellphone when he'd fallen asleep in the recliner, and they were currently sending text messages to some chick Gabe had hooked up with the night before. Adam had no idea how Gabe could sleep with the amount of sniggering going on around him. Maybe all that drumming had permanently damaged his hearing.

"Now type: *I'll show you mine, if you show me yours,*" Owen said as Kellen thumbed in his words. "Send it, dude." More sniggering.

Adam was glad they were occupied with Gabe's torture while he attempted to hide his current weakness.

"Hello," Madison answered in Adam's ear.

It had been too long since he'd last seen her. Just the sound of her voice made his jeans tight. "Hey, baby," he said quietly.

"I can't wait to see you after the concert," she said.

"That's why I'm calling."

"Oh."

The disappointment in her voice made his heart twist. Damn, but this woman could reduce him to mush with a single syllable. He considered teasing her and making her think they wouldn't be able to see each other that night, but if it had been the other way around and he'd thought she was breaking one of their far-too-infrequent dates, he'd be devastated.

"We should be in Dallas around five." Adam glanced at the bunk where Shade was resting. Sole Regret's nosy lead singer was probably asleep, but his curtain was closed, so there was no guarantee Adam's conversation wouldn't be overheard. He made sure to keep his voice down when he asked, "Do you want to meet for dinner before the concert?"

"Yes!"

Now he couldn't resist teasing her. "*No?* Why not?"

"Yes, Adam. I said yes. *Yes!*"

He chuckled. "*Yes?*"

"Y. E. S. Where? What time?" The fact that she was so excited split Adam's face in a truly embarrassing grin. Thank God no one was paying attention. If anyone saw him smiling like a lottery jackpot winner, his gig was up.

"Italian. Five thirty. Meet me inside." He didn't have to tell her which restaurant. For almost a year, he'd been seeing Madison whenever Sole Regret's tour bus blazed through Dallas. Their favorite place served fantastic breadsticks and had a family-style restroom with a sturdy lock. The hip-high vanity had come in handy for more than one quick reunion between Madison's insatiable body and his.

"Hey, Adam!" Owen called from his seat on the sofa. "Who are you talking to? Your *girl*friend?"

Adam cringed.

"No one would be stupid enough to date a man-whore like him," Kellen said.

Adam scowled at the wall and covered his cellphone with his hand, hoping Madison hadn't heard. "I have to go," he said.

"I can't wait to see you."

"Madison?" He wasn't ready to hang up yet.

"Yeah?"

"Will you make cookies?"

She laughed softly. "You don't have to ask, Adam. I already made them."

Her homemade gingersnaps were to die for, but he mostly loved the idea of her making them for him—especially since he pictured her baking in a frilly white apron, her black cowboy boots and nothing else. Her soft, round breasts would be fully exposed. When she turned and bent to slide the cookies in the oven, he'd have a clear view of her spectacular ass and more. The white bow in the center of her back would beg him to untie it and reveal what she was hiding beneath the front of that fantasy apron. Or maybe if he pleaded nicely, she'd lift the fabric and display her secrets to him. Mercy.

Lost in his fantasy, the crotch of Adam's jeans shrank an additional size.

"Are you still there?" she asked.

He snapped back to his uninspiring reality. "Yeah. Um, Madison?"

"Yeah?"

"Wear a dress for me?" She wouldn't agree to wear nothing but an apron in public, but a dress would at least give him a view of those spectacular legs of hers. "With a short skirt."

"Okay," she said breathlessly.

Dear lord, he was already picturing her skirt bunched up around her waist and her panties clenched in his fist.

"Later." He hung up and, nowhere near as trusting as Gabe, buried his phone deep in his pocket where pranksters couldn't get to it.

Adam adjusted his over-eager cock into a less tenting position, grabbed a Mountain Dew from the fridge and hopped into the empty chair across from Owen and Kellen. He tried his damnedest not to smile like a dipshit, but it was a challenge with thoughts of Madison filtering through his head. Gabe was still out cold in the matching recliner beside Adam. Their drummer must've had one hell of time with that accountant babe the night before.

Still in Kellen's possession, Gabe's cellphone beeped to alert a new text message.

"What did she say?" Owen asked eagerly.

"*Show you my what?*" Kellen read from the screen.

"Boobs," Owen blurted.

Kellen rolled his eyes. "Gabe wouldn't call them boobs."

"Lady lumps."

Kellen shook his head.

"Tits?" Adam suggested.

Kellen texted a response.

"Breasts?" Owen read over Kellen's shoulder. "What kind of dude calls them that?"

"Gabe."

At the sound of his name, Gabe rubbed his nose with the back of his hand and inhaled deeply. His eyes opened a crack. He smiled trustingly at Adam and immediately fell back to sleep.

The phone beeped again. "Did she send a pic?" Owen asked in a whisper.

"Nope," Kellen said, "She says, *You first. Show me your nipple and I'll show you mine. Seeing your piercing makes my nipples so hard.*" Kellen read her text in a halting monotone, as if verbalizing stock quotes.

"Whoa," Owen said. "And she looked so sweet."

Adam knew just how naughty those sweet-looking ones could be. "Hey, Tex," he called to the driver. "How long until we reach Dallas?" *And Madison.*

"Couple hours," Tex called from the front of the bus.

"Anxious to see your *girl*friend?" Owen asked with a perceptive grin.

"Not my girlfriend," Adam said. "Just a great piece of ass I like to fuck." He knew they'd leave him alone if they thought Madison didn't mean anything to him.

"How do we get a picture of Gabe's nipple?" Kellen asked. He eyed Gabe's chest appraisingly, tilting his head to the left and right and using both hands to form a finger frame for his inspired masterpiece, *Guy with a Pearl Nip-ring.*

"You restrain him," Owen said. "I'll get the shot."

Kellen shook his head.

Adam chugged his liquid sugar rush and waited for Kellen and Owen to make their move on Gabe. He really couldn't wait to see Gabe's revenge.

"Fine," Owen said. "I'll jump him; you snap the picture and send it before he knows what's happening."

"Maybe we should tranquilize him first," Kellen said. "He hits fucking hard."

Gabe's hand suddenly covered his belly. His eyes snapped open. "Where's my phone?" he asked, his voice thick with sleep.

Kellen shoved it under Owen's thigh. "No idea."

The phone beeped with Gabe's characteristic tone from beneath their looking-entirely-up-to-no-good bassist. Gabe leveled Owen with a glare. Gabe looked badass. Black and crimson mohawk. Tribal dragon tattoos on his scalp. A long, wiry drummer's body—all lean muscle and sinew that packed a deadly punch. But they all knew Gabe too well to be intimidated by his looks. His fists on the other hand. . .

"What are you doing with my phone, assmunch?"

Owen, with his big blue eyes looking their most innocent, retrieved the phone from beneath his leg and glanced at the screen. "Oh yeah, now *those* are some nice-looking boobs. I could lick them for hours."

"I guess she didn't need to actually see Gabe's piercing to make her nipples hard," Kellen said as he viewed the screen over Owen's shoulder.

"Melanie?" Gabe's eyes narrowed dangerously.

"Oh yeah," Owen said. "I'd definitely love to squeeze those pretty titties together around my dick and give Gabe's sweetie a nice pearl necklace."

Gabe's face went as red as the crimson tips of his mohawk.

"Shouldn't have gone there, Owen," Adam said with a chuckle.

Gabe launched out of the recliner and onto Owen. Kellen had the sense to scramble out of the way.

"Oh Melanie," Owen egged Gabe on. "Yeah, baby, lick my dickhead while I fuck those plump titties."

"I'm going to make you pay!"

"Sure, I'll pay for it," Owen said, laughing through Gabe's hard jabs. "I've got your five dollars right here, baby." He grabbed his crotch suggestively.

Adam picked up Gabe's phone, which had landed on the floor near his feet. What better way to keep his own romantic interest under the radar than to join in on harassing Gabe? The picture of Melanie's breasts hinted at uncommon beauty, but Adam was sure the blurry shot didn't do them justice. Still, he whistled long and loud. "Nice. Maybe she'll show us more." Adam pressed reply so he could add to Gabe's misery. "*They're as beautiful as I remember from last night*," Adam said as he composed a new text message and thumbed it in, "*but you know what I really want to see*." He pressed *send* and handed the phone to Kellen, who was now standing between the two recliners to stay out of the way of the brawl between their drummer and bassist.

"*Show me what's in your panties*," Kellen said as he typed. "And send."

Kellen's diversion effectively got Gabe's attention. Gabe abandoned Owen, who lay immobilized on the floor by either pain or hilarity. He rubbed his ribs with one hand and clutched his stomach with the other as he gasped for air between laughs. Gabe stumbled to his feet and grabbed Kellen by the back of the neck. Kellen took his one-quarter Comanche heritage very seriously. In addition to always keeping his straight black hair long and well-kept, he also had a personal vendetta against wearing a shirt. It made getting a good grip on him a challenge.

"Give me my phone, Kellen."

Kellen handed it over calmly. "You should be thanking us," he said. "Now you have jack-off material to aid your attempt at long distance monogamy."

"He'll never last," Owen said, still lying on the floor,

gasping for air.

Gabe's phone beeped again, and he looked down at the screen. His eyes widened at whatever picture Melanie had sent him. "Sweet Jesus," he swore under his breath.

"Let me see." Owen used the sofa to haul himself off the floor. "Get his phone, Kelly."

The pair of friends cornered Gabe against the refrigerator.

Gabe held his phone out of reach over their heads. "Get the fuck away. No one sees this one but me."

Adam wondered if Madison would send him a sexy picture. He'd love something to remember her by on all those long, lonely nights on the road. Maybe she'd let him take a pic with his cellphone while they had sex—a shot of her beautiful pussy stuffed with his cock. Adam tugged at his fly. Damn, but these incredibly shrinking jeans were uncomfortable. And they had to be close to their destination by now. "Tex," he called to the driver, "how long until we reach Dallas?"

"One hour and fifty-nine minutes," Tex yelled. "Keep your pants on, stud. Her pussy will still be warm when you get there." Tex laughed so hard, Adam thought he might burst a blood vessel in his wide, ruddy neck.

Adam looked to the back of the bus to see if he was about to become the new target of his band's teasing. Fortunately, Kellen and Owen were too busy trying to pry Gabe's phone from his death grip to have heard Tex's barb.

Adam rested his elbows on his knees and took another sip from his can. The road between Tulsa and Dallas had to be the longest in existence.

CHAPTER TWO

Madison tried to stifle her excited flutters by covering her belly with both hands and taking several deep breaths. Her attempts to calm her jumbled nerves did no good. Between the butterflies and the perpetual grin, she was a giddy wreck. It had been weeks since she'd last seen Adam, and she hadn't been able to think of anything all day but being in his arms, in his bed and, hopefully someday, in his heart.

She was meeting Adam for dinner in half an hour. The seconds ticked by so slowly she wondered if the batteries in the large, wooden wall-clock were going dead. Though she knew her relationship with Adam was not exclusive—did world-famous rock guitarists *ever* have committed relationships?—she never felt alive unless he was near. Adam opened her eyes, her mind, her heart and *yes*, her thighs, to all that was wonderful in the world. Just the prospect of seeing him overwhelmed her with wonder, anticipation, joy and *yes*, panting lust.

"I'm not sure what you're smiling about, Madi," her twin sister said. Kennedy placed both hands on Madison's shoulders from behind and caught her blue eyes with her matching set in the antique dresser mirror. "All he ever does is hurt you."

Madison scowled. Being with Adam was her greatest joy in an already fulfilling life. Kennedy just didn't understand. "He only hurts me when he leaves."

"And that's what he does best. He leaves."

"He has to," Madison said. "Sole Regret is still on tour."

"Madi..." Kennedy's lower lip protruded in an unhappy pout.

"Don't do this to me, Kennedy. You know I love him.

There's nothing I can do about it."

"How about don't go running to him every time he calls? How about telling him if he doesn't commit to you, then you're through with him? How about remembering what he was like when you met him?"

How could she forget?

"He's clean now."

"You of all people should realize how unlikely it is for him to stay that way."

As a licensed chemical dependency counselor, Madison was well aware of how common it was for an addict to fall back into the web of drug abuse, but she never gave up on any of her clients—even the most hopeless of cases—and Adam was no exception. She would do anything to prevent him from falling into the deep, dark hell she'd found him in. "He's clean now," she repeated.

Kennedy's arms slipped around Madison's waist, and she dropped her forehead against the back of her sister's shoulder. "How long is he in town *this* time?"

Madison's heart squeezed in her chest, knowing how dismal she'd feel when she had to say goodbye to him in the morning. "Just one night. We're going to an early dinner before his concert and then afterward he promised to spend time alone with me. Tomorrow they leave for Austin."

Kennedy's arms tightened around her. "I guess I'll see you tomorrow then. We'll go riding this weekend. That should cheer you up a little." She snorted. "And maybe Daddy will get off our cases about how much the horses need exercise."

Madison really should visit her parents more often. They were just a few miles away on the southern half of the ranch her father had inherited from Madison's grandparents. Her father had gifted his daughters with the old farmhouse he'd grown up in after he'd built a new place down the road with large stables for their quarter horses. Commuting to Dallas each workday made life hectic, so Madison didn't have much time for the hobbies she loved. Even though she and Kennedy lived in the same house, they were both so busy with their careers that they rarely spent time together. She missed their long, dusty horseback rides through the countryside. "I'd like that," Madison said.

She turned to give her sister a proper hug. She knew Kennedy just wanted her to find true and lasting love. And Madison had found someone to love. Unfortunately, Adam wasn't the kind of man who could be tied down—not even by a former rodeo queen.

The hardwood floor creaked beneath her boots as Madison pulled away from Kennedy and checked her appearance one last time. She plucked a stray hair from her dress, smoothed a wrinkle and tugged at her skirt's short hem to make sure everything was concealed. She normally didn't wear sexy little black dresses that barely covered her butt. She felt half-naked in it. And naughty. The way she liked to feel when she was with Adam. The way no other man had ever made her feel.

"You look gorgeous," Kennedy said. "You always were the pretty one."

Madison laughed. They looked identical in every way except for the small mole at the corner of Madison's left eye. "And you always were the smart one, Dr. Fairbanks."

Kennedy had just earned her MD in psychiatry. She still had years of her residency to complete, but Madison couldn't have been prouder of her younger-by-seven-minutes sister. It was almost as if Kennedy's accomplishments were her own. Kennedy's happiness was her own. They shared more than just looks. Madison understood why Kennedy objected to her seeing Adam. If Kennedy had been the one dropping everything to spend one night with some man, Madison would have been the one trying to make her see reason. But understanding Kennedy's advice and following it were two different things.

"That goes without saying," Kennedy said. "I'm much too smart to let some selfish rock star lead me around by the nose."

"He *doesn't* lead me around by the nose." Madison scowled at Kennedy, but thoughts of Adam soon had her grinning. "His hold on me is a bit farther south. If you ever had sex with the man, you'd understand."

"I could always pretend to be you and find out what I've been missing." Kennedy winked at her.

Madison felt the blood drain from her face, leaving her slightly dizzy. It was bad enough that Adam undoubtedly slept with nameless women while on tour, but if he screwed her own sister, Madison would be devastated.

"You know I'd never do that to you," Kennedy said, her teasing smile fading. "You know that, right?" Kennedy bumped her in the arm with the back of her wrist. "*Madison?*"

Madison nodded.

"Now if his band's cute bassist wanted to introduce me to his psyche, I wouldn't refuse."

"Owen?"

"The gorgeous one with the pierced cock?" Kennedy grinned and wiggled her eyebrows.

Madison's face flamed. She wasn't sure why she'd shared that tidbit of privileged information with Kennedy. Madison had been so shocked by the very idea that she'd had to tell someone. "That's what I've heard."

"Are you sure you haven't *seen* it? You're blushing like mad."

Madison shook her head vehemently. She'd overheard Adam teasing Owen about it, that was all. Curiosity piqued, she'd done an Internet search to see what a pierced penis looked like and found there was more than one way to pierce a cock. Once she'd picked her jaw up off the floor and shoved her eyes back into their sockets, she'd told Kennedy about Owen's, um, *modification.* Her sister seemed a tad fixated on it. "I could introduce you to him. If you'd like."

"Maybe," Kennedy said. "I would like to know what drives a man to do something like that to his own body."

Madison chuckled. She should've known that Kennedy would be more interested in Owen's mental state than in his physical attributes.

Madison turned her head to check the time. While that damned clock had ticked forward at a slow mosey all day, it had inexplicably fast-forwarded fifteen minutes since the last time she'd glanced its way. Her fluttery stomach dropped. "I have to leave. I'm going to be late."

Kennedy crossed her arms over her chest and drummed her fingertips against her biceps. "Maybe you should keep *him* waiting for once."

Maybe. But the thought of missing even one moment with him made her eyes prickle with unshed tears. *Oh God, I have it so bad for him.* She knew she was a fool. What could possibly come from a one-sided love affair with a rock star?

"Next time." She hurried down the hallway, which was decorated with family pictures in mismatched frames. Out of habit, she kissed her fingertips and pressed them to the photo of her departed grandmother on her way into the dining room. Madison still felt the feisty matriarch's presence in the old house, which was why she hesitated to move to the city. "Bye, granny. Don't wait up." In the small, tidy kitchen, Madison grabbed her purse and the sealed container of gingersnaps she'd spent hours baking that morning, before dashing toward the back door.

"Call me if you need anything," Kennedy yelled after her.

"I will. Love you!" Madison was sure that Adam had everything she could possibly need pounding within his muscular chest. She had no hope of getting what she really wanted from him, though settling for what he kept in his pants wasn't too great a hardship.

CHAPTER THREE

There were few things that made Adam's heart thud like a bass drum at a metal concert: the first cheer of the crowd when he appeared on stage; watching Madison Fairbanks enter a room; any creature with six or more legs; watching Madison Fairbanks looking anxious and lost near a restaurant entrance; tornado sirens at night; watching Madison Fairbanks scan a room looking for him.

Madison hadn't spotted him yet, which gave him a moment to admire her innocent beauty. She wore a little black dress that clung to her slight curves and had a wide, low neckline that showed off the bronze skin of her throat and chest. Her collarbones were visible. He did have a thing for collar bones. Had he told her that? He must have, since she never disappointed him. He smiled to see her wearing her sexy, black cowboy boots. Adam's thighs tightened at fond memories of her legs around him and those signature boots digging into the backs of his legs. Even if the scuffed boots didn't exactly go with her elegant dress, they went with Madison.

Madison's dirty-blonde hair was drawn back by a clip at her nape. He couldn't wait to free those silky strands and run his fingers through them. To taste her sweet lips, her skin, her cum. To smell her delicate perfume, her fruity shampoo, the musky evidence of her excitement seeping from her sex. To feel her arms and legs wrapped around him, the timid touch of her hands, her nails digging into his back as her naked body thrashed against his in orgasm. Damn, he'd missed her.

Adam drummed his fingers on the surface of the table as if playing triplets on his fret board and waited for his hot date to spot him. A group of what had to be concert-goers—wearing Sole Regret T-shirts and an aura of anticipation—had entered the restaurant a few minutes before her, and he didn't want to draw attention to himself. He was glad he'd requested the back corner booth. He had a good view of the entrance, but the stained glass partitions at the top of each booth offered plenty of privacy from surrounding tables. The decor also made it difficult for Madison to find him. Apparently, she couldn't hear his telepathic mantra of *here, over here*.

Fuck it. He couldn't wait any longer. Just as Adam opened his mouth to call out to her, Madison said something to the hostess, who nodded in his direction. Madison turned and took a step in his direction. His heart skipped a beat. When her gaze located him, her pretty blue eyes lit up and a welcoming smile spread across her lovely face. Of all the people he knew, she was the only one who looked at him like that. The only one. She openly showed him how happy she was to see him, not because he was the lead guitarist of Sole Regret, not because she might gain notoriety or expensive gifts by associating with a rock star, but because she genuinely liked him for who he was. On the inside. Totally baffling.

Adam had no idea what she saw in him. When they'd met, he'd been at rock bottom. In the hospital recovering from a near-fatal overdose, he'd looked like hell. He'd felt like shit. He'd been so pissed off at the world and everyone in it that he'd acted like a complete asshole. Madison had talked to him for hours, never criticized, never given up on him, just talked. And more importantly, she'd listened. Not because she had to as part of her job, but as if she gave a shit. About him. About his problems. His pain and anger. She didn't trivialize any of it. She was the only reason he even tried to stay clean. The thought of disappointing her tore him up inside.

Clutching a plastic container of what he hoped was cookies, Madison hurried to his table, her sexy boots clomping across the tile floor. Damn, she rocked those boots. Her long legs were well muscled from years of riding. Seeing them made him want her on his lap. *Riding.* Adam's blood went hot and flooded his groin.

"Oh gosh," she said. "Am I late? I hope you haven't been

waiting long."

"You're right on time," he said. "I was early." He'd practically sprinted from the bus and into the limo, but she didn't need to know that. She thought he was cool. Madison leaned toward him to offer a chaste kiss, which he gladly accepted. Mmm. She was so sweet and pure. And so easily corruptible. Adam's hand moved to the back of her head as he coaxed her lips apart with his, seeking the deep, intimate kiss he craved. His tongue brushed hers, savoring the minty flavor of her mouth. She produced a throaty moan of longing. Fuck, she was sensual. And so unaware of her sensuality. He got off on awakening it in her again and again. Of discovering what she found pleasing—which usually surprised them both. It didn't take much to bring out Madison's naughty side and have her seeking new experiences. Adam let himself believe she showed her hidden side to him alone, because if any other man tempted her into getting down and dirty, he'd feel obligated to break the dude's face. Then his nuts. Then his face again.

"I missed you," she whispered when he drew away.

His heart warmed, and he grinned. He knew the feeling. "You did?"

She nodded and cupped his jaw, rubbing her thumb across his cheek as if she cherished him. She was the only one who ever made him feel cherished. The only one. She held his gaze as she asked, "Have you been taking care of yourself?"

He knew what she was really asking. Have you been clean and sober?

"Mostly."

She leveled him with an assessing glare, and he wanted to crawl under the table.

"You're supposed to call me when you get those urges," she said.

He'd rather call her when he had different urges. She had to be sick of listening to his problems.

Madison set her container on the table, slid into the booth across from him and took both of his hands in hers. She was the most caring person he'd ever met. He didn't understand how she handled being a substance abuse counselor. She'd seen more than one of her clients die of an overdose. She'd been yelled at, cursed out and even hit a few times. Some refused her help. Others took advantage of her infallible kindness. Madison took all of those occurrences as a personal affront, but instead of letting them destroy her, she used them as fuel. Her strength astounded him.

"Talk," she insisted, holding his gaze with hers.

He diverted his eyes to focus on her hands, which were holding his trustingly, and opened his mouth to lie. "I haven't taken anything since the last time I saw you." Considering the last time he saw her was when she'd entered the restaurant, that was true.

"Really?" She sounded so happy and proud that he couldn't bring himself to look her in the eye.

He'd enjoyed a couple of hits off a joint backstage the night before—nothing major. Technically, he hadn't even been high and it had been his first slip in weeks. So why did he feel like the biggest loser on the planet?

Because he had let her down. Gone back on his promise to stay clean. It didn't matter that he'd been strong when his father had blazed back into his life a few months ago in a purple haze. Adam hadn't been strong when Rico had produced that joint last night and cajoled him into smoking it. Madison had done so much for Adam—still did—and the only thing she'd ever asked was that he call her if the cravings got the better of him so they could talk about his choices. He hadn't even been able to keep that promise.

She squeezed his hand. "Tell me the truth, Adam."

He hadn't known what it felt like to be ashamed before he'd met Madison. Not a feeling he particularly cared for. Guilt clawed at his belly as he forced himself to look at her so she would believe him. The last thing he wanted was for his problems to intrude on their evening together. "There's nothing to tell."

Her eyes searched his—could she see that harmless lie behind his gaze?—but he held firm and eventually the tension drained from her slight shoulders. She gave his hands another squeeze. "I care about you, Adam. Please be good to yourself."

Words that inspired and crushed him in the same breath.

He turned his gaze to the ceiling, wishing he could tell her that he cared about her too, and that he was sorry he'd disappointed her by taking two hits off a joint, but the words caught in his throat. What did she see in him anyway? Didn't she realize what a bastard he was? Everyone else seemed to recognize it.

"Don't forget to call me if you're struggling. I can help."

She'd already helped enough. He could handle it from here. "Are you finished, Counselor? I didn't invite you to dinner so you'd ride my ass all night."

"I know," she said quietly, a delightful blush creeping up her neck. "I'd much rather *you* ride mine."

A spike of lust punched him in the gut.

She smiled gently and picked up her menu. "We should probably order soon," she said. "I need to be alone with you. Is the restroom free?"

Now sporting a throbbing stiffy, Adam turned his head to check the status of their favorite restroom. Even from a distance, he could see the little placard above the lock was red. His heart sank in disappointment. "Occupied."

"Let me know when it's free, would you?" The heated look she gave him could have melted iron. Madison opened up her menu and hid behind it to cover that devious grin he so coveted.

God, he loved spending time with her. He thought about her constantly, but didn't get to see her nearly enough. Since they'd become intimate, he hadn't even been sleeping around with other women. Much. No other woman excited him the way Madison did or made him feel so special. But he could never tell her that. He didn't need the headache of a permanent relationship. Or even a semi-permanent relationship. So he enjoyed her whenever he could and pretended he didn't miss her like crazy when he was on the road.

"Are those for me?" he asked. He nodded at the container sitting on the edge of the table. He could almost taste the spicy, sweetness of the treats he hoped were inside.

"That depends," she said. "Are you going to behave yourself tonight?"

He lifted an eyebrow at her and she giggled.

"Yes, they're for you," she said.

He opened the container and inhaled the heavenly aroma of ginger and brown sugar. "The guys are going to be so jealous when I eat these in front of them."

"You could share," Madison said, watching him over her menu. "There are two dozen cookies in there."

"I'm much too selfish to share. These are mine." Unable to resist temptation, Adam selected a cookie and shut the lid. He took a bite and the blend of molasses and spice that melted on his tongue made his eyes roll back in his head. "Oh God, Madison, you're so good to me."

She grinned. "I know how you can thank me properly. Bathroom?"

He checked the door. "Still occupied."

Their harried-looking server set two glasses of water on the table. "My name is James. I'll be your server tonight. Are you ready to order?" he asked.

Adam reached for his menu. "Order something quick," he said to Madison. "I have a sound check at six thirty."

"And what do you have to do after sound check?" she asked.

"You."

CHAPTER FOUR

Madison tried not to stare at Adam as he scarfed down his panini, but she wanted to commit everything about him to memory so when he was on the road she could torture herself wondering what he was doing, *who* he was doing.

Adam's thick black hair was cut in a shaggy style that framed his masculine features and brushed across his forehead. His nose was a bit too large, his lower lip a little too thick, his jawline too harsh to be considered model-perfect, but he took her breath away. Thick, dark lashes framed his steel-gray eyes. They were easily the most beautiful eyes she'd ever gotten lost in, but he had a tendency to glare, as if looking for a reason to become enraged. She wondered how many people got deep enough into him to see past that anger.

It hadn't taken Madison long to find the good in him. Those gorgeous, stormy eyes were always gentle when he looked at her. A single dimple teased the corner of his mouth, which only showed itself when he smiled broadly. Because he didn't hand out smiles on a regular basis, she'd only seen it a few times.

Adam's childhood had been a broken disaster. Only his music had kept him from falling apart. He'd used drugs because he'd learned from his father's example, and narcotics had become a crutch to cope with his turmoil. She knew all this because once she'd finally gotten him to start talking, he'd told her everything that he'd kept bottled inside for years. He'd trusted her with his secrets. She didn't take that trust lightly. And she couldn't deny that Adam's vulnerability, which he hid so carefully behind his tough-guy exterior, was her number one vice. He didn't let anyone but her see his weaknesses.

Yep, she had it bad for the guy.

Madison's fingers itched to trace the tattoos on Adam's strong forearm, to stroke his talented fingers, to tangle in those chains around his neck and pull him closer so she could kiss him with the maddening desperation she felt every time she looked at him.

She glanced over her shoulder to the bathroom across the way. She needed to be alone with Adam—submerged in him in a way she couldn't be in public. Just as she was about to inform him that the bathroom was free at last, someone entered and closed the door, switching the lock to occupied. *Darn.*

With a sigh, Madison returned her attention to the table. Adam picked up bits of chicken that had dropped out of his panini and stuffed them into his mouth with his fingers. Even his crude table manners made her smile. A man learned manners from his mother. If she hadn't already known that his mother had run off and left him with his drug-addicted father when he was seven, Madison would have guessed that the woman hadn't been in his life much. But Madison wanted to be in his life. Seeing him tonight cemented the feelings she'd been analyzing for weeks. She didn't feel only simple lust or affection for Adam. She loved him. No question. But was he capable of loving her?

This not knowing where she stood with him was eating her alive.

Madison turned her attention from Adam's gorgeous features to her plate and picked at her salad. She was almost certain that if she gave him an ultimatum, he'd run and never look back. She'd lose him forever. Just the thought of never seeing him again opened a deep empty chasm in the center of her chest.

Before they'd become intimate—when he'd still been in treatment—she'd asked him how he maintained romantic relationships while on the road. He'd responded that he didn't need nor want a relationship. He was content with sex. Relationships complicated things and were impossible to maintain.

Impossible.

Madison tried to convince herself that she was special to him. That a relationship *was* possible. Maybe he just needed time to realize he wanted only her and that she was worth the complications. She could give him time. She could be patient with him. As long as she had him when he was in Dallas, she could make do.

Coward, the little voice in her head accused. It always sounded like Kennedy. *You know you're worth more than this.*

Madison had never thought she'd end up in such a desperate situation. She never thought she'd so willingly hand her heart over to someone who didn't particularly want it.

"Everything okay?" Adam asked.

She looked up from her salad and nodded. Just a glimpse of his dimple as he smiled had her giddy. She grinned so wide, her cheeks ached. Her heart lightened and seemed to float in her chest like a helium balloon. She didn't want to give up this feeling. If she had an addiction, it was Adam Taylor.

"You're quiet tonight," he said. "What are you thinking about so hard?" He ripped a breadstick in half and placed a portion on her plate.

She hesitated. *Go for it, Madison.* "Us."

He stiffened and sat up straighter in his seat. "What about *us?*"

She could practically see him bolting from commitment. *Retreat, Madison. Retreat.* She shrugged. "I was just wondering how little sleep we could get by on. I'm really horny."

He laughed. "You looked pretty serious for someone who was thinking about getting laid."

"When you're involved, I take getting laid very seriously."

Adam's gaze settled on her throat, and he wet his lips. "None," he said.

"What?"

"That's how much sleep you can plan on getting tonight."

She laughed. "Good thing I don't have to work early in the morning."

Madison took a bite of her tangy Caesar salad, crunching on croutons and lettuce like a woman with a vendetta against the Roman Empire. It wasn't his fault that their relationship revolved around sex. Not when she balked every time she had the opportunity to tell him what she really wanted. Tonight she'd forget about her need for commitment. She had him here and now. She would make the most of their time together. And when he left again, she'd pine for him until the next time she could see him.

She had a powerful urge to bang her head on the tabletop repeatedly.

"Do you have a break from touring soon?" she asked, hoping she didn't sound as desperate as she felt.

"Why?"

"I could take some time off from work and we could spend a few days together."

"We'll be on tour all summer," he said.

Her heart sank. "Oh."

"But next time we're in Austin for a few days, I'll come visit you."

"I was thinking I could come visit *you*." She offered him a bright and hopeful smile.

"No."

Her heart was hanging somewhere around knee level now. "Oh."

"We could go on a trip," he suggested.

The man's hedging triggered suspicion. "Why don't you want me to visit you?"

Avoiding her gaze by staring blankly at the dessert menu, he shrugged.

She pictured a doting wife and three kids waiting for him in Austin. "Are you hiding something from me?"

He peeled his gaze off the photo of tiramisu and grinned at her. "Yeah." He snorted. "My apartment."

"What's wrong with it?"

He shrugged. "Nothing, as far as I'm concerned, but it's decorated with paintings of naked chicks."

She laughed. "I do know what the female form looks like. I happen to have one myself."

With a devious glint in his eyes, he gave her a twice-over. "I noticed."

As an expert at reading people who tried to hide things from her, she couldn't overlook his hesitation in answering her questions. "Is that really the reason? You don't have to make stuff up."

He reached for his beverage and slurped soda from his near-empty glass, his attention focused down his straw. Still not looking at her, he said, "That's really the reason."

"You could take the pictures down if they embarrass you."

"They don't embarrass me. I was more worried about you."

He *worried* about her? She reminded herself not to analyze his every word, looking for indications that he cared.

"It took me years to accumulate them," he said.

"You accumulate *porn?*"

His eyebrows drew together, and he shook his head. "It's not porn; it's art."

She figured his definition of art and hers were as different as bunnies were from tiger sharks.

"I promise I won't be embarrassed," she said. "I'd like to see where you live."

He trained his gaze on her at last. "Do you have plans to go paparazzi on me?"

"Of course not," she said. "Why would you think that?" Oh God, she must be coming across as some desperate stalker chick.

"I don't tell people where I live because I like privacy when I'm not on tour. I need to unwind from the insanity of this business. Plus, time alone reminds me that I'm actually a no-good loser whose only redeeming quality is an ability to make sound come out of six steel strings."

"You're an amazing talent, but there's more to you than music," she said, reaching for his hand and squeezing. "And you are not a loser. But you are good. You have a good heart, Adam."

He chuckled. "Do you actually believe that?"

"I do. I've seen it."

He held her gaze long enough that his attention triggered her heart rate to accelerate. *Oh God, his eyes.* She wanted to stare into them for eons.

"Are you trying to turn my head, Madison Fairbanks?"

"Only if it's working."

He lifted her hand to his lips and kissed her knuckles. "It's working. You always know exactly what to say."

So how did she say what was really on her mind? She stared at him, collecting her courage.

"Are you finished eating?" he asked.

She looked down at her nearly full plate and then at the still occupied restroom. *Go away, people.*

"Is it time to go?" Madison dug her cellphone out of her purse and checked the time. "It's not six yet." She glanced up at him and found him staring at her with hungry eyes. "I thought your sound check was at six thirty."

"I don't think I'm going to make it on time."

"AAC is only a few minutes from here," she said, pointing in the general direction of the arena. "I'll drive you. I know the best routes to avoid traffic."

"That's not why I'm going to be late."

His expression was entirely blank. Unreadable. In their early counseling sessions, he'd always looked out at the world from behind that wall, but why now?

"Is something wrong?" she asked.

"Just one thing that I can think of."

His hands slid to her wrists, his thumbs resting against her pulse points. Her body knew his touch and how well it pleased her. Just that small contact had her nerve endings thrumming with excitement and her muscles melting in surrender.

"What?" she asked.

"You're still in your dress."

She stifled a loud bark of laughter. Mostly. "Well, the damned bathroom's been occupied all night, and I'm not going to remedy that situation here at the table."

"That's why we're going to be late." He lifted a hand to a passing waiter. "Check, please."

CHAPTER FIVE

The band had rented a limo to take them to and from the hotel, but as Adam planned to hog it all to himself, the guys would have to find a different way to the venue.

"Are you sure it's okay to leave my car here?" Madison asked as they waited for the black stretch limousine to pull to a halt in front of the restaurant.

"If they tow it, I'll pay the impound fees."

"I could just follow the limo to the arena and—"

He silenced her with a kiss. When he drew away, she stared up at him with that trusting, sultry expression that made his heart pound and his cock pitch a tent. "It will be fine, Madi," he whispered.

She glanced at her dusty, pale blue sedan one last time and then climbed into the backseat of the limo. Adam slipped the driver a few hundred dollars. "Drive around for a while."

The driver nodded as if he didn't know why Adam wanted to spend alone-time with the beautiful woman waiting in the back of the limo. "Yes, sir. What time would you like to arrive at the arena?"

Adam estimated how tardy he'd have to be to cause a blood vessel to pop in Shade's head. Probably fifteen minutes. "A little before seven."

"Yes, sir. I assume you do not wish to be disturbed."

"You assume correctly," Adam said before climbing into the air-conditioned back seat with Madison.

She was inspecting the minibar. Glasses clinked as her slight figure straightened and she slammed the lid closed. Had she been snooping? Did she suspect him of hiding drugs or what? She'd been acting a bit strange all evening. Perceptive to a fault, she'd probably guessed that he'd lied about not doing any drugs, or maybe she was suspicious about his reason for refusing her visit to his apartment. He hoped she didn't press the issue. He wasn't sure how he'd hide his recently obtained roommate. Adam had promised Madison that his father was out of his life for good, and he didn't want her to know that he wasn't capable of confronting the man and telling him to get lost. She didn't need to know that. Madison thought he was strong.

Adam set his cookies on the seat and pointed at the minibar. "Would you like a drink?"

The driver shut the door and they were bathed in the soft glow of an overhead light.

She shook her head, clutching her hands in her lap.

"Good," he said. "I'm much too impatient to let you drink it anyway."

He reached for her and pulled her slender body against his. He always worried that he was too rough with her. He felt he should be gentle, but she liked the rough stuff. Begged for harsh treatment. It excited her. Made her insane with lust. Adam wrapped his hand around her hair at her nape and pulled her head back so he could suckle her throat and collarbones.

"Adam," she whispered, "should we be doing this here?"

He slipped the straps of her dress from her shoulders, revealing more flesh for him to feast upon. "Absolutely."

There was no way he'd make it through the concert tonight in his current state. Hell, he wouldn't even make it through the sound check. A quickie in the limo to make up for their missed opportunity in the restaurant's restroom wasn't ideal, but he was under a time constraint. He'd take his time with her later. Worship her body the way it was meant to be worshipped. Give her all the pleasure she deserved, because it was the one thing he did have to offer.

Adam kissed a path from the beauty mark beneath her left eye to her ear. "You have me ready to explode already," he said. "I can't think of anything but being inside you." *Twenty-four hours a day.*

A rush of air escaped Madison's sensual lips. "Yes." She shifted her hands under her dress and slipped her panties down her thighs. "Take them off."

"Woman, you tempt me beyond reason." He yanked off her black cowboy boots and tugged her panties down her legs. After he'd tossed the scrap of lavender-colored satin aside, he ran his hands up her thighs, drawing the skirt of her dress to her waist. Her bare butt rested against the edge of the pliable leather seat; her legs extended out across the spacious floorboard.

Adam knelt between her thighs and drank in the sight of her exposed flesh. She'd completely shaved her pubic region. The first time he'd eaten her out—on her office desk—he'd told her that he liked a clean-shaven pussy. She'd been mortified that he'd had to pause several times to remove stray hairs from his tongue. The next time he'd seen her, she'd gone Brazilian. He'd made her confess that she'd shaved herself before their appointment, hoping they'd go all the way in her office. After she'd admitted she been fantasizing about him fucking her for weeks, he hadn't disappointed her. Her office had been a complete wreck by the time he'd finished banging her on every available surface. A year and copious tumbles later, she still made his blood run hot.

Adam gazed at her feminine folds for a long moment, his mouth watering with anticipation. So sweet. So pure. So his. He committed the view to memory, knowing he'd have plenty of inspiration the next time he sat down with his drawing pad and charcoal pencil. He loved to draw her body from memory.

Unexpectedly, Madison's hands shifted to cover her mound, blocking the glorious sight of her sex. Such beauty should be celebrated, not hidden. He looked up at her and found her blushing, her gaze trained somewhere above his head.

"Don't stare at me like that," she whispered. "It's embarrassing."

"Why is it embarrassing? It's beautiful. The most beautiful thing God ever created." He urged her hands away and her knees farther apart. She scarcely resisted. Under his attention, her pussy grew redder, more swollen, wetter. Making her do things that she normally wouldn't always turned her on, and seeing her in this state had his cock straining his zipper. He had to have her. Now.

Adam unfastened his fly and pulled out his stiff and throbbing cock. "The only thing that could possibly be more beautiful. . ." He rubbed the head of his dick over her warm, slippery folds, brushing her clit, teasing her opening until she shuddered. " . . . is seeing it filled with me."

He entered her a few inches to prove his point, but got lost in sensation. His eyes drifted closed. *Bliss.*

"Adam?"

He opened his eyes, expecting her to be flushed with pleasure, but found her chewing on the end of her finger, looking uncertain.

"Relax, sweetheart," he whispered, his hands sliding over her hips, thumbs drawing upward along her hip bones.

He thrust deeper and glanced down to watch her hot sheath swallow his cock. His balls tightened. Fuck, he wouldn't last long. He wasn't sure what was about her that shredded his usual control.

Adam pulled back and plunged deeper, watching her body accept him. He loved how her flesh adjusted to his. Relished how her body was designed to give his ultimate pleasure. He wanted her to feel as much as she gave. Adam rubbed his fingertips over her clit to help her find release quickly. Later he'd tease her. Touch her. Please her. Later. Now, now he just had to fuck her. As he withdrew again, his cock, slick with her juices, was revealed an inch at a time, and then her pussy engulfed it as he thrust forward again.

Madison grabbed one of the chains Adam wore around his neck and pulled. "Adam!" she cried.

He tore his gaze from where their bodies were joined in splendid perfection. She wasn't looking at him; her horrified blue eyes were focused on the side window. "He can see us."

They were stopped in traffic. The driver in the next car was staring straight at them. Adam knew there was no way the man could see through the dark tint on the limo's glass. "He can't see us, sweetheart."

"Are you sure?"

Adam presented the dude with a stiff middle finger. The guy's curious expression didn't change. "I'm sure," Adam said.

She turned her head to look at him.

"You're not comfortable doing it here, are you?" he asked.

"It's just. . . I feel really exposed. Everything is showing out here in public."

He didn't consider this public, but he didn't want her to feel uncomfortable. He knew she had issue with public displays of affection. She probably didn't want pictures of her getting intimate with a guy like him showing up in the tabloids. He couldn't blame her. But when they were alone together—even in a place like a locked restroom in an Italian restaurant—all that shyness vanished. She became an uninhibited, sensual creature who wanted to experience everything he gave her. Must be the windows giving her pause. Even though no one could see in, she could see out.

"Baby, I promise no one can see in through those windows."

"Maybe if. . ." She pulled her skirt down to hide the spectacular view he'd been enjoying.

He tugged the fabric back up. "Careful, Madi. You'll get cum on your dress."

Her eyes widened. "Oh."

She pushed him away. He groaned when his cock fell free of her delightful body.

"Sit," she insisted, patting the bench seat beside her.

He wondered what she planned. He hoped she wouldn't make him put his dick away. It was so hard, he feared it might split its skin. When he settled on the seat beside her, she straddled his lap, facing him.

"Put it in," she whispered in his ear. "No one will be able to see that you're inside me under my skirt."

Including him, un-fucking-fortunately. He wasn't stupid enough to point out that even if a spectator couldn't actually see that she was impaled by him, they'd still be able to tell what they were doing under her dress. But if she was more comfortable doing it this way, he'd take what he could get. He could watch the action between their bodies after the concert, when they were alone in the hotel room and she gave herself to him completely.

"Can I fuck your ass later?" he asked as her slick heat engulfed him. He loved the way she responded to being pounded hard in the ass. He was pretty sure she liked anal more than vaginal sex. *It makes me feel naughty*, she'd whispered to him when he'd asked her why she kept requesting back-door entry. *Make me feel naughty, Adam.*

Can do.

Madison shuddered against him, his cock buried to the hilt inside her. "Don't talk about that now," she pleaded. "When you talk about it, it makes me want it and we can't do that here."

"What else makes you want it, baby? What about when we talk dirty on the phone?" he asked. "When I call just to tell you all the dirty things I want to do to you? Tell you how much I love to ram my cock into your hot little ass until you beg for more?" He knew the answer; he just liked to see her flustered. It turned him on. Just like everything about her turned him on. The fastest way to get her flustered was to talk dirty and try to get her to respond.

"After you hang up, I get into my bed and hide under the covers," she whispered in his ear. Her face burned hot against his.

"Naked?" he asked. When she didn't answer, he pressed her. "Do you get naked under the covers, Madison? Tell me."

She shook her head. "With my panties down."

"Do you use the toy I bought you on yourself? Do you fuck your ass hard with it?" He remembered when he'd given her that toy and made her use it on herself while he'd watched. She'd been embarrassed at first and then she'd really gotten into it. Given it to herself so good that he'd come all over himself just watching her.

"No," she said close to his ear. "I ordered a bigger toy. The little one you bought me isn't thick enough, not like your cock."

"Do you like a big, hard cock in your ass, Madison?"

She shuddered as if the thought had her close to orgasm. She nodded against his face. "Oh yes. I love *your* big, hard cock in my ass. None of those toys feel half as good as when you take me. You fuck it so good. So hard. Until I ache deep inside." She groaned. "Oh God, Adam, I want you in there now."

Damn, she made him hot. "Later. I promise." He burrowed his face against her neck, his hands tangled in her skirt. "You have to move, baby. I need to come inside you. If I don't soon, I'll die."

She kissed his cheek. "You're sure no one can see us in here." She checked the traffic out the back window.

"I'm sure."

She began to move. She rose and fell over his lap, caressing the entire length of his over-sensitized cock with her slick warmth. Made for him. Her body had to have been made just for him. She fit him so right. Felt so good. Adam wanted to look at her, touch her, taste her, but all he could do was cling to the crumpled dress at her hips and revel in the pleasure rippling through his flesh.

"Oh, Adam," she whispered breathlessly. "Feels amazing." She moved faster, burying him deep, riding him as hard as she could. Churning her hips. Working him inside her. Driving him mad with pleasure. He gripped her ass, pulling her cheeks apart to torment her. She grabbed his hair, fisting it in both hands. "God, yes. Finger my ass."

"Later."

"Please."

He inched his fingers closer to her back opening, and she squirmed. She rose and fell over him faster. Faster. Grinding her clit against him each time she sank. His pleasure built. His heart raced. He fought release, wanting her to find her orgasm before he surrendered to bliss. He knew slipping a finger in her ass would make her come. It always did.

His fingers inched closer to where she wanted them.

"Yes, Adam," she panted. "I need it."

The instant his fingertip brushed her empty hole, her entire body went rigid, arching backward. He moved his arms around her back so she wouldn't fall and hit her head on the console behind her. Her hot, tight pussy clenched hard on his cock in sucking spasms as she cried out in ecstasy. Adam was so consumed by his own pleasure that he couldn't force his eyes open to watch her expressions as she came. She made the sexiest faces when caught in the throes of an orgasm. Later. He'd watch her come later. Now, now he let go, calling her name as his seed erupted inside her. Each pulse of release drew a hard shudder from his entire body. Fuck, she always made him come so hard. He was so glad he didn't have to wear a condom with her anymore. So glad she'd trusted him when he'd promised to keep her safe. He would never break that trust, because being inside her sent him soaring—body and soul. There was nothing as thrilling as pumping his cum into her receptive little body.

Madison went limp, and she collapsed against his chest. Her hot, rapid breaths stirred the hairs along his neck. He inhaled her scent—a mix of sweet lilies and sex and Madison. God, he'd missed her.

The limo lurched to a sudden halt, sending them both tumbling to the floor. Adam landed on top of Madison between the seat and the wet bar. He instinctively cradled her in both arms.

"Sorry," Adam said. "Are you okay?" He kissed her collarbone gently.

"I think so. You're on my leg."

Adam shifted so she could free her leg and then struggled to rise from the floorboard. Still laboring for breath, Madison tugged him closer and buried her face against his neck. "Wait," she said, holding him tightly, "don't move yet. I need this part."

He relaxed and let her hold him. He'd never admit to her how much he needed this part too.

A cacophony of loud slaps came from outside the car, followed by the excited yells of what had to be fans.

His alone time with Madison had come to an end. For now. But later? Later he had a blow-your-mind agenda in store for her.

Adam kissed Madison's flushed cheeks and helped her find her panties. She struggled into them hurriedly and located her boots under the rear-facing seat.

"Rock star hazard," he joked as the crowd outside became even louder.

As hands and faces pressed against the windows from outside, Madison shrank against the corner of the seat. Adam rearranged his clothes and fastened his pants. "I'll go talk to them for a few minutes. You stay here and hide."

She lowered her gaze to her hands, which were clutched together in her lap. He touched her smooth cheek with the backs of his knuckles. "We'll continue this later," he promised. "I'll fuck you so hard in the ass you won't be able to walk. Would you like that?"

She bit her lip and nodded.

He moved to the seat closest to the passenger-side window and rolled it down a crack. "Hey," he said to the crowd surrounding the car. The limo was outside the arena now, so the crowd had guessed someone famous was inside the car. "Are you here to see Sole Regret?"

"Oh my God, it's Adam Taylor," someone yelled.

The small crowd became huge. Safely locked inside the car, Adam shook hands and signed autographs through the open window. He was glad that no one noticed Madison hiding in the shadows across from him. He tried not to draw attention to her, but her troubled expression as she stared at her hands baffled him. He had to force himself not to ask what was wrong. She wouldn't want everyone surrounding the car to know that she was with him. He had to protect her reputation. Any woman caught with him was automatically branded a slut, and he wouldn't be able to live with himself if she got hurt because he'd been born an asshole.

CHAPTER SIX

Inside the stadium, Madison stood among the stage equipment and watched Adam work with the sound technician. There was too much feedback in the amps, so it was taking much longer than expected for them to get the equipment ready for the show. A heavy black curtain blocked the fans' view of the stage, but they were already filtering into the arena for the opening acts. They must have recognized that Adam was the hidden guitarist, however, because every time he played a string of notes, they erupted in spontaneous cheers. Madison sometimes forgot he was famous. Not necessarily when they had sex in a limo—who did that besides famous people, horny newlyweds and the occasional prom couple—or when said limo was mobbed by fans and twenty-five security guards had to be called out to control the crowd, but these reminders made her feel even more conflicted about the status of her relationship with Adam.

In the limo, he'd made sure she'd stayed hidden from the crowd, obviously not wanting them to know she was with him. When they'd dashed from the limo to the back door of the arena, he'd made her cover her head with some security guard's jacket. Madison's pride had taken a beating because he hadn't publicly claimed that they were together, but she couldn't really blame him. He could have any woman he wanted—certainly more glamorous, sexier and richer women than Madison ever aspired to be. Why would he ever give that up for her? She knew he liked her. Knew they were compatible sexually and that they enjoyed each other's company. But she also knew the minute she started making demands on his time and required him to be true to her, he'd be gone. Maybe if she'd been a supermodel or a famous actress, he'd consider admitting they were involved. But she was just ordinary Madison Fairbanks, with ordinary aspirations and ordinary looks and an ordinary life. She'd never be enough for him.

Even so, how much longer could she remain in a relationship where she was the only monogamous partner? Maybe she'd feel better if she found another man to dally with in Adam's absence. She rejected the idea as soon as it occurred to her. She had no interest in other men. No other man made her burn and ache and long and... love. She'd have to be completely over him before she'd spread her legs for anyone but her unattainable rock god.

"Are you waiting for Adam?" Owen, the band's bassist, asked. She hadn't realized he was standing beside her.

Her gaze automatically dropped to his crotch, as if he'd have his pierced cock hanging out for her to gape at. She really wished she didn't know about that bit of hidden jewelry.

"Um..." She huffed, exasperated by her crude behavior, and lifted her eyes to his. They were a pretty blue, which went well with his handsome face, and lightly gelled brown hair. "Yeah. He didn't figure it would take this long." Otherwise he probably would've hidden her in a storage room with a bag over her head or made her wait for him at the hotel by herself.

"Some roadie knocked over a bunch of amps when they were unloading the truck this afternoon. They can't figure out which one was damaged. They sound fine individually, but when they're all connected to the soundboard, it picks up feedback."

"Oh."

Owen chuckled. "Like you care."

"It's interesting," she said. "I don't know much about music."

"Just how to keep a guitarist captivated." Owen nudged her in the ribs with his elbow.

She felt her face flame. "Not really."

"He likes you, you know. I've known him for almost ten years. He's never been interested in the same woman for more than a few weeks. How long have you two been seeing each other?"

"A year." She shook her head, because that made it sound as if he was serious about her. "But we don't see each other often."

"He never misses the chance to see you when he can. He's busy, right?"

"He does call when he's in town." And late at night when he wants to talk dirty.

"Yep, he likes you. But I have to warn you."

"Warn me?"

Owen nodded. "Don't pressure him."

"So it's not a good idea to force him to pledge his everlasting love and commit to me alone?" She was half-joking and half wanted to know the answer.

"No," he said, drawing out the syllable for an indecent length of time. "He'd break it off with you if you even suggest it. It's how he rolls."

"I was afraid of that. I hate that he has so many other women."

"So don't think about him with them."

Madison's heart twisted. She bit her lip to stop its trembling. Owen had basically confirmed her suspicions: Adam slept around on her. She'd known he did, but she'd been doing a pretty good job of pretending he was hers alone. Something hot streaked from the corner of her eye. She dashed the annoying tear away and concentrated on breathing regularly. She didn't want to burst into racking sobs in front of Owen. That would prove that she didn't have what it took to be a rock star's girlfriend. Because frankly, she didn't.

"Oh shit, don't look so sad, sweetie," he said, patting her back. "Just remember those chicks don't mean anything to him."

"So why does he bother sleeping with them?" she said much louder than she'd intended.

Owen shrugged and scratched his head. "Convenience?"

And that's all she was to Adam too. His *convenience* stationed in Dallas, Texas. "Excuse me," she said. "I need to use the restroom." *So I don't bawl my eyes out in public.* She couldn't do this anymore. It didn't matter how much she loved him if he didn't love her in return. A one-sided love affair would never be enough for her. Not even with Adam Taylor.

"Sure," Owen said, his attention already diverting to someone else.

Madison was allowed to navigate the backstage area without interference. Both security and the crew recognized her. A few even offered her a friendly nod in greeting, which was baffling. Didn't they realize she wasn't *famous* enough to be here?

She found a restroom and locked herself in an empty stall. She didn't let herself crumble, only allowed a few tears to fall. She didn't want anyone to know she'd even considered crying. Maybe if she'd been interested in Adam because he was legendary, this would be easier, but she didn't love him because he was a rock star. She loved him despite it. Before she'd been introduced to the band and interacted with the scene that surrounded his professional life, she'd thought of music as Adam's job. But it was more than that. Music was his life. And she didn't fit in that life.

It was different when they were alone together. During those moments, she felt connected to him, a part of him, and felt he was a part of her, but here, surrounded by the crew and the band and the fans and the press and the hundreds of other people who were necessary to help run Adam's career, she knew their relationship was an illusion. There was no way for them to be together in a normal capacity. She didn't even know if he remembered what normal was like.

She blew her nose on some toilet paper and let herself out of the stall. She gazed at her face in the mirror, wondering why she had to fall for someone as unattainable as Adam Taylor. Why couldn't she have fallen for some nice plumber? Or a civil engineer? Nope, she had to hand her heart over to one of the most famous rock guitarists in the world. And she knew she could never have him. Not entirely.

Staring at her stricken reflection in the mirror, she realized the only way she was going to get over Adam was if she broke things off. Quit him cold turkey. And she had to do it soon; there was no point in delaying the inevitable. This would be their last night together. And she would make sure it was a night to remember so she could treasure it forever.

Heart heavy, Madison took a deep breath, straightened her spine and left the restroom to find Adam. She knew he liked when she showed her naughty side and since she didn't want to be the only one who remembered their last night together, she'd use that to her advantage. He'd burn for her by the time he went onstage in two hours.

The sound of his guitar no longer filled the arena, but she headed that direction anyway. She wasn't sure if he'd be in the band's dressing room or on the bus.

Or talking to some gorgeous redhead in a short leather skirt.

Madison drew to an abrupt halt, staring daggers at the woman. She wondered how intimately Adam knew her. They sure were standing close together. And the woman sure was smiling at him in open invitation. Even though Madison couldn't see Adam's face, there was no mistaking him from behind. If the rocker hair and all black attire hadn't given him away, that hot ass of his did.

Madison moved to stand behind him. *You like sluts? I can pretend to be a slut.* She slid her hand down his ass and squeezed. He whirled around.

"*Madison?*" he said, obviously astonished that she was the one giving his ass a squeeze in public. He probably would have been less surprised if some woman he'd never met had done so.

"Are you busy?" she asked.

"I was wondering where you wandered off to," he said. He glanced at the redhead, who was scowling at Madison.

Sorry to get in the way of your good time, bitch, but he's mine tonight. Madison narrowed her eyes at the woman.

The redhead's eyes narrowed at her.

"I had to use the restroom," Madison said, her eyes practically closed they were so narrowed now. "I hope you didn't get too lonely without me."

The corner of the redhead's mouth turned up. "I'd never let that happen," she said in a low-pitched purr and ran her palm over Adam's thick-muscled arm.

Unless she squeezed her eyelids completely shut, it was physically impossible for Madison to narrow her eyes more, so she grabbed Adam's other arm and jerked him away from his predator.

"Is there anyone on the bus?" she asked him.

He shrugged. "Not sure. We can go check." He nodded at the redhead. "Later, um..."

"Sarah."

"Right," he said.

Madison forced herself not to give Sarah a smug look as Adam took her hand and led her toward the back of the arena where the tour bus was parked.

"You're not going to ask?" he said as they walked.

"Ask what?"

"How I know that woman. I thought you were going to scratch her eyes out for a minute there."

"I don't really *care* how you know her," she said, her spine so rigid she was surprised it didn't crack under the strain.

He shrugged. "If you say so."

Madison clung to his hand more tightly. She was such a liar. She did want to know how he knew her. If he was interested in her. If he'd ever had sex with her or if she'd sucked his cock or if he'd so much as kissed her, but it wasn't her business.

"Did you *fuck* her?" she blurted and then covered her mouth with her free hand. *Where in the hell had that question come from?*

"Nope," he said simply.

"Do you want to?"

"When I have you here?" He kissed her temple and squeezed her hand.

"But what if I wasn't here?"

"That would be different."

And that's why she had to say goodbye to him. Technically, they could continue this way—her dropping everything to be with him when he was in town and those being the moments she lived for—but she couldn't go on like this forever. She'd tell him that in the morning. She wasn't even sure he'd care. A line of women waited to take her place the second she stepped aside.

"But I *am* here," she reminded him.

"Exactly."

Madison was disappointed to find the bus jam-packed with the rest of the band, some other guys Madison didn't recognize and a group of girls who didn't seem to care who fondled what. One of the young women was obviously very drunk and completely topless. When she spotted Adam standing near the driver's seat, she staggered in his direction.

"My friend bet that I couldn't get all the band members to suck my tits. Your turn!" She cupped her breasts in both hands and offered them to Adam. "Someone take a picture of this! I need proof."

Adam lifted an eyebrow at her. "No thanks, sugar. Some other time."

"You guys are no fun," she declared.

"I'll suck them," offered some guy who was drenched in what had to be beer—he reeked of it.

"I don't want you to suck them, Henry," SureBet said. "Force," she called when she spotted the band's drummer coming out of the bedroom at the back of the bus. "You still haven't sucked them. What are you waiting for?"

He took one look at her, returned to the bedroom and shut the door.

"I don't want to go on a date with Katie's weird brother," she moaned. "Pleeeeeeease don't make me lose this bet." She stomped her foot in agitation.

"I'll take another turn," Owen offered with a crooked grin. He sat next to ever-shirtless Kellen on the sofa.

"Okay." She hurried to shove her boob in his face and didn't seem to care about the bet when Owen's mouth latched onto her nipple. "Cuff," she moaned, grabbing a handful of Kellen's long, dark hair and tugging him to her free breast. "You suck the other one."

Madison gaped at the three of them. Had they no shame? Is that what it took to hang around rock stars? Being shameless? She could do shameless.

Maybe.

She glanced at Adam, knowing she'd decided to let him go after tonight, but the very thought of this being their last night together stole her breath. Maybe she could try being more like the girl getting her tits sucked by two guys at once. Maybe that's what it would take to keep Adam's attention. Maybe if she let go of propriety a bit, she'd be okay with him living the life of a superstar and with him screwing around as long as she could be his Dallas hookup.

She was so mixed up she couldn't see straight. All she could see was how much she wanted him.

"Do you want to hang out here?" Adam asked.

She steeled her resolve and grabbed his crotch, knowing she was blushing to the roots of her hair, but she had no control over that. She did have control over her words. "Not unless you want me to suck you off in front of an audience," she said. She forced herself to look at him and tightened her grip on the growing bulge in his pants so her hand would stop shaking.

"I would love you to suck me off in front of an audience," he said in a low voice.

Oh God. What had she done? She'd never expected him to actually take her up on the offer. She slid her hand to his belt buckle and for a moment, as she stared up into his gentle gray eyes, she forgot he wasn't the only other person on earth. Suddenly, she wanted to suck him off. Madison unfastened his belt, and then her fingers fumbled with his fly.

He caught her hand. "Madison, what's wrong?" he asked. "You're not acting like yourself tonight."

Heart hammering, she opened the top button of his jeans. "I don't know what you mean. It's no big deal. Don't women do this for you all the time?"

"Not all the time."

"But isn't this what you want? A slut who gets your rocks off."

There was none of the usual gentleness in his eyes as he scowled down at her. "If I wanted that, I wouldn't be with you, would I?"

"*Are* you with me?" she said loudly.

"Yeah, you *see* me here, don't you?" His voice was raised in anger too. She'd seen him pissed off, but had never been the cause of it. "What do you want from me, Madison? You're acting so strange."

She realized the reason his voice sounded loud was because

the bus was suddenly silent. She glanced around Adam's body to the other occupants of the bus. Everyone was staring at them. She caught Owen's eye, and he gave a barely perceptible shake of his head. *Don't pressure him.* His words returned to her loud and clear.

"Can we go somewhere and talk in private?" she asked Adam.

"I have to be on stage in an hour."

"It won't take long," she promised.

"Is there anyone in the dressing room?" Adam asked the lead singer, Shade, who like the others was watching their little argument.

"If there is, kick them out," Shade said, looking at Adam as if he was the biggest idiot he'd ever encountered.

Adam turned and stomped off the bus. Because he was refastening his belt, he didn't hold Madison's hand as he strode toward the venue. She wondered if he hadn't stopped her, what she would have done. Would she have shamelessly sucked his cock just to keep his attention? She honestly didn't know.

Adam made the two crew members taking a break in the band's dressing room leave and then he locked Madison in the room with him. She opened her mouth to speak—having already concocted the perfect line of bull to feed him about her behavior—but before she could begin, he wrapped her in both arms and drew her against him. He buried his face in her neck.

"You're going to stop seeing me, aren't you?" he whispered.

She was so stunned that she didn't immediately deny it.

"Why, Madison? Is it because I was talking to some other woman?"

"Talking to another woman? No, I wouldn't stop seeing you over that."

His body sagged with relief, and her heart twisted.

She forced herself to continue. *Cold turkey, Madison. It's the only way.* "But tonight will have to be our last night together." Her heart was thudding so hard that it threated to break through her sternum.

His arms tightened around her. "No," he said harshly. "I won't let you go."

"Adam, I can't do this anymore."

"Do what?"

"Date you. I need to know you're committed to me. And I know you can't be."

He tugged away and looked down at her. "How do you know that?"

"Well, because, you're famous and women chase you and—"

"They'll always chase me, Madison."

And who could blame them? She stared up at him, knowing she wasn't even going to get one last night with him. This would be the last time she would see him. The last time he held her in his arms. Owen had warned her. Why hadn't she listened?

Trying to find the resolve to walk out the door and retain a shred of her dignity, she lowered her gaze to his chest and took a deep, shaky breath. The shards of her broken heart tore through her lungs, stealing her breath. Adam's black T-shirt blurred out of focus behind foolish tears. She squeezed her eyes shut. *Don't cry. Don't cry. Don't.*

Adam grabbed her by the arms and shook her.

"Damn it, Madison," he said in a harsh growl. "I don't have to let them *catch* me."

All the air whooshed out of Madison's lungs and her head snapped up so she could search for sincerity in his expression. "Adam, are you saying..." Already the shreds of her heart were mending. "Would you be willing to..."

"Madison, you're the only woman I give a damn about. If I have to give up fucking chicks I don't give a shit about in order to be with you, what do you think I'm going to choose?"

She lowered her eyes to stare at his chest again. "I don't know."

He released her abruptly and stepped backward. She forced herself to look up again. She wasn't prepared for the twisted look of anguish on his handsome face.

He shook his head at her. "You really don't know? Madison, I thought you were the one person who understood me."

"I hoped. I *hoped* you would choose me, Adam, but I didn't

know, so I... I was just going to quit you cold turkey without forcing you to choose. My heart couldn't take it, if you didn't choose me."

He fisted her hair in both hands and tugged her closer. "Of course I'd choose you."

He kissed her—a hard, deep punishing kiss that left her disoriented and breathless.

"How could you doubt me, Madison? Doubt your worth?" he whispered against her tender lips. "You're so much better than I am, baby." His voice cracked.

She shook her head. "You could have any woman you want."

"That doesn't matter. I want you. *Only* you."

Could she let herself believe that? She wanted to. But if she trusted him with her heart, held nothing back, gave it all to him, and he betrayed her... She clung to him, terrified that he'd crush her heart into a pulp.

Adam released one hand from her hair. He rubbed her flank, his hand sliding up under her skirt. A soothing touch, yet so very not.

"Do you believe, Madison?"

She wasn't sure. She'd never had these insecurities before. It had to be his fame that had her feeling so uncertain of herself. And the cheating. She couldn't stand the thought of him holding another woman like this. Touching her like this. But was it cheating? He probably hadn't thought of it that way, but even though they'd never forged a real relationship, it felt like he'd cheated on her. And that she wasn't good enough to hold his attention.

"Why aren't I enough for you?" she said, her eyes swimming with tears. "Why do you sleep with other women?"

"Baby, you're more than enough for me. It's just... I have a healthy sex drive," he said.

She chuckled half-heartedly, squeezing her eyes shut and swallowing the lump in her throat. "I am well aware of that."

"I didn't think you'd care about the other women. They kind of go with the territory and you never said anything about it. We never agreed that we're an exclusive couple."

Fair enough. "I know. But I *do* care," she said. Some part of her afraid that he would run from her, her fingers clenched in his T-shirt. She didn't want him to run and she didn't want to quit him cold turkey. She wanted what she thought he was offering. She wanted to be with him. She wanted to believe it was possible. "The thought of you with another woman is agonizing. It's been driving me crazy since our first kiss."

His eyebrows drew together as if he'd just had a most disturbing thought. "Have you been with other men since our first time?"

No. God, no. I only want you, Adam. I only ever want you. She couldn't get the words out. Trying to calm down, she lowered her gaze and took a deep breath. So many emotions were churning through her that she couldn't decide if she wanted to laugh or cry.

"Who the *fuck* is he?" His hand tightened in her hair and he tugged her head back. He glared down at her, and Madison's heart rate doubled instantly. Yes, she needed him to be rough with her now. All the emotions swirling within her were too much to bear. And that hand on her ass was deliciously, mind-bogglingly distracting.

"Would you spank me if I said that I spread my legs for another man?" she asked. Because lord, she could use a good, hard spanking right now.

"*Did* you fuck another man?" He ground his teeth together, a muscle twitching in his strong jaw.

"Did *you* fuck another woman?" she countered.

"Not as many as I have in the past," he said defensively.

In other words, yes, he had fucked another woman. Or more precisely, other *women*. She fucking hated this. "Is that supposed to make me feel better?"

His grip on her hair loosened, and he smoothed the long strands from her face. His lips brushed her forehead tenderly. "I wish it did. I'm sorry I hurt you. I didn't know it would matter to you. I should have realized, I just... I'm sorry, baby."

Overwhelmed with emotion, she jerked back. She couldn't stand him to be tender with her. Not when she was already this close to tears. "I need you to spank me, Adam. Right now."

His eyes searched hers for a moment, and then his hand tightened in her hair again. "I'll never figure out why you like the rough stuff, Madison." He swatted her ass with a loud crack and her pussy throbbed with excitement. Some of the heavy emotions churning through her body parted to make way for primitive lust. It was so much easier to deal with those feelings.

Oh, thank you.

"I only like it rough with you, Adam." Because he was the only man who had ever made her feel so many profound and confusing emotions. And he was the only man who made her feel secure enough in her sexuality to even ask for such treatment.

"How many men have you fucked, Madison?" he asked, his strong hand connecting with her stinging ass a second time. "Tell me."

She groaned, so aware of the empty ache in her pussy that she worked his leg between hers and rubbed her mound against his thigh. "In my entire life?" she asked. She kind of liked that he was jealous, even though he had nothing to be jealous about.

"Since we met." He spanked her again. Her entire body trembled with need.

She fumbled under her dress to push her panties down. They got caught on his thigh, but she couldn't find the strength to move away. She wanted him buried inside her while he spanked her.

"One," she admitted. "Just one."

His palm connected again, and she thought she might die if he didn't fill her soon.

"What was his name?"

"Adam," she said. "His name was Adam Taylor."

He went still, his hand resting on her sensitized ass cheek. Wanting him to continue, she whimpered.

Adam's eyes widened and he shook his head in astonishment. "I'm the only one?"

Tears flooded her eyes and she nodded. Damn it. She was an emotional wreck again. "Please, Adam, don't make me cry. I need you to fuck me and spank me at the same time."

He moved so fast, she stumbled. In an instant she found herself bent forward over the back of a sofa with her panties around her knees and a big stiff cock seeking entrance into her swollen pussy. He surged forward, filling her in one deep, hard thrust. "I always have the best intentions to please you with slow, tender lovemaking and end up driving my cock into you like an animal." His cock buried deep, he slapped her ass and she cried out, squirming against him. "Why is that, Madison? Why do you tempt me into taking you so rough?"

"I like it." She groaned, her face pressed against a sofa cushion. "I like you to fuck me, Adam. No one else has ever fucked me hard. Spanked me. Pulled my hair. Pounded me in the ass. I love it. All of it. Don't make me beg."

He slapped her ass again, and she whimpered. "Maybe I like to hear you beg, babe. Maybe that's why I hesitate and tell myself I should treat you gently. Because I know if I take it slow, you'll beg to be fucked."

She rocked her hips against him, impatient for the deep, hard thrusts she craved. Why was he holding still?

"Adam," she whispered desperately. "Please."

"Please what?"

"Move."

He rubbed her ass, which was stinging yet craving another swat. "Your ass is really red," he said. "Did I spank you too hard?"

Was he intentionally trying to drive her insane? "No, I like it. I want you to spank me hard. And I want you to fuck me even harder." She wriggled her hips, hoping he'd take the hint.

Finally, he began to thrust. Deep and forcefully, just as she wanted it. When his hand slapped her ass again, she cried out, her pussy clenching his cock.

"Damn, that feels good," he said. He spanked her yet untouched ass cheek and she clenched again, the stinging pain causing her muscles to contract automatically. Within a few thrusts and swats, she peaked and was screaming her release into the sofa cushion.

"God, I wish I had some lube with me. I want to punish your ass so bad right now."

He rubbed her puckered hole with his finger, and she moaned. She didn't think she could want more after the amazing orgasm she'd just experienced, but her ass suddenly felt hopelessly empty. She squirmed, trying to get his finger to dip inside her. She whimpered. "Please. Take my ass."

He pulled out. She was lightheaded from standing bent in half for so long, so it took her a moment to realize the soft, warm, wet thing rubbing against her aching asshole was his tongue. He'd never licked her there before. Her legs began to tremble as pleasure raged through her core. The naughty, dirtiness of his actions fueled her excitement into an inferno of lust.

"Adam," she called breathlessly. "Oh God, that is the hottest thing ever."

His tongue dipped inside her and her knees gave out. She clung to the back of the sofa so she didn't sink to the floor. He kissed a trail up the crack of her ass and lower back as he rose again. She heard him open a condom and her pussy clenched. He only wore condoms when he fucked her ass. Oh yes, she couldn't wait.

"Hurry," she pleaded.

He rubbed his cock through the juices wetting her seam and then the head of his cock brushed her saliva-slickened hole. He struggled to enter.

"Not wet enough," he said. "Even with the lubricated condom."

She didn't care. She pushed back against him, taking him inside a few inches. She loved that full, hot feeling that made heat prickle her skin as he slipped into her receptive ass. Even the soles of her feet tingled in awareness of his invasion.

"It's good enough," she insisted. "Go deep."

His fingers slipped inside her pussy, collecting her cum and rubbing it over the connection between their bodies. His cock slid an inch deeper.

"Are you sure?"

He was always so worried that he was going to hurt her. That she was fragile. That she'd break. She supposed she should be grateful that he was so careful, but she didn't need him to be. If she wanted him to stop, she'd tell him. Maybe that's why he held back. Maybe he didn't think she was capable of telling him no, because she never did. Not because she couldn't or because she was afraid to. She never wanted to.

"I'll tell you if I need you to stop," she said breathlessly.

"Promise?"

She nodded.

He didn't take her as deep as she liked it, but his shallow rapid thrusts tugged at her ass just right and she was soon writhing against the back of the sofa in ecstasy. With each thrust, he inched deeper. Deeper. *Yes! Deeper, Adam.* She wasn't sure if she was thinking the demand or chanting it aloud.

When he swatted her ass unexpectedly, her back arched and she felt him inside her even more distinctly. Oh! She straightened her back slowly and rose to standing, each of his deep thrusts stimulating her in a slightly different place as the angle of his penetration changed.

"God, Madison." Adam groaned. One of his hands threaded through her hair and tugged her upright, the other moved to her breast, kneading her sensitized flesh, plucking at her tender nipple until it ached almost as much as her empty pussy.

She didn't know why this turned her on so much—to be filled from behind. Her vagina rippling with spasms of unfulfilled need. Her ass protesting the invasion.

Adam's hot breath came in jerky gasps against her shoulder. He was getting close. His hand moved from her breast to between her thighs. The heel of his hand ground into her clit; his strong, calloused fingers slid through her center, dipping sporadically into her wet opening.

"Fly with me, babe," he said brokenly, giving her hair a demanding tug. "Fly."

She let go, straining against his hand and his cock as she took her release. The pleasure was so exquisite that tears streamed from her eyes. "Adam," she whispered as his body jerked behind her.

He gasped brokenly and cried out an indistinguishable mantra of curses and disjointed syllables.

How could she have ever thought she'd be able walk away from him? He left her incapable of walking. Figuratively and, after that wonderfully rough fuck in the ass, literally.

CHAPTER SEVEN

Adam released his hold on Madison's hair and tugged her body closer, his hand still cupped possessively over her mound. He stroked her drenched lips with two fingers, drawing intermittent shudders from her slight frame. He loved that he could give her such pleasure. Loved that she opened herself to him. Loved *her*.

He'd never felt this all-encompassing need to possess a woman before. It had to be more than lust. More than affection. More than friendship. More even than gratitude for all she'd done for him. A hell of a lot more than simple infatuation. There was no other word for it. He loved her. Why had he not realized it until he'd been threatened with her leaving him?

"Madison?" he murmured against her sweat-damp neck. His arm squeezed tighter just beneath her ribs.

"Y-yes?"

Did she love him? Could any woman as wonderful and as fundamentally good as Madison Fairbanks give a shit about someone like him?

Adam took a deep breath. "I lo—"

A sharp knock rattled the dressing room door. "Ten minutes," someone called from the hall outside.

Madison tensed and jerked away. Watching her struggle to pull her panties up her trembling thighs nearly broke his heart. Her inability to meet his eyes. The blush of shame on her beautiful face. After the concert, he'd take her to bed, hold her naked body against his for as long as he liked, take her gently, tell her he loved her. A thousand times. A thousand ways. Tell her. Show her. Love her.

"You're beautiful," he said, kissing her bare shoulder as she worked to return her dress to its proper location.

She smiled shyly, and his heart panged. He had it so bad for her.

Her blue eyes flicked up to meet his briefly and her blush deepened. "Thank you."

"Do you want to watch the concert tonight?"

"Of course. I wouldn't miss it." She kissed his cheek. "Is there a bathroom in here? Or do I have to take the walk of shame?" She took a step to the side and winced. "Hobble of shame?"

"Are you okay?"

"Never better," she said breathlessly.

He settled a hand on her lower back and directed her to the restroom. She locked herself in one of the two stalls while he disposed of his expended condom and cleaned up in the sink.

Another knock sounded on the dressing room door. "Adam, are you in there?"

"One minute," he yelled.

"You don't have a minute."

"Madison, are you ready?" He hurriedly tucked his recently washed and still damp dick into his pants.

"Go on ahead," she said. "I'll catch up."

He really wanted her on his arm when he'd arrived backstage. Wanted to show her off. *This beautiful, wonderful, sexy-as-sin woman is mine. You may look—and seethe with envy—but never touch.* Since they'd met, she'd only given herself to one man. Him. And it was going to stay that way. Should knowing she'd been true to him, even though he hadn't asked it of her, make his chest swell with pride? Maybe not, but it did.

"They won't start without me," he said. "I can wait a few minutes."

"I... uh... need a bit of *privacy*."

He chuckled. How could she still be shy around him about anything her body did?

"Okay, I'll go, but I want to see you standing in my corner of the stage by the end of the first song."

"I'll be there."

When Adam arrived behind the stage, the entire band was waiting in the wings. Their pointed glares bounced right off him. Adam didn't give a shit if they were pissed. He was in love.

Jack handed him his silver guitar and attached his wireless transmitter to the back of his belt.

"The show started five minutes ago," Shade grumbled.

"I don't hear any music."

"I know your dick means a lot to you, but you need to get your priorities straight."

"Don't start with me," Adam warned. Could they get through a single day without arguing? Yeah, he was five minutes late, so what? He'd been concerned for Madison. She had to be hurting. In the future, he'd make sure he carried lube in his pocket whenever her sexy and always eager ass was within reach.

Owen, who started the show, shook his head at both of them. "Are we going to stand here and listen to you two bitch at each other, or should I proceed?"

Adam stuck a sound feed into one ear and an earplug into the other. "What's the hold-up?" the head of their sound crew shouted into his ear.

"Adam was getting laid. Again," Shade said. "You know what he's like. Two girls a night. Three. Four. He doesn't discriminate if it has a vagina."

Like he could talk.

"Shut up," Adam said. He wasn't sure if he deserved his reputation. Especially in recent months. A year ago? Sure. He'd fucked anything that stood still long enough for him to mount it. But now? He was getting his priorities straight. Or trying to. No one seemed to take notice of his efforts to keep clean and sober or to forge a steady relationship. He wasn't an irresponsible kid anymore. Would he ever live down the mistakes of his past? Madison seemed to be the only one who saw who he was becoming. Everyone else had pegged him long ago and held him down in the hole they'd chosen for him. Was it even possible to dig himself out of that hole at this point?

"Go, Owen," Hawkeye, their soundboard operator, said into their feed. "The rest of them will figure it out."

Owen entered the stage, playing his bass solo backed by the hard and heavy beat of Gabe's drumming.

Adam plucked a guitar pick from the tape attached to the neck of his guitar. He scratched his nose with the back of his wrist and was instantly engulfed in Madison's scent. He inhaled her essence deep into his lungs and fought the urged to lick his fingers. How was he supposed to concentrate on the show with the smell of her sweet pussy all over his left hand?

"So fucking selfish and irresponsible," Shade muttered under his breath.

Adam stiffened and lowered his hand so he could concentrate on dealing with Shade. "What is your *problem?*"

"You, Adam," Shade said. "Let's review your behavior in the past twenty-four hours alone. Smoking weed backstage before a concert." He ticked off Adam's crimes on his fingers. "Taking the limo without telling anyone so the rest of us had to find a cab. Thirty minutes late for sound check. Almost starting a riot in front of the stadium. Too busy fucking some slut to show up for the concert on time."

Adam took a swing at him. Busting his balls was one thing; calling Madison *some slut* was going way too far. Unfortunately, Kellen stepped between them before Adam could connect his fist with Shade's face.

"Now is not the time for this," Kellen said. "Adam, your cue."

Fuck the concert. Adam wanted to beat the shit out of Shade. Just because Adam had wanted to spend time with Madison at the expense of his other responsibilities did not make him irresponsible. Did it? And even if it did, why did Shade think it was any of his business? Adam wasn't Shade's responsibility. Fuck him.

Adam heard the drumbeat that signaled the start of his guitar intro. His hands found familiar strings and began to play automatically. He should already be on stage in the red spotlight over his stomp pad. If Shade would stop sticking his arrogant nose where it didn't belong and making Adam's blood boil, Adam might be able to concentrate on what he was doing. He played his way up the stage steps and pretended his entrance was part of the show. The crowd wouldn't know any different. When the spotlight bathed him in an aura of crimson, the crowd erupted in screams of excitement. *Yeah, just try continuing this band without me, asshole.* Shade darted across the stage and stood at its center, belting out a battle cry that would have made Spartans tremble. The crowd roared even louder. *Son of a bitch.*

If Adam didn't love Sole Regret's music so much, he'd have left the band—and Shade's bullshit—long ago.

Fingers flying over the strings near the body of his guitar as he played one of his most elaborate solos, Adam caught movement at the corner of the stage. He turned his head to find Madison watching him with her hands clenched together over her heart. He should play something just for her. He wondered if she'd like that. Near the end of his solo he lifted the neck of his guitar vertically next to his face and caught her scent on his hand again. He drew a deep breath into his lungs and his eyes drifted closed. Mercy, she smelled like honeyed sin.

Reluctant to move his hand, Adam took his time lowering his guitar to rest in front of his suddenly attentive cock. Not the best time and place to become aroused, but he couldn't help it. Her scent did that to him. Everything about her did that to him.

The stadium erupted in cheers as he completed his solo and stepped back from the front edge of the stage. As loud as the crowd was, the only cheer that made his heart thud was Madison's fist thrown in the air with excitement. She'd never cheered like that at one of his shows before. She'd always hung back away from the action and tried to remain unnoticed. He wondered about the sudden change in her. He was glad she was having a good time, but he wasn't sure if he wanted her to change. She was his anchor as well as the wind in his sails. He needed to know she was there for him even when he didn't see her for weeks, sometimes months, at a time.

The song ended, and Shade stalked the front of the stage, talking to the crowd as vocalists were prone to do. "How are we feeling tonight, Dallas-Fort Worth?"

The crowd roared on cue. Adam stole a glance at Madison. She offered him a timid wave and then smiled and lowered her gaze. He couldn't see the color of her face from this distance, but he knew she'd be blushing. He loved it when she blushed.

Shade was still jabbering at the crowd. He might as well have been talking like an adult in a Peanuts cartoon for all that Adam heard. The heavy thud of Gabe's bass drum snapped Adam to attention when the next song started. He really was out of it tonight; he needed to step up his game. He did have fans to entertain. He could concentrate on entertaining Madison in about an hour.

Adam trotted to the front of the stage next to Shade the-attention-whore Silverton, and bent forward to play a hard and heavy riff to a cluster of fans in the pit.

"Adam, you're a god!" someone yelled.

He grinned. *Did you hear that, Shade? They think I'm a god.*

"I love you, Shade," someone else yelled like a banshee with a megaphone.

Son of a bitch.

Adam noted the amused grins on the faces of several people in the audience and knew Kellen was mocking him behind his back. He did it every show. The crowd thought it was hilarious, so Adam let it slide. He knew Kellen would never do something to intentionally harm a person—well, except maybe those lovers he tied to his bed. But they begged to receive his punishment. Adam wondered if Madison would enjoy something like that. All indications pointed to *hell* yeah.

Shade charged in front of Adam so he could sing to the fans that Adam was favoring with personal attention. *Seriously, dude?* Adam rolled his eyes at Shade and jogged to the opposite end of the stage, climbing up on a platform and playing to the audience in the stadium seats. He pointed his guitar stock at the excited crowd and they yelled in enthusiasm. He pulled the neck of his guitar back and then thrust it forward again. Half the stadium roared on cue. He soon had them chanting at will. And when he bounced up on his toes, they jumped in unison.

A rush of adrenaline flooded his body, and he bounced in time with the beat. His audience followed his cue, jumping up and down with the music. Adam loved interacting with the crowd. Especially one so eager to follow his lead. Occasionally they got a dud of an audience, but most of their fans were crazy fun. The audience on the opposite side of the stadium began to roar, and Adam glanced over to find Shade standing near Madison, who was barely hidden in the wings. Shade was thrusting his fist in the air to get the other half of the audience worked into a frenzy.

And then the competition began. Who could get their side of the stadium to scream louder, to jump higher, to go crazier? Owen and Kellen moved down stage center to involve the audience members writhing in the pit. The craziest mother-fuckers always rocked general admission. Several mosh pits formed on the floor, and bodies were soon ricocheting off each other in utter pandemonium.

By the end of the second song, Adam was already drenched in sweat. His shirt clung to his back and his hair to his face. He wiped his palm on his jeans so his fingers wouldn't slip on his guitar strings when he played their next song. He'd like to say his half of the stadium was the most worked up now, but he had to admit the entire audience was in an uproar.

Adam moved back to Owen's live microphone and shouted, "You fuckers know how to rock!"

By the roar the audience produced, they obviously agreed.

Shade offered him a smile. "What do you say, Adam? Are you ready to set your fingers on fire?"

Like steam, the tension between them evaporated. At that moment, all that mattered was the music they shared. "Light me," Adam said.

The crowd roared its approval as Adam started the intro to "Light Me." By the time the rest of the band entered the song and he gave his left hand a half-second of rest, his fingers did feel like they were on fire. He loved the challenge of playing that intro live. Only the song's minute-long solo offered a greater test of his skills. Adam had been so high when he'd written "Light Me," he was surprised he'd been able to find the strings, much less compose his most inspired piece of music. He wondered what magic he'd be able to create now that he was sober. He only had one person to thank for the blessing of his sobriety.

Adam searched for Madison in the wings and found her gazing at him in worshipful awe. He'd much rather put that look on her face in bed, but of the fifteen-thousand people giving him their undivided attention, it was her opinion that mattered most.

By the end of Sole Regret's set, Adam was overheated and his clothes were soaked through with sweat. Despite the amount of energy he'd expended, he was too amped to be tired. He had plenty of energy to spare and when Madison took several steps onto the stage so she could wrap her arms around him, he knew exactly what he wanted to do to drain his remaining strength.

CHAPTER EIGHT

Madison didn't mind the dampness of Adam's T-shirt as she wrapped him in a tight embrace and buried her face in his shoulder. She couldn't stop her tongue from collecting the salty tang of sweat from his neck. The guitar cutting into her belly only increased her awareness of him.

Watching Adam perform and seeing how much his music meant to so many people infused her with pride. And worry. She couldn't compete with the crowd or his music. Maybe she could steal him away from the world and keep him all to herself, but she had no business getting in the way of his music career. No right to make demands on his time that might interfere with his continued success. Yet could she give everything to this relationship and expect so little in return? Would she *ever* be happy with him? Would she ever be happy *without* him?

Her arms tightened, drawing him closer still. She never had these confusing thoughts when they were alone together, just when she was confronted with his infamy. And fame was part of who he was. She had to come to grips with that somehow or this relationship would never work.

"I need a shower." He rubbed his nose against her ear, his labored breathing stirring stray hairs against her neck. "Care to join me?"

She nodded and held him more tightly.

"Let's go to the hotel," he whispered into her ear. "I can't wait to be alone with you. I can smell your pussy all over my left hand. Every time I caught scent of it, I wanted to say screw the concert and drag you off to a secluded corner for another vigorous fuck."

She didn't know whether to celebrate him telling her how much he wanted her or if she should feel guilty for breaking his concentration on stage. He had a lot of people who depended on him to perform at his best.

"Sorry," she said to his chest.

"For what?"

"Making things difficult for you."

He pulled away and captured her face between both hands, tilting her head back so she had no choice but to look into his eyes. "I'm not sure what you're so worried about, but stop it. It's starting to piss me off." He didn't sound the least bit angry. He smiled and kissed the tip of her nose. "I don't want you to worry about anything for the rest of the night, except how you want me to make love to you next."

She forced her concerns to the back of her mind. She knew when they were alone together all the worries that weighed her down wouldn't even be considerations. He had a way of making her forget everything but the moment. Everyone but him.

"Maybe the hotel suite has a bathtub made for two," she whispered.

"Baby, as far as we're concerned, *all* bathtubs are made for two."

He handed his equipment to an anxious roadie, took Madison's hand and led her toward the back of the stadium, where the limo was waiting for the band. Owen and Kellen were already inside the car.

Owen had discovered Adam's container of gingersnaps and was scarfing them down one after another. He seemed oblivious to the young woman tugging on his belt.

"I want to see it," his companion said. She had his zipper undone and her hand down his fly before Madison and Adam had even settled in the seat facing them. Adam cleared his throat to gain Owen's attention and then nodded in Madison's direction with his eyebrows lifted.

Owen caught the lady's hand and tugged it out of his pants. "Later," he said. "We have company."

Apparently Kellen didn't count as company. Madison

realized Owen would be having a lot more fun right now if she hadn't shown up.

"Don't mind me," Madison said. In actuality, she wanted to see it too—assuming the woman struggling to return her hand to Owen's crotch was interested in his piercing.

"Are those my cookies?" Adam yelled and yanked the container out of Owen's hands. A single gingersnap rattled around at the bottom of the bowl. Adam stuffed it into his mouth and then threw the container at Owen's head. "Fucker," he said through a mouthful of cookie.

"They were delicious. Did your *girl*friend make them for you?" Owen said in a teasing tone.

"Yeah, she made them for *me*. Not you."

The fact that Adam hadn't denied she was his girlfriend had Madison struggling to find air. He took her hand and gave it an encouraging squeeze. Did she look that freaked-the-fuck out? She felt like a skittish horse being saddled for the first time. Was this really happening? Was Adam claiming her as his girlfriend? Publicly? What would her life be like if the media discovered they were dating? Would her face be posted all over the Internet and the tabloids? Would jealous fangirls find Madison's every fault and insist she wasn't good enough for the perfection that was Adam Taylor? Was she ready for this? There was no question that she was ready to love the man, but she wasn't so sure about loving the rock star.

"Where are Force and Shade?" Adam asked. He craned his neck to look out the window.

"Don't like waiting around for other people?" Owen asked. "Does it piss you off when your bros don't value your time?"

Adam huffed and shook his head. "Don't you start in on me too."

"What's he talking about?" Madison asked.

"Shade was pissed that I was five minutes late to the show." Adam rolled his eyes as if Shade was the inconsiderate ass.

"Were you late because of me?" Madison asked.

"It's fine," Adam said. "He'll get over it."

"Oh wow, I feel it, Tags," Owen's female companion said. She had her entire hand down Owen's pants and was moving it around inside the front of his jeans. "What's it feel like when you're hard? Oh! Do you leave it in when you screw?"

"That's the only reason to get one. It feels fantastic."

Madison made a mental note to share that tidbit of information with Kennedy. Her sister would be relieved to know Owen had pierced his fifth appendage for pleasure not pain.

The young woman's free hand moved to Kellen's crotch. He was sitting next to Owen, shirtless and sweaty, his long dark hair sticking to his bare shoulders. A heated flush made his strong cheekbones appear even more pronounced. "Do you have one too, Cuff?" she asked, fondling him through his jeans. "Can I feel it?"

"Uh, no." Kellen lifted her hand from his crotch and dropped it on Owen's thigh.

She then turned and reached across the limo toward Adam. Recognizing her intent, Madison slid onto Adam's lap, blocking Miss Touchy Feely from finding her target. Madison glared at the bold woman, whose gaze lifted from Adam's suddenly hidden lap to Madison face. "Does Adam have his cock pierced?" she asked.

"None of your business," Madison said.

"I'm sure his fingers move really fast when he strokes you down there, huh? You should ask him to play the solo to "Light Me" on your clit. That should get you off in, like, five seconds." The fangirl nodded at Madison's lap, lifted her eyebrows up and down and then laughed until she snorted.

When Madison just stared at her as if she'd escaped a loony bin for sluts, Miss Touchy Feely stopped laughing and blew a raspberry. "Old prude."

Madison bristled.

"You're really getting on my nerves," Owen said, pulling his fondler's hand out of his pants, rearranging himself as discreetly as possible and securing his fly. "Bye now."

He leaned out the open door, said something to one of the security guards just outside and in an instant, the girl was gone.

"Since when do you care how obnoxious a babe is behaving as long as you're getting laid?" Kellen asked.

"Madison doesn't need to see someone acting like that," Owen said. "She's... nice."

Nice. It didn't feel like a compliment. Madison kept encountering the women who naturally hung around the band and *nice* wasn't the first descriptor that came to mind. Maybe that was why she felt so out of place.

"She also makes the best gingersnaps I've ever tasted," Owen added.

Adam growled and tried to kick him, almost unsettling Madison in the process.

The band's drummer, with his black and red mohawk, tattooed scalp, and startlingly green eyes, slid into the seat next to Owen. If Adam was damp, and Kellen was wet, then Gabe was drenched. Madison wasn't sure how Owen managed to look like he'd just stepped out of a styling salon. He didn't have a single hair out of place.

"Hey, Gabe, where's Shade?" Adam asked.

Now that Miss Groupie, make that Miss Grope-y, was out of the car and Adam was no longer in danger of sexual harassment, Madison tried to shift off his lap. He wrapped his arms around her to keep her from moving away.

"I think he's on the phone arguing with Tina again," Gabe said.

"He can do that at the hotel," Adam said. "Let's go."

"Keep your pants on, Adam," Kellen said.

"If you had this woman on your lap, would you want to keep your pants on?"

Madison flushed. She could *not* believe he'd said that.

"Well, no. I'd already have my pants off if I was in your situation," Kellen said, "but you might not want to piss Shade off any more than you already have. He's having a bad day."

"Which I'm sure he blames on me," Adam said. "Just like he blames everything on me."

Shade slid into the car next to Adam and the door shut. Someone slapped the roof of the car and it moved forward.

Shade was still clutching his cellphone and didn't spare any of them a glance, not that it was easy to tell what his gaze was fixed on as he always wore a pair of aviator sunglasses. While Owen enthusiastically described some sex club in San Antonio to Kellen, who seemed interested, and Gabe, who did not, Adam's hand kept wandering under Madison's skirt to stroke the inside of her thigh. Shade stared out the tinted window and didn't say a word to anyone. Madison's need to counsel Shade was overwhelming. She extended a hand in his direction and opened her mouth to ask him a question, but thought better of it and pursed her lips.

"Come on, Gabe," Owen said. "You'll have a great time."

"I told you," he said, running a finger along his head at the boundary of his mohawk. "I have this *thing* I'm working on with Melanie."

"What thing?" Owen asked with a smirk. "Does it involve batteries or a gas-powered generator?"

Brows drawn together, Gabe bit his lip and punched Owen in the thigh. "A relationship. You know, *commitment?*"

"Never heard of it," Owen claimed as he elbowed Kellen in the ribs.

Madison's attention turned to Gabe. She'd never known any of the band members to commit to a woman in the entire year she'd been acquainted with them. If Gabe could manage it, then maybe Adam could hang out with him while the other three went out and fooled around with their grope-ies. Or went to sex clubs. Or whatever other activities they partook in that might involve the indiscretion of Adam's dick.

Owen's blue eyes shifted to Adam and then immediately diverted to Shade. Apparently he knew better than to ask Adam in front of Madison. "You'll come, won't you, Shade?"

As the sound of his name, Shade pulled his strict concentration from the dark streets outside the car. "What?"

"This club I heard about in San Antonio. You're coming, right?"

"Sex club?" Shade asked, as if it was their most typical excursion.

"Oh yeah."

"When?"

"Day after tomorrow."

"Exclusive?" Shade asked.

"Yep."

"I'm in."

Owen glanced at Adam again. Madison could tell he wanted to ask Adam if he was going, and she wanted to hear Adam's response. Did he go to sex clubs often? Was that where he'd learned to be such an amazing lover? She wasn't even sure what went on at sex clubs. Sex, she presumed, but would it be like a brothel or a free-for-all orgy or what?

"What do you do at a sex club?" Madison asked Owen.

Adam's thighs stiffened beneath her.

Owen glanced nervously at Adam. Madison turned her head and found Adam staring ice daggers at the bassist.

"Nothing that would interest you, sweetie," Owen said. "Or Adam," he added with a wave of his hand.

Of course Adam would *never* be interested in something like that. *Sure.* She wasn't going to be deterred that easily. "Do you just have sex with strangers out in the open in front of everyone?"

"If that's your kink," Kellen said.

Madison's heart rate accelerated. "Is it yours?" she asked him, lost in his dark brown eyes. The man had an unquestionable strength about him. He didn't say much around her, but she was always aware of him. Owen drew attention with ceaseless interaction, Kellen by his presence alone.

"Performance sex?" Kellen shook his head. "Not particularly, no. That's more Adam's thing."

"Don't tell her that," Adam said. "She's liable to believe you."

Shade leaned across the back seat and slid a hand onto Madison's knee. "I think you should come down to San Antonio and join us, sweetheart. I always wondered what it was about you that kept Adam interested. You seem pretty vanilla to me. What are you hiding behind that innocent act? And beneath that skirt?"

Adam grabbed Shade's hand and crushed his fingers. "Don't touch her."

Shade chuckled. "See? He's all pissed-off now. Hey, Adam, what's so great about her anyway? Does she give good head or what?"

Before she could tell Shade to go fuck himself, Madison found herself bouncing across the seat beside Adam when he tossed her off his lap and jumped on Shade. Within seconds, a full-out brawl raged in the back of the limo. Adam got in a few good punches before Shade found enough leverage to send him flying toward the backseat. Adam careened into Kellen's and Owen's legs before launching himself in Shade's direction again.

Heart thundering out of control, Madison grabbed the back of Adam's shirt to try to pull him off Shade. "Stop!"

She instantly found her back secured against a hard chest with both wrists trapped at her sides.

"Let them fight," Kellen's deep voice said in her ear. "This has been building for weeks."

Madison struggled to be set free, but not only was Kellen strong, he seemed to know some technique for keeping her easily immobilized. "One of them is going to get hurt," Madison said.

Adam and Shade's rapid-fire punches were already slowing and becoming less punishing. After less than a minute, they separated, glaring acid at each other. Shade's sunglasses were bent and askew. Adam's full lower lip was bleeding. A red mark darkened his cheek.

"I am sick of your bullshit, Shade," Adam yelled. "I've fucking had it."

"What? You gonna leave?" Shade returned. "Go ahead. Leave. Then maybe we could find someone to take your place who shows up for sound checks on time, doesn't think fucking is more important than breathing, isn't stupid enough to smoke pot backstage while on probation, and isn't the all-around most inconsiderate *asshole* I've ever met."

Madison's heart slammed into her ribcage. What did Shade mean about Adam smoking pot backstage? Recently? Why would he keep something like that from her? Why would he *lie*? And if he lied about something like that, how could she believe anything he said to her?

"Yeah, maybe I will leave," Adam yelled. "At least I won't have to put up with getting bitched at by an egomaniac like you."

"No one is leaving," Kellen said. "You two need to stop pissing each other off on purpose. It's juvenile."

Adam and Shade gaped at Kellen in astonishment.

"It's fucking obvious that you do it," Owen said. While

Adam and Shade agreed on nothing, Owen and Kellen seemed to agree on everything. "Adam knows how much it pisses Shade off to be late, so any opportunity he has to be late, he takes it."

Adam lowered his gaze and stared at his reddened knuckles.

"And Shade will do anything to get Adam riled," Owen continued. "He knew it would piss Adam off to make a move on his girl, so what does he do? Makes a move on his girl."

"Maybe I'm genuinely interested in her," Shade said, his deep voice gruff. He removed his ruined sunglasses and stuffed them into a pocket.

Shade had gorgeous dark blue eyes set off by thick, black lashes. There were all sorts of emotions swirling around in their depths. Madison wondered why he hid those beautiful eyes behind sunglasses at all hours of the day and night.

"Yeah?" Adam asked. "If you're so interested in her, what's her name?"

Shade shrugged and shook his head. "Like I give a shit."

Owen released a heavy sigh. "Maybe it's time for you two to apologize—"

"I'm not apologizing to *him*," Adam grumbled.

"What the fuck do *I* have to apologize for?" Shade bellowed.

Owen rolled his eyes and shook his head in annoyance. Gabe, who was sitting directly across from Shade, lifted a foot and nudged Shade in the knee with his toe. Gabe gave Shade a pointed glance, and Shade sank back against the seat to stare out the window again. Madison released the breath she hadn't realized she was holding.

The limo slowed and turned into a drive. When the car pulled to a halt in front of the hotel, Shade was out the door before the driver could come around to open it for him.

"Jacob," Gabe called. "Wait up." He unfolded his long and lean frame from the back seat and jogged after Shade.

Madison could hear Shade muttering under his breath to Gabe, "I'm going to *fucking* kill him."

"You know he does this," Gabe said. "Don't let it get to you."

Kellen's hands loosened from Madison's wrists, and she

darted across the seats to dab at Adam's lip with her thumb. "You shouldn't fight. Someone could have been seriously injured."

"Don't start," Adam said. He pushed her aside and climbed from the car.

She hesitated. Should she go after him? He seemed awfully upset, and she didn't want to make matters worse. She was pretty sure the animosity between Shade and Adam wasn't a recent development.

"Go talk to him. He listens to you," Owen said. "Maybe you can help him figure out why Shade has been pissed off at him for four years."

Four years? "Do you know why?"

He shrugged. "Nope."

"Maybe I should talk to Shade about it. I don't think Adam knows what the problem is."

Kellen grimaced. "Not a good idea. Adam has a hair trigger as far as you're concerned. Just go cheer him up. You're the only one who ever makes him smile."

She wasn't sure anything would make Adam smile tonight. Especially not when she had to get on his case about smoking pot. What the fuck was he thinking? If his parole officer found out, agreeing to drug counseling would not keep him out of prison this time. She hoped Shade had been blowing hot air and Adam hadn't slipped up—especially somewhere he could get caught so easily—but she remembered how guilty Adam had looked at dinner when she'd asked how he was making it. She'd been suspicious then, but had decided to trust his word because she knew he needed that trust as part of his treatment. And she needed to extend her trust because she loved him.

"Are you coming?" Adam said, peering back into the car, his eyes seeking her in the dim interior.

Her heart skipped a beat. She didn't have a choice but to confront him. She had a feeling things were going to go from tense to disastrous, but she couldn't let this slide.

"Yeah," she said. She scooted across the seat and out into the warm night air.

Adam took her wrist and stalked toward the building. She had to jog—boots clomping on the cement—to keep up with him. He didn't say a word to her in the lobby, the elevator or the corridor. Why was he pissed at *her*?

He unlocked the door to his suite and opened it. When she paused to stare up at him, he avoided her gaze and ushered her inside.

The door closed and before she could turn, he stepped up behind her, wrapped his arms around her waist and held on to her like a drowning man clinging to a capsized boat. His entire body trembled against her.

"You okay?" she asked after a moment. She stroked the tense muscles in his forearm.

He released her abruptly and moved into the spacious room. "Why wouldn't I be?"

"You seem upset."

"The vocalist of my band, who used to be my best friend, basically told me he wanted to replace me. Why would I be upset?"

She knew he was being sarcastic, but she needed to get him to talk seriously about this issue with Shade. "I'd be upset," she said. "And hurt."

"I'm not hurt, I'm pissed. I'm not sure why he thinks I'm the one who needs replacing. Maybe if he didn't try to lead the band like a dictator instead of considering us all equals, I wouldn't feel the need to get under his narcissistic skin."

"So you do show up late on purpose?"

"Not always." He took a deep breath. "Consciously."

"What started the animosity between you? Owen says Shade's been pissed at you for four years. It must have been something pretty substantial."

"I don't remember," Adam said. He scrubbed his face with both hands. "I was having a rough patch at the time. Doing lots of drugs. I don't remember much of anything from those few years. Bits and pieces of disagreements, but nothing that would give him a reason to hate me so much. When we started the band we were best friends, but now?" He shook his head.

"Have you asked him why he's angry with you?"

"Yeah, I ask him *what the fuck* his problem is all the time."

She stepped closer and laid a gentle hand on his chest. His heart thudded hard against her palm. "Have you asked him in a non-hostile manner?"

Adam drew away and sank onto a sofa. "We can't interact without being hostile."

"Except on stage." For nearly half an hour, both men had looked genuinely pleased to be in each other's company.

Gaze distant, Adam scratched the nape of his neck. "We kind of lose ourselves onstage."

"But offstage your egos get in the way."

Adam smirked. "What egos? We don't have egos."

Madison chuckled. "Oh no. You're both exceedingly humble."

"You've seen me humble," he said, slipping an arm around her waist and directing her to sit on his lap. "No one else gets to see me like that."

Which was probably one reason why Shade busted his balls all the time. "I like that humble guy," she said.

"Yeah?"

She nodded.

"But not the egotistical guy," he said.

"I like that guy too, but he's not as loveable. Probably why Shade punches him in the mouth."

"I don't want to talk about Shade now," Adam said. "I want to get lost in you and forget about all this bullshit."

She turned sideways and leaned against his chest, snuggling into his warmth. "Did he hurt your face?"

"Not too bad." He chuckled. "Couldn't get a wide enough swing in the car, or he would have nailed me to the floor."

"I hope you two can make amends," she said. "I think you'll both feel better if you talk things through."

"Maybe." He was quiet for a long moment. The only sounds were the hum of a mini-fridge somewhere in the room and the occasional voice in the hall. He stroked her arm with the back of his hand as he collected his thoughts. "I'll try to talk to him without goading him into a fight," he said. "His attitude just pisses me off."

Madison could tell the feeling was mutual. "I'm sure you can find a way to reach him." And she needed to find a way to reach Adam. She hated to hit him with a second confrontation now, but she couldn't ignore what Shade had said in the limo about Adam's drug use. They had to face this issue before drug *use* became drug *abuse.* The difference was a slippery slope for an addict; it didn't take much for one to lead to the other. "So has smoking pot backstage become routine or was it more of a onetime thing?"

The hand methodically rubbing her bare arm went still. "I didn't—"

"Don't lie to me, Adam." She could deal with his problems, but not his lies. She wanted to trust him—about everything—but she couldn't trust a liar.

"I wasn't going to lie. I was going to say I didn't tell you, because... I don't like to disappoint you. It makes me feel guilty. I don't like that feeling."

"You feel guilty for disappointing me? Is that why you've been working so hard to stay clean?"

"Yeah."

She cringed. He still had some work to do. "Am I the *only* reason you fight addiction?"

"It's a good enough reason for me." His lips brushed her hair. "You're the best reason I've ever met."

The woman in her wanted that dependence—that tie between them—but the counselor knew it wasn't healthy. "Adam." She turned on his lap and cupped his face in her hands. Her feelings for him bubbled to the surface, making her chest ache and her voice raw. "Baby, you need to stay clean for yourself, not for me. You can't fully recover that way. What happens to you when I'm no longer in your life?"

He went very still, his eyes clouding with hurt or anger or some combination of the two. "Are you still planning on leaving?"

"Breaking it off would be the most logical thing to do," she said. Especially now that she knew he had latched on to the wrong reason to fight his addiction.

His gaze shifted to her forehead, and he sucked a deep, ragged breath into his chest. "*Fuck.*"

She touched her fingertips to his chin and waited until his stormy gray eyes focused on hers. "Sometimes a girl has to listen to her heart instead of her head." Because even though her heart was blind and dumb, it was still clever enough to befuddle her head with constant thoughts of Adam.

His arms tightened around her. "What's your heart say?"

She clutched the fabric of her dress over her chest. "My heart says you rock."

He chuckled and pressed a kiss to her temple. "But your head doesn't say that?"

"Nope. My head says you're trouble."

He chuckled. "Smart head." His hand slid over her breast and squeezed gently. "So what does your body say?"

Arousal uncoiled low in her belly as her breast swelled in his hand. "My body screams you rock."

His thumb slipped inside her clothes and brushed her nipple, rubbing it until it puckered and strained against his maddening touch. She failed to stifle a groan of longing.

"That's two out of three. Majority rules," he said.

Adam eased her onto her back on the sofa and shifted his hips to rest between her legs. Supporting his weight on his arms, he stared down at her with the strangest expression on his face.

"Madison?" he whispered.

She couldn't find the presence of mind to answer—could only stare up into his handsome face with her pulse thrumming wildly in her ears. He'd never looked at her with this level of intensity in the past. She wasn't sure if her pitter-pattering heart could take the passion behind his gaze.

"I have something I need to tell you. I want you to promise you'll believe what I say. Don't question my words the way you question everything."

"I don't ques—"

"Shh, baby. Listen and accept."

"Adam?"

"Believe, Madison. Promise."

"Okay. I promise."

He took a deep breath. "I lo—"

A loud knock at the door cut him off.

CHAPTER NINE

Adam closed his eyes and swallowed. "Fuck," he growled, squeezing his eyelids together as tightly as possible. "I've lost my nerve again."

Usually overflowing with confidence, his inability to say three simple words—or *not so simple* words—rattled him to the core. True, he'd never said them to anyone in his life, but he knew love was what he felt for Madison. It was more than gratitude for saving his life and his career and his sanity, he loved her. Not for things she'd done for him or the things she continued to do for him, but because she was his heart. He'd been missing that fragile organ for so long that he hadn't realized it was gone until she'd filled the hole inside his chest. And now whenever she so much as hinted at taking his heart away again, he couldn't tolerate the pain. It clawed at him, deep within his chest, threatening to leave him the shell of a man he'd been before he'd met her.

So why couldn't he just say the words? *I love you, Madison.*

Because maybe she wouldn't say them back.

A second more vigorous knock rattled the door. "Yo, Adam!" someone called from the hall. "Before you get too naked, I've got your stuff out here."

Maybe this wasn't the best time to tell her. So far their night together hadn't been the romantic rendezvous he'd envisioned. Life kept kicking him in the nuts.

Adam pecked Madison on the lips and climbed from the sofa. He yanked open the door and grabbed his bags from Jordan, who was usually in charge of the beer. Knowing Jordan was one of their more incompetent crew members, Adam glanced down to make sure the bag he'd delivered was the right one. "Thanks."

Jordan beamed and opened his mouth to speak, but Adam closed the door in his face before the guy could get a word out. Didn't these people understand that he wanted to be alone with his woman? Fuck, did he have to hang a sign on the door *or what?* He tossed his bag on the floor and took a step in Madison's direction, before he realized a sign on the door was *exactly* what he needed. Clutching the *do not disturb* sign as if it were a golden ticket, he opened the door and hung it outside. Jordan was still standing there, looking more befuddled than usual. He opened his mouth to speak again, and Adam pointed at the sign before slamming the door in Jordan's face a second time. Adam locked the deadbolt and turned toward the living area of the room. Madison lay sprawled on the sofa, one booted foot on the floor, one resting on the sofa arm, and her skirt hiked up just high enough to show the juncture between her thighs. Those panties needed to go.

So he couldn't tell her his feelings, and he couldn't erase her disappointment in him, but he *could* give her pleasure. He knew that for certain. He crossed the room and paused at the end of the sofa, admiring her disheveled appearance and committing it to memory.

"What were you going to say before you were interrupted?" she asked.

His heart slammed into his ribcage. "Um, why are you still in your dress?"

And why was he such a coward when it came to this woman? What was the worst she could do if he confessed his feelings? Okay, he didn't even want to contemplate possibilities.

Madison offered him a sexy grin and rose from the sofa. She slid her mass of dirty-blond hair over one shoulder and presented her back to him. "Unzip me?"

When his fingers brushed the skin along her spine, her soft, pliable flesh warmed beneath his fingertips. At last, she was allowing him to be gentle with her. Heart full to bursting, Adam pressed his lips to the nape of her neck and kissed a trail down the center of her back as he slowly lowered the zipper of her dress. Her throaty moan grabbed him by the balls and made his cock rise inside his jeans. Lower and lower he went—tasting and sucking the sweet skin down the length of her back—until he ran out of zipper and was on his knees behind her.

He released her dress and it dropped, pooling around her feet. She took a step forward. Her luscious ass entered his view, and he couldn't keep his hands off it. He cupped her bottom in both palms and squeezed. He then leaned forward to brush his lips against the smooth skin just above the elastic of her panties.

When she took another step, he murmured a protest and slid his hands forward over her hips to keep her close. He wanted to devour her ass whole. Those silky, purple panties were in his way. He caught the top of her undergarment in his thumbs and eased the scrap of lavender satin down. He left her panties at the top of her thighs while he kissed and suckled and squeezed the cheeks of her ass. He avoided pleasing her asshole, knowing withholding what she most desired would make her want him. He loved that it took so little to make her beg.

"Adam," she said breathlessly. "Have you ever gone to one of those sex clubs Owen was talking about?"

What? How could she be thinking about what Owen had said in the limo at a time like this? He paused, wondering what he should do next to excite her. Making out with her ass obviously wasn't doing what he'd intended. "Do you want me to lie?"

"No, don't lie. No need to spare my feelings. I know you sleep around. I just wondered if going to them is fun."

He could tell that she still didn't trust him. How could he prove that he wasn't interested in anyone but her? "I'm not going to sleep around anymore, Madison."

"I know. I didn't mean now. I meant before. Have you been to a lot of sex clubs? How do you even find one? They're not in the phone book, are they?"

Adam's heart kicked in his chest. He'd been to plenty of sex clubs, and they weren't the kind of places his sweet Madison should explore on her own. "You aren't thinking of going to one, are you?"

She shrugged. "I'm just curious. What do you do there?"

"Depends." He pressed a hand against her back and urged her to bend forward. He drew his tongue through her juicy lips, glad to know she was turned on, even though she insisted on talking. He wondered how she'd respond to being gagged.

"What's your favorite thing to do at them?" she asked.

She obviously wasn't going to let this rest. "Perform."

"Perform?" She went utterly still. "What do you mean?"

He sat back on his heels and sighed. "If I explain it, it's going to make me want to go to one. Are you prepared to come with me?"

"I always come with you," she teased. "Usually more than once."

Grinning, he landed a playful swat on her butt. "I'll tell you," he said, "but only after you tell me your dirtiest fantasy." If they were going to talk during sex, it had to be dirty talk. When his cock was hard, his brain didn't function well enough for more sophisticated conversation.

"Never mind," she said, her face suddenly beet red. Her head swiveled to face away from him.

He grinned. Now he had the challenge of wringing a dirty fantasy from her reluctant lips. He did enjoy a challenge. Kneeling on the floor behind her, he reached up and rubbed her back opening with two fingers. "I'll bet it involves this insatiable hole."

Her ass tightened, and she groaned. "Yes."

"What am I doing to it, Madison? Am I licking it? You liked that, didn't you?"

"Yes, but that's not my fantasy."

"Tell me what it is, and I'll make it a reality."

"I'll tell you, but don't be mad," she pleaded.

"Why would I be mad? I love to give you pleasure."

"I..." She swallowed and covered both eyes with her hands. "I fantasize about having two cocks fucking me at once."

Two cocks? But he didn't *have* two cocks. How was he supposed to...

He stared at her ass in astonishment, trying to come to terms with the fact that his woman wanted to be fucked by two men. After a moment, she lowered her hands and peered over her shoulder at him.

"Um, let me explain," she said in a tremulous voice. "When you're fucking my ass, I want you in my pussy. And when you're in my pussy, I want you pounding my ass."

He didn't blink or meet her eyes. His woman wanted to be *fucked* by two men. To be double penetrated.

She pressed on. "So I thought maybe if I had both holes filled at once..." She shuddered and creamed instantly, so turned on by thoughts of someone else fucking her that cum flowed from her sex and wet the insides of her thighs.

He couldn't believe that he wasn't enough.

"Forget I said that," she said.

He took a deep gasping breath. "Are you serious?" he sputtered, still struggling to wrap his head around the idea. And there was no way in hell he'd ever let another man touch her, even if that fantasy did make her pussy swell and seep cum as if he'd been sucking on her clit for an hour.

"Forget I said that," she repeated.

"I'm glad you told me, but sweetheart, if another man touched you, I'd have to break his face. And his nuts. Both arms. All of his fingers. His fucking neck."

Her brow twisted with confusion. "What are you talking about?"

"I want to make your fantasies a reality, baby. But I'm not sure I can handle giving you that one. Let me think about it. Maybe Owen would..."

"Owen? Wait." Her eyes widened and her hands flew up to cover her gaping mouth. "You didn't think I wanted two *real* cocks at once, did you?"

Isn't that what she had said?

"Oh God, no. Adam, I can't even think about being with another man."

Adam almost dissolved into a puddle of relief on the floor.

"I wondered if you'd..." She covered her mouth with one hand so that he barely heard her request. "...wear a strap-on for me."

Fuck, he'd wear *three* strap-ons if it turned her on.

She shook her head as if horrified by her own words.

"Forget I said that," she said. "Maybe a butt plug will be enough."

He laughed—not at her, but in relief—and stood from his kneeling position. He drew her body against his length. "You've become so much more open since we first met. I doubt you even knew what a butt plug was and now you're talking about using them. And a strap-on? Where did that come from, Madi?"

"I saw one in the catalog when I ordered my eight-inch dildo." Her face reddened to a deeper shade. "Oh God. I can't believe I told you that."

Damn, if she kept looking all sweet and flustered while she said such naughty things, he was going to bust the zipper right out of his pants.

"Have you tried it on yourself when you masturbate?" he asked. "One toy up your pussy and another up your ass?"

She shook her head and, unable to meet his eyes, talked to the loop of chain at the base of his neck. "I've thought about doing it, but... I like trying things for the first time with you."

He crushed her against his chest and kissed her forehead. "Baby, I wish I had something with me to give you what you want, but I don't."

"That's okay. I shouldn't have—"

He squeezed her tighter. "Yes, you should have. I'm glad you can tell me your fantasies." And as far as fantasies went, that one wasn't too extreme. He could give her that one. Letting another man touch her? Not happening.

"You've made me naughty, Adam Taylor."

He chuckled, his heart warming in his chest. "You're going to blame this on me?"

She nodded. "It's your fault I'm so horny all the time."

He had no problem taking the blame for that.

"You should take responsibility for making me like this."

"Hmm." He glanced reflectively at the ceiling. "I thought we'd already established that I'm irresponsible."

"You have to start somewhere."

"You're right. Okay, I take complete responsibility for your horniness *and* your naughtiness."

She snuggled into his chest. "And what are you going to do

about it?"

"When we see each other next week, I'll bring you a surprise," he said. "You're going to find out what being fucked with two cocks feels like."

She tugged away, her eyes lighting up with excitement. She gave him a quick squeeze. "Oh, I *love* you." Her breath caught and she covered her mouth in horror. "I didn't mean to say that."

His heart, which had been about to burst with happiness half a second before, twisted in his chest. "You didn't?"

She shook her head. But he had hope. Because she hadn't said she didn't mean those three amazing words. Just that she hadn't meant to *say* them.

"That's too bad," he said. "I've been trying to say that to you all night."

She stared at him—eyes wide, mouth agape. "W-what?"

"Madison." He cupped her face with one hand and stared down into her wide, blue eyes. *Say it, asshole. Just say it.* He swallowed. "Madison?" His voice cracked. He took a deep shaky breath. "Madison, I love you."

Tears flooded her eyes, and she squeezed them shut. *What? What did that mean?* Oh God, if she dumped him after he'd found the balls to tell her he loved her, it would kill him.

CHAPTER TEN

This much happiness couldn't be right. Joy flowed through Madison from head to toe. "Oh, Adam, I love you so much!"

She reached for him, seeking his mouth to seal their declarations. She kissed him once on the lips. Once on the chin. Repeatedly at the base of his neck between his collarbones. "I've loved you for so long."

He wrapped his arms around her and crushed her to his chest. "Why didn't you tell me sooner?" he asked breathlessly.

"Because... Because I didn't think you wanted anything serious."

"There you go thinking again. Have I ever done anything that made you feel I didn't adore you?"

She looked up at him, and she could see it—*adoration*—in his eyes.

"Kennedy said—"

"I'm not Kennedy."

"But Owen told me—"

He lifted an eyebrow at her.

She lowered her gaze. "I know you've been with other women."

"I can't deny that."

Her heart squeezed up into her throat until she thought it would suffocate her.

"But that was before I realized I love you," he said. "I couldn't figure out why I was losing interest in sex. Not with you." He tucked her hair behind one ear and gently stroked her cheek. "When you're around, all I can think about is sex. But any other woman I was with didn't do for much me. My performance has been—how do I say this—*subpar.*"

She frowned up at him, confused.

He flushed and stared over the top of her head. "Not every time, but um, *limp* noodle?"

"You mean you couldn't get a boner?" She'd thought erect and ready was pretty much a permanent condition for him.

He laughed. "Hey, easy on the ego, babe. The past few months I haven't slept around much at all. I was always wishing whoever I was with was you and when it wasn't..." He cringed. "I guess the little head figured it out before the big head did."

That made her feel marginally better. "I can't even think of being with anyone but you. I've felt that way since the first time you made love to me on my desk."

He kissed the tip of her nose. "I didn't realize you had such strong feelings for me, Madison. It's a good thing that you waited to tell me until I understood what I was feeling, or I probably would've been an idiot and dumped you for pressuring me."

"I was afraid of that." Her heart thudded, because she needed to pressure him now. She had to put her conditions all out on the table. Let him know exactly what she wanted. "I want to be with you, Adam, I do. I can't even express how much I want to be with you. I just..." She licked her lips, her mouth impossibly dry all of a sudden. She pushed forward with what she had to say. "I love you, but I can't be with someone who sleeps around on me or even *tries* to sleep around." God, it was hard to think she might have to give him up when she'd just heard him speak the words she never thought he'd say to her. "If you can't be mine alone, I can't be with you at all."

She took a deep breath and waited.

He gazed into her eyes for seconds that felt like days.

"I can be faithful to you, Madison. I *will* be. It won't even be a challenge. Do you believe me?"

How could she not when he looked at her with such promise? And love. Overcome with emotion, she blinked back tears. Adam loved her. He pledged to be faithful to her. And he loved her. He *loved* her.

Even more baffling, she believed him. Believed in him.

Believed in them. She didn't have to let him go after tonight. He was hers. All hers.

"I do," she said.

His eyes widened, and then he chuckled. "Now let's not get ahead of ourselves here."

She flushed. "I wasn't thinking marriage I-dos or anything," she said. "I meant, I do believe you. I do believe you'll be faithful. I do believe we can make this work."

He squeezed her against him so tightly, she could scarcely draw breath. "We'll make it work," he said. "We have to. I can't live without you."

Face buried in his strong chest, Madison inhaled his scent, drawing it deep into her lungs. She wished more of him were within her. Wished all of him were within her. She wanted to be as close to him as physically possible. "Can we take that bath now?" she asked hopefully.

He laughed and released her just enough to gaze down into her eyes. "I do stink, don't I?"

She shook her head. "That's not why. I like the way you smell." She pictured him with his ink-decorated skin all exposed, and her nipples tightened in anticipation. "I just want an excuse to get naked with you."

He smiled and touched the tip of his nose to hers. "You don't need an excuse."

He reached behind her and unfastened her bra with practiced ease. He stripped the garment from her body and gazed down at her exposed breasts. "Beautiful." He sank down and sucked her nipple into his hot mouth, rubbing the sensitive tip with his tongue. She fisted her hands in his thick hair and allowed her head to drop back in wonder. He released her nipple with a loud sucking sound and turned his attention to her other breast. Fingers of pleasure licked through her breasts, down her quivering belly and to the juncture between her thighs. Her pussy tightened with need.

"Oh God, Adam, I need your cock inside me."

"Mmm," he murmured around her breast. She pulled at his shirt until he released her throbbing nipple and stood straight. He helped her remove the sweat-damp garment and tossed it on the back of the sofa. Madison stared at his bare chest, tracing the heavy, dark lines of his tattoos with her fingertips. Something about the ink decorating his skin always got her blood pumping.

"Adam?" she whispered.

"Yeah, baby?"

"Why aren't you naked yet?"

He laughed. "I thought you needed to talk."

"I did," she said, reaching for his belt. "But now I need what's in here."

Her fingers trembled as she unfastened his pants and jerked them down over his hips. Her pussy clenched at the sight of his rising cock. It wasn't nearly hard enough for what she craved. She sank to her knees and captured his shaft between her palms before caressing its sensitive tip, with the flat of her tongue. He groaned and placed his hands on the crown of her head.

Thumbs stroking the ridge on the underside of his thickening erection, Madison trailed sucking kisses in a circle along the rim of his cockhead. His hips rocked rhythmically as she teased him. Her tongue flicked over the tip and then she blew a hot breath over the moisture left behind. She licked. Kissed. Rubbed. Purposely didn't suck.

"Madison," he whispered brokenly. "Please."

He tried to thrust into her mouth, but she turned her head and his cock brushed against her cheek. She moved one hand aside so she could lick and kiss her way up his shaft from the thick base to the slightly upturned tip. He tightened his grip on her head and directed her to take him into her mouth. She resisted.

"God, Madison. Stop fucking around and suck it."

She squeezed her thighs together, her pussy so swollen and achy she couldn't stand it. When he said things like that to her, it only turned her on more. With gentle fingertips, she traced the veins straining against the skin of his now rock-hard erection. She did good work, if she did say so herself. She circled his thick shaft with both hands and tugged gently. She wondered how long it would take him to come if she just played with him like this.

"If you don't stop teasing me, I'm going to fuck you right

here on the floor," he said in a dangerous growl.

She peered up at him as she licked the underside of his cock—a slow, sensual dance from base to tip. He had to know that was what she was after. She wanted to tempt him into losing control. Wanted him to fuck her. Holding his gaze, she opened her mouth wide as if she planned to suck him inside. His cock twitched with excitement. She closed her empty mouth and grinned deviously.

"Fuck!"

He tackled her to the carpet between the sofa and the coffee table. Gasping for air and muttering under his breath, Adam fumbled with the panties at the tops of her thighs for a few seconds before getting frustrated and pushing the crotch to one side. He entered her with one penetrating thrust. She cried out, her pussy convulsing with delight as he took her fast, driving his cock into her hard and deep.

"Yes, Adam, fuck it. It's greedy and it needs fucked."

Her back scraped across the carpet as he pounded into her with greater and greater force. His hands tangled in her hair; he rubbed his face against her neck; his saliva wet her skin. She wasn't sure if he realized how hard he was pulling her hair or that he was banging into her cervix with each deep thrust, but God, she loved it. She wrapped her legs around him, her boots digging into the backs of his thighs, and held on for the ride. They strained against each other as they sought quick release. Their breaths came harsh and rapid. Madison feared her heart would burst, it was beating so hard.

"Come," Adam demanded. "Madison, come."

She obeyed, spasms of intense pleasure clenching deep in her pelvis, around his thrusting cock, through her clit, up her belly and down her thighs. She cried out, her back arching off the floor, every muscle in her body taut with ecstasy. His shoulders tightened beneath her fingertips as he thrust deep a final time and shuddered with release.

He spoke her name—might have even whispered words of love against her throat—as he pumped his seed into her.

Breathing hard, he collapsed on top of her, gathering her in his arms and holding her tight.

"Damn it, Madison," he said breathlessly. "Why do you

have to get me so worked up that I jump you like some animal?"

"I like it," she said, squeezing him in gratitude.

"I want to be gentle with you, baby, and treasure your body, but I always end up fucking you like a maniac."

She kissed his shoulder. "I promise I'll let you be gentle with me in the bath," she said.

"You'd better."

She laughed. "But I'm going to need another good hard fuck afterward."

He groaned against her throat. "Will you listen to that dirty mouth?" he muttered to himself. "And she looks so deceptively sweet and innocent."

"And then I'll need you to hold me facedown so I can't move while you pound your cock into my ass as deep as you can."

He shifted to cover her mouth with one hand. She could smell her sex on his skin. Her eyelids fluttered as her inner muscles clenched hard on his softening cock.

"Stop saying things like that." Adam stared down at her with an intense, angry expression. "That's what gets me so worked up in the first place."

She was well aware of that; she loved to get him worked up. When he couldn't keep his hands off her or his dick out of her, it made her feel sexy. Irresistible.

"I love you," she said against his hand.

His expression softened, and his entire body melted into hers. "I love you too."

After a lengthy kiss that made her toes curl inside her boots, he pulled out and rose to his feet. He removed his shoes and shucked his jeans, which had settled around his knees. He stretched his arms over his head, and she drank in the sight of his lean torso, solid chest, muscled arms and thighs, and that delightful trail of hair on his lower belly that drew her attention to his softening cock—still wet with her juices. Maybe she should offer to lick them off. Would that make him grow hard again?

"I hope that tub has jets," he said, stretching his lower back by tilting side to side. "I'm getting too old for hot monkey sex on the floor."

She hoped it had jets for different reasons. He leaned forward to offer her a hand up. She wouldn't have minded enjoying the view for a few more hours, but a bath did sound heavenly. She struggled to her feet and when she moved, discovered her back was deliciously raw with rug burn. She wouldn't be able to get Adam out of her thoughts for days with that reminder on her skin.

She tugged off her boots, but left her panties at the tops of her thighs, and followed him to the bathroom, eager to see what he had in store for her next. She wondered how long it would take her to tempt him into fucking her senseless again. He seemed determined to take it slow, which meant she was going to have to up her game.

CHAPTER ELEVEN

Adam turned on the faucets and adjusted the temperature of the water. With Madison in the tub with him, he should probably set it to frigid so he could keep his wits about him longer than ten seconds. Her hands slid up his ass as she moved to stand behind him. Case in point. When her fingertip pressed into exit-only territory, he jerked upright and spun around to capture her by the arms.

"What do you think you're doing?" he asked.

"Repaying the favor?" She smiled up at him hopefully.

He didn't have the heart to tell her he didn't enjoy being penetrated. Not even by her sexy little fingers. "Get in the tub."

She wriggled out of her panties and bent over to check the water. Luscious ass in the air, her legs were spread just enough to give him an eyeful of her hidden delights. A mixture of her cum and his dripped from her pussy. *Jesus.* Had her view of him a moment ago been that revealing? No wonder she'd tried to press a finger into his ass. She didn't protest a bit when he followed her example. He'd just spent himself inside her, but the sight of his finger penetrating her rear had his cock rising with excitement again. And the sexy little *oh* she vocalized before rocking backward to take him deeper formed an undeniable knot of need low in his belly.

Yeah, should have gone with the cold bath.

He freed his finger and playfully swatted the gentle curve of her butt. "Into the tub, Miss Fairbanks," he said. "You've been a dirty girl."

"If I disobey, will you punish me, Mr. Taylor?" Her hips

writhed suggestively. "I loved it when you spanked me until I made you come last time."

He remembered the way her pussy had clenched around his cock with each swat—how fan-fucking-tastic it felt to come with her squeezing him inside her so tight—but he was determined to be gentle with her this time. To show her that sex didn't have to be rough to be fun and exciting.

"No, I won't spank you for disobeying, Miss Fairbanks. I'll just get in first, knowing you won't be able to resist joining me." He climbed into the tub and sank into the water with a contented sigh. His weary body melted into the warmth. He switched on the jets and a mechanical rumble accompanied the water pounding against his lower back. He sank a bit lower and closed his eyes. Very nice.

Within seconds, Madison joined him, splashing his chest as she settled on the opposite side of the tub. When the level of the water reached his shoulders, she turned off the taps and sat before him with her back facing his chest, leaving at least a foot of distance between them. He knew what she was after. She liked that he couldn't keep his hands off her. Since he wouldn't want to disappoint her, he tugged her back against his front and waited for her to relax before he released his hold. They were both used to fucking like rabbits whenever they were naked and in each other's sights, so it took her a moment to go limp against him and just enjoy the soothing heat and Jacuzzi jets. The weight of her body felt wonderful against his chest and belly. She felt so right and real tucked against him, as if she belonged in that exact spot.

Adam didn't mean to get sexually excited again, but he couldn't stop his cock from finding the rump pressed against it extremely arousing. And damned if his hands didn't have minds of their own as they moved to gently massage the soft globes of her breasts. His disobedient fingers couldn't help but toy with her nipples when those delightful buds hardened into tight tips against his palms. It was totally not his fault that he couldn't be around her for any length of time without wanting to sample every delight her body so willingly offered him.

"Adam?"

"Hmm?" he murmured, not sure how it was possible to be

relaxed and excited at the same time.

"Will you show me more naughty things?"

He grinned and rubbed his nose against her neck just behind her ear. "What kinds of naughty things?"

"Everything. I want to experience everything with you."

"I don't know everything."

"You know more than I do. And I could look some things up and we can try them out," she said.

He couldn't see her face, but he knew she'd be blushing.

"I mean, if you want to."

"If I was a betting man, and I am, I'd put my money on you being far kinkier than I am."

She giggled. "I'll make that a goal."

Dear lord, he'd created a monster—a very sweet and sexy monster, one he was more than willing to experiment with sexually, but a monster just the same. Her fingertips lightly stroked his outer thighs beneath the warm water. Every inch of him was aware of every inch of her.

"What goes on at those sex clubs you go to?" she asked.

"Used to go to," he corrected. "Why do you keep asking about it?"

She shrugged. "You said you liked to perform, but never explained what that means, so I figured I'd go find out for myself."

Absolutely not. He knew what those places were like, and he didn't want her anywhere near one by herself. "I'd be happy to show you."

"No arguments from me. Every time you show me something new, I'm rewarded with mind-blowing orgasms."

"Are you sure? It requires an audience."

She went still. "An audience?"

He could already picture her tangled in the bed sheets on the stage, her thighs spread wide, his mouth working fervently to make her scream so all those watching knew how hard he made her come.

"I know of this really great place in New Orleans," he said. "It's fairly exclusive; they don't let just any average Joe off the street join. I have a few days off tour next week. If you want to go, I'm sure I could get us in."

"What would I have to do?"

"Nothing. Let me please you. Let me perform."

"Would I have to be naked?"

He chuckled. "Mostly."

"And people would see me naked? People I don't know?"

"We'll both wear masks. No one will know it's you, except me."

"But *I'll* know it's me."

He kissed the crown of her head. "It's okay. It's not for everyone."

She didn't say anything for a long moment, so he figured she'd let the idea drop. He should have known better.

"I want to be open to try things you like Adam. You're always willing to give me what I like. Do you really like to perform in front of an audience?"

He chuckled. "Let's just say before I met you, it was my favorite sex act."

"And now?"

"*You're* my favorite sex act."

"So if you performed on me..."

His entire body stiffened, splashing water out of the tub as he reached for solid porcelain to steady himself. "I'd probably come so hard my balls would launch into outer space."

She laughed. "We don't want your balls to end up in orbit."

"You're right. That doesn't sound pleasant."

"But I do want to see how hard I can make you come," she said. "I could give performing a try. Next week in New Orleans?"

"No pressure," he said.

"If I change my mind, I can back out, right?"

"Of course," he said, but he had some ideas on how to get her excited about the idea so she wouldn't change her mind.

Madison sat there for several minutes and he gave her the time to think it through. He didn't want her to feel like she couldn't tell him no. When he said no pressure, he meant it.

"Okay, New Orleans next week. I'm in." She sounded like she'd just agreed to a bank heist. She took a deep breath. "Tell me what to expect."

He withheld his victory dance and played it cool. "Not

saying. I want you to be surprised." He pressed his hands between her thighs and forced her legs apart. "But I know you'll like it," he whispered in her ear. "You'll like strangers watching you beg for penetration. You'll like when they watch you come." He stroked her clit, and she thrashed in the water. "Their attention will make you so hot."

"I'll be embarrassed," she said.

"Just remember, I'm the only one who will know it's you."

"Everyone wears masks?" she asked.

"Except for the director." He smirked. "He wears a hood."

"What?" Her entire body trembled against him. "What do you mean? Who's the director?"

"You'll find out next week. I'm not saying any more."

"Adam! Don't tease me. Tell me what will happen."

But he had plans to tease her all week with hints and messages so that by the time they arrived at *La Petite Mort*, she'd be so excited by the idea of performing, she wouldn't even question it.

"Every man in the room will be jealous of me eating out this pussy," he whispered into her ear. He cupped her mound and squeezed, his fingertips sliding between her swollen folds. "I'm going to hold you wide open so they can see my tongue licking your sweet cum. They'll see how much I relish it, and will be salivating for a taste, but only I can have it. It's mine."

She groaned. "How many will be watching?"

"We won't know until the time comes. It might be a few or as many as thirty. And they'll all have their cocks in their hands by the time I'm finished with you."

She rocked her hips, rubbing her mound against his hand. "Oh God, just the thought is making me hot."

He stroked her swollen clit rhythmically beneath the water. He wasn't quite ready to make love to her yet—he was really enjoying the water jets against his back—but he loved that she was getting all hot and bothered by making future plans. Mostly because it meant they *had* a future.

He caressed her clit faster—*faster*—until her hips bucked and she rocked her mound against his hand as she came. The back of her head crashed against his shoulder as she cried out in ecstasy.

"You're going to give all of our spectators raging hard-ons when you come all sexy like that." It certainly made his cock stiff. "Make lots of noise for me, Madison. Don't hold it in. You have to let our audience know how much I please you."

"I'll be loud," she said breathlessly. "I'll scream if you want me to."

Her body went limp, and he held her against his chest, nose buried in her fragrant hair. She relaxed and let him hold her. This was what he'd been craving all evening—calm, quiet closeness. He had no doubt that she'd soon have him worked into a frenzy again, but for now this was nice. Sometimes nice was exactly what he needed.

They sat for a long while in silence. His eyelids were drooping lethargically when she asked, "Are there other kinds of sex clubs?"

He chuckled. Yep, his sexually curious little monster would definitely have him pawing her like an animal in record time. "There are the ones that Kellen prefers."

She tilted her head to look at him over her shoulder. "What is Kellen into anyway?"

"His nickname didn't give it away?"

"Cuff? Don't you call him that because he wears those leather cuffs on his wrists?"

"That's exactly why we call him Cuff."

She looked completely perplexed—her forehead furrowed and lips pursed. As adventurous and sexy as the woman was, he loved these glimpses of her innocence. She was losing a bit of the quality as her eyes opened to experiences beyond the ordinary, but he doubted she'd ever completely lose her basic purity, and he didn't want her to.

"He loves to restrain a woman so she can't resist all the dirty, kinky things he does to her body," he whispered in her ear.

Madison shuddered against him. "Oh! Does he spank them?"

"If they ask nicely."

"I want you to do that to me," she said.

Adam visualized her with her arms restrained behind her back and her legs secured spread so that her scrumptious ass and sweet pussy were exposed to his delight. He could lick and suck on her for hours, and she wouldn't be able to get away or tempt him into taking her quickly. He doubted he'd spank her at all. Even if she asked nicely. He nibbled gently on her ear, as if blood wasn't surging into his cock at the thought of her bound and at his mercy. "If that's what you want."

She nodded eagerly.

"But not tonight. Tonight I get to be gentle with you."

"I'm not sure if I'll be able to stand it, Adam."

"Why not?"

She took a deep breath. "Because... Because when you're tender with me, I get so overwhelmed with emotion that I'm likely to burst into tears."

His heart twisted unpleasantly. He wasn't sure how he'd react if she cried during sex. "Happy tears?"

"Yes, happy tears."

"Then that's okay. I'll kiss them away. I love you." Those three words were becoming easier to say, but he meant them a little more with each passing moment.

Madison turned around to face him, kneeling between his thighs. She cradled his face in her hands and touched her nose to his, her eyes drifting closed. "Is this real?" she asked. "I've dreamed of you saying you love me so many times, I'm worried that I'm dreaming."

Normally if a woman had said something like that, he'd be reaching for his clothes and bolting for the door, but this was Madison. She wouldn't hurt him. It was okay to love her. Okay to tell her.

"If you're dreaming, then I'm dreaming too," he said. "I've never told anyone I love them."

Her eyes opened, and her pupils adjusted as she focused on him. "No one? Not even family?"

"No one," he said.

She looped her wet arms around his neck and pressed her breasts into his chest. "Then I think you need to say it some more. Just so you get used to it. Think of it as therapy."

He chuckled. "I love you."

Her fingers burrowed into his hair. "Again," she whispered.

"I love you." It felt good to let her know. He could say

these things when they were alone together. He wouldn't want others to recognize his weakness, but if only she knew, that was okay.

"Again."

"I love you. Your turn."

She stared intently into his eyes and said, "I love you." She didn't look away for several moments and then out of nowhere said, "I wonder what it feels like to have a pierced cock rubbing inside you."

"Woman," he said, "you had better stop thinking about having sex with my band. First Kellen and now Owen?"

"Oh, I wasn't thinking of having sex with anyone but you."

Though his dick was hidden beneath the churning water, there was no doubt where she was directing her pointed look. His balls tried to crawl up into his pelvic cavity. "Absolutely not, Madison."

She stuck out her lower lip and blinked her beguiling blue eyes at him.

"That look will get you diamonds, baby," he said, "but not my cock pierced."

She laughed. "I guess I'll just have to imagine what it feels like. And I bet it makes giving blow jobs a challenge."

He threw back his head and laughed. "You'll have to ask one of Owen's playthings. I've never blown him."

She grinned crookedly. "Have you ever done anything sexy with another guy?" she asked, rubbing her breasts against his chest. For fuck's sake, was she getting turned on by thinking of him with another man?

"No, I'm not into guys."

"Would you like to see me do something sexy with another girl?"

Whoa. What in the hell had he awoken in this once sheltered woman? And why was he so glad to have corrupted her innocence? "Such as..."

"Kissing?" She had the same expression on her face that she wore when she questioned him in a counseling session—all serious and attentive.

"Yeah, I'd like to see you kiss a girl."

"Playing with each other's breasts?" She cupped her perky

tits and rubbed her thumbs over her nipples. "Licking them?" Her tongue traced her upper lip, not in an intentionally seductive way, but as if she was imagining the best way to use it on another woman.

Welcome back, raging hard-on. Where have you been for the past five minutes?

"That would be sexy," he said, his breath already hitching with excitement.

She glanced up and caught his titty-roaming gaze. "Would you rather watch another woman eat me out or me eat her out?"

Both scenarios played in his mind, and he found that an easy question to answer. "You eat her, so I can fuck you from behind while I watch."

Her hand slid from her breast and into the water. He couldn't see what she was doing clearly, but he was pretty sure she was exploring the folds of her sex.

"Does a woman's cum taste like a man's?" she asked.

How the hell would he know? He'd never tasted his own, and he sure as hell had never tasted another dude's.

"I don't think so."

"I want to taste it. A woman's cum." Her hand lifted out of the water, and she slipped two wet fingers into her mouth.

Adam's gut clenched, and his balls threatened to explode.

"I can't taste it," she said, pouting. "I know my pussy is wet enough. I guess the water washed the cum off my fingers."

A flood sloshed across the bathroom floor. Adam hadn't meant to tackle her backward into the tub. His intention had been to be gentle for the rest of the night, not to find the hot, slick sheath between her thighs and drive his throbbing cock into it over and over and over again. But damn it, if she kept tempting him, what the hell did she expect? She knew what it did to him when she acted all sweet and innocent, dirty and naughty at the same time.

She clung to him as he plunged into her, moaning encouragement as she moved with him. When his urgency receded enough for him gather a thought, he paused and frowned down at her.

Her eyes blinked open. "Is something wrong?"

"You did that on purpose," he accused.

"Did what?"

For once, he wasn't buying her look of innocence.

"Acted sexy so I'd jump you again. You knew I wanted to be gentle with you."

She grinned crookedly. "Was it sexy when I tasted my cum?"

"Fuck, woman, you know it was."

"Are you expecting me to apologize for tempting you?"

"You *are* manipulating me."

"And I so like the outcome," she said, her grin widening. "Don't stop."

He didn't plan to stop, just calm his motions a bit. He moved his hips slowly, churning inside her. Her eyelids fluttered. He repeated the motion—deeper, wider—holding her tightly for leverage in the give of the water. Each time he withdrew, one water jet massaged his foot and another jet stirred a stream of water against his balls, encouraging him to move faster. He fought the urge, watching Madison's face as she relaxed and let him carry a languid rhythm.

"That feels so good," she whispered, staring up into his eyes. "Oh, Adam."

He kissed her soft lips, continuing his pattern of slow, deep, gyrating thrusts. Giving her time to focus on sensation. To feel how perfectly their bodies came together. To recognize his love for her, which must be apparent on his face and in every motion of his body. The enormity of his feelings swelled in his chest. He was starting to understand what she meant about the need to always rush, so there wasn't time for this profound connection to overwhelm the physical pleasure. She felt so perfect against him, around him. Looked so wet and sexy—her face flushed, breasts exposed, hair floating like a cloud of dark silk in the water. Her head tilted back a little more with each churning thrust. Her mouth opened a bit wider each time he withdrew.

"Adam, I think... I think... I'm gonna come soon. Oh God, the slow build feels so good. Don't stop. Almost."

She continued to encourage him with gasping words as he took her higher and higher. Her body began to tremble uncontrollably as her orgasm eluded her. At last, she caught it. "Oh!"

When she squeezed her eyes shut in ecstasy, he said, "Don't look away."

Body straining and lungs gasping for air, she forced her eyes open.

"I love you, Madison," he whispered. "Do you feel it?" He felt it—as if his buoyant soul was going to float out of his chest and into the heavens.

"Y-yes." When the first tear slipped from the corner of her eye, his thought he'd somehow hurt her. By the second drop, he realized those were the happy tears she'd been worried about spilling. Just as he promised, he kissed them away.

When her orgasm subsided, she lifted her head from the tub—a torrent of water pouring from her long hair—and pressed kisses to his throat and shoulders. "You were right," she said. "It's just as good, maybe better, when it isn't quick and rough."

"You're not telling me anything new. I *know* what makes sex great," he boasted. "You." He couldn't imagine how hard the guys would rip on him if they heard him say that. But here with her, he could be as repulsively sappy as he wanted to be. Here with her, appearances didn't matter.

"You're right about that too," she said, snuggling her face into the crook of his neck. "The partner makes all the difference."

Why in the hell had he waited so long to admit he had feelings for her? He'd wasted months that he could have been loving her and being openly loved in return. He kissed her with all the passion he could muster and then pulled out of her body before collapsing against the back of the tub again.

Madison struggled to orient her body in a kneeling position between his legs.

"You didn't come, did you?" she asked.

Apparently she couldn't see how stiff he cock was beneath the surface of the water. "No. I can only do that so many times a night. I figured I better save something for later."

"Last time we spent the night together, you had seven orgasms."

He chuckled. "You counted?"

She nodded. "And I had ten." She shifted both hands out of the water and wiggled all ten fingers at him.

"No wonder I always sleep for two days after I see you."

"And I can feel you deep inside for days."

"Do I make you sore?"

She bit her lip and nodded. "I need that part. It makes me miss you less." She took a shaky breath. "For a little while."

Her sad little frown about broke his heart. *Damn.*

He grabbed her wrist and tugged. With a startled cry, she slipped on the bottom of the tub and collided sideways with his chest. Instead of righting herself, she melted against him, her head resting on his shoulder and her warm breath blowing gently against the wetness on his chest. Her hand moved to his erection, stroking his length absently. Her gentle touch wouldn't make him come, but it would definitely keep him hard.

"Madison," he said, enjoying the relative calm between them, but needing to share something he'd been hiding from her.

"Hmm?"

"I wasn't exactly truthful with you earlier."

She stiffened. "You don't really love me?"

"*What?*" He couldn't believe that was the first thing she'd think he'd lie about. Hell, it was probably the only thing he'd *never* lie about. "No. That's not it."

"I don't care about any other lies right now as long as you truly love me."

"Too bad, I'm telling you anyway." He rubbed a hand over her upper arm. Her smooth, damp skin was chilly to the touch. Perhaps he should concentrate on keeping her warm instead of troubling her with his problems. "I lied about the reason I don't want you to visit me in Austin."

"The porn on the walls?"

"Madison, it's not porn. It's my artwork. *Mine,*" he clarified. "I didn't buy it; I created it."

"You're an artist?" She shifted away from his chest so she could look at him. "Why didn't you ever tell me that?"

"Hey, baby," he said in a creepy stalker voice, "I draw and

paint portraits of nude women from memory. Wanna come view my collection?"

"Yeah, actually, I *do* want to see your work, naked chicks or not." Her eyes lit up. "Have you ever painted me?"

The heat of embarrassment rose up his neck and face. Was he seriously blushing? "Yeah, far more than I should. I have at least five paintings of your left breast alone."

"But not the right?" She looked down at her perfect breasts. "Is the left one better or something?"

"Nope, it's just usually in my dominant hand."

She laughed. "Well, now that I know your secret, I can visit, right?"

"Someday." He had started this thread of conversation to tell her that his father had moved back in, but that feeling of not wanting to disappoint her made him hesitate. He decided it would be easier to get rid of the old man than to remind Madison that he wasn't as strong as she seemed to think he was. "But not next week. Next week it's you and me in New Orleans. Did you forget?"

"How could I forget? I wonder... While you eat me out at the club, should I do this?" Leaning her back against his chest, she cupped her breasts and tugged at her nipples, making them hard and rosy pink. "If I play with my boobs, will our audience think it's sexy?"

She was totally getting into it. He couldn't imagine anyone not thinking his Madison was the sexiest woman alive. And she was his. How did he get so lucky? She lifted her breasts in both hands, pressing them together into tit-fucking cleavage. "Or is it sexier to hold them together like this? Adam, tell me what looks hotter."

Jesus. His cock pulsed, protesting its mistreatment. He covered her breasts and massaged them roughly. "Fuck, woman, why do you tempt me? Now I want to come all over your tits."

She treated him to a deep, throaty laugh. "Well, what's stopping you?"

CHAPTER TWELVE

Madison wore a T-shirt she'd borrowed from Adam—one day she'd learn to bring an overnight bag when she had a date with him—and was resting on her stomach on the bed next to him. He was gloriously naked, which tended to make her hands wander. She'd yet to tempt him into tossing her on her back and possessing her body as he consistently possessed her soul, but she was working on it.

He'd made her all hot and bothered in the tub, stroking his cock within the pulsing jets of the Jacuzzi until he'd erupted all over her chest. Then he'd insisted on washing every inch of her body and encouraging her to return the favor. After getting her worked up again, he hadn't offered her release. Instead, he'd decided it was time to munch on snacks and watch TV.

They sampled from the banquet laid out before them on the end of the bed—an assortment of junk food Adam had purchased out of a vending machine while she'd dried her hair. Some show about a tattoo artist was on the flat-screen, but Madison couldn't concentrate on television with Adam's toe rubbing the instep of her foot and his arm resting against hers. All she could think about—all she *ever* seemed able to think about—was him. She pressed her head against his shoulder and closed her eyes. All the anxiety, the loneliness, the jealousy and the uncertainty had been worth it just to experience this perfect moment. And she had so many more perfect moments to look forward to.

"I think you need a tattoo, Madi," Adam said. Unlike her, he was very into the program. He munched another nacho-flavored tortilla chip and licked the psychedelic orange cheese from his fingertips.

"I'm too squeamish to get a tattoo."

He chuckled. "As much as you like being spanked? You'd love it. You'd get so hot and bothered, you'd probably jump me in the tattoo parlor."

"I'd probably jump you in the tattoo parlor without any provocation."

He kissed her with salty lips. "How about a practice run?" He leaned across the bed and snatched a ballpoint pen off the side table. Holding it in his teeth, he flipped her onto her back and ran his hands lightly over her skin as he lifted his T-shirt to reveal her bare belly. "Such beautiful canvas," he said. He placed a kiss just beneath her belly button. "I think right here. What do you want as your design, Miss Fairbanks?"

"You do tattoos?"

He shook his head. "Nope. I just like to draw. How about a little pussy just above your pretty pussy?" His tongue flicked over the cleft at the apex of her thighs, and her body jerked. She hadn't been able to locate her panties and was pretty sure that Adam had hidden them from her when she'd insisted on wearing one of his clean T-shirts after their bath.

"Adam," she admonished. "Don't you think that's a little crude?"

He chuckled. "Absolutely." He uncapped the pen and drew a curved line from her belly button to her mound.

She giggled and squirmed. "That tickles."

"Hold still," he said.

She tried, but his hand stretching the skin of her belly taut and the tip of the pen rubbing against her sensitive flesh had goose bumps rising, her nipples hard and her pretty pussy drenched. The intensity of his expression as he worked, with his tongue pressed against his upper lip, excited her further. He wore the same air of concentration when he played a guitar solo.

"Hot and bothered yet?" he asked, flicking his gorgeous gray eyes upward for a brief instant.

She moaned in the affirmative.

"I can smell your excitement. It's making it hard to concentrate."

She eased her legs open and was rewarded with a groan of approval and a tongue flicked over her swollen clit.

"That isn't fair," he said. "You know what your scent does to me."

She grinned and spread her legs wider. She lifted her head and caught sight of his half-finished drawing. She'd expected perhaps a stick-figure cat, but the image was amazingly detailed, three-dimensional and realistic.

"Oh, Adam, how do you do that?"

"Well, I just sort of tighten my tongue and then flick it up and down, then—"

She laughed. "No, I don't mean how you lick my clit. How do you draw so realistically? It's amazing."

He shrugged. "Don't know. It's just something I've always done for fun. I mostly draw naked women. And for *some* reason... animals."

"You're fantastic. Finish it." She nodded toward her lower belly. "Please."

He grinned at her, obviously pleased by her compliment. "Okay."

"Now I really want to visit your place to see your artwork."

"I carry some of it with me at all times."

"Really? Is it in your suitcase?"

He shook his head. "On my skin."

"You designed your tattoos?"

She giggled as he drew on a particularly ticklish spot on her pubis.

"I designed the dragon on my back, but not my sleeve; a real artist drew that." The tattoos that covered his right arm from shoulder to wrist were abstract, where Adam's drawings were realistic. She still remembered how breathless she'd become the first time she'd seen the tattoo that covered most of his back. She couldn't believe he had drawn it. She would have bet her left kidney that a professional artist had designed it. The man was definitely multi-talented. "You drew your dragon?"

He nodded. "I also drew some of the band's tattoos. Especially Gabe's. The phoenix on his back, the cougar on one side of his chest and the wolf on the other. I designed the shark on Kellen's calf and the stallion on his shoulder, the snake on Owen's... uh, hip region, and Shade's..." Adam scowled.

"What's the matter?"

"Nothing. He just pisses me off, is all."

She lifted a hand to stroke his hair, which was still damp from their bath. "You need to talk to him, sweetheart. Try to sort things out."

His scowl deepened. She hated to see him in turmoil, wanted him to smile more. "So I'm guessing that you designed the turtle Shade has inked on ass."

Adam's features softened, and he chuckled. "Shade doesn't have a turtle on his ass."

"Are you sure? I think I heard that somewhere. Well then, did you draw the butterfly on his lower back?"

He laughed. "Nope."

"Hmm. Maybe the hummingbirds on his chest. Or the little piglet on his belly?"

"He must have some new tattoos I haven't seen."

"They're all adorable," Madison said, glad she'd made him laugh. "What did you draw for him?"

Adam sighed. "A lion. It's on his chest, over his heart." Adam licked his thumb and rubbed it over her belly to correct a mistake he'd made with his pen. "He probably wants to have it removed."

"I doubt that. I'm sure it's special to him."

And he was scowling again. Maybe it was best to leave the real world outside. She'd hate to upset him now and ruin their limited time together. "Almost finished?" she asked. "I have a powerful need to suck your cock while you use that tongue on my pretty pussy."

His grin returned. "Oh yeah?"

She nodded.

He tossed the pen aside. "All finished."

She rose up on her elbows and admired the fuzzy kitten on her lower belly. It seemed to stare up at her with an impish grin. "Maybe I do need a tattoo," she said. "Then your artwork would become a permanent part of me."

"We need to experiment with more designs first. Then I

can draw on you as often as I like and never run out of canvas." He looked up at her. "But I am going to take a picture of this before I make you sweat it off." He leaned off the bed and found his cellphone among the clothes he'd discarded after his trip to the vending machines. He lifted it high and aimed the lens at his drawing.

She knew there was no way for him to get a picture without including her exposed private area just beneath it.

"Wait," she said, "let me cover..."

Before she could position her hands, he snapped a picture. Her face flamed. She tried to grab his phone, but he held it above his head and looked up at the picture he'd taken. "Now *that's* art," he said.

Her face felt as if it would burst into flame. "Please delete it."

He smiled down at her. "Are you blushing, Madi?"

"It's embarrassing. Someone might see it."

"Do you really think I'd let anyone look at it besides me? I won't."

She relaxed slightly.

"But you'd better get used to people looking at your body if you still want to go to that sex club next week."

"But they won't be able to see my face."

He chuckled. "Can't see your face in this shot either."

She supposed that was true. "Can I see it?"

He showed her the picture, which was erotic in that her shaved pubis was visible just beneath his drawing, but the photo was also tasteful. Artistic. Looking it at made her pussy throb.

"That's kind of hot," she said breathlessly.

"Kind of? It's on fire, baby. God, it makes me hard."

He shifted onto his side, and she zeroed in on the evidence of his desire for her. His cock *was* hard, and she really did have a powerful need to suck it. She rolled onto her side upside down beside him and directed him into her mouth, sucking hard and bobbing her head rapidly because she wanted to taste his cum. The sooner, the better. He grabbed her hips and shifted her closer so he could suckle her clit and flick his tongue over it as hard and fast as she was giving it to him.

She shattered almost instantly, the ripples of pleasure causing her to buck against his face.

He pulled out of her mouth and leaned off the bed to retrieve a condom and a tube of lube.

Her ass tightened with anticipation. *God, yes!* But...

"I wanted you to come in my mouth," she said.

"I will, but not just yet."

He yanked the oversized black T-shirt off over her head and pressed her onto her back. Lifting her legs straight up, he rested her heels on his shoulders and slipped a pillow under her hips. He handed her the condom. "Open it," he said. "Hurry." He twisted the cap off the tube with his teeth and applied lube to her twitching ass with his hand. When his slick finger slid inside her, she shuddered. "Hurry," he pleaded.

Her fingers were trembling so hard, she couldn't get the damned package open.

"Can't wait." He filled her pussy with one deep thrust. Kneeling between her thighs, he held her legs open and wide, churning his hips as he thrust. He was watching himself fill her, his bottom lip trapped between his teeth. She wished she could see what he was looking at, what had him broken out in an instant sweat, what had him shuddering and making sexy murmurs of pleasure in the back of his throat.

"I wish there was a mirror over the bed," she said.

He paused. "I'll have one installed at my place. You need to see how sexy your pussy looks with my cock working it."

She groaned, loving when he said such things to her. She tried to imagine what something that felt so good looked like from his perspective.

"Wait. I know..."

He reached for his cellphone and before she could freak-the-fuck-out, he snapped a picture. He handed her the phone, and she gawked at the sight of her red and swollen pussy stuffed with his thick shaft. *Dear God.*

"Gorgeous, isn't it?" he asked, meeting her eyes for a moment before returning his gaze to where his cock was plunging into her.

"Is . . . Is this what they'll be watching at the sex club next week?"

"That and more. I definitely want them to witness you getting it from behind. Not many performers do live anal sex."

Her core clenched. "Will we be able to see others doing it?" She took another look at the picture on the screen and groaned.

"If that's your kink." He grinned crookedly and winked at her. "You'd better get that condom open if you want me back here." He slipped a finger into her well-lubed ass.

She dropped the phone and fumbled with the condom wrapper. Finally, she was able to open the little package. She tried to hand the condom to him, but he was still gripping her legs, still staring at where their bodies were connected.

"Adam," she whispered. "Take it."

"Okay, just give me another minute."

His motions became more vigorous, his breathing more ragged. Just when she thought he was going to let go, he pulled out, gulping desperately for air, his body twitching, his eyes squeezed tightly shut.

"Oh God," he said. "I could look at that for a lifetime."

She was perfectly okay with that. "I love you," she said.

He opened one eye and grinned. "Love you too. Where's that condom?"

She'd accidentally dropped it while she'd been watching him get off on the sight of their joined bodies. The cream-colored circle was stuck to her chest. Chuckling, he retrieved the condom and fumbled between her legs as he unrolled it over his length. With her hands, Madison held her legs up and wide while he readied himself. While he applied more lube, she trembled with anticipation. She wondered how two parts of her, which were so close together and so similar in design, could feel so very different when filled with him.

He nudged against her ass and entered her slowly, applying even more lube as he penetrated deeper. She really didn't mind the soreness produced by too little lubrication, but loved that he cared about her comfort. He plunged inside with little resistance. Buried balls deep, he paused.

"Okay?"

She nodded. "Love it."

"I thought you might be too tender from earlier."

"I feel great. I want it hard."

"Hold your legs for me, okay? I'm going to try something. Tell me if you want me to stop."

Oh hell yes. He'd never once disappointed her when he tried something. She nodded eagerly.

His strokes were deep and straight, and oh so hard. He pulled out completely several times driving her to blissful moans. Her pussy was starting to protest its emptiness. That was why she thought being filled with two cocks at once would be spectacular. Already, her vagina was jealous because her ass was getting all the attention. Adam slipped two fingers into her emptiness and tugged them in and out with the same rhythm he was using to take her ass.

"Oh God," she moaned.

Another finger joined the first two. She screamed her encouragement, rocking with him to work against his hand, his cock.

"More!" she demanded.

He rotated his hand and filled her more. Most of his hand—all four fingers—plunged in and out of her clenching pussy. It sucked at his hand greedily, wanting still more. She fleetingly hoped he'd fist her, but before she could beg him to do it, his thumb brushed her clit and she exploded into a million pieces of blinding ecstasy.

Her body was still seizing with the hardest orgasm of her life when he pulled out, stripped off the condom and positioned the head of his cock over her trembling lips. He pumped himself twice and let go, his fluids squirting into her mouth and across her face. She was breathing too hard to suck the head of his twitching cock, but she rubbed him with her trembling lips, wanting to give him at least a fraction of the pleasure he'd given her.

He collapsed on the bed beside her. Madison straightened her legs, smiling because she could still feel that he'd been inside her, in her naughty, wet hole. She licked his salty cum from her lips, pleased he'd remembered to give her what she'd asked for.

"Fuck, Madison. You're too hot for your own good." He groaned. "For *my* own good."

She'd never had a man call her hot before. Pretty. Sweet. Cute, even. But never *hot*. She squirmed around on the bed so she could rest her head on his heaving stomach and traced the narrow strip of hair on his lower belly with one finger. "That was amazing," she whispered. "I've never come that hard before."

"I'm glad I satisfied you."

"I had no doubt. You never disappoint me."

He placed a hand on the back of her head and pressed her face against him. "I do love you, Madison Fairbanks. I wish this night would never end."

She wished that too.

Using Adam as the sexiest pillow in existence, Madison had almost drifted to sleep when the phone rang and shattered the tranquility of the moment.

Adam groaned in protest. "Don't answer that," he said. "It's probably Shade. He can't sleep unless he bitches me out right before bedtime."

"It's almost two," Madison said. "It might be an emergency."

She scrambled across the bed and lifted the receiver. "Hello?"

"Oh, hey there, baby," a man said in a grizzly voice. "Is my son around?"

"I think you have the wrong number." Madison knew for a fact that Adam did not associate with his father. It had been his father who'd gotten him addicted to drugs in the first place.

"This isn't Adam Taylor's room?"

Her forehead crinkled. "Yeah. This is Adam's room."

"Well, let me talk him," he said loudly. "I need him to get me something special on his way home."

Adam sat up beside her on the bed. "Who is it?" he asked.

She wasn't sure how it was possible, but... "It's your father."

CHAPTER THIRTEEN

Fuck. Why did the old man have to ruin everything? It wasn't enough that his father had run off Adam's mother, ruined his childhood and introduced him to drugs. Nope, he had to call his hotel room at two o'clock in the goddamned morning and make his unwanted presence known to Madison. So much for getting rid of the bastard before Madison could find out his toxic existence was back in Adam's life.

"What do you want?" Adam said into the phone.

"Cocaine," his dad answered in his two-pack-a-day rasp.

"I'm not getting anything for you. We've been through this." No matter how many times he told his father that he was clean now, the man didn't believe him. He thought Adam was holding out on him.

His father clicked his tongue. "What good is it to have a rock-star son if he doesn't share his prime drug sources with you?"

Adam couldn't bring himself to look at Madison, because even though she'd *said* he never disappointed her, he knew this would.

"I have to go," Adam said.

"Will you be home tomorrow?"

"Yeah." His stomach twisted in knots, Adam hung up.

"When were you going to tell me he was back in your life?" Madison said in her calm, professional voice.

Damn it. Adam shrugged, turned off the TV and switched off the lamp on his side of the bed. "Let's go to bed. I'm tired."

"Adam!"

"I'm working on getting rid of him, all right? Give it a rest."

"I'm not going to give it a rest. Is he the real reason you didn't want me to visit you in Austin?"

He plumped his pillow and stretched out on his side with his back to her.

"Don't you fucking shut me out, Adam." There was no calm professionalism in her tone now.

"I don't want to talk about this."

"You told me he was out of your life. Did you lie to me about that too? How can I believe *anything* you say?"

"That wasn't a lie. He was out of my life. He came to visit a few months ago and he's been staying at my place ever since." He impersonated his father's grating voice to say, "About time you were good for something, boy. You rock stars have access to all the best drugs. Do your daddy a favor and get me some choice cocaine. Been way too long since we snorted a line of blow together, son. It'll be just like old times."

"So you've been doing drugs with your father again?"

He hadn't, but guilt clenched his gut as if he had. He shook his head. "No, but he has drugs stashed all over my house. I hope to fucking God my parole officer doesn't decide to drop in for a visit. The only reason I didn't do any jail time last year is because I agreed to see you. If they find drugs in my house, I'll do time behind bars for sure."

"Adam, you have to get rid of him."

Adam flopped onto his back and stared at the ceiling. He still couldn't bring himself to look her in the eye. He couldn't handle the disappointment he feared he'd see in her gaze. Or the mistrust.

"Ideally, yes. Realistically, the man does whatever the fuck he wants to do. That will never change."

"I could try talking to him. Does he even realize how much trouble he can get you in?"

"Does he care, Madison? Does a man who shoots up his thirteen-year-old son with heroin as his rite of *manhood* care about anything but an altered state of mind?" Adam had broken down the first time he'd told Madison about his thirteenth birthday. And then he'd cussed her out for making him cry. And then he'd cried again. It had been his first step to healing and the first time she'd held him. Maybe that was when he'd fallen in love with her.

"I could turn him in when you're out on the road," Madison said. "You wouldn't be the one to get busted then. He would."

"I don't want him in jail. Has jail ever helped an addict? It just turns people with addictions into criminals with addictions."

"I can help him the way I helped you, but you're my priority. We have to keep him away from you until he's clean."

He sighed. "Madison, I don't want you to get involved. This is a family issue."

"That's bullshit!"

He didn't argue. He knew it was bullshit, but he didn't want her to get involved. He had this situation under control.

"Adam," she said, "you had to know if you told me, I'd get involved. It's my job. No, more than that." She slapped his belly. "It's who I am. I have to help."

"But it won't help anything, Madi. For an addict to become clean, he has to want it. And my father loves his lifestyle." Loved it more than his wife and his son.

"Sometimes we have to force them to want it."

He shook his head at her. "You don't really believe that. You're too smart to believe you can force it."

She released a heavy sigh. "Will you at least let me talk to him? Try to reason with him. For *your* sake."

Adam rubbed his left eyebrow with the side of his index finger. He always got a headache behind his left brow when he was stressed. "I'll talk to him," he said, "and if he won't see reason, I'll let you try to gain his cooperation."

Madison pursed her lips and then nodded. "Okay. I trust you'll do what you have to do to get him out of your house. I do know some good counselors in Austin. If you want, I could have someone—"

"I'll handle it."

Her entire body was tense as she struggled to maintain her composure. Adam knew it was killing her to leave this up to him, but he also knew his father, and the man wasn't ever going to change. The best thing would be to get him to move out. If threats didn't work, maybe bribes would.

Adam suddenly found himself buried beneath Madison and enveloped in her tight embrace.

"This must be so hard for you, sweetheart," she whispered and kissed his temple. "I know you were just coming to terms with him being out of your life for good. Do you want to talk about it?"

He drew a deep breath into his heavy, aching chest. "When it's over."

She rose up on her arms and gazed down at him, nodding in understanding. "Okay. Day or night, I'll be here when you need me."

This. This is why he loved her with every particle of his existence. What would he ever do without her? He wished he'd told her the instant his father had darkened his doorstep. He didn't have to go through this alone. He had Madison. Madison who understood him. Madison who helped him find his way. He'd never had anyone to depend on before. It was both terrifying and a huge relief to realize that she was there for him when he needed her. "I love you," he said. "How can I ever repay you for everything you've done for me?"

She kissed him gently and stroked his hair back from his eyes. "You already have. In just three words. It's enough."

He tugged her against him and pulled the tangled sheets to cover their entwined bodies. She switched off the lamp on her side of the bed and snuggled closer to his chest. "I love you," she whispered in the darkness.

His heart swelled. If only he could hear those words from her every night before he closed his eyes. She was right—three words were enough. But as her hand stroked up and down the bare skin along his spine, he realized he'd hadn't yet had enough of her body.

"That feels nice," he said. "I hope you weren't actually planning on getting any sleep."

CHAPTER FOURTEEN

A loud banging pulled Adam from a deep sleep.

"Get the fuck out of bed," Shade bellowed from the hallway. "We were supposed to leave an hour ago. Are you even in there?"

Adam reached for Madison's sleeping body and tucked her against his chest. *Nope,* he thought. *No one's home.*

"You didn't have another fucking overdose, did you? If you don't open this door, I'm calling an ambulance."

"Go let him know you're all right," Madison murmured. "He's worried about you."

Adam rolled his eyes. "Yeah, I'm sure that's it."

He stumbled out of bed, his thighs, buttocks and lower back protesting their strenuous workouts from the night before. He stretched as he crossed the hotel suite, not bothering to find clothes on his way to the door.

He yanked it open. "Did you not see the do not disturb sign?"

"It's after noon."

"So?"

"So we've all been ready to leave for hours. Everyone is waiting for you. As usual."

Adam supposed everyone but him was looking forward to spending a night at home in Austin. "Yeah, all right. I'll be right down." He closed the door and rubbed his face with both hands. He wasn't sure what time he'd finally fallen asleep, but he remembered the orange glow of dawn seeping into the room from around the edges of the black-out curtains.

"Did he say it was *after* noon?" Madison said, bolting

upright in the middle of the bed and trying to focus on the clock on the nightstand.

Hair tangled, nipples red, lips swollen, marks on her chest from his sucking kisses, mascara in dark half-moons beneath each eye, Madison looked positively well-fucked. Adam was seriously considering adding another layer to that look.

"I'm going to be late for work," she said as she collapsed in an exhausted sprawl on her back. Adam stepped on a half-eaten bag of chips. The wrapper crinkled, and the chips crunched beneath his foot as he returned to the bed.

"I'm not sure how my dick is even functional after last night, but it would very much like to show you a good morning."

She groaned and threw a pillow at him. "I don't think I can open my legs to accept its good morning."

"I'll just bend you over the back of the sofa then."

She cringed. "We have to go."

He knew she was right, but that didn't mean he had to accept it was time for his interlude with Madison to end. He climbed onto the bed beside her and drew her against him. "Just let me hold you for a few more minutes," he whispered into her hair.

She snuggled closer.

His eyes opened and closed lethargically.

A loud banging started Adam awake some time later. "What is taking you so long?" Shade yelled from the hallway. "There are other people on the planet too, you know. The entire world doesn't revolve around you."

"We fell asleep again?" Madison said in a slurred voice. "What time is it?"

Adam tilted his head back and squinted at the glowing numbers of the alarm clock. "One oh four."

"Shit!" Madison struggled out of the tangle of his arms. He helped her free her legs from the knotted sheet and watched her stumble around the room looking for her clothes. He knew the hesitance in her steps was his doing. Rock on.

"Adam, get dressed." She threw his jeans at his face.

She fought to get her bra in place and then slipped her dress over her head. It gaped open in the back.

"Where are my panties?" she said.

He grinned. Right where he'd put them.

Hands on her hips, challenging glare on her face, she pursed her lips at him. "I can't wear this dress without panties. All it would take is a gust of wind and..." She lifted her skirt, and he caught a glimpse of her mound.

His cock twitched to life, drawing her attention.

"Don't you *dare* get a hard-on, Adam Taylor. I'm supposed to be at work in forty-five minutes, and the entire band is waiting for you so they can leave."

"What can I say?" He shrugged. "You're a worthy distraction."

The corner of her mouth twitched with the hint of a smile, and her cheeks pinked in a most beguiling blush.

Adam heard the suite's door unlock.

"Thank you," Shade said to a harassed-looking maid. "I think he's dead in here or something."

"I'm not dead," he assured the maid, whose eyes widened when she noticed him lounging on the bed sporting a half a hard-on. "Just naked."

The maid gasped, hurried from the room and shut the door.

"I'm so sorry, Shade," Madison said, holding the front of her dress against her chest with one hand. "We accidentally fell back asleep."

Adam's gaze drifted to the tops of Madison's thighs and the hint of her luscious bare ass peeking just beneath the hem of her skirt. She was right about needing her panties.

He supposed he could no longer avoid the inevitable. He had to say goodbye to the spot of radiance in his dark existence, find out what the fuck Shade's problem was once and for all and bribe his father into moving to Amsterdam. Or maybe he'd just sleep on the tour bus tonight and continue to practice avoidance.

Adam tugged the pair of lavender, satin panties from the pocket of his jeans.

He held them up with one finger. "Looking for these, Madi?"

She turned in his direction, her eyes widening when she saw

what he was offering her. Blushing furiously, she snatched the tiny garment from his hand and rushed into the bathroom.

"You know, the only reason we even stayed in Dallas last night instead of going straight to Austin is because we all knew how much you need to see that woman," Shade said.

Adam's face fell. They *knew*? How could they know? "So you should have just left me here to find my own way home."

Shade nodded. "Yeah, I realize that now. I keep hoping you'll learn some consideration for others, but you're a lost cause."

Adam didn't care what Shade thought of him. "I don't need a sermon. Thanks."

"Julie's birthday is today. I missed her party because of you," Shade said.

Adam's heart sank into the pit of his stomach. He knew how much Julie meant to Shade.

"I didn't realize," Adam said.

Shade didn't say anything. He just left Adam sitting in the center of the crumpled bed, feeling like the most self-centered asshole on the planet.

Adam was sorry. So sorry. Why hadn't he told Shade he was sorry before Shade had turned his back on him again?

Hands trembling, Adam got dressed. He recognized the craving crawling along his skin. He knew this feeling. This gnawing hunger. This need for something to numb his pain, his troubles, his worries. His father would have any mind-altering substance he wanted waiting for him at home. All he had to do was ask. Take. And he could create the illusion that everything was right in his world.

It would be so easy. So *familiar*.

Adam took a deep, steadying breath and sat on the edge of the bed. He clenched his still shaking hands together and struggled to find air. He recalled the allure of that illusion so well. Living in a world without problems.

"Adam?" Madison called from the bathroom. "Will you zip me?"

A world without light.

He had something better than illusion now. He remembered the way Madison had looked as she told him she loved him last night. As she climaxed with him and for him. As she slept trustingly in the circle of his arms. As he'd loved her. That had been no illusion.

Adam rose from the bed and headed for the bathroom. Madison stood at the mirror with her back exposed. He paused in the doorway and watched his world scowl at the smudge under her eye. She licked her finger and rubbed at it to no avail. Peace settled over him, spreading out from his chest in soothing warmth. This feeling wasn't found in a pill or a powder or a needle. This feeling was all Madison's doing.

She noticed him standing there and smiled at him over her shoulder. Heart in his throat, he smiled back.

"Is everything okay?" she asked.

He stepped up behind her and slowly zipped her dress. "Yeah, baby. I've got this."

She met his eyes in the mirror and, for a second, he thought she was going to call him a liar and point out how easily his resolve could crumble. How easily life could break him into a thousand jagged pieces and toss him back into the pit of despair he knew so well. She smiled instead. "I know you do."

Her belief in him gave him strength. He would make amends with Shade and he would deal with his father and he didn't need drugs to get him through tough times. They were no longer necessary to numb his pain. Not when he already had bliss. Madison Fairbanks was in his life. Not an illusion. His reality. Everything was right in his world as long as he had her.

"You'd better hope my car wasn't towed last night," she said. "If I'm late, I'm going to be fired."

He hugged her from behind and splayed his hands over her belly. "You could quit that job and go on tour with me as my personal sex slave."

She laughed. "Don't tempt me, Adam Taylor. I might just take you up on that offer."

He grinned. Now there was a challenge he was up for. So, how did he tempt the master temptress? He'd think of something before he saw her again. After all, New Orleans was six very long days away.

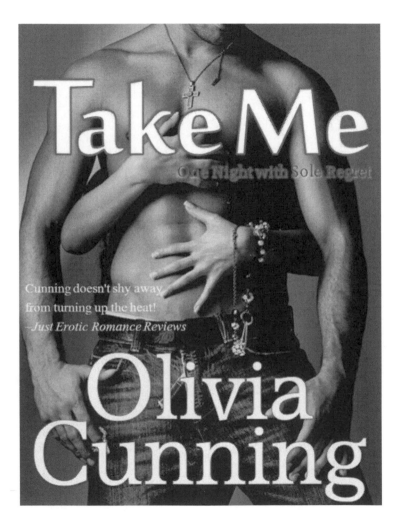

Take Me

One Night with Sole Regret

Cunning doesn't shy away
from turning up the heat!
—*Just Erotic Romance Reviews*

Olivia
Cunning

Take Me
One Night with Sole Regret #3

CHAPTER ONE

Shade's day had just gone from crap to shit. A hollow feeling of disbelief spread from his throat to his chest, and then rage crawled up the back of his neck. He stared at the empty parking spot between Kellen's Firebird and Owen's Jeep, trying to comprehend the absence of the ton of steel he'd left there. Shade glanced around the parking lot. Maybe his memory was fuzzy. Maybe he hadn't parked in his usual space. Two semi-trucks containing Sole Regret's equipment and stage setup had already been backed into the fenced lot so they'd be ready to head to San Antonio the next day. Their tour bus was on the opposite side of the lot. The band's drummer, Gabe, was pulling his overnight bag from the luggage compartment beneath the bus. Everyone else—band and crew—was already heading for their vehicles. The only distinctly empty spot on the lot was the one where Shade had parked his favorite toy.

"Okay," he yelled. "This isn't funny. Who hid my car?"

"I'm not a rocket scientist or anything," Kellen said, "but I'd say it's been stolen." He tossed his overnight bag into his Firebird's trunk.

"That's what you get for being a douche and buying a

hundred-and-fifty-thousand-dollar vehicle," Owen said with a smirk.

"You should call the cops and report it," Kellen said. He secured his long black hair at the nape of his neck with a leather strap he'd collected from his bag. Then he opened his car door and said, "I'd stay and wallow in your misery, but I'm late for an appointment."

Shade knew the feeling. "I don't have time for this right now," he said. "I have places I need to be. I've already missed my chance to crash Julie's party, but I don't want her to think I forgot her birthday entirely." He tossed his overnight bag on the ground where his car's trunk should have been. "Fuck!"

"Where's your car?" Adam paused between Owen and Shade.

Adam was the band's lead guitarist and in second place on Shade's shit list, right after whoever had stolen his ride. The three musicians stared at the empty parking spot as if expecting the car to suddenly uncloak itself and come out of hiding.

Shade was already pissed at Adam for making them hours late getting home. Adam had spent over half the day lounging around a hotel with his drug abuse counselor—who obviously wasn't very good at what she did, because Shade had caught Adam using drugs backstage just two nights before. It would have served Adam right if the band and crew had left him to find his own way from Dallas to Austin. Maybe that would've taught the selfish prick a lesson. Everyone else had been looking forward to this day off in their home town, but the only person who mattered to Adam was Adam.

"I swear if I miss Julie's birthday, you're going to need a very good dentist," Shade said to Adam.

"Why? I didn't steal your car," Adam said. "But I will give you a ride."

Shade was surprised he'd offered, but Adam rode a motorcycle, and Shade didn't think it was wise to be that close to him at freeway speeds. As pissed as Shade was, he'd probably strangle him to death from behind.

Owen slapped Adam in the center of the chest. "Hey, don't worry about it. I already said I'd drive him. Julie's house isn't far from mine."

And technically, Adam's was even closer, but Owen knew how ticked off Shade was, and if the band lost both its vocalist and lead guitarist in a fiery motorcycle crash, they'd be shit out of luck.

Adam shrugged. "All right. But, Shade, once you cool down a bit, we need to have a man-to-man."

Shade didn't want to talk to him. His blood pressure was already high enough to cause a massive stroke. Nothing Adam could say would ever earn Shade's forgiveness.

Adam turned and walked toward his bike, his head low, shoulders hunched. Kellen had already backed up his Firebird and was heading out of the lot with a rubber-burning squeal.

Owen retrieved Shade's overnight bag from the asphalt and tossed it into the back seat of the Jeep. After throwing his own luggage inside, he climbed behind the wheel and waited. Shade took one last look at the empty parking space, thinking perhaps he'd somehow overlooked the ton of black shiny metal that should be sitting there, and slid into the passenger seat next to Owen.

"Is Tina going to be pissed that you missed Julie's party?"

"Tina is pissed that I breathe," Shade said. His ex-wife hadn't actually invited him to the party. Not that her wishes were going to stop him from showing up.

Owen chuckled. "Ain't that the truth?" He started the Jeep, put it in reverse and backed out of his spot. Owen waved at Gabe, who was climbing into his obscenely large pickup, ducking his head low to keep his six-inch-high red and black mohawk from scraping the roof of the cab. Gabe saluted Owen with two fingers before shutting his door.

Owen switched on the radio, and a hard and heavy song blared from the speakers. "So what did you get Julie for her birthday?" he yelled over the road noise and music.

Shade's heart sank. "*Fuck.* I completely forgot to get her a present." She'd be expecting a gift. Shade wasn't even sure what she'd like. But every female on the planet liked sparkly things, didn't they? "I can't show up empty-handed. Find the nearest jewelry store."

Owen sighed heavily. "Sure. Why not? I obviously don't have anything better to do with my night off than taxi you around. No family to see. No trouble to get into." Owen grinned.

Shade knew exactly what kind of trouble Owen wanted to get into. He was the biggest skirt chaser Shade had ever met. Even more so than the man Shade faced in the mirror.

Shade took several deep breaths to calm his frayed nerves. "Sorry," he said after a moment. "I didn't mean to order you around." He attributed his shitty attitude to Adam, who was one hundred percent at fault, as usual. Shade's car could be replaced, but his limited time with Julie could not be. "I'm a little keyed up at the moment."

Owen chuckled. "Just a little."

"Would you mind stopping at the mall on the way to the house?" He took another deep breath. "Please?"

"Not for you," Owen said, checking over his shoulder as he merged onto the freeway.

"Seriously? Son of a … I should have called a fucking cab." *Let's make this day suck a little more, shall we?*

"I will, however, stop at the mall for Julie." Owen smiled, the deviousness behind it frankly disturbing. "What a little heartbreaker. I'm going to marry her someday."

Shade shoved him into the door. "Don't you even think about touching her."

Owen elbowed him in the ribs. "Really, dude? What the fuck is wrong with you tonight? You better calm down before you see her. You've completely lost your cool."

Owen was right. And he knew that Owen wouldn't ever become romantically involved with his Julie. But Shade had lost the rest of his depleted sense of humor when he'd been forced to have a maid let him into Adam's hotel room so Shade could get his sorry ass out of bed at one o'clock in the afternoon. God, why did the guy always have to fuck up his plans? And get him so riled up that he took out his frustration on people who didn't deserve it? "Shit."

Owen took the next exit off the interstate. They drove around the mall area until they spotted a jewelry store. Once inside, it didn't take Shade long to find something he thought Julie would love. He left the store with both his wallet and his mood lighter than when he'd arrived. He couldn't wait to hold his angel in his arms and see her face when she opened his gift. He smiled at his thoughts.

"Feeling better?" Owen asked.

"Yeah. It's been much too long since I've seen her. I miss her so much."

They returned to the Jeep, and Owen drove him to see the only girl who would ever own his heart.

Several cars were parked in the long driveway of the house that had once been Shade's residence. His ex-wife had received most of their joint material possessions in the divorce settlement. He hadn't fought her on that; he knew he'd done her wrong. It was easy for a rock star to stray on the road. Way too easy. He'd tried not to cheat and had been successful for over a year, but she'd become bitter about his career and he'd lost interest in his own wife. Instead of trying to prove that he wasn't a cheater—which she'd falsely accused him of every time he'd gone on tour—he'd lived up to her expectations and become an unfaithful jerk. He knew it. He owned that. He wouldn't make the mistake of getting married again. He wasn't the type of man who could make a woman happy outside the bedroom and he knew that too.

"Do you want me to wait for you?" Owen asked as Shade opened the door.

Shade hesitated. He wasn't sure what he'd do if Tina refused to let him in the house. She didn't want him there. She would have invited him to the party if she'd wanted him there. He was sure she'd thought he'd be out of town and unable to attend. If her sister, Amanda, hadn't texted Shade about the party, he never would have known about it.

"No. I'll find my way home. You don't have to taxi me around all night. Go have some fun."

"I don't mind. I know this shit weighs you down."

Shade smiled at Owen. "I appreciate you having my back, but you deserve a night off. Go on home."

"If you're sure."

"Yep." Shade didn't care if Tina refused. He would see Julie on her birthday and give her the present he'd just bought. He wasn't going to take no for an answer. "Thanks for the ride. Do you mind swinging by my place to pick me up tomorrow?"

He was sort of without a car.

"No problem. I'll be there around noon."

"Thanks." He had no desire to deal with the police and the insurance company tonight. Maybe he could convince one of the band's assistants to report the car theft for him. Didn't they pay them to deal with this sort of bullshit?

Shade swung his overnight bag over one shoulder and shut the Jeep door behind him. He headed up the wide walk to the front door with the most ridiculous pink bag in existence dangling from one hand. He fleetingly wondered if Julie would like what he chose. All girls liked diamonds, right?

Standing on the front step trying to find his courage, Shade heard laughter from inside the house. There hadn't been much of that when he'd lived here. Arguing had been the norm. Accusations. Name calling. And a whole lot of angry sex. Shade pressed the doorbell and waited.

After a moment the door opened, and Tina's cold blue eyes narrowed the instant she recognized him. A blond-haired, blue-eyed bombshell, the woman was centerfold gorgeous. At least until she opened her mouth. "What *the fuck* are you doing here?"

"I came to wish Julie a happy birthday." He lifted the shiny pink bag. "I brought her a present."

"From a *jewelry* store?" Tina rolled her eyes at him. "Just as stupid as always. She's four, Shade. She's too young for jewelry."

His heart faltered. He hated when Tina called him stupid, and she knew it. Even if it was true, he didn't like to hear it. And now he was even more worried that Julie wouldn't like her present. When he'd seen it, he'd thought it perfect for her. Now he wasn't so sure. "Can I see her?"

"It's not your weekend." Tina tried to shut the door in his face, but he lifted an arm to block it.

"I haven't seen her in weeks."

"Whose fault is that? You're never home. You're always off touring with your band, shoving your dick into anything with holes."

"Mommy." Julie's sweet voice drifted from the foyer behind Tina. "I want more ice cream, pwease. Just the stwawberry kind."

Shade smiled at her slightly fuddled words. His little girl was talking so much better than the last time Shade had seen her. He wondered how much she'd grown in five weeks.

"In a minute, baby," Tina called.

"Just let me talk to her," Shade said. "I won't take long. I want to wish her a happy birthday."

"Seeing you confuses her, Shade. She hardly knows you. Everyone would be better off if you just sent money and got lost permanently."

Probably, but he was a self-centered bastard, and he wanted to see his daughter on her birthday. He wasn't leaving until he did.

"Mommy? Who is it?" Julie appeared at her mother's side. She paused when she saw her father standing halfway in the door. Her ice-blue eyes grew wide, and she slid her hand into her mother's. She had pink icing all over her face and was wearing fairy wings with her pink princess dress. Shade melted. Every time he looked at her, he turned to mush. His daughter looked like him. She had her mother's blond hair, but the bright blue eyes, the straight nose, the stubborn chin were all him.

"Happy birthday, baby," he said.

"Hi, Daddy. Are you singing songs at the loud place today?"

He smiled. She hadn't enjoyed the Sole Regret concert she'd attended because the volume of the music bothered her. But she did like his music when it wasn't too loud. His baby rocked. He assumed it was genetic.

"Not tonight, princess. But I brought you a birthday present." He lifted the pink bag in her direction.

Sucking an excited breath into her narrow chest, Julie beamed and released Tina's hand to reach for the bag.

Tina grabbed her wrist. "No. Go find your grandma, and she'll get you more ice cream."

"I want my pwesent," she said.

"Julie, I said no. Go find your grandma."

"You can't tell her she can't have her birthday present," Shade said. That old anger he felt toward his ex-wife rushed to the surface. Like Adam, Tina knew exactly how to push his buttons.

"You can't barge in here whenever you feel like it, Shade. The custody order—"

"I just came to give her a present," he interrupted. "Why do you always have to be such a b—?" He caught himself just in time.

Julie burst into tears. He knew better than to yell in front of her. Damn it. He had such a difficult time controlling his temper where Tina was concerned.

"If you don't leave, I'm calling the cops," Tina said and lifted Julie into her arms, cradling the back of her head to hold her face against her shoulder.

"For *what?*"

"I'll think of something."

"I just want to see my little girl on her birthday—"

Tina covered Julie's ears with her hands. "What about the other three hundred and sixty-four days of the year when you're too busy fucking whores to even call her?"

"I try to call her, but you won't let me talk to her."

"She's in bed. Three-year-olds don't party until two a.m."

"One time I called that late. I didn't realize how late it was because we were in California."

"She doesn't party until midnight either."

"Don't yell," Julie cried, pushing her mother's hands away from her ears. "Don't yell. Don't *yell!*"

"I'm sorry, baby," Shade said.

"Do you see how upset you make her?" Tina wiped at Julie's runny nose with a pink napkin she pulled from her pocket, and then scrubbed the frosting off Julie's cheek with an unused corner.

"*Me?* I just came to see her for a few minutes, and you act like I'm some sort of criminal."

"Not a criminal," Tina said coldly, "just an idiot. Leave. Now! I mean it, Shade."

"I want my daddy," Julie wailed. Sobbing uncontrollably, she stretched her arms in his direction.

Tina released a heavy sigh of exasperation. "Are you happy, Shade? You've ruined her birthday. She was having so much fun until you arrived."

Shade was too flustered to defend himself. He hadn't done anything wrong. He knew Tina liked to make his life miserable, and sometimes he felt he deserved it, but she was a good mother to Julie. Tina was the one who'd gotten Julie so upset this time. She was the one who refused to let her have her present. She was the one who hadn't even invited Shade to his own daughter's party. He was not at fault here. Or was he missing something?

"Can I sit out on the step with her for a minute?" Shade asked. "I won't even come inside."

"Daddy!" Julie screamed.

He wasn't sure if he was capable of calming Julie at this point, but he couldn't stand to see her so distraught. Maybe it would be better if he stayed away. Maybe they were all better off without him. But just the thought of missing these few stolen moments with his princess made his eyes sting and his chest ache.

"Fine. Ten minutes, Shade. And then you're leaving."

He nodded, willing to agree to any concession.

A sobbing little girl was thrust in his direction.

Shade held Julie perched in the crook of one arm. Her arms tightened around his neck and she buried her wet, little face against his shoulder.

Julie gasped and sniffled for several minutes, but she'd stopped wailing immediately. Shade just held her, rocking her slightly and stroking her silky blond hair. He heard the door close, and was surprised that Tina didn't think she needed to supervise the two of them.

"Mommy said you forgot about my birthday," Julie said.

"Of course I didn't forget about your birthday, princess. I tried to get here as soon as I could."

"She said you had to sing at the loud pwace today, so you wasn't coming."

"No, I don't have a concert tonight, but I do have to sing. I have to sing to the birthday girl."

Julie drew back and looked him in the eyes. Scowling, she grabbed his sunglasses by the nosepiece and pulled them off. "Take these off. I can't see you."

Eyes exposed, he stared down at her, his heart filled with love and loss, joy and sorrow all at once.

"Can you see me now?" he whispered.

She nodded and squashed his face between two sticky hands. He made fish lips at her until she giggled.

"What do you want me to sing?"

"The Cinderella song!"

He chuckled. "I don't think I know that one."

"I'll teach you."

"Okay."

"A dweam is a wish when you fast asweep," she sang, using her arms and hands expressively to punctuate her heartfelt words. He'd have paid for front row seats to watch her perform.

Shade opened his mouth to sing after her, and she covered his mouth with her hand. "Wait. I messed up."

"I know," he said when she moved her hand. "How about some Aerosmith?"

She sucked in a deep excited breath, her eyes alight with eagerness. "Yes, Daddy. Sing the angel song. See my wings." She reached over her shoulder and tugged at one of her flimsy, sparkly wings. "I'm an angel."

"You sure are," he said. "An angel princess."

He cleared his throat and sang to her, backing the lyrics, as always, with his entire heart and soul. "I'm alone, yeah…" By the time he was belting out the end of the second line, she was squirming in anticipation. He knew what she wanted. She just liked the chorus, so he skipped the majority of the first stanza and went straight to her favorite part.

Julie beamed as he sang to her. She looked at him with such utter adoration that his throat closed off and he choked over the next few words. She bounced excitedly, and he lifted his free hand to support her back so she didn't jostle her way out of his arms and onto the brick steps at his feet. She hugged him when he'd finished and fisted her little hand around the cross hanging from the chain at his neck.

"Now sing the babe song," she requested.

He smiled. Couldn't help it. She always called Aerosmith's "I Don't Want to Miss a Thing" the babe song.

"Don't you want to open your present?" he asked.

She jerked backward and smiled up at him broadly. She nodded, squirming to get down. He set her on her feet and squatted down in front of her to hand her the pink bag. He wished his gift was better wrapped, something Julie could tear into the way a little kid was supposed to open a birthday present. She tugged out the tissue paper and struggled to remove the large square box wedged inside the gift bag. Shade helped her. When he opened the lid for her, her jaw dropped.

"Oh, *Daddy*!" she squealed.

"Do you like it?"

She couldn't seem to form words. But she could run in place excitedly, her entire body quivering with glee. Shade removed the diamond and pink-sapphire tiara from the box and set it on her head. Her hands flew upward to touch the little crown. "Now I'm a really, really real princess." She nodded and looked up at him with expectant wide eyes.

"The most beautiful princess who ever lived."

Her dazzling smile did things to his heart that would cause any cardiologist to cringe.

"I want to see my princess crown in the mirror!" She turned and started to rush for the front door, but he caught her and lifted her into his arms again.

He knew if she went into the house, his time with her would be over. He wasn't ready to say goodbye yet. "Can I sing the babe song first?"

She held onto the tiara with one hand and nodded. "Yes, yes. I love the babe song." She hugged him with one arm. "And I love my princess crown. And I love you, Daddy."

He wished he had his damned sunglasses on. What kind of bad-ass rock star stood outside his ex-wife's house, clinging to a little girl, with tears swimming in his eyes? "I love you too, baby."

"Mommy says I can't be a baby anymore. I'm a big girl now."

"You are a big girl," he whispered to her. And he wasn't sure when it had happened. He'd missed so many of her milestones. "But you can be a baby when you're with me, if you want to."

"Sing."

He sang "I Don't Want to Miss a Thing" as if entertaining a crowd of twelve thousand. When he reached the chorus, Julie acted out the lyrics by offering him one smile and one kiss on the cheek. At the appropriate times, she held him close. She felt his heartbeat with one tiny hand and her own heartbeat with her other hand. He experienced this song on an emotional level whenever he sang it to her. He'd sung it to her in the middle of the night when she'd been an infant; it had never failed to soothe her. As the last line of the chorus rang from between his parted lips, he realized he did miss her. Even though he was holding her, he missed her. Terribly.

And he'd missed so much of her young life already. Too much. Those moments were lost forever. He needed to find a way to be home more often. His baby was growing up without him. There was no way to put her childhood on hold until he could find the time to enjoy it.

The front door opened, and Shade's arms automatically tightened around the little sweetheart in his arms.

"You sing good," Julie said. "I want to sing when I grow up. I want to be just like you, Daddy."

When had all the oxygen evacuated the atmosphere? Shade struggled to suck air into his suddenly nonfunctional lungs.

Standing in the doorway, Tina huffed out a breath of annoyance. "You want to be a cheating, no good, high school dropout? I don't think so, Jules. You're going to college."

Shade didn't know why she had to keep busting his balls. It was hurtful enough when she did it to him alone, but when she did it in front of Julie, he couldn't stand it. He wondered what kind of bullshit the woman said about him when he wasn't around. It was a miracle he had any sort of relationship with his daughter.

"Time to go inside, Julie," Tina said.

"Do you want to see my new dollhouse, Daddy? It looks like a palace. And it has a princess doll. And it has a bed in it for she's apposed to sleep." She yawned at the mention of sleep.

"Daddy has to leave now," Tina said.

"Are you coming back tomorrow?" Julie asked.

"I have to sing at the loud place tomorrow," he said.

"Are you coming back in two more sleeps?" she asked.

He shook his head.

"Three more sleeps?" she bargained, holding up three fingers.

"Six more sleeps."

Her slim eyebrows crinkled in confusion. She held up five fingers, and he added one of his own. She gave him a horrified look. "That is too many sleeps, Daddy."

"Is that thing *real?*" Tina sputtered, plucking the tiara off Julie's head and gaping at it.

"Of course, it's real. I'm not going to give her junk."

"She can't wear this."

"Give it to me," Julie insisted, making a grab for it.

"Just great, Jacob. You come here, disrupt everything, give her something she can't possibly keep, and now I have to be the bad guy and take it away from her."

"Why do you have to take it away from her? It's not yours. It's hers."

"What if she loses it? Or if the stones fall out? Or someone takes it? Or if she's kidnapped because of it? Jesus, Shade, this thing must've cost you ten grand."

If she knew what he'd spent on it, he had no doubt that she'd hock it and buy herself another hundred pairs of shoes she never wore.

"Just let her wear it around the house," Shade said. "It's insured if it gets damaged or lost. She'll be fine."

"Give it to me," Julie wailed. "I'm a princess. A really real princess. My daddy said so."

"Now you've got her crying again," Tina grumbled and jerked Julie out of his arms.

"*Me?*"

"Why do you have to be so stupid, Shade? It's as if you were born without a brain."

"Don't frickin' call me stupid in front of Julie, Tina."

"The truth hurts, doesn't it?"

"Daddy!" Julie screamed as Tina carted her into the house and slammed the door in Shade's face. "I want my princess crown. I *want* it!" He could hear Julie's tantrum through the door.

He hadn't meant for his gift to be a problem. He'd just thought Julie would like it. The cost hadn't been a consideration. Maybe he should have bought her some rhinestone piece of junk instead. Julie would have never known the difference. She was three. Four, he reminded himself. Fuck. He really was stupid.

Cursing at himself under his breath, he picked up the empty box, stuffed it into the pink bag with the crumpled tissue paper and hung it on the doorknob. Julie was farther from the door now, so he couldn't hear what she was screaming, but there was no doubt she was still upset. Maybe he *should* do everyone a favor and get lost permanently.

Shade snatched his sunglasses out of his pocket and put them back on. He wasn't sure how he was going to get home. He supposed he could call a cab. He turned to start down the driveway; he'd figure it out once he was far enough away that he couldn't hear Julie's crying. Because God, that sound was like a knife stabbing and twisting into his chest, and he knew Tina wouldn't let him do anything about it. He felt so fucking powerless.

The door behind him opened.

"Jacob?" a gentle voice said from behind him.

He paused and turned slowly. He probably should've expected her to be here, but he was in no way prepared for his body's reaction to her. His heart leapt, gut clenched, balls tightened. Her shoulder-length brown hair swayed gently in a warm breeze. Her hazel green eyes brightened as her lovely face broke into a genuine smile. Time stood still as he allowed his gaze to travel down her lean body. Those long tanned legs just might be the death of him. It had been a long time since he'd seen her.

"Amanda."

CHAPTER TWO

Amanda probably shouldn't have watched Jacob's private moments with his daughter through the window, but she couldn't help it. She had wanted to open the window and listen to his gorgeous voice, but Tina had been pacing the room, calling him every lewd name she could think of, and he didn't need to hear that. Amanda understood why Tina hated Jacob. He'd hurt her by cheating on her with another woman. Well, *several* other women. Amanda didn't expect Tina to forgive him, but trying to keep him away from his daughter? That wasn't right. Especially when it was so obvious that they adored each other. He needed that little girl in his life. And despite what Tina thought, Julie needed her father.

Amanda stepped out on the front step and closed the door behind her. She hoped their mom talked some sense into her sister so she'd let Julie wear her tiara. Jacob had done a wonderful job picking out something Julie would love. He obviously knew his daughter well and had put some thought into the gift.

"Once Tina cools down, she'll let Julie wear it," Amanda said. She wished he hadn't put his sunglasses back on. He had the most beautiful blue eyes. And his short black hair, tanned complexion and thick black eyelashes made them even more striking. She had every inch of his handsome face memorized—sexy lips, straight nose, high forehead, strong jaw, stubborn chin. She'd wanted Jacob "Shade" Silverton for so long, she couldn't remember a time when thoughts of him hadn't flitted through her head constantly.

"I wouldn't be so sure," he said.

"How's the tour going?" she asked. Small talk to keep him

close for as long as possible. If Tina knew Amanda was out here talking to him, she'd have a coronary. That was the problem with being infatuated with your younger sister's ex-husband. There was no way to make it work without someone getting hurt or someone going crazy.

Jacob smiled gently. "It's going great. Music is the only thing that goes great for me."

He glanced up at the big brick Georgian-style house. Julie could no longer be heard screaming. Maybe Tina had relented already.

"You don't have a show tonight?" She knew damned well he didn't. She bought tickets every time Sole Regret performed in Austin. She kept close tabs on the band's touring schedule, because the next best thing to hanging out with Shade Silverton was watching him perform on stage. If Amanda hadn't figured he was going to be in town today, she wouldn't have bothered getting into a huge fight with Tina for not inviting him to Julie's party. Instead of doing as Amanda had suggested, Tina had conveniently forgotten to tell him anything. So in the interest of her niece's happiness, Amanda had meddled. She hadn't told Tina that she'd sent Jacob a text about the party. While she sometimes felt compelled to stick her nose in other people's business, she didn't have a death wish.

Jacob shook his head. "We're in San Antonio tomorrow, so we decided to stay the night at home. The drive between here and there isn't bad."

She nodded in understanding and glanced down the driveway looking for his sexy-as-sin, electric sports car. There was no Tesla Roadster in sight.

"Where's your car?"

"Someone stole it."

She gaped at his nonchalance. "Someone *stole* it?"

"Yeah." He shrugged. "It can be replaced."

"So how did you get here?"

"Owen dropped me off. I was just going to call a cab to take me home. I'll be out of here in a few minutes."

"I'll drive you," she offered much too eagerly. She needed to be careful, or he'd figure out how much she desired him.

She didn't want things to be awkward between them. It had to be impossible for him to forget that she was sister to the woman who made his life hell.

"That's not necessary. You should go back to the party."

"It's over. All the kids are gone. I was just helping clean up."

"Oh."

"This will give me a great excuse to get out of washing pink icing off the walls."

He grinned, and she melted. It was as if the man had some magical ability to remove her bones.

"All right," he said. "As long as it helps you out."

"I'll go grab my purse and keys." She darted into the house and found her mother in the rocking chair holding Julie. The little birthday princess was wearing her new tiara and fast asleep with her thumb in her mouth. Amanda melted. Julie must've inherited that magic from her father. God, she loved the kid.

"I have to leave," Amanda whispered to her mother.

She nodded. "I'll let Tina know. She's upset about Jacob again."

"She's always upset about Jacob." Amanda leaned over to kiss her mother's cheek and then her niece's temple before grabbing her purse and dashing back outside.

She found Jacob where she'd left him. He was staring up at the house as if in a trance. She wondered what he was thinking about behind those dark sunglasses.

"Julie's asleep already," she told him. "And wearing her tiara."

Jacob released a deep breath. "I don't like it when Tina jumps on me like that, but I really hate it when she does it in front of Julie. Your sister probably talks bad about me all the time."

Amanda didn't want to confirm his suspicions. Though they'd never been exactly close, Tina *was* her little sister. But still, Jacob was right. Tina did talk smack about him all the time. That was the main reason why Julie got confused about the role her father played in her life. Jacob could make an effort to see his daughter more often, but the amount of crap he had to take from Tina every time he showed up would have turned most men away.

"Julie loves you," Amanda said, unlocking her car doors with the button on her key fob. "That's all that matters."

"I just hope she doesn't change her mind."

"You don't have to worry about that."

Amanda opened the trunk, and he leaned toward her to put his bag inside. When she caught the spicy scent of his aftershave, her knees went weak. It took every shred of her willpower not to bury her face in his neck and inhale. She wished she wasn't so attracted to him. His utter masculinity made it so hard for her to behave herself.

When Jacob didn't move away immediately, Amanda dragged her gaze up his body. His six feet of hard muscles and his broad shoulders completely overwhelmed her senses. For a minute, she thought he was leaning closer with the intention of kissing her, but as she couldn't see his eyes through his dark sunglasses, she couldn't know for sure if he was even looking at her. She plucked his disconcerting eyewear from his nose.

"Not sure why you always wear these damned things," she said, folding them and tucking them into the neck of his white T-shirt. She forced her hands not to explore the distractingly cut chest muscles defined beneath his shirt. The man was gorgeous. Perfect. And she *liked* him. Always had. Couldn't help herself.

"Because."

She tore her appreciative gaze from Jacob's body and peered into his eyes. She *did* know why he always wore sunglasses. He had expressive eyes that quickly made a person realize that he wasn't the heartless, narcissistic son of a bitch he pretended to be. And that's why she wanted him. Not because he was the most eyegasmic man ever to walk to earth, but because he felt. Deeply. And those pretty blue eyes of his revealed everything he tried to hide.

"Have you eaten?" she asked. "I'll take you out. My treat."

"I was planning on just hanging out at home. Maybe order a pizza. Eat it in front of the TV. Have a beer. Get in a good workout followed by a swim. Then I'm going to sit in the hot tub and vegetate."

It sounded as if he would be busy being sweaty, wet and potentially naked for most of the evening. Holy hotness. Amanda suddenly needed a panty change. "Oh."

"I wouldn't mind some company though." Before he could turn away, she'd caught his forlorn expression. Ah God, he was lonely. She wasn't sure how a man who was surrounded by a perpetual crowd could ever be lonely, but even though those kissable lips could lie, those expressive blue eyes didn't.

Amanda closed the trunk. "Do I count as company?" she asked.

"Can't take a hint?" he said with a grin. He climbed into the car and shut the door.

A hint? What did he mean? That he wanted to spend more time with her? If only. Amanda was the smart, quirky sister. Tina was the hot sister who all the guys wanted. Jacob included. Amanda had come to terms with Tina's appeal—and her own lack thereof—after the fourth time Amanda got dumped so her boyfriend could pursue Tina. It didn't matter to them that Tina wasn't interested in anyone who didn't have a fat wallet.

Amanda got behind the wheel of her sensible Toyota, shut the door and fastened her seat belt.

"Did you need to stop anywhere before I drop you off at home?" she asked.

"You really can't take a hint."

He chuckled; the rich, deep sound made Amanda's belly quiver.

"Say, Amanda, do you want to hang out with me and have some pizza and a beer? Watch a movie?"

"What kind of movie?"

"I don't care." His eyes widened as if he was struck by a horrendous revelation. "Just no chick flicks."

Her heart was thudding like a jackhammer, but she somehow managed to play it cool and start the car. "I don't know, Jacob. I'm pretty picky about the movies I watch. I have a chick-flick only policy."

"I guess we'll have to watch golf instead. I don't do chick flicks."

Golf? Snore-fest. Though if she was with Jacob, she couldn't imagine even televised golf would be boring. "Well in that case... I guess I can tolerate a bit of testosterone. I do, however, draw the line at movies with fist-fight sound effects."

He grinned, and the ambient temperature inside the car increased at least ten degrees. "Slasher horror movie it is."

She laughed uneasily. She was a certified coward when it came to scary movies. "Sure. As long as you don't mind me clinging to you in terror and hiding my face in your chest." She couldn't stop her gaze from wandering to that big, muscular chest. Yep, it looked perfect for hiding one's face. Also perfect for fondling. And licking. Kissing. Caressing. Sucking. Massaging. Nib—

"I wouldn't mind that at all," he said.

Her eyes lifted to meet his. Wait just a second. "Are you hitting on me, Jacob Silverton?"

"I thought that was obvious."

Oh *hell*, yes. "I'm not sure if I should be alone with you. You might try to get in my pants."

He chuckled. "I might."

She knew he was teasing her, but that didn't stop parts in her pants from readying themselves for a welcome invasion.

"I guess I'll have to risk it," she said, as if her heart wasn't about to thud itself out of her chest. "You've given me a powerful craving for pizza. And a cold beer."

She started the car and shifted it into drive.

"And burying my face in your chest," she added.

He laughed. "I can hook you up with all three."

His knuckles brushed the side of her leg, and she nearly leapt out of her skin. She praised her wise decision to wear shorts that morning.

"Hey, thanks for letting me know about Julie's party."

"No problem!" she squeaked.

Jacob's thumb rubbed a small spot of skin just above her knee. Amanda's panties were going to need scuba gear if they got any wetter.

"I wish I could have made it earlier," he said. "Adam seems to think he's the only one in the band who has a life. I get really sick of trying to get him to see beyond himself."

Amanda chanced a glance at him. He was staring at where

his thumb was igniting the nerve endings in her skin, but he didn't seem to be seeing what he was doing.

"You didn't miss much. Ten obnoxious screaming kids, sticky hands covered in pink frosting, a few tantrums, and one stomachache that ended badly in the kiddie pool."

"Did Julie make a wish and blow out her candles?"

Amanda smiled, fighting the urge to stroke his dark hair. She adored that the man's biggest weakness was a thirty-pound girl who loved strawberry ice cream. "Yeah. She got them all in one breath. She's windy like her father."

He laughed and jerked his hand from her knee as if he'd just noticed he was still touching her. "That probably wasn't a good trait to inherit."

"Sure it is. It's part of what makes you an amazing singer." She took her eyes off the road and found him staring at the dashboard. The turmoil in his pretty blue eyes broke her heart. "You know, I recorded Julie blowing out her candles on my cellphone."

He sat up straighter, and a smile softened his hard features. "You did?"

"Get my phone out of my purse and you can watch it."

He scowled at her purse, which was squashed between the front seats. "There are few things I won't touch. A woman's purse is one of them."

"Why?" she asked. "Afraid you might find a tampon in there or something?"

"Ever since I saw the movie Mary Poppins as a kid, I've been leery of women's purses. I don't know if you have a coatrack in there or an alligator or a chainsaw."

"Nope," she said, "no chainsaws. No tampons either." Just to make it perfectly clear that it was *not* her time of the month. In case he wanted to check out all the hot, throbbing wetness going on in her shorts.

He chuckled and stuck a tentative hand in her purse. His startled yell caused Amanda to stomp on the brakes. The horn of the car behind them blared.

"Oh, it's just your wallet," he said. "Thought it was an alligator."

She slapped him in the arm repeatedly. "You scared the

crap out of me."

He poked her in the side, and she squirmed, the friction against the seat drawing her attention to how inappropriately turned on she was. Another horn blared as she drifted toward the oncoming lane. She was surprised she hadn't hit a phone pole yet. It was exceedingly difficult to concentrate on the road with Jacob Silverton sitting next to her, smelling as amazing as he looked. She could only imagine how good he felt. Damn, she was horny. She needed to find the time to date more often.

Jacob located her cellphone and flicked his finger over the screen. "Hmm," he murmured. "What's this? A sex tape starring Amanda Lange?"

"What?" She made a grab for her phone—knowing damned well there weren't any X-rated videos of herself stored on it. "I thought I erased that."

"Ooo," he said, holding the phone cradled in both hands. "I want to see this."

An off-key rendition of "Happy Birthday to Julie" came from the tiny speakers on her phone. Jacob stared down at the screen completely mesmerized and if Amanda wasn't mistaken, a teensy bit misty-eyed. She smiled. All talk. The man was all talk.

"Make a wish, Julie," Tina's voice said from the phone's speaker.

"Like Aladdin?" Julie asked.

"Hurry, the candles are dripping."

"I wish I is a princess. A really real princess." There was a pause and then everyone clapped.

"See, you made her wish come true without even knowing about it," Amanda said.

"This kid is going to be the death of me," Jacob said. He replayed the video. Twice.

Amanda's hand hovered above his thigh. She so wanted to touch him but ultimately couldn't find the courage to do it and so fiddled with the air conditioner instead. She fleetingly wondered if it needed repaired. She was strangely overheated though the vents were directed toward her and blowing air at full blast. "I could send you videos of her, if you'd like."

She turned onto the road that led to Jacob's house, thinking that she should have driven like her grandfather—as if trying to throw a race to a snail. The drive had been much too short. She slowed until her foot was off the gas and they literally rolled the length of the final block. "I do babysit her a lot, you know. She thinks her Aunt Mander is *pretty* cool." And someone had to look after the kid when Tina went shopping. Tina loved spending Jacob's money. She tackled the task as if competing in an Olympic event.

"You'd do that for me?" Jacob said, turning in his seat and leaning into her field of view so he could look into her eyes.

"Yeah, of course I would. I should've thought of it sooner."

"Thanks, Amanda. You're a real sweetheart."

She stifled a cringe. She didn't want him to think of her as that one *nice*, forgettable girl. The one who guys always seemed to think of as their *friend*. Their buddy. She didn't want to be called a real sweetheart. Not after Jacob had flirted with her ever so briefly moments before and made her believe *her* fondest wish could come true.

Amanda turned into Jacob's drive and coasted to a halt behind his car.

"Um, Jacob?" she said. "Isn't that your car?"

He didn't answer her, just tore open the door and leapt out of her car. He was hugging the shiny black hood of the roadster before she could release her seat belt. She climbed out and went to stand beside him.

"I thought you said it was stolen."

"I thought it had been."

"Then how did it get here?"

"No idea."

Amanda noted the piece of pink paper stuck under one wiper. She pulled it free and read the note aloud. "*Shade, I know you won't mind that I borrowed your car to beat you home. I'll be in the hot tub waiting to rock your world, stud.* It's signed Veronica. And she dotted the i with a heart. How precious." Amanda pretended not to be affected by the note, but she'd really been looking forward to spending the evening with him. Unfortunately, some other woman had beaten her to it. And unlike Amanda, Veronica probably had the self-confidence, beautiful face and hot body to actually attract someone like Jacob.

"Fuckin' Veronica," Jacob bellowed. "I wondered where I'd left my spare set of keys."

Probably in her skirt the last time she'd been in his hot tub.

"I guess I'll go on home," Amanda said. "I'm glad you got your car back. It was good to see—"

Jacob moved to stand in Amanda's path. She wasn't sure how he managed to so easily trap her between one gorgeous hunk of metal and one gorgeous hunk of metal vocalist, but it got her attention. With her back pressed against the side of the car, she tried to regain her senses. No good. Her heart thundered out of control as she slowly lifted her gaze to look him in the eye.

"You're staying," he said. "I invited you. She's leaving. No one invited her."

"Maybe I don't want—"

Jacob touched her cheek, and her breath stalled in her throat. "You're staying."

She couldn't look away from his intense blue eyes. "I'm staying," she said obediently.

He smiled crookedly, plucked his sunglasses out of the neckband of his T-shirt and put them on. She stared at the cross around his neck.

"Do you want to wait out here while I call her a cab or would you rather wait in the house?" he asked. "She's sure to cause a scene."

"Um."

"You could go to the family room and pick out a movie to watch or scrounge in the kitchen for food. It won't take me long to get rid of her."

"Well, okay. Do you have the movie *Steel Magnolias*?" She kept her poker face firmly in place as she blinked up at him. "It's been ages since I've seen it, y'all."

He laughed. "I thought we agreed no chick flicks."

Amanda huffed as if she was very put out by his demands, when in truth she just wanted to put out. She couldn't blame Veronica for inviting herself to a night in a hot tub with this man, but Amanda was oh so glad that Jacob was making the woman leave.

"I suppose we did."

He tucked his forefinger under her chin and stroked the skin just beneath her lips with his thumb. "I'd kiss you," he said, "but I don't want Veronica to think I'm sporting a hard-on for her."

What?

Had he actually just said that? He couldn't possibly have meant it. Too flabbergasted to form a comeback, Amanda gaped at him.

He laughed. "What a priceless expression."

He squeezed her shoulder, and her legs began to tremble uncontrollably.

"I'll see you inside."

"Uh huh," she might have said around her mouthful of drool.

Jacob turned and hurried to front door, unlocking it and leaving it open so she could go inside. He then strode to the walk along the side of the house that led to the pool and hot tub out back.

It was all Amanda could do to keep from sliding to the ground in a puddle of lust.

CHAPTER THREE

Shade covered the distance to his back yard in long, angry strides. He couldn't believe Veronica had had the audacity to *borrow* his car without asking. And then she thought he'd be happy enough about it to fuck her? Not tonight. Maybe not ever again. Of course, if she hadn't taken his car, then Amanda wouldn't have driven him home and he wouldn't be anticipating an evening with one of the few people who allowed him to let his guard down.

A trail of discarded clothing started at the back corner of the house and continued to the hot tub that was surrounded on three sides by a cedar privacy fence. As he continued around the house, he picked up her clothes one sexy item at a time. Lace-topped stocking here. Black satin thong there. Shade dumped the clothing on the slate patio at the bottom of the hot tub's wooden steps.

Veronica was right where she'd said she be. She had a glass of wine in one hand, her ebony hair piled on top of her head, her eyes closed and her beautiful naked breasts hovering above the surface of the water. She had a fantastic set of tits. Yeah, he noticed. There wasn't a heterosexual male alive who wouldn't have found her sexually inviting. And if Amanda hadn't agreed to stay, Shade would have undoubtedly stripped off his clothes to join Veronica. But Amanda *was* here and strange as it seemed, he'd much rather spend the evening teasing her than fucking the hot-tub sex goddess until he couldn't move.

He cleared his throat, and Veronica's sultry brown eyes blinked open. An inviting smile spread across her lush lips. "There you are, lover," she said. "I was starting to regret not just waiting for you in the parking lot, but you were hours past due and I was all hot and sweaty." She pouted. "And not because you made me that way." She took a sip of her wine. The green bottle sat in a Styrofoam cooler of ice behind her. "Would you like a drink?"

"I have company, Veronica. You need to get dressed and leave."

"Company? What kind of company?"

He struggled to come up with the best way to describe Amanda. Friend? Family? Long-time crush? "*Female* company."

"So? I have no problem with her joining us, Shade. Is she sexy?" Veronica emitted a throaty chuckle. "You know how much I enjoy women."

While normally he'd have thought that would be a great idea, he didn't think Amanda would be into threesomes with a woman she didn't know. Shade loved to flirt with Amanda, tease her, but she was off-limits. He had no intention of *ever* sleeping with her. Which made him wonder why he would rather spend the evening with her than enjoying the tits and ass in his hot tub. Probably because he was still recovering from that crazy chick in Tulsa. What had her name been? Nikki. Damn, the woman had tried to wear his dick down to a nub.

"No, Veronica, I came back here to tell you to leave. You can't just take my car without asking. You're lucky I don't call the cops and have you hauled in for grand theft auto."

"Did you expect me to wait out in the parking lot for hours?"

"Why were you waiting for me in the first place? I didn't ask you to."

"Now you're just being a jerk."

He'd been called worse. "How did you get my keys?"

"You left them at my place. Remember?"

"No."

"You were too drunk to drive, so Selene took you home and the next day you came and picked up your car. I wasn't home, so you must've used your spare set."

While he remembered little of his drunken evening with Veronica and Selene, he did recall waking up with Selene in his bed and then picking his car up the following morning. He'd completely forgotten to get his extra keys from Veronica. Sole

Regret had been back on tour by the next day, and recovering his keys hadn't been a priority. "That was over a month ago. You've had them all this time?"

She smiled. "And don't think the idea of taking your car for a joyride every night didn't cross my mind. I didn't though. Until tonight. And I wouldn't have taken it tonight if you hadn't been so late."

And he wouldn't have been so late if the lead guitarist of his band wasn't such an inconsiderate ass.

Julie's birthday wasn't the only major event he'd missed because of Adam. He'd missed Julie's *birth* because he'd been accompanying Adam's unconscious ass to the hospital. Back in those days, Adam had had a tendency to overdo the heroin. While waiting in the emergency room for Adam to be revived, he'd missed the call that Tina had gone into premature labor. By the time he got the message, Julie had already been born in a different hospital, in a different state—three weeks early, but healthy. He'd never forgive Adam for making him miss his daughter's first breath. Never. Especially since the jerk didn't even understand why Shade was so angry with him. Maybe someday Shade would give up on Adam and just let him destroy himself, but the guy was a walking disaster and Shade felt responsible for him. If someone didn't keep tabs on Adam, he'd likely end up dead. As much as the guy ticked him off, Shade wouldn't want that. They'd been through a lot together. And not all of it bad. In fact, Adam had been the one to give Shade a dream to pursue. Before Adam had convinced Shade that he could sing, Shade had been on the fast track to working in some factory—if he'd been *lucky*.

"Why don't you go ask your female company if she'd like to join us?" Veronica said. "I'm so comfortable and so in the mood. Seems a shame to waste a pussy this hot and juicy for you." Her fingertips moved to stroke her nipple. "We can call Selene over if your company is too shy to get busy with us."

Veronica and Selene would keep him up and going all night. He couldn't say he wasn't tempted. But he wasn't sold. "I'll call you a cab while you get dressed," he said.

He turned to go into the house, and a glass of wine hurtled past him and crashed onto the slate at his feet. "You fucking jerk!"

"Be sure to clean up that broken glass before you go. I'll have the cab wait for you at the end of the driveway." He started up the deck steps to enter the house through the door off the kitchen.

"Wait, Shade. I'm sorry," Veronica called after him. Water splashed as she exited the hot tub. Wet feet landed on the cedar decking. Shade didn't make the mistake of turning around. He let himself into the house. Amanda was peering out the kitchen window.

"I know it isn't any of my business," she said. "But your hot, naked babe seems a bit perturbed at you."

He chuckled. "I inherited the piss-off-women gene from my father."

"You must be homozygous dominant for the trait."

"Huh?"

She laughed and smoothed her silky brown hair with one hand. "Sorry. Biology teacher humor."

Shade had never liked school, but he respected teachers. Smart chicks intimidated him a bit. Not that he'd admit that to a smart chick. Especially not a smart, *hot* chick like Amanda Lange. "How's the job?" he asked, tugging the door closed behind him and locking it.

"Oh it's great. Especially in June, July and August."

He chuckled. "All that time off would be a nice perk. You know, those are the months I work the most."

"As if strutting around on stage for an hour a night is work. Puh-lease." She rolled her eyes.

He stood up straighter and scowled. "I don't *strut.*"

"Yeah. You do." She grinned. "But it's hella sexy, so don't ever stop."

He laughed. It was refreshing to flirt with a woman who didn't think it meant she had to fall on his dick with a missile-seeking vagina.

"Let me call a cab for Veronica, and then I'll order a pizza."

Amanda nodded toward the window overlooking the backyard. "I think she already left."

Shade's heart dropped. "Shit! She still has my keys."

He raced through the house and yanked open the front

door. Standing next to the driver's door of his car, Veronica threw one of her high heels at him. "Asshole!"

He easily sidestepped her projectile and dashed across the driveway. Veronica tore open the door and was halfway into the car before he reached her. He pulled her against him and closed the door with his foot. One disaster avoided. One instigated.

Veronica struck him in the chest with surprising strength. "Don't touch me. Don't touch me."

He released his hold on her arm, and she collapsed against his chest, sobbing uncontrollably. *Fuck.* He was on a roll with making females cry today, and he had a pathological weakness to tears. *Double fuck.*

He wrapped Veronica in a loose embrace and stroked her back. "Don't cry."

"Y-you, you-you think I'm *ugly*," she wailed.

"What? No. I don't think you're ugly at all. You're beautiful. Perfect."

"Then w-why-why-why won't you sleep with meeeeeeee?"

He bit his lip so he didn't laugh. She sounded absolutely ridiculous. "I told you: I have other plans."

"Are-are-are you going to sleep with herrrrrrrrr?"

He had no intention of sleeping with Amanda. He liked her too much to fuck her. "That's not any of your business."

Veronica clung to him. "Don't send me away. Please. I need to be with you."

"It's not going to happen tonight, Veronica. Maybe some other time."

She pulled away and looked up at him. Her nose was red, and black streaks ran down each cheek. "Is it because I took your car? Are you mad at me?"

It was much more complicated than that, but he took the easy way out. "Yes. And if you take off in it now, I'll be so mad that I won't call you again."

She whimpered.

He searched her face. "You aren't upset because you have *feelings* for me, are you?" Because he didn't *do* feelings anymore. Not since his botched marriage. And Veronica knew that. That's why he hooked up with her regularly. Casual sex was the only way to go, and he'd thought she was in agreement.

Veronica wiped her tears with the back of her wrists and said, "Of course not. I just wanted to get laid. I've been horny all day thinking about your big, thick cock."

He somehow managed not to roll his eyes at her. "That's what you say, but you're acting jealous."

Veronica took a step back, straightened her spine and returned to the self-confident woman he knew well. "Not jealous, Shade. *Envious.* I was really looking forward to being fucked senseless tonight. No one has your stamina, baby."

Well, his dick was looking forward to a night of rest.

"Will you take me home at least?" she asked. "Selene isn't off work yet. She dropped me at the parking lot to wait for you. That's why I took your car."

Shade glanced over his shoulder at the house. Taking Veronica home would cut into his time with Amanda, but it was only a ten-minute drive, and it would take longer than that for a cab to arrive. "Yeah, okay. Just give me a minute."

Shade picked up Veronica's discarded shoe on his way into the house. Amanda stood in the foyer with her arms crossed over her chest and looking very awkward.

"I should go," she said.

"Please don't. I'm just going to give her a ride home. You can come along if you want."

"Your car is a two-seater, Shade."

Shade? She was one of the few people who called him by his given name, so her using his stage name set off all sorts of warning bells. Shade rubbed his forehead. He was really fucking things up. "Right."

"I thought you were going to call her a cab."

"It'll take longer for a cab to get here than for me to drive her home. She doesn't live far."

Amanda shrugged. "Whatever. I understand. Maybe we'll do this some other time."

Shade took his sunglasses off and looked down into her eyes, hoping she could see the sincerity in his expression. "I don't want you to leave, Amanda. I want *her* to leave."

She surprised him by blushing and lowering her gaze. "Okay." She took a deep breath and then smiled up at him.

"I'll order the pizza while you're gone. I hope you're a fan of anchovies and pineapple."

"I like them almost as much as I like *Steel Magnolias*."

She laughed and patted his chest. His heart leaped, and his dick decided it no longer wanted the night off. *Down boy. Hot or not, Amanda is off-limits.*

"Go take Naked Babe home. I've got you covered."

He fought the urge to kiss her gently smiling lips and instead put his sunglasses back on. "I'll hurry." There were benefits to owning a car that went zero to sixty in under four seconds.

By the time he closed the front door behind him, Veronica was waiting in the car. He climbed inside and dropped her shoe on her lap.

"I'm sorry if I upset you," she said. She leaned close and kissed his neck. Her hand slid over his thigh and between his legs. "Forgive me?"

"Yeah. Whatever."

He started the car, and its quiet, electric engine purred. He'd owned bigger, louder cars in the past, but he actually liked the calm power of his Tesla. It rode fast, like any sports car, but the engine was almost silent and it shifted seamlessly, taking the handling out of his hands and putting it in the car's control. He mostly loved this car because it made him feel he was driving a vehicle from the future and because he never had to fill it with gas. He would have to charge it when he got home, however. The battery was low on juice.

"I could make it up to you." Veronica's hand slid to his crotch. "Would you prefer a hand job or a blow job?"

"Not interested right now," he said, but his already engorging cock was making a liar out of him. Sometimes his libido was a liability.

"I can feel that," she said and produced a throaty chuckle. "I'll take care of you. Big-eyes doesn't have to know about it."

"Big-eyes?"

"The pretty little thing you have waiting back at your place."

"You saw her?"

"She has a tendency to watch things, through windows, that

are none of her business."

"Well, I'm sure she'll thank you for getting me hard. Keep on doing what you're doing and I'll be ready to fuck her as soon as I walk in the door." He figured that would be more affective at getting Veronica to stop fondling him than if he asked her to stop. She jerked her hand from his crotch and put distance between them in the close quarters of the car by leaning against the passenger door and crossing her arms over her ample bust.

"You really are an asshole." She tried to glare a hole through the dashboard.

"And you don't know how to take *no* for an answer."

"I don't understand why I should have to. We always have a good time in the sack."

And that was the only thing they had in common. Tires squealed as he turned into her driveway. He stopped in front of her garage door. When she continued to glare at the dashboard and didn't make a move to get out of the car, he leaned over her and opened the door.

"You aren't even going to get out of the car?"

"Nope, I've got a raging hard-on now and am eager to get back to *Big-eyes*." Which was true, but the two statements weren't linked. Not that Amanda and raging hard-ons didn't go hand in hand. He just wanted to be with her for reasons other than what was going on in his pants.

"I hope your dick falls off," Veronica said and stumbled out of the car with one shoe on her foot and the other one in her hand.

He chuckled. "No you don't. Then you wouldn't be able to fuck it."

She growled at him and then slammed the door. Smiling at her, he waved goodbye, backed the car out of the driveway and headed for home. Another good thing about having a fast sports car was that when a spiteful woman threw her shoe at it, she missed.

Shade was relieved to see Amanda's car was still in his driveway when he returned. He'd expected her to have left. He could understand why she'd feel uncomfortable enough to split. What woman wanted to hang out with a guy who came home to uninvited naked chicks in his hot tub? Amanda probably thought he was the biggest man-whore on the planet. And maybe he was a contender for the top ten pussy chasers of all time, but he didn't think with his dick. He just liked to keep it happy by giving it what it wanted. It was an entirely conscious decision on his part. He didn't have a problem telling a woman no. Just like a woman should never have a problem telling *him* no. Easy come, easy go. But mostly easy cum.

Shade pulled into his garage and plugged the car into the charger before entering the house through the mudroom. He could hear Amanda singing in the kitchen as soon as he stepped inside. She was screeching the eighties song "Walking on Sunshine" entirely off-key. He smiled and followed her voice to the chef's kitchen. He watched her from the doorway. She had ear buds in her ears and, unaware of his presence, treated him to a little dance as she helped herself to the fresh fruit in his fridge. She did a sideways shuffle to the sink and washed grapes, strawberries and apples before tossing them into a bowl and opening several drawers until she found a knife.

As she sang the perky chorus, her cute little butt wiggled side to side. Her dancing was a hell of a lot better than her singing.

"Whoa-o." Shade couldn't resist joining her.

Amanda whirled around, knife in hand. Her face went instantly red, and she yanked her ear buds out. "When did you get back?" she asked.

"Put the knife down, lady, and we'll talk."

She glanced down at her hand, which was holding the knife like a weapon, and then dropped it on the dark granite of the kitchen island. "Oh God, how long have you been standing there?"

"Long enough to know you sing sharp. Way sharp."

"You weren't supposed to hear that. I figured it would be at least an hour before you got back."

His brow crinkled. "I told you I'd hurry."

"Yeah, but I didn't take you for a minute-man."

"What?"

"Oh, come on, Jacob, I know why you wanted to take her home. I'm not dumb."

"You think I wanted to be alone with her?"

"Well, didn't you?"

"No. I wanted to be alone with *you*."

She stared at him with wide eyes and her fist over her heart, apparently dumbfounded.

Shade circled the island's counter and pulled out a towel to dry off the fruit sitting in the big bowl in the sink. His cleaning lady always stocked his fridge with fresh fruit because she knew how he craved it whenever he was home. He popped a grape into his mouth and tossed Amanda a golden delicious apple. He sang the first line of "Walking on Sunshine's" chorus.

"Whoa-oh," Amanda sang.

He repeated his line.

"Whoa-oh-oh," she sang with even more gusto.

They sang the next line together, grinning at each other like a pair of insane hyenas.

Shade plucked grapes off their stems and tossed them into the bowl while Amanda cut the cores out of several varieties of apples—red, yellow, green—and sliced them. She settled for singing backup while they worked.

He wondered what his fans would say if they heard him singing a girly pop song. His band was known for creating melt-your-face-off metal, but he was having such a good time goofing off with Amanda, he'd risk any public outcry.

Amanda tackled a pair of oranges next, while he removed the greenery from the strawberries. They had enough fruit in the bowl for ten people by the time they finished and had sung the chorus of the same song at least twenty times, but Shade was reluctant to end the easy camaraderie between them and checked the fridge for fruit they might have overlooked. He didn't get to do this kind of thing often. Especially not with a woman. He had a certain reputation to uphold, but with Amanda, he could let go and just be himself without worrying about what she thought of him. It had always been this way between them. Even when he'd been engaged and married to her sister, if he'd wanted to have a little goofy fun, he'd seek out Amanda's easy-going companionship.

Something ice-cold blasted him in the back of the neck. He yelled and spun around only to get hit with a stream of water in the face. Brandishing the water sprayer from the island sink, Amanda laughed and sprayed him in the ear.

"Shit, that's cold," he protested, covering his ear with one hand and rubbing the liquid out of it.

She made a sad puppy dog face at him, her lower lip protruding in a pout. "Oh, poor baby," she said and then squirted him at the base of his neck.

"You," he growled, though he couldn't wipe the smile off his face.

Laughing gleefully, Amanda dashed around the island and when the counter was between them, turned and sprayed him again.

He circled the counter at a run. She squealed and skidded out of reach, squirting water in all directions. The icy liquid caught him on the arm. Despite getting drenched, he didn't back down, not even when he had her trapped against him and she directed a steady spray of water down both their bellies.

"That's cold," she squealed and released the nozzle.

Shade wrested the sprayer out of her hand. "You're damned right it's cold." He held her tightly with one arm and sprayed water down her shirt. Which drew his attention to her now sopping wet breasts, transparent pale pink T-shirt and hard nipples. His body's reaction was instantaneous. His brain was a few seconds behind.

She yelled, "Cold, cold, cold. Jacob! Stop!"

He dropped the hose and cupped the inviting succulence of one breast in his hand. His thumb brushed the hardened nipple, and she shuddered. There wasn't enough cold water in the Arctic Ocean to cool the hot lust flooding his groin.

Amanda needed to slap him, and soon, or he was going to do something they'd both regret. She lifted her hand and instead of delivering a stinging palm to his cheek, she pulled off his sunglasses and tossed them across the counter.

Their eyes met. He couldn't look away. She moved closer. Or he moved closer. He wasn't sure which. Didn't care. All he knew was that he had to sample her lips. He'd dreamed of kissing her so many times… He wondered if she'd taste as sweet as she looked.

His heart thudded faster and faster as he leaned closer. He hadn't felt this giddy since his first kiss in junior high school.

His lips were a hair's breadth from hers when the doorbell rang and he came back to his senses.

"Sorry," he said and jerked away.

No matter how much he wanted her, Amanda Lange was off limits.

Yeah, tell that to his dick.

CHAPTER FOUR

Amanda had never wished harm to a pizza delivery person before, but as Jacob stepped away and she was robbed of the heat of his hard body and the scent of his delectable flesh, she started compiling a list of tortures.

Jacob had almost kissed her. *Almost.* And she could still feel the weight of his hand on her breast. Oh God, she wanted the man. And for about thirty seconds, she'd thought she might actually have her wish fulfilled.

Leaning against the kitchen island for support, she watched him leave the room to answer the door. Why hadn't she been more aggressive? She should have just grabbed him and kissed him. Made it perfectly clear that she wanted him.

As usual, her tendency to hesitate and think things through left her without the prize she craved. She needed to let loose. Get aggressive. Paw the man like a sex-starved lioness. Yeah, right. Even if she could find the courage to throw caution aside, those kinds of tactics didn't work with Jacob anyway.

With a sigh, Amanda reached for a towel and began to mop up the water covering the kitchen. It kept her hands occupied so she didn't start peeling off her clothes so she could wait for him, naked, like the woman he'd ditched earlier. She wouldn't put herself in a position to be rejected by him. Amanda had felt bad for Veronica—not that she'd wanted Big Boobs Maloney to stick around, not that she wasn't glad that Jacob had rejected her and taken her home—but Amanda was desperate enough for the man to do something like wait for him naked in a hot tub, so she empathized with the woman.

The smell of pizza accompanied Jacob back into the kitchen. Amanda tossed the wet dishtowel in the sink and turned to face him, pretending she didn't feel awkward by forcing a smile. "Smells great."

Avoiding her eyes, he stared over her head as he slid the pizza box onto the still-damp island counter. He was not so good at hiding his own awkwardness. "I guess you decided against the pineapple and anchovies."

"Yeah, I had that a couple nights ago. Thought I'd mix it up a little."

He reached for his sunglasses, but she snatched them up before he could get his hand on them. No way was she letting him hide behind them. She didn't care if it made him uncomfortable to look at her after he'd almost kissed her.

"No sunglasses for you tonight," she said, stuffing them down the front of her shirt. His gaze landed on her chest and her damp T-shirt. This time when her nipples hardened, it wasn't from the cold. It was from the heat in his eyes.

"Um." He jerked his head up and took a step backward. "I'll get you something dry to put on."

He fled the room before she could tell him she was more than happy to wear a wet shirt if it made him look at her like *that*. She sighed, hid his sunglasses in a random drawer and then searched the cabinets for plates. A few minutes later he returned with a bath towel and a button-down man's flannel shirt. "I figured you were probably cold."

Oh sure. So she was supposed to wear a big flannel shirt that covered her from neck to knee while she was forced to look at him in his skintight T-shirt that pulled against his well-defined muscles every time he moved? And he expected her not to tackle him to the floor and get her hands on every bulging inch of him? Her eyes dropped to his crotch. Yeah, she especially wanted to get her hands on that particular bulge.

"Thanks," she managed to say.

She pulled her T-shirt off over her head and reached for the shirt he was holding in her direction. He gaped at her as if he'd never seen a chick in her bra before. As soon as she had his shirt in her possession, he spun around and faced the opposite direction.

"Amanda," he said breathlessly, "what are you doing?"

She smiled, glad he was at least a little flustered. "Putting on your shirt so I don't catch cold." She buttoned it to the middle of her chest and then wriggled out of her wet shorts. She tossed them at him, and they smacked him in the back before falling to the floor. "Should I take off my panties too? They're positively drenched."

"No!"

She bit her lip to hold in a laugh. Why was he acting so embarrassed? Amanda imagined women threw their panties at him all the time.

"I'm decent," she told him. Not that she wanted to be.

He took a deep breath and turned to face her, as if dreading a walk to the guillotine. His gaze slid from her feet up her bare legs and to the large, shapeless shirt that fit her like a muumuu.

"Mercy," he said under his breath. He squeezed his eyes shut and then bent to retrieve her wet shorts and shirt. "I'll put these in the dryer for you." He fled the room again.

Perplexed, Amanda scratched her head. What the fuck was his deal? She wasn't *that* unappealing, was she? For a few minutes she'd actually thought he was attracted to her. Now he was treating her like she had a communicable disease.

Oh well. She wasn't going to let his lack of interest ruin her evening. Even if he didn't want her in a sexual capacity, they could still have a few laughs together. She searched the fridge for a couple of beers, tossed several slices of pizza on a plate and grabbed the bowl of fruit before carrying it all to the family room off the kitchen. She set everything on the coffee table and knelt in front of his shelves of Blu-ray discs, scanning titles for something that would give her an excuse to bury her face in his chest. Just because he wasn't attracted to *her* didn't mean she couldn't enjoy being close to *him*. Right?

Desperate much, Amanda? She released a heavy sigh.

On her elbows and knees, she swayed back and forth with nervous energy as she read titles. She wouldn't have known he'd entered the room if he hadn't muttered, "son of a bitch," under his breath. What was his problem now? She pulled a case off the shelf and tossed it on the coffee table.

"How about that one?"

"Fine," he said, without looking at it. He crossed the room to the large ottoman at the foot of an oversized blue chair. He opened it and pulled out a blanket. "Have a seat."

When she sat on the sofa in front of the television, he unfolded the blanket over her lap and then went so far as to tuck it in around her legs. "That's better," he said.

"What's better?"

He paused. "I figured you were cold."

"In a flannel shirt?"

"Your legs, I mean."

"It's June."

"The A/C is on."

"Okay, I get it. I'll keep covered up," she said testily. "Sit down and eat."

Scratching the back of his neck, he eyed the chair on the opposite side of the room. If he sat all the way over there, she was going to punch him in the nose.

"Put the movie in," she said and loosened the blanket so she could reach for a slice of pizza.

He obeyed. She glowered. They hadn't even kissed, yet all of the easy friendliness between them had vanished as if he'd just discovered he'd been making out with his first cousin. She paused with her pizza dangling from her mouth. Oh God. Maybe he thought of her *like a sister*. She suddenly felt like throwing a Julie-sized tantrum.

Jacob got the movie going and then settled at the opposite end of the sofa from where Amanda was wrapped up like beans in a burrito.

"Uh, no," she said, "if you're making me watch a scary movie, then you're sitting within grabbing distance."

He inched closer but looked none too happy about it. She munched her pizza and sipped her beer while pretending she didn't feel like an ugly duckling. The room darkened as the sun slipped beneath the horizon. The surround sound and the suspense soon had Amanda so engrossed in the movie that she couldn't look away from the wide screen. *She* was the woman lost in the woods. *She* was the woman who kept glancing over her shoulder. The sound of crunching leaves grew louder behind her. Closer. Louder. Something grabbed Amanda's shoulder. She screamed.

Jacob burst out laughing.

She smacked him on the arm. "You scared the shit out of me." Her heart was racing out of control.

"Hey, you were the one who wanted to sit within grabbing distance."

"So I could hold on to you when I was afraid, not so you could *scare* me."

The blue light of the television cast an eerie glow to his grinning face. "Sorry."

"No, you aren't." She took another sip of her beer only to find it empty. Her pizza had also disappeared into her stomach while she'd been absorbed by the movie. She noticed Jacob had finished all the slices she'd brought from the kitchen and she did not want to move from her spot.

Amanda reached for the bowl of fruit, setting it between herself and Jacob on the sofa. They both reached into the bowl at the same time, and the back of his hand brushed hers. Her entire body tightened in response. He yanked his hand from the bowl and reached for his beer. Jeez, was it hot in here or was it just him? Most likely it was the fucking blanket she was smothered under. She kicked it off and tucked her legs beneath her, which moved her closer to Jacob. He didn't seem to notice, but his scent engulfed her, mixing with the mouthwatering scent of strawberries and oranges wafting up from the bowl.

The unlucky woman on the TV screen was being brutally murdered, but Amanda didn't find it nearly as frightening as the build-up. Blood and guts didn't bother biology teachers. The being stalked in the darkness part terrified her, however. So when the next unlucky woman found herself being pursued down dark alleys in the wrong part of town, Amanda leaned toward Jacob until her temple rested on his shoulder.

He tensed, but didn't push her away.

"God, don't these women carry a damned cellphone?" Amanda said. To the woman on the screen who was breaking into an abandoned warehouse, she yelled, "Don't go in there, you idiot."

Jacob pulled the bowl of fruit from between their hips and set it on the table. Then he did an entirely baffling thing. He wrapped an arm around her and cradled her against his side.

Her heart was definitely pounding now. Blood rushed through her ears, stifling the screams of the woman in the movie. *Movie? What movie?* Amanda's awareness focused entirely on the hard male body pressed against her. She didn't mean to turn her head and kiss his neck, but once she'd crossed the line, there was no retreat.

CHAPTER FIVE

Every nerve-ending in Shade's body was already in tune with the woman beside him, so when her soft lips brushed his throat, the last shred of his self-control snapped like an overstretched rubber band. He'd thought covering her with a big, shapeless flannel shirt would keep his raging hormones in check, but seeing her looking so small and feminine in his shirt had unleashed a second battery of hormones. The blanket he'd used to hide her sexy bare legs hadn't helped smother the lust in his groin. And now? Now there was no way in hell he'd be able to get through another moment without tasting her. Every inch of her. He didn't care if she was off-limits—he was on fire.

She gasped when he deftly shifted her onto her back and covered her tempting little body with his. He buried his hands in her hair and tilted her head back. She stared up at him with her soft green eyes wide with shock.

"You shouldn't have done that, Amanda," he said. "I only have so much self-control." He claimed her mouth in a deep, hungry kiss, not knowing if he wanted to punish her for being irresistibly unattainable or if he wanted to devour her whole. He groaned when her mouth opened to his. Fuck, she was even sweeter than he imagined.

He tore his mouth from hers and kissed and suckled her throat.

"Jacob," she whispered breathlessly.

Most women he bedded called him Shade because that's what they thought his name was. Hearing his given name made him feel vulnerable and unbalanced. It didn't do a damned thing to calm his excitement though. If anything, it fueled the inferno already blazing inside him. His fingers curled into the soft flannel at her shoulders. Kissing her hadn't been enough, but necking, necking was plenty. He could stop here. Not take it any farther. He could stop before he destroyed their cherished friendship with mindless fucking. He could stop.

His fingers fumbled with the buttons of her shirt. He just had to feel the give of her soft breasts against his palms. That was all. He'd hold her luscious breasts in his hands for just a moment and then he'd stop. Shade opened the shirt and shifted onto his elbows so he could cup her breasts. Her back arched, pressing the soft globes more firmly into his hands.

"Jacob," she moaned.

Oh God. He couldn't let her call his name like that again, or the hardened nubs of her nipples that were burning holes through her bra and into his palms would have to be sucked and licked and nibbled. He wasn't going to take it that far. He had to stop before... She shifted her back from the sofa and unfastened her bra.

"Amanda," he murmured. He'd meant it as a reprimand, but it sounded like a lover's caress. *Shit.*

Okay, he'd massage her bare breasts with his hands and then he wouldn't go farther. He pushed her loosened bra up to free her breasts. Lord, they were perfect. He covered them with his hands so the sight of them didn't tempt him into sucking on them for hours. He occupied his mouth with hers, though his disobedient thumbs insisted on stroking the taut buds of her nipples until she began to writhe beneath him, rubbing her mound against what had to be the hardest erection he'd ever experienced. Her legs parted, and he sank between her thighs. He could feel the molten heat of her sex and couldn't keep from grinding his cock against her soft flesh. Damn it. *You can't take this any farther, Silverton. You have to stop. Stop now. Stop before you go too far.*

"Take me, Jacob," she moaned into his mouth.

His mind was saying no, no, no, but his body had already surrendered.

He tore his mouth free, ending their heated kiss, and rested his cheek against hers, trying to collect his breath. "We can't do this, Amanda."

"Why not?"

"Because… because it will complicate things."

"It doesn't have to. It's just sex."

That's what he was used to, *just* sex. *Just sex.* But not with women he cared about, enjoyed outside of the bedroom and had been inappropriately crushing on for years. No, he'd never had just-sex with someone like Amanda. He had just-sex with women like Veronica. He preferred it that way. So why was he so excited that he expected to blow his load down his thigh at any moment?

"Jacob, please don't leave me like this. I'm about to explode."

Yeah, he knew the feeling.

Okay, he'd give her relief by making her come and then he'd stop. That was doable. Sure.

"Easy," he whispered into her ear. "I've got you."

He kissed a slow path from her ear to her collarbone. He massaged both breasts in easy circles, deciding he'd allow himself the pleasure of sampling her nipples. Sucking them. They were so hard. So in need of proper attention. And pleasuring them would help her reach orgasm. And then, by God, he would put a stop to this madness.

When his lips drew one tight bud into his mouth, she shuddered and clung to the back of his head with both hands.

"Jacob," she whispered. "Yes."

At the sound of his name, his cock jerked, and he felt the dampness of pre-cum against his thigh. He rocked his hips, rubbing himself against the sofa cushions, because no matter how much he wanted to plunge his throbbing cock into her wet heat, he wasn't going to take it that far. He needed to make her come quickly so he could go jerk one out in the bathroom. He couldn't remember the last time he'd masturbated, but he was sure he remembered how to do it.

He shifted one hand to her mound and rubbed its heel against her, massaging her clit gently through her satin panties.

"Jacob!"

She had to stop saying his name like that. He was going to lose all control. His cock ached, protesting its uncomfortable position trapped inside his jeans. He moved his hand to loosen his fly. He sighed in relief when his cock sprang free. Much better. With his dick in a less painful and distracting position, he might regain a semblance of control. Still sucking her nipple, he flicked his tongue over the sensitized flesh in his mouth, and she shuddered. Amanda clung to his scalp, her fingertips holding him to her breast, while he moved his hands to slowly lower her panties. She wriggled out of them eagerly, and he lifted his hips so he could free the garment from her legs. He quickly pressed his cock against the sofa cushions again so he didn't do something truly stupid and thrust deep inside her.

Lord, he could smell the musk of her excitement, feel the heat of her pussy against his belly. If he moved just a foot upward, he could plunge into that inviting warmth. And plunge into it again and again and again. Harder and faster.

Fuck, he had to stop thinking about the slick, warm pussy at his disposal. Instead of doing what his body demanded and surging up into her, Shade moved down instead. He gave her nipple a sharp nip with his teeth before sucking a trail of open-mouthed kisses down her belly. If he didn't taste her sex soon, he just might go insane. Or maybe he'd already lost his frickin' mind.

Amanda opened her legs wide for him, and he groaned at the sight of her submissive position in the dim light of the television. He spread her wet lips with two fingers and then rubbed his tongue against her swollen clit. She cried out and rocked her hips as her entire body went taut with release.

"Oh God, Jacob. I'm coming. I'm coming."

Okay, he'd made her come. He'd promised himself that he'd stop after she'd finished, but shit, that had been too fast. What, five seconds? That didn't count as a real orgasm. He'd make her come again—harder this time—and then he'd go take care of himself in the bathroom.

"Take me, Jacob," she said, rocking her hips as involuntary spasms shook her. "Please. Take me."

He slipped two fingers inside her, and her slick heat engulfed them, tightening, pulling at them, trying to draw them deeper. His cock throbbed in envy.

She went limp. Her breath came out in labored gasps. "Do

you have a condom? If not, I have some in my purse."

He didn't answer her. He wasn't taking this that far. Kissing. Necking. Sucking her tits. Fingering her. Tasting her cum. Okay. Thrusting his cock into her until he erupted with much needed release? Not happening.

He used his fingers in the way he wished he could use his dick, thrusting them into her silky tunnel hard and rhythmically. He suckled and licked her clit at the same time, until her muscles went taut again and she began to rock against his face.

"Jacob," she called to him. "Oh God. I'm close again. Take me now. Please."

His cock was primed and ready to pump. He shifted onto his side, drawing her with him as he turned. He continued onto his back, easing her up and over so that she was kneeling over his face. He positioned her so he could suckle her clit and slide his fingers in and out of her without having to use his other hand to hold her because, dammit, he needed his other hand at the moment. He introduced his twitching cock to his fist, wrapping his hand loosely around himself and stroking with the same rhythm he was using on her sweet, slick pussy. He allowed himself to fantasize that he wasn't thrusting into his hand, but into her body. It was okay to think about it, just as long as he didn't actually do it. Right? Yeah, that was fine. Oh God, he was going to come so hard. *Amanda. Amanda.*

Her pussy tightened around his fingers, and she cried out somewhere above his head as another orgasm ripped through her. He stroked himself faster, wanting to join her, but he wasn't quite there yet. He tore his mouth away from her clit, trying to catch his breath, trying to find release, realizing all at once that his hand was no substitute for her tight pussy. And then she did something he never expected. She turned to face the opposite end of the sofa and sucked the head of his cock into her mouth.

Okay. That was okay. He'd given her oral pleasure. She could do the same for him and it wouldn't be an utter violation of his promise to himself not to have just-sex with her. Oh God, her hot mouth tugged on him just right. He was so excited he couldn't stop stroking himself with his hand, so she covered his hand with both of hers and pumped him hard until he erupted, his seed shooting into her mouth as he found release at last. He couldn't see what she was doing with his eyes rolled into the back of his head and his head tossed back in blinding ecstasy, but he was pretty sure she was swallowing all of what had to be twelve gallons of cum pumping out of him.

"Oh God, Amanda," he said, his voice a breathless rasp. "Amanda."

When the pulsing spasms of pleasure abated at last, he relaxed into the sofa with an outrush of air. Amanda's lush mouth popped free of his cock, and she turned to cuddle up against his side on the large sofa. She rested her head on his shoulder and her hand on his belly. He didn't have the energy to put any appropriate distance between them. Ah fuck, he was in trouble.

CHAPTER SIX

Amanda needed to get the condoms out of her purse, because she was not going to be satisfied with a couple of fingers after getting her eyes and hands and lips on the monster in Jacob's pants.

"Oh shit," he said. "I shouldn't have done that."

Amanda stiffened and then lifted her head to stare at him. He refused to meet her eyes. Was getting busy with her on the couch *that* embarrassing?

"Shouldn't have done *what?*" she said, her voice laced with the building anger she felt.

"I had no intention of making a move on you, Amanda, I swear. I apologize."

Jacob "Shade" Silverton was apologizing for sexual contact? Had the world ended without her knowing it? Or was he truly disgusted that *she* was the one who had had two mind-blowing orgasms under his attention and not that Busty Lusty McGillicutty who undoubtedly knew her way around a penis?

"Why wouldn't you make a move on me?" she said, mentally cursing the emotional hitch in her voice. "Do you find me that sexually unappealing?"

"*What?* No," he said and squeezed her against his side, "I can scarcely keep a grip on myself when you're within the same county. It's just... I *like* you, Amanda. I shouldn't have touched you."

"You *like* me, so you shouldn't touch me? Jacob, that makes absolutely no sense whatsoever."

"I don't sleep with women I like."

"Why not?"

"Because..."

This was a side of him she'd never seen before, and she wasn't sure how to handle this guy. The cocky jerk? Yeah, she understood him. But she'd never imagined there was a heart under all of Shade Silverton's pomp and pageantry. Well, that wasn't exactly true. She had seen his heart. He wore it like a huge target on his chest when he was with his little girl. But could he care for a woman with the level of devotion he showed Julie?

"Because *why*?" she pressed.

"Because I wouldn't want to hurt a woman I like. Not the way I hurt Tina. And I would. I'd tear her heart apart. I can't help it. I'm an asshole that way."

She chuckled and relaxed against him. "What if I promised that you wouldn't hurt me, Jacob? Because even though I like you too, I would never in a million years think a serious relationship would work out with you. I just want to hang around with you. Have fun with you."

"Have sex with me?"

"Yeah, there's that."

"You're sure?"

"Why wouldn't I be? It's just sex. It doesn't have to mean anything."

His tense body relaxed. "Just-sex."

"Yeah, nothing more."

"All right, we're on exactly the same page then."

"You'd better stop acting all caring and sensitive. You wouldn't want me to fall in love with you, would you?"

"No," he said quickly, "that would be a bad idea."

"Agreed."

"Are you sure just-sex won't hurt your feelings?"

"I'm sure."

"All right then." He sat up and pulled his shirt off over his head. "Then these clothes need to go."

Oh God, the man was a genius. Not to mention gorgeous. He shucked his pants next and then settled back on the sofa with her tucked along his side. He slipped her borrowed shirt from her shoulder. "You won't need this for the rest of the night."

"What if I get *cold*?" she said with a smirk.

"Not an option."

She removed the rest of her clothes and snuggled up against him with his arm around her. With his free hand, he reached for the bowl of fruit, set it on his sculpted stomach and began to feed her bites. She allowed her hand to wander his body, wondering if she was dreaming, or if she really was naked in Jacob Silverton's arms, supposedly watching a movie, and doing her damnedest to make that magnificent cock of his rise again.

When she got brave enough to run one fingertip down the length of his limp cock, he said, "Trying to watch a movie here."

She smiled when she received the appropriate response out of his fifth appendage and it began to harden and thicken.

"Oh, I'm sorry," she said, "am I bothering you?"

"You are being a little distracting, Miss Lange."

"Only a little?" She wrapped her hand around his thickening length. "It looks rather big from my perspective."

He chuckled, smoothed her hair and kissed the top of her head. "We have all night for that. I mean, if you want to stay."

Fuck yeah, she wanted to stay. "Are you inviting me?"

"We've already established that you can't take a hint."

She tore her gaze from the beauty that was his now fully erect cock and angled her head to look into his eyes. "Well?"

"Will you stay the night with me, Amanda?"

"That depends," she said.

He scowled. "On what?"

She grinned at him. "How many erections you can get in one night."

He grinned back. "One won't be enough?"

It would take him years to satisfy every fantasy she'd ever had about him. "Not for what I have in mind."

"And I assume I'm supposed to figure out what you have in mind by trial and error?"

And she was sure he was going to treat her to fantasies she'd never dreamed of. "Normally I don't like people to put ideas in my head, but that sounds like a plan."

"Three."

She supposed she could live with that. "I guess I'll stay."

He kissed her forehead tenderly. "Then you can relax. No need to rush."

She supposed that was true, but she'd wanted him for so many years, now that he was literally at her fingertips, she didn't want to waste any time. Maybe if she thought they'd have anything beyond one night together, she wouldn't feel so desperate to spend the entire time with him between her thighs.

Jacob munched fruit and watched the continuing adventures of a psychotic serial killer while Amanda gently massaged the length of his cock. She was surprised when he continued to thicken beneath her persistent touch. She'd incorrectly assumed that he was as hard as he could get.

His skin was so smooth. Veins strained in tortuous paths just beneath the surface. She would have believed he was mostly unaffected by her touch if not for the little hitches in his breathing each time she discovered new ways of touching him. When she enclosed the head of his cock in a loose fist and stroked him rapidly, his belly tightened and breath caught in his throat.

She glanced up at his face and found his eyes closed, lips parted, expression tense. Dear lord, she'd never seen a sexier man in her life. Amanda's pussy swelled and moistened instantly and began to throb in protest of its neglect.

He took a sudden deep breath and forced his eyes open. The predatory look in those eyes made her belly quiver. He set the bowl of fruit on the floor and then in one swift movement flipped her onto her back and covered her body with his.

"All right, Amanda. I get it. Unlike you, I *can* take a hint."

She smiled up at him. "Oh? What was I hinting at?"

"You want to be fucked senseless."

"Maybe," she said. "Or maybe I just like the feel of your cock in my hand."

He lowered himself onto her. Belly to belly, chest to chest. His hard body made her feel soft, feminine. The coarse hairs on his legs made hers feel smooth, sensual. His skin felt cool everywhere they touched. Most likely because she was on fire.

"I think you'd prefer the feel of my cock buried deep inside you," he whispered in her ear. He nibbled her earlobe and then dropped soft, sucking kisses along the side of her neck. She moaned and wrapped her arms around his body, splaying her hands over his lower back. His hands rested on either side of her ribcage, each thumb stroking the outer curves of a breast.

Blood raced through her body as her heart beat faster and faster. Her flesh heated. She wanted every inch of her body to know every inch of his. His mouth shifted to the other side of her neck, drawing a groan of torment from the back of her throat. Just that amount of contact had her nipples hard against his muscular chest and her core achy and as hot as molten lava. She spread her legs, opening herself to him, wanting just what he'd said she was after—the feel of his cock buried deep inside her.

"Jacob," she whispered. "I'm ready for you."

"That's nice," he murmured, sliding downward. He dragged his mouth over every inch of her shoulders, her collarbones and the depression between them where her pulse was racing out of control. Beneath his kisses, her flesh came alive, every nerve-ending in tune with pleasure and need. The thumbs still stroking the sides of her breasts were starting to drive her crazy. She needed those rhythmic caresses against her throbbing nipples, not the less sensitive sides of her breasts. Jacob moved down to rub his sensual sucking lips against the tops of her breasts. His thumbs shifted closer to her nipples, still stroking back and forth, still making her acutely aware of how hard her nipples were. She could probably cut diamonds with those things.

"Jacob, please."

"Please, what?" he said against her breastbone.

"My nipples."

"Are beautiful," he said.

His hands shifted beneath her breasts, lifting them, pressing them closer together. His thumbs stroked the inner, under-curves of the over-sensitized mounds of flesh, and his tongue darted in and out between them. Impossibly, her nipples hardened even further. Her womb clenched. Oh God, if he'd just brush one peak at this point, she'd explode.

Still holding her breasts together, now massaging just beneath her straining nipples with both thumbs, Jacob moved his mouth to her belly. She moaned in protest.

"Please, Jacob."

"Please, what?"

"My nipples are driving me insane."

"That's nice." He rubbed his lips over every inch of her stomach between her ribs and her navel. When he started nibbling just beneath her belly button, she moaned. Her fingers dug into his scalp, and she pushed down. *Go down, Jacob. Down.* His thumbs brushed over the peaks of both breasts, and her back arched. She tried to tug his head up. *Come up, Jacob. Up.* Up or down, she didn't care, as long as he stopped making her crazy with need and gave her aching, throbbing parts some relief.

He continued lower, and her hands slipped from his head. She clung to the sofa cushions to keep herself from plucking desperately at her nipples. Jacob spread her legs wide and sucked on the insides of her thighs. She became delirious, her hips rocking involuntarily, her head tossing back and forth, a constant stream of moans and groans erupting from her parted lips. Jacob's tongue traced chaotic patterns inches from her swollen pussy. Sweet, torturous agony. She'd never needed to be fucked so badly in her life.

His tongue brushed her clit. She jerked, her butt rising off the sofa to angle herself for easy penetration. He licked the center of her sopping wet seam. One long continuous brush of his tongue. Oh God, finally, yes. Amanda shuddered hard, seeking orgasm, so close, so close. If he would just... His mouth moved to the shaved area of her mound, right next to the narrow strip of hair at the middle. He suckled and nibbled either side, drawing her attention to the wet, achy center of her body.

"Jacob, please."

"Are your nipples still driving you insane?"

"No, yes. Please. Just..."

His tongue brushed her clit, and her pussy clenched hard.

"Yes, that. Don't stop."

"Oh. I thought you were ready for me."

She could hear the teasing in his voice and wanted to slap him in frustration. Unfortunately, her mind seemed incapable of controlling her body at the moment.

"I'll keep going then," he said.

Jacob sucked one of her outer lips into his mouth. Pleasuring it with nibbles and licks and suction until Amanda's pussy was clenching rhythmically with the tease of an orgasm that just would not come.

Jacob's hand moved from her breast; she heard the slide of a wooden drawer. Both of his hands were off of her now. The rustle of a wrapper reached her ears. He pulled his mouth free to suck a breath through his teeth. "Fuck, I'm hard for you."

He shifted up the sofa, settling his hips between her thighs. His knee slipped under one side of her ass, lifting her at an angle. He had the other foot on the floor for leverage. Entranced, she stared at him as he grabbed his cock in one hand, opened her pussy wide with the other and then slipped inside her. She exploded instantly, her body jerking with hard spasms of dizzying release. She screamed his name, hands reaching for him desperately but unable to find him.

"You really were ready for me," he said, shifting his leg out from under her now so he could thrust more easily.

All the things he'd denied her before, he gave her. He leaned over her to suck her nipples, filled her deeply, rubbed against her clit with each deep churning stroke. She sobbed as her body fought to find a second release. One hadn't been enough to break all the tension he'd created in her body.

"Shh," Jacob whispered. His tongue flicked her nipple. "I won't leave you like this."

He rose up and leaned back, his balls bumping her ass with each deep thrust. He moved his hand to her clit and tapped it with two fingers, before rubbing in deep, massaging circles and then tapping it again. He was playing her body like an instrument, and he knew exactly how to get the most sound of her. When she attained her peak again, he pinched her nipple with a harsh twist, adding to the hard, rhythmic pulsations gripping her womb, making her pussy clench his pounding cock as if trying to suck it dry. Pleasure, unlike anything in her experience, ripped through her.

"Fuck *yes*, Jacob. Yes!"

"That's it, Amanda. Come hard. Come so fucking hard."

She had no choice but to obey and when her body decided it had had enough, she collapsed into a trembling mass of boneless flesh on the sofa.

"Dear God, dear God," she said between gasps. Her body, every part, quaked. She tried to open her eyes to look at the man responsible for her absolute rapture, but couldn't get her eyelids to function properly. She hadn't known it was possible to come that hard.

He pulled out and sat at the far end of the sofa.

What? "Aren't you going to finish?" she said. Her voice was slurred, as if she'd had one too many margaritas.

"I think I'm ready for a dip in the hot tub. Care to join me?"

"Does a pig's orgasm last thirty minutes?" She was pretty sure she'd just topped that.

His eyebrows drew together. "Um, *yes?*"

She smiled. "Yes."

CHAPTER SEVEN

How had this happened?

Shade sat in the steamy water of the hot tub, his delighted cock buried deep in Amanda's warmth. Facing his, her exhausted body rested against his chest, her head against his shoulder. He hadn't still come—not for lack of pleasure. Shade wasn't ready for this to end yet, so he relished the stall of his release. That meant he got to enjoy being inside Amanda all that much longer. But he was starting to worry that she was going to go into a coma. She'd been riding him with the determination of a second-place racehorse for well over fifteen minutes.

"Why haven't you come yet?" she whispered. "I can't move anymore."

"It's always like that for me. My first orgasm comes easy. The next one always takes forever. That's why I was trying to finish watching that movie. I figured you'd need to conserve your energy."

"Well, I'm glad I interrupted your plans." He couldn't see her face, but he could hear the smile in her voice. "God, you made me come hard."

"No need to call me God," he teased.

He lifted a hand out of the water to stroke her hair, which was wet at the ends and sticking to her bare shoulders.

"My body disagrees."

"Don't wear yourself out. Relax for a little while." He kissed the top of her head, confused by the tender feelings she evoked in him. It wasn't that he never had feelings for a woman. Tenderness wasn't usually one of them.

"Don't you have a concert tomorrow night?" she asked.

"Yeah. In San Antonio."

"Then you're the one who needs to conserve your strength."

"It doesn't take too much energy to—what did you say I did?—*strut* around on stage for an hour."

She laughed. "I was just poking at you."

He shifted his hips to burrow deeper into her silky heat. "And now I'm poking at you."

She laughed again and hugged him. "You can poke at me all you want, Mr. Silverton."

"It's a good thing you have summers off then."

She shifted away to look at him with wide eyes, and he realized he'd allowed himself to get too comfortable. After tonight he wouldn't be poking her at all. Why had he brought up the summer?

"Uh…" How in hell was he going to cover up that slip?

She collapsed against him again. "Not nice to joke about things like that, Mr. Silverton. My vagina has just found a new best friend. Don't give her false hope that she's going to get to hang out with him all summer when you know damned well she'll be flying solo."

Shade chuckled and gave her a squeeze. She'd let him off the hook so easily, which he appreciated, but part of him wanted her to demand he hang out with her all summer even if she kept her vagina to herself. "I have never met a woman like you, Amanda Lange."

"I don't believe that. I'm sure lots of vaginas consider your cock their best friend."

"Maybe, but they wouldn't crack corny jokes about it."

She shifted back to sit on his thighs and looked him in the eyes. "This isn't good pillow talk, is it? Very unsexy. Sorry."

"There isn't a pillow in sight," he said. "And even if you weren't the sexiest woman who has ever been in my hot tub, I'd still enjoy your company."

"Puh-lease," she said, rolling her eyes. "I saw that woman who was waiting for you when we arrived. She was gorgeous. And she had enormous boobs." Amanda held both hands in front of her chest, approximating the size of Veronica's double D's.

He grabbed her ass with both hands and pulled her down on his cock. "And yet you're here, and she's not."

"Which makes me think it's all about conquest for you."

He laughed until he was blinking tears out of his eyes and holding the stich in his side. "If I'm the one being hunted, then I guess that's the case."

He didn't have to chase women, they always chased him. And he didn't mind it one bit.

"Maybe I should have posed more of a challenge and played hard to get."

Seeing as she was currently sitting naked in a hot tub with him, impaled by his cock, it was too late for that. And he didn't need the game, but he had to admit he'd wanted her for so long that having her was far more thrilling than his usual hook-ups.

Shade shifted forward so he could steal a kiss. "I waited for you long enough."

"Five minutes? Or was it ten? Must be a new record for you. Would you prefer a medal or a trophy for your achievement—Jacob's Longest Seduction?"

He chuckled again. "Stop making me laugh so much. I'm getting a stomach ache."

"If I had the strength, I'd find myself otherwise occupied, but my legs refuse to move. My mouth seems to be working just fine though. If I had gills, I could go down on you."

If she didn't get serious, he was going laugh until he hurt something. Time to take matters into his own hands. He wrapped his arms around her and rolled so that she was the one sitting and he was between her legs, kneeling on the floor of the hot tub.

"I did wait for you long enough," he said, beginning to thrust into and withdraw slowly from her body. "I've wanted you since the first time you made me spew iced tea out my nose."

She gave him a look that called him on his bullshit—eyes lifting skyward, lips pursed, head shaking.

"Whatever. The last thing on your mind was me that night. Tina was not too happy with you for getting tea on her wedding gown. You spent the next hour promising her you'd make it up to her during the honeymoon."

"That's because she lacks what you have."

Amanda looked perplexed. Her brows drew together as if she were trying to solve a complex problem. Shade had married what most people considered the prettier, more fashionable, *trophy* sister. Tina looked good—he couldn't deny that—but she had the personality of a cactus.

"A *job*?" Amanda said finally.

He chuckled. He felt Tina's entitlement in his wallet every month. "Well, there is that. But I meant a sense of humor."

"Oh." She lifted a wary eyebrow. "Yeah, that has the guys beating down my door."

He imagined it did. He wanted to beat her door down. Since he couldn't tell her that, he'd have to show her with physical attention.

Shade took her slowly, lost in her pretty green eyes as she accepted him. And not only with her body. She accepted all of him. Even the parts he tried to conceal. The parts he didn't share with anyone while he fucked them. He should probably be more careful—he didn't want either of them to get the wrong idea—but for a few moments, he let himself feel more than her body. He let himself feel her on a much deeper level.

He knew Amanda was exhausted, so he tried to hurry. Watching her blissful expression as his pumping hips brought her closer and closer to orgasm aided his own search for release. Her hands roamed his back, his chest, his shoulders and his arms as if she were committing his body to memory.

When she squeezed his ass in both hands, urging him to take her faster, he complied, allowing her to drive his rhythm. He couldn't look away from her eyes as the urgency overwhelmed him and he sought release with rapid, shallow strokes. The angle of her hips worked his cockhead inside her so perfectly that he couldn't concentrate on anything but coming. Coming inside her while locked in her gaze.

His orgasm took him by surprise. He tried thrusting deep and holding still so he could regain his control, but it was too late. Hard spasms of pleasure pulsed through the base of his cock, driving him beyond the brink of restraint. He ground his hips against her, hoping she'd join him in bliss. He'd been so wrapped up in her gaze that he'd ignored her body. He ground into her again, not certain he was even stimulating her clit. *Come on, baby. Let go now.* As if she'd heard his instruction, her back arched, slapping her belly against his as she cried out. For a second he thought she was faking an orgasm, which was about the biggest insult she could have given him, but he felt her pussy clench around him in hard spasms, drawing out his orgasm as she took hers.

Spent and content, Shade collapsed against the back of the hot tub, still breathing hard. He slipped the condom from his cock and tossed it over the side of the tub. After a moment, he spotted the wine in the Styrofoam cooler of melting ice and grabbed the bottle to take a swig. Amanda was slumped sideways against the side of the tub, barely keeping her head above the roiling water.

"You okay?" he asked.

"Hot."

"It is pretty warm in here," he agreed.

"You. You're *hot.*"

He reached for her and tugged her around the slippery seat until she was beside him. They might only get to be intimate like this for one night, so he was going to take full advantage of their naked time together. "Have some wine."

Her arm was shaking when she reached for the bottle.

"Sure you're okay?" he asked "You're shaking."

"Just exhausted. I should have started training for this months ago."

He chuckled and helped her lift the bottle of wine to her lips. She took one swallow before pulling the bottle away and collapsing against the back of the tub with her eyes closed.

He set the wine on the deck behind the tub and wrapped an arm around her. His lips brushed her forehead. "Do you want to take a little nap?"

"Mmm hmm," she murmured, leaning into him.

"You'll need to recover some strength. I last even longer the third time."

Her eyes popped open. "Third time?"

And she'd acted as if three erections wouldn't be enough

for her.

He grinned. "The night is young. I might be able to pull off four if you're lucky."

"Dear lord. If I didn't thoroughly enjoy every minute with you, I'd put my pussy on strike."

He chuckled. Most women couldn't keep up with his libido, but that didn't mean he was going to take it easy on her. She was his for the night. The *entire* night.

Amanda was quiet for so long that he thought she'd fallen asleep. "How did your band come up with the name Sole Regret?" she asked. "Is there a meaning behind it?"

He wondered where that question had come from. "Yeah, but it's a secret. We all promised to keep it to the grave."

"Sounds extreme."

He smiled at memories of how passionate they'd once been. "We were young. *Everything* was extreme."

"Did *you* come up with the name?"

"Kellen did, actually. He was having one of his philosophical moments. Said there was only one thing in his life that he ever truly regretted, all the rest of the bullshit was secondary."

"His *sole* regret."

"Exactly. We'd all had a few too many beers that night. Each of us shared our biggest regret and then made a pact to never tell anyone about them. We named the band Sole Regret to remind ourselves of that promise."

"So what was your sole regret, Jacob?"

"Not telling."

"Why not? I can keep a secret."

"Because it's personal."

"More personal than sex?"

He nodded. "Way more personal than sex."

"Does it have something to do with your divorce?"

"Nope, it happened before I even met your sister."

"You were like twenty-two when you met her. So it must have been something that happened in high school then."

He had the feeling she wasn't going to relent until she figured it out. "I said I'm not telling."

"Did you beat up someone? Steal something? Spend time in

juvenile hall?"

"*What?*" he said. "No. Why do you think it was something bad?"

She shrugged. "Because you won't tell me. It makes me assume the worse."

He took a deep breath. "I regret not finishing high school," he said. "That's it. It's not even a secret. Most people just don't realize how much I regret dropping out." He wasn't sure why he'd told her. Probably because the truth was far less criminal than what she was imagining.

"So go finish."

He'd expected disdain or pity, not a solution. "I'm too old to finish."

"You're kidding, right? You could get your GED. You're smart enough. You probably just need a refresher course."

"I'm *not* smart enough. I was flunking out of high school. That's why I quit. I was going to have to retake my entire senior year, and at the time, quitting seemed better than failing."

She shifted in the water so she could meet his eyes. "You *are* smart enough."

Lost without his sunglasses, he stared over her head. "No."

"Jacob, I'm a teacher; I know what I'm talking about. You *are* smart enough."

He knew his personal limitations. Her insisting things that weren't true only managed to tick him off. He was done talking about this. "No."

"One of my best friends teaches an accelerated GED prep course," she pressed. "You should take it. She's a really great teacher."

"I'm not taking it, Amanda, and I'm not going to bother taking a test I know I'll flunk. Drop it."

"You shouldn't go through life with regrets, Jacob. Especially not ones you can fix."

"Amanda." He gave her a stern look, and she matched it with a death glare that undoubtedly made the most unruly of teenaged students take notice and obey.

"Just think about it," she said. "If you decide you want to try, I'll get you signed up for Leah's class. She usually has a waiting list, but I'm sure she'd squeeze you in if I asked her for a favor."

"Why does it matter to you so much? Are you ashamed to be fucked by a high school dropout?" Her sister certainly used it against him.

"It doesn't matter to me at all. You're obviously doing well for yourself. I'm being a nosy, pushy bitch because it matters to *you*."

"You're not a bitch," he said. He'd encountered plenty of them in his travels.

"Just nosy and pushy."

She looked at him expectantly and had he been wearing his sunglasses or if she'd been a less perceptive woman, he might have stood a chance of fooling her into thinking he didn't give a damn about any of this. He hated being told what to do more than anything, but had to admit her idea was a good one. He didn't know why he hadn't thought of it years ago. Getting his GED would give Tina less ammunition to use against him and maybe she'd stop reminding Julie that he was stupid.

"If I say I'll think about it, will you get off my back?"

She smiled. "I'll call Leah tomorrow."

"I didn't say I was doing it for sure."

"Just in case." She kissed him and then shifted to lean against him with her head on his shoulder again.

He squeezed her upper arm in one hand and then gently stroked up and down while his mind turned over possibilities. Dropping out of high school was his only real regret, and he didn't need the diploma to make a living, but he did *want* it. A piece of paper might prove he wasn't as stupid as everyone thought he was. He didn't have the time to study while he was on tour but maybe in a few months when the band took a break, he could squeeze a refresher course into his schedule. Sole Regret would be in the studio cutting a new album in the fall, but during the coming winter he might find the time. He hoped this Leah woman was patient and a miracle worker because it would take both to get the brain tucked inside his thick skull to retain information. He'd never been good at school stuff. For years he'd barely scraped by. His teachers had taken pity on him and let him move up through the system one frustrating year at a time.

He wondered what kind of teacher Amanda was. He imagined her class would be challenging and a lot of fun. Even so, he probably would've flunked it. Especially since he would have spent the entire period fantasizing about her hot body.

"Do you like being a teacher?" he asked.

"Yeah, I do. Well, I like most parts about it. I like my students and finding new ways to excite them about science, but all the extraneous administrative bullshit becomes exhausting."

"I had quite a few crushes on my teachers." He grinned.

"Why's that? Do you like women with authority, Mr. Silverton?"

"Nope. I like big brains." He kissed the top of her head. "Sexy."

"Oh really? I thought you liked big boobs."

"Hey, I can like more than one part at a time."

She laughed. "You can also please more than one part at a time."

"A man has to draw attention to his talents."

"You definitely have my attention."

"Oh, good," a deep voice said from the shadows next to the house. "You have company. I need to ask her something."

CHAPTER EIGHT

At the sound of a man's voice, Amanda jerked upright with a splash. She gasped when cool air hit her naked breasts, and she sank deep beneath the steaming water to hide.

"You could *call* before you drop by," Jacob said. "I have better things to do than hang out with you on my night off."

The drummer of Shade's band, Gabe, stepped into the dim light given off by several solar lights. Amanda hadn't noticed how dark Jacob kept the area around his hot tub until their uninvited guest sneaked up on them. She was sure the poor lighting was intentional. Probably kept the neighbors from seeing what Jacob had going on in his backyard.

"Looks like an intermission to me," Gabe said.

Gabe was tall and lean, with a red and black mohawk that would have gotten him kicked out of Amanda's class for being disruptive to the educational process. She didn't know him very well, had only met him a few times when Jacob had hosted parties tame enough for extended family—which had once included her. His band had been surprisingly well behaved. Amanda's mother had particularly enjoyed the bassist, Owen, who could be quite the sweet-talker. That had been before Jacob and Tina had split, of course. Every time Amanda had met Gabe in the past, he'd been wearing a baseball cap over his hair, but tonight he had it spiked straight up. He approached the hot tub and sat on the edge, kicking off a pair of flip-flops and easing his feet into the water. He was wearing a pair of board shorts, so sank his legs into the water to the knee.

"I need to get one of these," he said.

"You need to get lost," Jacob said.

"You know a lot about women," Gabe said to Jacob. His gaze dropped on Amanda, who was using Jacob's arm to shield as much of her body as possible. Gabe's jaw dropped and he pointed a finger at her. "Wait? Aren't you Tina's sister?"

"You didn't see her," Jacob said in a low voice.

"Fuck, Jacob," Gabe said, his head swiveling in Jacob's direction. "Are you a *complete* idiot?"

"It's none of your business." He scowled. "And don't call me an idiot."

Amanda's fingers curled into his belly, and she gave him a weak hug. She was too exhausted and relaxed to give him proper support. She hated that he believed he was stupid and wondered how many people had made him feel that way over the course of his life for him to be so sensitive about it. Especially since she knew it wasn't true.

Gabe ran a finger along the margin of his hairline. "I came over here to ask your advice about a woman, but I think I'll go ask one of the roadies. You obviously don't have a lick of good sense when it comes to females."

Interest piqued, Amanda straightened. "What kind of advice about a woman?"

Gabe stared into the water and then lifted his gaze to meet hers. He had the most striking green eyes she'd ever encountered. Perhaps it was the contrast of the black and red tattoos on his scalp and his equally bright mohawk that made his eyes look so green, but she got sucked into his gaze and couldn't look away.

"Maybe it would be better to ask a woman's advice instead of a dude's," he said. "I'm dating this woman from Wichita."

"By dating, he means he had a one-night stand with her." Jacob chuckled.

"Fuck you," Gabe said. "This is why none of us date regularly," he said to Amanda. "Ever since Jacob's divorce, everyone in the band seems to think women are only after one thing."

"Sex?" she blurted. Because that's what she was after.

Gabe's eyes widened, and then he laughed. "I meant money."

Amanda's face went hot and she couldn't blame it on the

heat of the water. "Oh."

"We have each other's backs now," Jacob said.

"Except when we find someone we *do* want to get serious about, the rest of the band tries to fuck it up as soon as possible," Gabe said. "Anyway, I'm dating this girl who lives near Wichita." He paused and stared at Jacob as if daring him to deny his claim. "Named Melanie." He paused again. When Jacob didn't tease him, Gabe shifted his gaze to Amanda. "She's all pissed off because I didn't invite her down to hang out on my one night off this week."

"I'm sure she just wants to spend time with you," Amanda said.

"She thinks I'm fooling around on her."

"Well, you are in hot tub with a naked woman," Jacob pointed out.

Gabe jerked his feet out of the water and extended them across the deck. Amanda stifled a chuckle. This was obviously bothering him.

"When did you meet her?" Amanda asked.

"Two nights ago."

Shocked, Amanda blinked at him. Why was he so concerned about a woman he just met? But he was worried if he was here asking for advice. Most guys would try to muddle through and then fuck things up before they started. "Maybe she's worried that you're just stringing her along. Do you have plans to see her again soon?"

"Yeah, the band has a three-day break next weekend and she's planning to visit me here in Austin for the duration."

Jacob stiffened beside Amanda, and she looked at him to find him offering Gabe pointed shut-the-hell-up looks. So he didn't want her to know that he'd be home next weekend? Not that she expected this hook-up to lead to anything even remotely permanent, but if she was good enough to fuck, she should be good enough to know such a small tidbit of information. She wasn't going to stalk him or anything. Or try to trap him. They were going to have a talk as soon as Gabe left so he realized that she wasn't like her sister. She wasn't a gold-digger. She didn't want anything from him but a good time.

"Tonight I was working on a surprise for Mel," Gabe said. "That's the main reason I didn't want her here. Plus it's a long trip to take to spend only a couple of hours together."

"Did you tell her you were working on a surprise for her?" Amanda asked.

Jacob stifled a chuckle. Now Gabe was sending him pointed shut-the-hell-up looks. "It wouldn't be a surprise if I told her about it," Gabe said.

"You don't have to tell her what it is," Amanda pointed out.

"True." He scratched behind his ear. "Um, say, Amanda," he said, "what do women find more pleasing? Length or girth?"

Jacob burst out laughing. "Are you lacking in both departments, Force?" he asked, using Gabe's stage name.

Gabe kicked water at him. "No. I just wondered."

"A bit of both," Amanda said. "Too long and it can beat the hell out of your cervix. After a while it starts to hurt. Too thick... Well, I've never had one that was too thick."

Jacob stared at her in astonishment and then laughed even harder. His arm tightened around her to press her into his side. "Woman, I never know what to expect out of you."

Gabe seemed to be taking mental notes. "That's what I thought. So in regards to the motion when it's inside the vagina, what's best? Repetitive, equally spaced thrusts or more variety in the rhythm? Shallow or deep? Fast or slow? And is it better to drive it straight in, at a certain angle, or move in circles?" He mimicked various erotic motions with two fingers.

Amanda had no idea why he was asking her advice on pleasing a vagina, but hers was starting to swell again at all the thoughts he suddenly had churning through her mind. "Um, why don't you ask her what *she* likes?"

"I do," he said, "but this is for her surprise."

"What, are you going to jump on her the moment she steps through your door?" Jacob asked. Beneath the water, his hand skimmed over Amanda's hip. Was Gabe's battery of questions turning him on as much as it was her? She'd never met a man who was so openly inquisitive about such things. At least not with a woman he scarcely knew.

Gabe ignored Jacob and stared at Amanda as he waited for her to respond. "Best to mix it up a little," she said finally.

"Why are you asking Amanda these things?" Jacob asked. "Call your chick and ask her."

"I already told you I want to surprise her."

"Surprise *her*? Or her vagina?" Amanda asked.

Gabe chuckled. "Well, mostly her vagina, but other parts too. I have to program one thing at a time though." He lifted both eyebrows. "What do you think about the girth continuing to increase? While it's inside, I mean. Thicker and thicker and thicker."

Amanda's jaw dropped.

"That's what I thought," Gabe said and chewed his bottom lip as he pondered his idea.

Jacob laughed. "Sounds as if you're working on some sort of sex machine."

"It's going to blow her mind." Gabe grinned wickedly. "Thanks for the input." He stood and descended the steps connected to the hot tub's decking.

"You are such a fucking pervert," Jacob said.

"So now *I'm* a pervert?" Gabe said, locating his flip-flops and sliding them on his feet. "Has Amanda seen your bedroom yet?"

Amanda's head swiveled in Jacob's direction.

"Not yet," Jacob said, "but she's about to."

CHAPTER NINE

Amanda wasn't sure what she expected Jacob's bedroom to look like, but she wouldn't have put her money on what she discovered. She'd figured he'd have a huge bed, which he did, but all the kinky toys she had anticipated were missing. There were TVs of various sizes around the periphery of the heavy wooden canopy above the bed. There was even a monitor above the pillows so you could watch the screen while you were flat on your back. It looked more like a sports bar than a bedroom.

"I had no idea you were such a big fan of television," Amanda said.

"Only when it's live."

"Like golf or something?"

"Or something." He drew her damp body against his, one large hand splaying over her lower back and the other between her shoulder blades. "If it makes you uncomfortable to watch it, let me know and I'll shut it off." He kissed her temple.

"Watching television in bed?"

"No, sweetheart," he said. "Watching me fuck you senseless."

He reached over and pressed a button on a panel next to the door. TVs flickered on. She barely heard the sounds of auto-focusing cameras. When she realized that the bed displayed on all the screens was *Jacob's* bed, her breath caught.

"You're going to record us having sex?" she squeaked. She could totally get fired over something like that.

"No, I never record it. Too much of a liability."

He cupped the back of her head, and she looked up at him. Why was her heart thudding out of control? He kissed her, lips stroking hers in sensual, sucking caresses until her entire body was tingling with pleasure and her knees were wobbly. Dear Lord, the man could kiss. She would give up food and drink until she died just so she could keep kissing him for the rest of her life.

The rest of *her life?* Where had *that* thought come from? That would never work, no matter how well he kissed her or how much she liked being with him. Just tonight. She just wanted him for tonight. Her arms went around him and drew him closer. Just tonight. That's all she needed, and then she could give him up. She'd promised herself that she wouldn't get attached because she knew he'd break her heart.

Amanda squeezed her eyes shut against the sudden sting behind them. Oh sure, her path would cross Jacob's occasionally—there was no way around that—but they couldn't be intimate again. She couldn't get emotionally involved. Could. *Not.*

Amanda kissed Jacob more passionately, more desperately. Her hands began to roam over the hard contours of his body. His firm ass tightened beneath her exploring palms. He tugged his lips free and grinned down at her.

She caught movement in the largest video screen that hung over the head of the bed. Displayed was a fantastic male ass and a pair of familiar hands massaging the firm buttocks. She slid her hands up to Jacob's lower back, and the image changed with the movement.

"What in the world?"

"The cameras have motion sensors."

She laughed. "Very sci-fi."

"Sole Regret's security chief is into this high-tech stuff. He set it up."

She watched the monitor, which would be much easier to see when she was sprawled on her back on the bed. There was something undeniably sexy about feeling his cool skin beneath her hands and watching herself touch him on the screen. She wondered how much she'd be able to see when they got down to business.

"You okay with this?" he asked.

She couldn't tear her attention away from the display of her hands stroking his ass.

"Amanda?"

She jerked at the sound of her name and forced her gaze to meet his. "Yeah, as long as there's no recording made."

"No recording," he promised.

"Then I'm more than okay with this. Your ass looks amazing in my hands." She gave his cheek a swat, and the muscle tensed. That sight did all sorts of things to the throbbing, swollen, heated flesh between her thighs.

Jacob released her, turned to the control panel near the door and started pushing buttons. The lights around the periphery of the room dimmed, casting shadows over the black satin sheets on the bed. The wooden canopy above the bed opened and some sort of contraption lowered out of the ceiling. Black padded straps flopped down to hang above the center of the bed, swaying beneath heavy chains that affixed the collection of loops to a heavy spring.

Amanda lifted an eyebrow at the contraption. "Oh sure, you get me to agree to one kinky thing and then you think it's okay to bring out the torture devices."

"It's not for torture. It's a sex swing. I figured you were getting tired. This will make my mad sex skills easier on your body."

She chuckled. "*Mad sex skills?*" While she didn't deny that he had *mad* sex skills, she couldn't help but find it hilarious that he referred to them that way. She'd always imagined Jacob would be suave in bed. Impersonal. She was actually relieved that he was as fun inside the bedroom as he was out of it.

"Are you *laughing* at me, Amanda Lange?" The corner of his mouth twitched. His own attempts to keep a straight face weren't working out so well for him.

"Of course not."

"No one laughs at Shade Silverton." He scooped her up in his arms and carried her to the bed.

"Do they laugh at Jacob Silverton? Because he's fuckin' hilarious. *Mad* sex skills. Oh Lord." Amanda looped both arms around his neck and buried her nose against his throat. She inhaled deeply, and her eyelids fluttered in bliss. Even with the hint of hot-tub chlorine on his skin, she couldn't get enough of the man's scent. She wanted to bathe in it.

"They laugh at the guy all the time," he said. "But I've retired Jacob for the evening. Now it's time for Shade to come out and play."

"I prefer Jacob. He's fun."

"But he doesn't have *mad* sex skills. He's sort of a dork." Shade lowered her to the mattress and kissed her gently before she could protest that Jacob did *indeed* have mad sex skills and was *not* a dork.

Shade opened a side table and retrieved a pair of sunglasses. She pouted when he put them on. One of the motion detecting cameras caught the movement of his hand and zoomed in on his face. On the screen above, he grinned. Not Jacob's easy-going grin. Shade's *you have no idea what I'm about to do to you* grin.

Amanda's belly clenched, and she shivered.

Shade pulled out a drawer beneath the bed and withdrew a wedge-shaped cushion. He placed it in the middle of the bed beside Amanda. Her attention was divided between the view of the front of his body as he leaned across her and that of his back, which was on the monitor overhead. She liked getting two views of him at once. She just wished she had more eyes, so she didn't miss anything. The monitor at the foot of the bed displayed an interesting angle of his ass. She could just see his package hanging freely between his legs as he shifted. Though she was in most of the camera shots as well, she couldn't have cared less about looking at herself. She wanted to look at him at every imaginable angle. The anticipation of seeing what he'd look like as he fucked her was making her squirm.

Shade covered the wedge with a silky red sheet and then carefully lifted her into his arms. He shifted her so that her hips were at the apex of the wedge and her back angled down toward the mattress. Knees bent, she kept her feet pressed against the bed to keep her back on the cushion. It conformed to her body and would have been incredibly comfortable if the tops of her thighs hadn't been protesting their overstretched position.

"How's your neck?" Shade asked. He rearranged her hair to fan out around her head.

"My neck is fine. My thighs won't be able to hold this for

long, however."

"We'll take care of that." He grinned, and she saw herself reflected in his sunglasses. She so wanted to look into his eyes, but she had to admit there was something sexy about not knowing what was going through his deviant mind.

Shade reached up and grabbed one of the swing's padded straps. Her eyes focused on the tensing muscles of his fantastic abdominal region until the hard ridge of his hip bone drew her attention lower to his cock, which was showing signs of renewed excitement. God, the man was exquisite. He slipped her foot through one loop and then reached for a second to hold her other foot. Ducking under the swing, he shifted to kneel between her legs. She stared at his sunglasses, feeling his gaze on her eyes even though she couldn't see it. He slid both loops up her calves to just under the backs of her knees. Her feet came off the bed. The swing took all the pressure off her hips and thighs. She could probably hold this position for hours.

And didn't *that* sound promising?

"Better?"

"Yes."

He smiled. "Good."

He ducked under the straps suspending her legs from the ceiling and climbed from the bed. He waved a hand at the main camera at the end of the bed and it tracked his motion. He slowly lowered his hands to between Amanda's parted legs. She watched the entire thing on the screen directly above her. Her breath caught when his fingers brushed her clit and then separated her swollen lips to fully display her slick pussy.

"So this is what my gyno sees beneath that paper sheet," she said.

"Lucky man."

"Woman," she said, losing her train of thought as the feel of his fingers against her sensitive clit overwhelmed the sight of him touching her.

She groaned when he removed his hand.

"Get your pussy wet for me, Amanda. I want cum dripping off your ass before I bother eating you out."

"*What?*"

He stretched out on his back beside her and tucked his folded arms behind his head. He stared up at the monitor above, which was still focused on her swollen, aching pussy.

"I'm waiting," he said after a long moment of her gaping at him in disbelief. She'd never masturbated in front of anyone before. She sure didn't want to watch herself do it on a widescreen TV. But she *did* want him to eat her out and see what that looked like from a different angle.

She closed her eyes and slid her hand down her belly. Her fingers found her clit and she rubbed it, hard and fast. Her thighs quivered as orgasm approached quickly. She hadn't realized how turned on she'd become.

"Don't make yourself come," Shade said. "Just get it wet."

Breathing hard, seconds from sending herself over the edge, she stopped. She rotated her hips in unfulfilled need, wanting something big and hard to fill her emptiness.

"Wetter," Shade said beside her.

After her excitement waned a bit, she rubbed her clit again. Fingered her opening. Rubbed her clit. She could hear how wet she was as her fingers worked her sensitive flesh harder and faster and harder and—

She moaned as she stopped her motions the instant before orgasm.

"You should open your eyes," Shade said quietly.

Amanda's eyes blinked open and focused on the monitor overhead. She bit her lip at the sight of her own red, wet and swollen flesh. Her French manicured fingertips looked incredibly erotic buried in her folds. She watched herself work her pussy this time, hoping this turned on Shade as much as it turned her on. A camera at the side of the bed caught motion and displayed the sight of Shade's rapidly rising cock. She licked her lips. He wrapped a hand around his impressive length and began to stroke it slowly. Up and down. Up and down. Now *that* she wanted to watch.

She was so caught up in touching herself and watching him touch himself that she nearly didn't stop in time to keep from coming. When her entire body quivered on the brink of orgasm, she tried to clamp her thighs together to hold it back, but the straps on her knees held her wide open.

"Oh shit," she gasped as pleasure licked its way up her spine, and her core tightened. She squeezed her eyes shut against the intensely erotic images overwhelming her.

"Don't come, Amanda," Shade demanded. "Just make it wet."

"I can't *get* any wetter," she complained as the throbbing ache inside became unbearable. "Please, Shade."

"Okay, but only if you promise to keep your eyes open."

"I promise." She'd have promised him anything for relief.

"Move your hand away."

She moved her hand.

"Open your eyes."

She forced her eyes open. He shifted so that he was leaning over her body. His tongue laved the moisture between her pussy lips.

"Tastes even better than it looks," he said.

Amanda fought to keep her eyes open as Shade devoured her pussy. Occasionally his head got in the way of the camera, but she could see most of it—his tongue feverishly stroking every wet inch of her flesh. When her gasps became screams of ecstasy, he latched onto her clit with a tight suction and plunged two fingers deep into her body. She felt it. Saw it. And the stimulation of both senses sent her spiraling out of control. He fucked her with his fingers while she came. She tried to keep her eyes open, to watch those fingers sliding in and out of her clenching pussy, but the pleasure was so exquisite she lost her ability to control her body, including her ability to draw breath. When she slowly drifted back to Earth, Shade tugged his fingers free and licked at her sensitive opening until she whimpered in protest.

"Now it's wet enough," he said, collecting her free-flowing cum with the flat of his tongue.

After a moment, she regained the ability to open her eyes, but she didn't watch the monitor above. She zeroed in on the thick, hard cock bobbing slightly each time Shade moved. She reached for him, surrounding his length in a loose fist. He rocked his hips, thrusting into her hand gently. She wanted to watch him thrust into her.

"Jacob?"

"I'm not answering to that name right now."

Exasperating man. "Shade?"

"Hmm?"

"Take me."

"In the encore," he said. "Are you light-headed?"

"A little," she admitted, but she didn't think it was from her position. The man was simply overwhelmingly virile.

Shade moved away and pulled a remote control from the side table drawer. He pressed a button and the familiar intro to Sole Regret's "Elevate" poured from hidden speakers. Another button press caused the room lights to go dark and multicolored lights around the top of the bedframe to brighten. Like a stage lightshow, they alternated between red and blue with the beat of the drums.

Wide-eyed, Amanda studied Shade's set-up. What in the *world?* "Is sex some sort of performance to you?"

He chuckled and removed the loop from one of her legs. He massaged its length from ankle to thigh as he said, "Haven't heard any complaints about it yet."

She wasn't complaining, just wondered at his reasoning. This must be why he'd insisted she call him Shade when they'd entered his room. He had some link in his mind between his stage performance and his performance in the bedroom. Was this his way of keeping all emotional connections out of sex?

"The ladies love to be reminded that a rock star is fucking them," he said.

She couldn't read how that made him feel because he had his stupid sunglasses on and she didn't have the strength to lift a hand to remove them.

"I don't need the reminder," she said. "I prefer the real you."

"I think I'm about to change your mind."

He removed her other leg from the sex swing's loop and massaged it before lifting her off the wedge-shaped cushion and lowering her flat onto the mattress. He pushed the wedge off the bed and settled his big, muscular body over her. His weight made her feel grounded. Protected. Petite. She stared up at him, her heart thudding out of control. This man, *Shade,* was a stranger to her, and as exciting as that was, she wanted to look into his eyes. She wanted Jacob.

When she reached for his sunglasses, he caught her wrists and pressed them against the mattress on either side of her head. The long intro of "Elevate" segued into the first stanza and he started to sing. Amanda's breath caught. Shade's low, sensual voice washed over her, making every inch of her skin tingle with delight. The flashing lights, the throbbing music added to her immersion in her private serenade. Oh God, his voice was as smooth and rich as butter. The sound of it caressed her spine. Her muscles tautened. Her nipples strained toward his naked chest. Her pussy throbbed in time with the deep, rich sound of the bass guitar. As Amanda stared up at him, she realized she no longer wanted Jacob. She wanted Shade. She wanted the rock star. She wanted him to fuck her hard.

In the pause after the first stanza, he kissed her deeply before taking a deep breath. With the chorus, he released her wrists and slid down her body. He cupped her breasts in both hands, singing the building chorus until he was screaming, *"Elevate from deep. Elevate from dark. Elevate. Elevate."* The deep low growl he produced at the end of the chorus made her shudder.

He sucked one breast into his mouth, stroking her nipple with his writhing tongue throughout the next guitar piece. Damn, his entire band was phenomenal.

Her attention was riveted to the screen above, where she got a spectacular view of Shade's mouth doing amazing things to her sensitive breast. Another camera caught the movement of his thumb on her other nipple. But her favorite shot of all was the one of his fantastic ass and the expanse of bronzed flesh that was his back. The flickering lights reflected off his skin, highlighting the contours of his muscles, keeping her attention on his gorgeous body.

Shade lifted his head, took a deep breath and sang the next chorus. Amanda felt she was in some highly erotic music video. She was surprised by how excited this made her. His music had never been the attraction, but she couldn't deny that it now added to his immense appeal. She'd always loved his voice, but had never thought of it as sexual before. She was sure every time she heard this song in the future, she'd cream her panties. And she planned to have this song on a continuous loop on her stereo system.

He flicked his tongue over her nipple in time with the beat, making the music come alive, making her feel part of it. Her hands moved to the back of his head, holding him to her breast, encouraging more pleasure.

"Shade."

He nipped her tender flesh and then soothed the flicker of pain with the flat of his tongue. His breath stirred across her aroused and sensitive nipple as he sang the final chorus. Her heart had taken on the beat of the music. Every inch of her was in tune with the rhythm and the man. When the song ended, Amanda took a deep breath, almost relieved that it was over so she could collect her scattered senses.

She sucked in a deep, shuddering breath when the next song began. "Darker" was even faster than the previous song—the vocals prominent and edgy. She imagined he'd chosen a certain order of songs for a reason. To excite his one-woman audience. Had it been designed like a set list for a concert? To build and build until the climax of the performance? He'd said something about an encore. All attempts to form a logical stream of thought vanished as he made her body part of his music once again. His thumbs stroked her nipples while his lips, teeth and tongue concentrated on the undersides of her breasts and her ribs. He moved to her belly on the next song. Then the insides of her thighs. He didn't take her, even when she begged. She expected him to please her swollen achy center on the next song, but he turned her onto her stomach and caressed and nibbled on her ass until she began to writhe, her aching nipples and sensitized mound rocking against the satin sheets.

The song ended and the room went quiet. The only sound was her own ragged breathing. The lights went dark. Shade moved away. Amanda lifted her head to locate him, but he wasn't beside her. He'd left the bed. She blinked her eyes trying to get them to adjust to the sudden lack of light, but everything was blurry, disorienting. She felt intoxicated.

Was it over? Surely he wasn't planning to leave her this

excited without offering her some relief. She rolled onto one side, looking for him in the direction she thought he'd moved.

"Shade?"

A drumbeat sounded, and a white light pulsed once with the beat. She caught sight of Shade standing beside the bed, unrolling a condom down the length of his cock. It stood hard, thick and proud, angled slightly upward. Amanda's pussy clenched at the sight. An instant later the room went dark again.

Another drumbeat. A blue light pulsed. Shade had one knee on the bed. Then again, darkness.

Another drumbeat. A green light pulsed. He was closer now. Darkness.

Amanda's heart thudded out of control. She felt exposed. Hunted. *Catch me, Shade. Devour me.*

Another drumbeat. White light. He tossed her onto her back and jerked her legs apart. Darkness.

Fuck me.

A bass riff began; the lights flashed in time with the complicated line of notes.

Shade's cock found her opening. He surged forward, filling her at last. He plunged into her with the song's fast and furious tempo. He was too intense, too breathless to sing. He just fucked her—*rough*—and she shattered with an orgasm that gripped her so long and so hard she screamed.

"That's it, baby," Shade said in a growling rasp of a voice somewhere above her. "Come harder than you've ever come in your life."

He didn't have to encourage her further; she was there. *Holy shit!*

She clung to his shoulders with both hands, her back arching off the bed, her entire core clenching at the rock-hard cock pounding into her. Even after the intensity waned, her body shuddered intermittently as she went limp. Her eyes blinked open and she stared up at Shade, sunglasses in place, sweat dripping down his face, neck and chest. Here in her afterglow she wanted her Jacob back, even though Shade was still fucking her like a beast.

She reached up and snatched his sunglasses off and tossed

them across the room.

He lost his rhythm and then went entirely still, staring down at her with a wide-eyed shell-shocked expression. "Why did you do that?"

"I want to look into your eyes."

"Why?"

Because I still prefer the man over the rock star, but she couldn't say that. "Because they're such a gorgeous blue."

He lowered his body over hers, his thrusts slower. He rotated his hips to grind deeper and then buried his face in her throat as he continued.

So even without the sunglasses he wouldn't look her in the eye while he had sex with her on his bed. His *stage*. Did he ever let anyone connect with his heart? Amanda's throat squeezed, robbing her of air. She wrapped both arms around Jacob to hold him as close as possible. After a moment, she opened her eyes and watched the monitor that was focused on his tight, pumping ass as he thrust and churned his hips. The song ended, the lights died.

He collapsed on top of her.

His body, so heavy.

His ragged breathing, so loud.

"I usually time my orgasm with that final drumbeat," he said.

She wondered how many performances he'd had in this bed. "I don't mind you taking as long as you need," she said. Nope, she didn't mind one bit.

"You're going to regret saying that." He pulled out and rose up to reach for the sex swing above him. "Let's get you up off that bed."

Amanda didn't resist being hooked into the straps and harnesses. She didn't have the strength or the desire to protest.

When he'd finished, she found herself suspended facedown above the bed. Amanda extended her arms in front of her. "I'm like Superman."

He chuckled. "I guarantee you'll be flying soon. Do you want the cameras on?"

She craned her neck to look up at the monitor. Gravity was not kind to her boobs in this position. "Um, maybe we should turn those off for now."

"They do tend to break my concentration after a while," he said. "Music helps it though."

"I like the music."

He used his remote control to turn the cameras and TVs off. The dim lights above the canopy scarcely provided any light. If she hadn't been tethered to the ceiling by something resembling a crazy piece of exercise equipment, she might have thought the mood was romantic. When music flooded the room with sound and the melody registered in her addled mind, Amanda could scarcely believe her ears.

"*Classical?*"

"You don't like classical music?" he asked.

"I do. I'm just surprised that you like it."

"It has great build and crescendos. Just like good sex."

She chuckled. "I never thought of it that way."

"Anyone ever tell you that you talk too much?" he asked. At her back, he grabbed the strap that was wrapped around her midsection and hoisted her up into a forty-five degree angle. Her knees were still several inches off the bed. She was surprised at how weightless she felt.

"Yeah," she said. "All the time."

"I'd kiss you quiet, but I'm going to be back here for a while. Hold your questions until the end."

She laughed. "I'll try."

He positioned himself to kneel behind her, lifted her by the hips and slowly lowered her until his cockhead was probing her opening. Shifting his hips to find a better angle, he placed both large hands to her breasts and pulled her down onto his shaft. He used the momentum of her weight and the recoil of the swing's springs to find a rhythm. The angle of his penetration felt amazing. The ease of movement kept her muscles from tiring. And the damned thing was just a lot of fun. In fact, she didn't know if she should moan in pleasure or giggle in glee as her body bounced with the action of the spring. It took her less than a minute to decide that moaning was the best response. Once Shade had his rhythm in tune with the music, he continued to use one hand to pull their bodies together. The other began to roam her heated flesh—breasts, belly, thighs, hips. Suspended as she was, she had no choice but to give herself over to the pleasure. There was no fighting Shade's experienced delivery. When the music built toward the crescendo, his fingertips sought her clit and sent her flying. Her body strained to find grounding as she soared into nirvana. The only thing solid she felt connected to was him.

"Oh!"

When she'd recovered her breath, he shifted her position so that she was still suspended, but now on her side. Startled by the loss of her center of gravity, she clutched at him for balance.

"Easy, baby," he said. "Trust the swing to hold you. Trust me to guide you. You won't fall."

Her breathing slowed, and she removed her death grip from Shade's forearm. She did trust him. She wasn't so sure about the collections of straps wrapped around her body.

He took her from the side in a position that would have been impossible to maintain for more than a few seconds without the assistance of the swing. She loved this position because she could see some of him. See the blend of concentration and pleasure on his strong, handsome face. See the sweat dripping from his brow. See the flexion of his bulging biceps as he tugged her body toward him and thrust in time with the music. She was floating on air. She wondered how long he could keep this up. While it was easy on her body, he had to be getting tired.

Amanda soon learned that a man with a sex swing, stamina, and fantastic upper body strength could fuck a woman into a state of delirium. Especially a man who knew at least forty-five positions. She lost count of how many times he brought her to orgasm. When he claimed his own release at last, she strained against him as he brought her to the pinnacle once again. "Jacob."

After his shaky breathing quieted, he released her from the swing and gently lowered her to the bed. She tried to lift her trembling arms to hold him. She wanted so much to hold him. "I can't move," she whispered.

He cradled her body against his sweat-slick body, her head resting on one of his arms, and then folded the bed sheet over

their entangled bodies. "Sleep now," he whispered.
Her eyelids were minutes ahead of him.

CHAPTER TEN

Someone cuddled up against Shade's side, and his eyes flipped open. Sunlight streamed from between the window blinds and across the tangled black and red sheets of his bed. Okay, he was going to look down at the warm, soft body pressed against his side and it wasn't going to be Amanda. Because if it was her, if last night had really happened and not just been the most amazing wet dream of his life, he'd fucked things up big time.

He tilted his chin, praying it was some random groupie using his shoulder as a pillow.

No such luck. His heart skipped a beat as Amanda's beautiful face, peaceful in sleep, graced his vision. It skipped a second beat when the enormity of their situation settled in his thoughts.

Shit. Shit. Shit. What had they done? What had *he* done? He'd touched the untouchable. *Touched?* Hell, he'd fucked her to the point of unconsciousness. And now he felt how much he'd relished their physical contact in every aching, weary muscle of his body. But just because he'd enjoyed it, just because being with her had surpassed all expectations, didn't make it right. What was it about sunlight that brought him back to his senses? And made one of the most wonderful nights of his life seem like a mistake.

He lay there for a long while, staring at the ceiling and stroking Amanda's arm absently, trying to sort through the mess he'd made. He knew they had to keep this from everyone, especially Tina. The woman would use his indiscretion with her sister against him. He knew that. She'd use it as an excuse to keep him from Julie and as much as he adored Amanda, he couldn't do anything to jeopardize his already limited relationship with his daughter.

Shit. Shit. Shit. Why hadn't he thought of these things last night before he'd acted on impulse?

Amanda murmured in her sleep, "Dogs don't have money for rent."

He smiled, wondering what she was dreaming about. Not him, apparently. Which was for the best. As much as he hated the idea of never spending another night engulfed by her heat and her heart, this couldn't go any farther. And they couldn't do this again. Ever. He had to make that clear to her. God, he hoped she didn't cry when he made his lack of intentions clear. He wasn't sure if he could handle her tears. He squeezed the bridge of his nose between his thumb and forefinger and took a deep breath.

If he stayed in bed with her any longer, his resolve would crumble. He'd have her on her back and his hands filled with her soft curves before she could blink. Shade carefully slid from beneath her body, settling her head on a pillow, and climbed from the bed.

"Don't give that schnauzer a flea bath in cottage cheese," she said and hugged her pillow.

Shade bit his lip to stifle a laugh. Even in her sleep, she made him smile. And warmed his heart. And made part of him wish he could wake up beside her every morning.

Not good.

He watched her for a long moment, her looking all tousled and sexy and unattainable. Even after they'd spent the night together, he still thought of her as beyond his reach. And she should have stayed out of reach. God, he really was an idiot. What in the fuck had he been thinking? He hadn't. He'd been *feeling.* Shit, when would he learn to stop doing that? When would he figure out that feelings, any feelings, always led to complications he wasn't prepared to deal with?

He put on a pair of swim trunks and headed for the pool. There was nothing like an hour of vigorous exercise to get a woman out from under his skin. But he wasn't even a half a lap down the pool's length when he realized that busying his body had freed his mind to churn over images of Amanda's body as he took her, Amanda's face as he made her come, Amanda's eyes as she gazed into his soul.

Shit. Shit. Shit.

What was he going to do? He could handle being used for sex—woman used bedding him as some sort of ego trip on a regular basis—but this was Amanda. *Amanda.* Even though she'd said that she was good with sex for the sake of sex, he didn't really believe it because for once, *he* wasn't okay with it. He couldn't push her away and forget she existed, because she was already too close. She'd been too close even before her soft lips had brushed his throat and every bit of common sense between them had spontaneously combusted.

After several laps, he stopped at the shallow end of the pool and stared blankly at the blue water. Maybe they could pretend last night had never happened and go back to just being friends. Maybe he could pretend that all they'd shared was physical intimacy.

No, he knew better. It hadn't been just-sex. Not for him. For him, his time with her had been more. He wasn't afraid of her getting hurt by a night of unrestrained passion. He was concerned for himself.

He'd just have to deal with these feelings in private. He had to be careful not to hurt her. He didn't like to hurt the women he cared about, and yeah, he cared about her. He wouldn't deny it, not to himself. He'd cared for a while now. Even before he'd started to lust after her, he'd known she was special. He liked her as a person first and a woman second. And that was the entire problem.

He didn't know if she felt anything for him beyond friendship and temporary sexual infatuation, but if she fell for him, he'd eventually end up doing something that hurt her. Something he'd regret. Because when it came to women, he could play them, but he had no idea how to forge a serious and lasting relationship. He was too easily distracted. That's why he'd sworn off relationships. And it had been a smart move on his part.

So why was he sitting here shivering on the edge of the pool with a full head and an empty heart? He'd just treat Amanda the way he treated all of his lovers—as temporary and exchangeable diversions.

And he hoped like hell she fell for his ruse because if she called him on his bluff, he wouldn't be able to deny that he thought of her as more than a bedmate. And *that*—being honest with her about his feelings—was a truly terrifying proposition.

Shade returned to the house and went to the kitchen to make breakfast. If he started to act unlike himself, she'd figure out that he was hiding something. She was a smart woman and for some reason, she read him like a book. Most people believed his devil-may-care act, but not Amanda.

He'd just finished frying turkey sausage and was adding pancake batter to a hot griddle when she entered the room. She'd borrowed one of his white dress shirts, but her legs were bare. He pretended she wasn't the sexiest thing he'd ever seen just so he wouldn't intensify the morning-after awkwardness between them by staring at her. By stalking her across the kitchen. By pressing her up against the counter and fucking her senseless again.

"Good morning," he said. "I hope you're hungry."

"Morning. And yes, I'm starving."

Shade's belly tightened when Amanda's hands slipped around his waist from behind.

"I didn't know you knew how to cook," she said in a sleep-slurred voice. Her hands roamed his abdomen. "Do your talents know no bounds?"

"I'm sure there's something I suck at," he said with a grin.

"I could figure out something for you to suck *on*."

He was surprised she was still capable of playful banter; he'd expected her to be embarrassed and ashamed. But he should have known better. Amanda always went with the flow. If she felt any awkwardness at all this morning, she hid it well.

"If you don't stop coming on to me," he said, "I'm going to think you're attracted to me or something."

"An amazing voice, gorgeous body, great in bed, a talented cook *and* smart. Who wouldn't be attracted to you?"

Shade scowled. *Smart?* Not even. He'd take credit for those other traits—they happened to be true—but he wasn't smart. He could barely read.

"What did I say?" Amanda said.

God, he kept forgetting he wasn't wearing his fucking sunglasses. "Nothing." He shoveled several pancakes onto a plate and added more batter to the pan.

"I said something. You're broody all of a sudden."

"Your pancakes are ready."

She sighed. "You don't have to be guarded with me, Jacob. I'm not going to poke holes in your oversensitive ego."

He chuckled. He'd never had anyone accuse him of being oversensitive. Just the opposite. Cold. Self-centered. Hard. That's why the sunglasses came in so handy.

"Go eat your pancakes."

"I want to eat with you. I'll wait." She pressed her forehead to his shoulder while he flipped the pancakes in the pan.

"You're not supposed to get attached, Amanda." And neither was he. Damn. What had he started here? Something he couldn't possibly finish. *Boneheaded move, Silverton.*

"I'm not." Her hands slid up over his belly. "My hands just refuse to trade the feel of this luxury for something as ordinary as a fork."

He smiled. How did she do it? Make him feel so good about himself? Just being in her company made him happy. And had him contemplating ways to see her again.

See? Not smart. He turned off the burner and scooped pancakes onto a second plate.

"I suppose this means I have to let you go now." Her hands wandered up his bare chest.

"I did go to the trouble of making you breakfast." Which went against all his rules about morning-after routines. Get them up and out of the house as fast as possible. Or better yet, leave on the tour bus as soon as the sun rose over the horizon.

"I appreciate that. I definitely worked up an appetite last night." She stepped away and smacked his ass.

He sat across from her at the small round table in the breakfast nook. It overlooked the pool, so he stared out the window instead of meeting her eyes.

"You regret it," she said after a long moment of uncomfortable silence. Neither of them had even touched their meal.

He jerked his gaze from the pool and concentrated on his breakfast.

He did regret it. Not the amazing time they'd had together, but the complications it brought. He wasn't sure how to proceed, because all signs pointed to getting her out of his life as soon as possible, but his foolish heart was breaking at the very idea. He could get by without ever having sex with her again but never seeing her smile or hearing her laugh or having her tease him mercilessly in a way that no one else dared to? Those were the things about her that he couldn't do without. And by making things physical between them, he was certain that he'd have to give up everything else he adored about her.

"What in the fuck is your problem this morning, Jacob?"

He didn't look at her. Didn't want to see her righteous anger. "No problem." He took a bite of his pancakes. He had a hell of a time chewing and forcing himself to swallow.

"What? Do you think I'm going to try to force a commitment out of you? I know you don't have it in you. I knew that from the beginning."

Her words should have appeased his fears. Instead they slashed his soul. But she was right. He didn't have the ability to commit, so why did her saying it hurt? He should be relieved. He had a powerful need to put on his sunglasses. She had to be able to see the turmoil in his eyes. He supposed he should be glad that she'd misinterpreted it for once.

"That's a relief," he said and forced a laugh that he hoped didn't sound as false to her ears as it did to his.

"You don't look relieved."

So much for fooling her.

"I didn't mean to get intimate with you, Amanda. It just sort of happened."

"Well, I meant to get intimate with you," she said. "I've been wanting to bone you for years."

She grinned at him, and his heart took its first unrestricted beat since he'd opened his eyes that morning. He attempted a smile. It felt slightly more natural. His shoulders and back, however, were still all sorts of tense.

"So where in the world did you come up with the idea for making your bed into a stage?"

He blushed. Lord, no one ever made him blush. "Uh, Adam and I used to frequent this sex club in New Orleans. It's performance based. There's a stage and a director who tells you how to fuck your partner. People watch. It's quite a head rush. I liked the performance part, but not having a director."

"That's because you need to be in charge." She smirked at him.

The tension continued to slowly drain from his body. He found he could chew naturally and even swallow without activating his gag reflex.

"Yeah, I don't take directions well. I was told that if I couldn't follow the director's instructions, then I shouldn't come back. I haven't been back since. I think Adam still goes. He likes to be watched. I just love to perform onstage; I don't need the audience to get off. Some woman said how her biggest fantasy was for me to fuck her onstage during a concert—to sing to her—and have every move displayed on the big screens in the stadium so everyone could see it. That's when I decided to turn my bedroom into a private stadium. I like to please the ladies." He winked at her.

"And we thank you for that."

"Did you enjoy your time on stage, Miss Lange?"

"You deliver an amazing performance."

Pleased by her compliment, he smiled broadly and took another bite of his pancakes.

"I wouldn't mind another encore," she said.

He choked.

"What time do you have to meet the tour bus?" she asked.

"Around noon."

She grinned. "I'm not sure if two hours gives us enough time. I've never met a man who could go at it as long as you can."

"Practice makes perfect." He paused. Why had he said that? Expecting retaliation, he cringed and forced himself to meet her wrathful glare.

She was grinning at him. "I'm willing to volunteer my body to help you perfect your skills."

Again he relaxed. She always put him at ease. "I thought I'd already perfected them."

"I'd definitely give you an A," she said.

He chuckled. She could stroke his ego all day; he never tired of it.

"But with a little extra credit, you could get an A-plus."

"Extra credit, huh? How much work are we talking about? I'm satisfied with an A." He cocked his head at her and licked pancake syrup off his thumb.

"I wouldn't want to tell you what to do and stifle your creativity, Mr. Silverton, but seeing as I didn't bother to put on any panties this morning, it wouldn't take much effort on your part to get into them."

He grinned, completely at ease now. How did she do it?

"So how much extra credit would I earn if I bent you over this table and fucked you from behind?"

"I couldn't say until I saw the quality of your work."

He moved swiftly. Her naughty teacher act already had his cock straining against his swim trunks. He pulled her from her chair and pushed her face down on the table. He lifted her shirt up over her ass and sought the heat between her legs with his fingers. She was as turned on as he was. He yanked his swim trunks down to his knees and rubbed his cockhead against her opening.

Fuck, he needed to get a condom out of his bedroom. He couldn't just plunge into her unprotected, no matter how much he wanted to.

"Hold that thought," he said.

She grabbed his wrist before he could move away and stuffed a condom into his hand. The little minx had planned this all along. Unlike him, she thought ahead. And he loved that she knew how to get what she wanted. He quickly applied the condom and then filled her with one deep thrust.

She rocked back to meet his thrusts. "Take me, Jacob."

His balls clenched at the sound of his name on her lips. "Jacob."

The doorbell rang.

Amanda tensed. "Who could that be?"

Shade thrust harder, trying to regain her attention. "Don't know, don't care." He rotated his hips. Amanda moaned and relaxed against the table.

The doorbell rang again and then someone pounded on the door.

"Jacob, get the door," Amanda pleaded.

"I'm in the middle of something."

"Yeah, me. Now go answer the door."

"Bossy damned woman," he grumbled and pulled out with a wince of protest.

The doorbell rang several times in rapid succession.

"This better be fucking important," he grumbled as he stripped off the condom, pulled his swim trunks up and tucked his stiff-as-a-board cock inside them.

"If it's not, I'm going to kick someone's ass," Amanda said as she pulled his shirt down to cover her beguiling ass.

Damn, she looked good in that shirt.

More pounding. Shade stomped off to see who dared interrupt his attempts to earn extra credit with Amanda against the kitchen table.

Shade opened the door to Adam. Should have known he'd be responsible for Shade's discomfort.

"This better be an emergency," Shade said.

"I need to talk to you."

Shade took a moment to look Adam over more carefully. He was wearing the same clothes he'd had on the day before, and he looked as if he'd slept in them. Or as if he hadn't slept at all.

"You look like shit," Shade said. He stepped aside and allowed Adam to enter the house.

"Yeah, that sometimes happens when you're up all night."

"Let me guess: you drove back to Dallas to hook up with your counselor again."

"Actually I was in the emergency room, but that's not why I'm here." Adam's gaze moved to a point behind Shade, and his eyes widened. "Amanda?"

"Hey, Adam," she said. "Did I overhear that you were in the ER? What happened? Are you hurt?"

"No, my dad's in the hospital."

"Oh," Amanda said. "Is he okay?"

"Sort of."

"Shit, man. Why didn't you call last night? Do you need a

few days off?" Shade asked.

"No, that's not why I'm here. They assure me he'll be fine. I came over here to talk to you. We need to clear the air, Shade. I can't take this anger between us anymore."

"Clear the air?"

"I need to know what you think I did that was so wrong."

Shade's spine straightened. He had no idea why Adam would choose *now* of all times to pick a fight. "What I *think* you did wrong?"

Adam closed his eyes and took a deep breath. "Apparently, you think I've done something truly horrible, but I don't even know what it is. So you can tell me and we can hash this out here. Or, if you'd rather, we can keep pissing each other off for reasons I don't understand."

Shade was flabbergasted. All this time he'd thought Adam was an inconsiderate prick, selfish and callous about stealing one of the most significant events of Shade's life from him, and now Adam was saying he didn't know *why* Shade had been infuriated with him for years?

"You really don't know what you did?"

"I'm pretty sure it has something to do with my drug abuse. I was wasted all the time when it all went down, but no, I don't remember."

"You don't remember me shoving my finger down your throat in Nashville so you'd purge whatever cocktail of pills you'd ingested that night?"

Adam gave a barely perceptible shake of his head.

"You don't remember throwing up all over me and me dragging you out of the tour bus because the EMTs couldn't fit the gurney up through the door?"

"No, I don't."

"You don't remember calling me a meddling asshole and telling me to mind my own business and that you could get high if you wanted to?"

Adam smirked. "I do remember that."

Shade scowled at him. "You don't remember dying in the ambulance? You don't remember them defibrillating you back to life?"

Adam's jaw dropped. His breath caught. He went white.

"I died?"

"Yes, Adam, you fucking died and while I was watching your own selfish stupidity kill you, my baby was taking her first breath in another hospital. I missed Julie's birth because you were so insistent on destroying yourself."

Adam ran a shaking hand through his thick black hair. "Shade, I don't remember much of anything from those days. I was in a bad place then."

"Now is different?"

Adam's hands clenched into fists. "Yes, now is totally different! I'm not doing drugs anymore. You're too busy to notice. Or care."

Shade closed his eyes and shook his head. He wished he was too busy to care. He was just so tired of this. So tired of Adam's denial. His lies. "You're still doing drugs, Adam. I caught you smoking pot two nights ago. So soon you forget."

Adam rubbed his haggard face with both hands and then crossed his arms over his chest. "It was just a little. And it was only pot. I mean..." He scowled, obviously still in denial. "*You* smoke it."

"I haven't smoked pot in years, Adam. Not since Julie was born. I grew up while you were stoned out of your mind. You just didn't notice."

Adam released a heavy sigh. "I'm not going to do drugs anymore, Shade."

Shade lifted an eyebrow at him.

Adam stood there with his hands clenching and unclenching. His entire body was tense. Shade had seen this behavior before. Adam got this way right before he started swinging his fists. Shade waited for him to snap. He'd knock him on his ass if he had to. Wouldn't be the first time. Adam's intense, gray-eyed gaze bored into Shade's, but instead of lashing out at him, he said, "Fuck, Shade. Why can't you give me a second chance?"

Adam was still blaming his difficulties on everyone but himself. Was the guy incapable of seeing reality?

"A second chance?" Shade yelled, unable to keep his temper in check any longer. "I've already given you a second chance, Adam. And a third chance. And a hundredth chance."

Shade shoved him in the shoulder, forcing Adam to take a step back. "Just how many fucking chances do you think you deserve?"

Adam's features hardened. "You don't believe I've changed. You don't believe I'm taking control of my life. The only one who sees the real me is Madison."

Shade released a derisive snort. "Your counselor? The one you're *screwing*?" Shade shook his head at him. "She's going to see what she wants to see. She's become your biggest enabler. There are some women you should *never* fuck."

Adam tilted his head toward the doorway that Amanda had graced only moments before. "Such as your ex-wife's sister?"

Touché.

"Fuck off, Adam. You don't know anything about my life."

"And you don't know anything about mine."

Shade narrowed his eyes. He really wished he could give the guy the benefit of the doubt, but he could only try to put a broken train back on its track so many times before he had to believe the engine's only course was derailment. And as much as Adam liked to think his life was proceeding smoothly now, Shade could see disaster coming from a mile away. He wasn't going to be the one who tried to save Adam anymore. Been there, done that, bought the T-shirt. It didn't fit anymore.

"Why is your dad in the hospital?" Shade really didn't need to ask. He knew the answer.

Adam lowered his eyes, going from pissed to defeated in the span of one breath. "He got his hands on some bad drugs and had an adverse reaction. Blames me for not hooking him up with my dealer."

"Wonderful." Shade snorted. "Why hold out on him?"

Adam scowled. "I don't have a fucking dealer, Shade. When did you turn into such an asshole?"

"When you took one too many things from me that I can never get back." Shade squeezed the bridge of his nose. He was not going to punch Adam today, no matter how much he wanted to. "Have you said your piece?"

Adam nodded. "Yeah. I'm sorry I died and made you miss Julie's birth. I would have waited until the next day to end it all had I known Tina was going to pop out your baby three weeks early. At least I understand why you hate me now. I'd hate me too."

That was the most mature observation Adam had made in years. And an actual apology instead of defensive avoidance? Maybe Adam was making progress. Maybe he was getting his life together. Maybe Shade could let himself care about the guy again. He had to be sure Adam was on the road to recovery before he trusted his progress, because Adam had had ripped out Shade's heart a million fucking times in the past, and he couldn't let him do it again.

"I don't hate you," Shade said. He never had.

Adam closed his eyes and drew a deep breath into his chest. "I don't hate you either."

Uncomfortable over exchanging feelings with a dude, Shade stared at the floor and stood in silence for several minutes.

"I'll, um, see you on the bus," Adam said. He also seemed to find the hardwood at their feet utterly fascinating.

"Yeah, good. Hope your dad gets better soon."

"Thanks. I should dump him off somewhere and hope he doesn't find his way back, but I just can't do it. Not even after all the shit he's put me through."

Shade knew more about the shit Adam's father had put him through than anyone. When they'd been back in high school, Shade had no idea how many times Adam had hid out at his house just to feel a bit of security. Shade's family had welcomed Adam. Shade's mother was some sort of stray magnet, be the strays broken people or lost animals. Shade had been disappointed and yeah, *hurt*, when Adam had chosen to follow in his father's footsteps. Shade hadn't wanted that for Adam and hadn't known what to do. How to help. He'd tried to force Adam to see the light, but it hadn't worked. Adam had always said he wanted to build a better life for himself, that he didn't want to be anything like his father, and yet he'd followed—almost to the *letter*—the failed life of the man he resented. The only thing that had kept Adam from sending himself to an early grave was that his bandmates happened to give a shit about him, whether Adam saw it that way or not.

"You really should get the man out of your life," Shade

said. "He's never going to change."

"I don't need him to be perfect," Adam said quietly. "I just want him to be my dad. After all this time, I still want that."

Shade leaned forward and squeezed Adam's shoulder. He wished he could say he understood what Adam was going through, but he didn't. He could support him though. Or try to. "If you need something, you can call me."

Adam's head lifted and he met Shade's eyes. He chuckled half-heartedly. "You don't mean that."

"Yeah, I do. I know how hard it is to deal with an addict who doesn't see he's destroying himself."

Adam grinned crookedly. "They're a total pain in the ass."

"But they can get better." Shade hoped. *Please, let him be better.*

"Yeah." Adam took a deep breath and glanced at the front door. "I'm going to go now. And it's none of my business who you mess around with, but *Amanda?*" Adam shook his head. "Didn't you learn your lesson with the younger Lange sister?"

"I think I chose the wrong one." Shade sighed. He knew he couldn't be with Amanda in any serious capacity, but the woman brought him joy, which was a good enough reason to keep his hands off her. He knew he'd fuck things up with her spectacularly, and she'd take that good feeling with her when she left.

"Just don't do anything stupid."

Too late. "I'll see you later," Shade said. He was ready to continue being stupid with the lovely woman in question. At least until he had to leave to meet the tour bus.

Shade and Adam exchanged an awkward bro-hug, slapping each other's backs with enough force to knock the wind out of an elephant, and then Adam let himself out of the house.

Smiling, Shade went in search of trouble. He found her in his shower.

CHAPTER ELEVEN

Amanda didn't know why she'd felt so uncomfortable when Adam had recognized her. Sure, he'd undoubtedly figured out why she was at Jacob's house borrowing his shirt, but they were both single, consenting adults. It wasn't any of Adam's business what they did in the semi-privacy of Jacob's breakfast nook. It hadn't bothered her nearly as much when Gabe had shown up the night before. Why not? She froze, her hands tangled up in hair and shampoo. Probably because she'd been so lost in a haze of lust that she hadn't been thinking clearly.

She scrubbed at her scalp. Eyes closed, she rinsed her hair beneath the steamy water.

She needed to go home and collect her scattered thoughts. Something about Jacob sent her logic on a short flight to nowhere-land.

When he stepped into the shower behind her, her senses boarded the plane. She turned so that the spray hit her shoulders and she wrapped her arms around his neck, standing on tiptoes to press her breasts against his chest.

"Everything okay with Adam?" she asked.

"One conversation can't solve years of conflict," he said. His hands slid over her back, and he drew her closer. "But it's a start."

"He wouldn't tell Tina that I was here, would he?"

"Nah. He can't stand her. That's why he refused to be the best man at our wedding. Said I was making the biggest mistake of my life."

"In hindsight, do you agree?"

"Nope. I have no regrets there. If I hadn't married Tina, I

wouldn't have Julie. And she's my heart."

Amanda kissed the center of his chest, right on the proud nose of his lion tattoo. "Way to dissolve me into a puddle of mush, Silverton," she said.

"I also might have never met you."

She grinned at him. "Are you trying to earn extra credit with words instead of actions?"

"Actually, I was hoping to finish what we started in the kitchen." His hands slid down over her butt, and he tugged her closer.

"I have one issue with that."

"What's that?" He lowered his head to nibble on her ear, and she almost forgot her teasing remark.

"There's no table in here," she said breathlessly.

"No, but there's a perfectly good wall."

It turned out walls weren't quite as much fun as swings, but detachable shower heads made for an enjoyable experience. Sex was fun with Jacob, and she didn't need more than a good time at the moment.

Yeah, keep telling yourself that, Amanda, and maybe you'll start believing it.

While he was in her arms, she was going to let herself enjoy being with him. She'd sort out any developing feelings later—he didn't need to hear about them. The man felt guilty enough for having sex with her in the first place.

Plus she wanted him to remember their time together as a blessing, not a burden. She could hide how she felt, keep him believing that she only wanted sex. There was no reason to complicate things with talk of relationships and the future. Neither of them wanted that—too many people would get hurt if they ever tried to be together in a serious capacity.

Amanda kept talking to herself, convincing herself that she was right, because her thoughts were the only obstacle keeping her from revealing her heart.

By the time she was sexually satiated and dressed in the clothes she found in the dryer—she'd nixed pulling on her dirty panties, so she was a bit light on the bottom end—it was time for him to meet the bus and go back on tour.

She wasn't sure what to say. Should she say anything? Not

goodbye. That was too final. She sat alone in the living room while he packed his overnight bag in the bedroom. Dare she ask him out the following weekend? She knew he'd be in town. She also clearly remembered his reaction to Gabe when he'd spilled those particular beans.

He won't want to see you again, fool. Don't set yourself up for that kind of heartache.

So, no, she wouldn't ask to see him again. She wouldn't put him on the spot. She would keep her word and not try to make something out of their one night together. It had just been an amazing night—and morning—of casual sex, and this would be the end of it.

When Jacob entered the living room, he dropped his bag on the floor and stood in the doorway. He was wearing his sunglasses again, so she couldn't be sure, but he seemed uncomfortable that she was there.

"I guess I'll be going," she said, rising to her feet. "I won't have to go to the gym for a *month* after that workout."

He smiled tersely.

She should have gone while he was packing. She collected her purse from the end table where she'd placed it the night before and walked past him with a stiff spine and an aching heart.

"Amanda?" he said.

Her heart lurched, and she stopped in the middle of the foyer. *Please ask to see me again. Please.*

"Good to see you."

Her hopes plummeted. "Yeah."

She opened the door just as a Jeep sped by the end of the front walk, hopped the curb with two wheels and stopped just in front of Amanda's car. The driver, Owen, blared on the horn.

Amanda hurried to her car. She could feel Owen's eyes on her as she prayed for invisibility and climbed behind the wheel. He'd blocked her in with his haphazard parking job, so she sat staring at the dashboard, trying not to watch Jacob stride confidently down the walk to Owen's Jeep. She could barely hear his words through the closed windows.

"I should have called and let you know I found my car,"

Jacob said. "It slipped my mind."

Owen said something she couldn't hear. Cranking the key, but not starting her knock-ridden engine, she lowered the passenger side window slightly.

"I'll still ride with you since you're already here," Jacob said. He dropped his bag into the open back of the Jeep and then opened the door to climb in the vehicle. He didn't look in her direction. This really was the end of their time together.

Amanda watched Owen's Jeep pull away. Her heart sank to the middle of her belly. She wasn't sure what she'd expected from Jacob. She'd known he wasn't interested in anything substantial, and she wasn't either. So why did it hurt so bad to think that all she'd ever have with him was a single night? Why was she paralyzed by the ache in her heart?

Pull it together, Amanda. This isn't the first time you haven't gotten the guy you wanted. It won't be the last.

She took a deep breath and started her car. Before she could put it in drive, Owen's tail lights brightened, the passenger door flew open and then Jacob was out of the car and jogging toward her. Her heart skipped a beat. He'd probably just forgotten to tell her something, but she couldn't help but hope.

He paused outside her door and tapped on the glass. She fumbled with the button that lowered her window. She looked up at him expectantly.

"Just so you know, I really am stupid," he said and before she could protest, he leaned into her open window and kissed her.

What? What did he mean? She lost her train of thought as he deepened the kiss and her body melted.

Jacob.

He tugged his mouth from hers and stared down into her eyes. At least she thought he was staring into her eyes. He was hiding behind his damned sunglasses again.

"I have Julie next weekend," he said. "I thought she might like to go to the zoo. What do you think?"

"Um…" So he'd dashed out of the car to ask her if Julie would like to go to the zoo? Not exactly what she'd hoped for, but she smiled for Julie's sake because she cherished that little girl more than her own life and she knew Julie would love to spend the day at the zoo with her father. "She'd love that. She really likes animals and is always full of questions."

He smiled. "Which I'd never be able to answer. Will you come with us?"

The air rushed out of Amanda's lungs. "Um... I wouldn't want to intrude on your time with her."

"Nah, you'd be helping me out. You're into animals and stuff, right, biology teacher?"

"Are you sure this isn't an excuse to see me again?" she asked.

"You really can't take a hint, can you?"

Hint? "I don't know what you mean."

He leaned his forearms on the doorframe and gently stroked a strand of hair behind her ear. "It's really stupid of me to do this, but I just couldn't stand the thought of not spending more time with you. Even though I know staying apart is for the best, I don't give a damn."

She smiled, her chest ready to explode from the joy blossoming in her heart. "I don't think you're stupid at all, Jacob Silverton. I think the smartest thing you've ever done is get out of that Jeep and kiss me."

He grinned. "So you'll join us?"

"I'd love to. I always have a great time with Julie at the zoo."

"And with me?"

She grinned. "Yeah, I guess you're all right."

"We don't have to have sex," he said.

"Uh, but we could. If the mood strikes us." She was going to start training to increase her stamina immediately. So much for getting out of a month's worth of workouts.

He laughed and kissed her again. "I have to go."

This time when Amanda watched the Jeep drive off with Jacob Silverton inside, she had a smile on her face and hope in her heart. She just had to ensure her sister never found out that she was seeing Jacob, even on a cursory level. The man didn't need another reason for his ex-wife to hate him.

CHAPTER TWELVE

"You are the biggest idiot on the planet," Owen said to Shade as they pulled out of his driveway. "I don't know what you have floating around in that big head of yours, but it sure as hell isn't a brain. Why are you fooling around with Amanda Lange?"

Shade shrugged. He was in too good of a mood to let Owen's words bother him. He was going to get to see Amanda again in less than a week. Spend the day with his two favorite females on the planet. Nothing anyone could have said would have darkened his mood. And before Owen could try, Shade changed the subject.

"Adam stopped by this morning. He looks like shit. Didn't get any sleep last night. His dad is in the hospital."

"Well, *fuck*, why didn't he call us? We could have been there to support him."

"You know he's ashamed of his father."

"I don't know which one of you is the bigger idiot," Owen said.

"He is," Shade assured him.

Owen laughed. "You two really need to stop going at each other constantly. It stresses us all out."

"We talked a bit about that this morning too. I think things will start to smooth out between us a little." Shade doubted they'd ever be as close as they'd once been, but he didn't want to fight with Adam anymore. Shade would work at not losing his temper. He'd find ways around Adam's inconsiderate behavior to make his own life easier. And he would no longer take it upon himself to garner Adam's cooperation; it wasn't his job to teach Adam responsibility. Maybe Adam would recognize how he was burdening everyone if Shade kept his cool instead of adding to their problems by always confronting Adam.

Shit, none of it would be easy, but Owen was right: everyone was stressed out by the constant strife between Shade and Adam. Shade promised himself that he wouldn't blow up the next time Adam did something selfish and inconsiderate. They were in an endless loop of animosity, and one of them had to step up and break the cycle. He wouldn't argue with Adam anymore; he couldn't control another man's actions. Shade wondered how long he'd be able to remember that.

"I hope you're all rested up for tonight," Owen said.

"I have plenty of energy left for the concert." But not an ounce extra. Amanda had been amazing. She'd taken everything he was willing to give. Most of his lovers made him stop before he was truly satisfied because he wore them out.

"And the sex club afterwards. Don't forget about that."

Shade's nose crinkled. There was no way in hell he would be in the mood to hook up with some stranger that night. Not after he'd had such a wonderful time with someone who mattered to him.

"I'm not going," Shade said. "Not in the mood."

"What? Are you fucking kidding me? First Gabe and then Adam and now you're swearing off perfectly good pussy? What is wrong with you guys?"

"I don't know about them, but my dick needs a few days to recover."

"Since when?"

"Drop it, Owen. I'm not going."

"At least I still have Kellen," Owen grumbled.

"You two will have more fun without me. You know I'm the biggest pussy magnet in the group. You might get to hook-up with someone half-way attractive if I'm not there stealing all the hotties." Shade somehow managed not to laugh as he taunted Owen.

Owen punched him in the arm and hit a curb with the front passenger-side tire. He returned the Jeep to his lane, managing not to hit any pedestrians in the process. "Bullshit, Silverton. I'm the biggest pussy magnet in the group."

"Yeah," Shade said with a hearty chuckle, "if you like cougars."

"I do like cougars." Owen grinned deviously. "They're not afraid to sharpen their claws on my back."

"To each his own," he said. Shade had an unnaturally strong attraction to smart chicks. Well, *one* in particular. He was glad he'd done the wrong thing, gone against every shred of his common sense, and asked Amanda to see him again. Now he had something to look forward to all week.

"That I-got-laid smile of yours looks fucking ridiculous," Owen said, rolling his eyes skyward.

"You're just jealous." And he had every reason to be. Shade would have to play this thing with Amanda by ear, one day— one night—at a time, but for the first time in forever, he had hope that he might be able to make a relationship work.

Assuming the woman in question wanted him as much as he wanted her.

"Jeez, will you stop smiling like that," Owen said. "You're starting to worry me."

Shade should probably be worried how his decision to pursue Amanda would complicate his life, but he was too happy to care.

"Shut up and drive, Owen. We have a concert to get to."

Everything else would sort itself out with time. He didn't have to be a genius to figure that out.

ABOUT THE AUTHOR

Combining her love for romantic fiction and rock 'n roll, Olivia Cunning writes erotic romance centered around rock musicians. Raised on hard rock music from the cradle, she attended her first Styx concert at age six and fell instantly in love with live music. She's been known to travel over a thousand miles just to see a favorite band in concert. As a teen, she discovered her second love, romantic fiction—first, voraciously reading steamy romance novels and then penning her own. Growing up as the daughter of a career soldier, she's lived all over the country and overseas. She currently lives in Galveston, Texas. To learn more about Olivia and her books, please visit www.oliviacunning.com.